OXFORD WORLD'S CLASSICS

THE RAID
AND OTHER STORIES

COUNT LEO NIKOLAYEVICH TOLSTOY, the youngest of four brothers, was born at Yásnaya Polyána, his father's estate in Tula province, about two hundred miles from Moscow. His mother died when he was 2, and his father when he was 9. He revered their memory, and they were the inspiration for his portraits of Princess Mary and Nicholas Rostov in *War and Peace*. Both his mother and father belonged to the Russian nobility, and Tolstoy always remained highly conscious of his aristocratic status, even when towards the end of his life he embraced and taught doctrines of Christian equality and the brotherhood of man.

He served in the army in the Caucasus and the Crimea, where as an artillery officer at the siege of Sevastopol he wrote his first stories and impressions. After leaving the army he travelled and studied educational theories, which deeply interested him. In 1862 he married Sophia Behrs and for the next fifteen years lived a tranquil and productive life as a country gentleman and author. *War and Peace* was finished in 1869 and *Anna Karénina* in 1877. He had thirteen children. In 1879, after undergoing a severe spiritual crisis, he wrote the autobiographical *A Confession*, and from then on he became a 'Tolstoyan', seeking to propagate his views on religion, morality, non-violence, and renunciation of the flesh. He continued to write, producing parables, tracts, and morality plays, but also a late novel, *Resurrection*, and some of his finest tales, including *The Death of Ivan Ilych* and *Master and Man*. Because of his new beliefs and disciples, and his international fame as pacifist and sage, relations with his wife became strained and family life increasingly difficult. At last in 1910, at the age of 82, he left his home and died of pneumonia at a local railway station.

P. N. FURBANK is Professor Emeritus in Literature at the Open University. His books include *E. M. Forster: A Life* (1977–8), *Unholy Pleasure: the Idea of Social Class* (1985), and *Diderot: a Critical Biography* (1992).

OXFORD WORLD'S CLASSICS

*For almost 100 years Oxford World's Classics have brought
readers closer to the world's great literature. Now with over 700
titles—from the 4,000-year-old myths of Mesopotamia to the
twentieth century's greatest novels—the series makes available
lesser-known as well as celebrated writing.*

*The pocket-sized hardbacks of the early years contained
introductions by Virginia Woolf, T. S. Eliot, Graham Greene,
and other literary figures which enriched the experience of reading.
Today the series is recognized for its fine scholarship and
reliability in texts that span world literature, drama and poetry,
religion, philosophy and politics. Each edition includes perceptive
commentary and essential background information to meet the
changing needs of readers.*

OXFORD WORLD'S CLASSICS

LEO TOLSTOY

The Raid
and Other Stories

Translated by
LOUISE AND AYLMER MAUDE

With an Introduction by
P. N. FURBANK

OXFORD
UNIVERSITY PRESS

Oxford University Press, Great Clarendon Street, Oxford OX2 6DP

Oxford New York

Athens Auckland Bangkok Bogotá Buenos Aires Calcutta
Cape Town Chennai Dar es Salaam Delhi Florence Hong Kong Istanbul
Karachi Kuala Lumpur Madrid Melbourne Mexico City Mumbai
Nairobi Paris São Paulo Singapore Taipei Tokyo Toronto Warsaw
and associated companies in Berlin Ibadan

Oxford is a registered trade mark of Oxford University Press

Published in the United States
by Oxford University Press Inc., New York

These translations first published by Oxford University Press
in the World's Classics hardback series between 1906 and 1935

Introduction © P. N. Furbank 1982

This selection first published, with a new introduction,
as a World's Classics paperback 1982
Reissued as an Oxford World's Classics paperback 1999

British Library Cataloguing in Publication Data

Data available

Library of Congress Cataloging in Publication Data
Tolstoy, Leo, graf, 1828–1910.
The raid, and other stories. (Oxford world's classics)
Contents: The raid—Sevastopol in May 1855—Two hussars—[etc.]
I. Maude, Louise Shanks, 1855–1939. II. Maude, Aylmer, 1858–1938. III. Title.
IV. Series
PG3366.A15M38 1982 891.73'3 81–16982
ISBN 0–19–283808–3 AACR2

1 3 5 7 9 10 8 6 4 2

Printed in Great Britain by
Cox & Wyman Ltd.
Reading, Berkshire

CONTENTS

INTRODUCTION

THIS selection from Tolstoy's short stories falls into two well-defined parts, one belonging to the 1850s and the other to the 1880s and 1890s. The explanation of this, from one point of view, is the quite simple one that during the period of the great novels *War and Peace* (written 1863–9) and *Anna Karenina* (written 1873–7) Tolstoy largely stopped writing short stories. This indeed was natural, since his early stories were closely akin to his novels and could be thought of in a sense as a preparation for them. Take, for instance, *The Raid* (1852), in the present selection. It is perfectly easy to imagine it, with a few changes in externals, as a chapter in *War and Peace*; and this says much both about it and about *War and Peace*. For the Tolstoy of this period is determined, for profound reasons, to do without 'plot'. *The Raid* has shape, through and through, just as *War and Peace* has, but in both there is a refusal of contrivance. Nothing is 'planted' for later use; there is no suspense; the reader is stationed squarely in a moment, or a succession of moments, with no more power to see round and beyond it than the characters. And it is for these very reasons that events in Tolstoy's stories can have such a shattering effect. For the reader is unprepared; he or she can make no calculation, based on past experience of plot devices, as to what kind of thing lies ahead. Most nineteenth-century novels – shall we say, for instance, *Mansfield Park* or *Wuthering Heights* or *The Idiot* – are guessing-games, in which at least we know where the enigma lies. It is 'What are the Crawfords *really* like?' or 'What lies hidden in Heathcliff's heart?'. There are no such games played in Tolstoy.

On the other hand, this does not (as you might for a moment be tempted to think) make him a twentieth-century novelist before his time. For, though resolutely psychological in his method, he is not what used to be called (in a now rather *démodé* phrase) a 'psychological novelist'. For the assumption of the 'psychological novel' (in the hands of Woolf or Lawrence) is that only psychological events count. No such assumption was made by Tolstoy. He aspired to be an epic novelist, and this meant opening his mind impartially to events of every kind. (It so happened that, despite efforts by certain poets in the eighteenth century, Russia did not possess a classical epic, and it was left to Tolstoy to produce one, in the age of the railways and newspapers.)

That gap or pause between our two groups of stories is, however, from another point of view intensely significant. For during that pause Tolstoy went through a devastating middle-life crisis, far-reaching in its consequences. The story, as related in his *Confession* of 1879–82, is well known: how, during the time that he was writing *Anna Karenina* he began to experience strange moments of 'perplexity and arrest of life', when he asked himself what his existence was for, what sense it could possibly have – seeing that, whatever he did, it would end equally in death; and how the moments came more and more often, until his life came to a standstill, and the thought that death made life pointless made him want to end his life here and now.

It had come to this, that I, a healthy, fortunate man, felt I could no longer live: some irresistible power impelled me to rid myself one way or another of life . . . The power which drew me away from life was stronger, fuller and more widespread than any mere wish. It was a force similar to the force striving to live, only in a contrary direction.

(*A Confession*, trans. A. Maude, section IV)

The Tolstoy who emerged from this crisis was, superficially at least, a totally altered man – a rigid moralist who held that ethics were, not merely the most important thing in life, but the *only* important one. He was the prophetic Tolstoy who dressed in peasant blouse and made his own shoes, the man who inspired innumerable disciples, among them Gandhi and Wittgenstein, but also the one towards whom we occasionally feel as did G. K. Chesterton:

When we put beside [Tolstoy's fables] the trumpeting and tearing nonsense of the didactic Tolstoy, screaming for an inhuman peace, hacking up human life into small sins with a chopper, sneering at men, women and children out of respect to humanity, combining in one chaos of contradictions an unmanly Puritan and uncivilised prig, then, indeed, we scarcely know whither Tolstoy has vanished. We know not what to do with this small and noisy moralist who is inhabiting one corner of a great and good man.

(G. K. Chesterton, *Twelve Types* (1902), p. 149)

The new Tolstoy condemned his *War and Peace* and *Anna Karenina* as frivolous and worthless. 'What difficulty is there in writing about how an officer fell in love with a married woman?' he would grumble. 'There is no difficulty in it, and, above all, no good in it.' Literature, to be of any profit, he now held, must have an absolutely clear moral purpose, and moreover should be simple and direct and understandable by anyone able to read. The greatness of Tolstoy as a man, you might say, was that, for him, the only point of forming an opinion was that you should act on it. Thus he set to and wrote a number of tales according to his new prescription – of which *What Men Live By*, first published in a children's magazine in 1881, was the precursor (becoming perhaps the most famous of them all), and of which *The Three Hermits* and *How Much Land Does a Man Need?* (both 1886) are also examples. (He got the basic idea for several of them, including *What Men Live By* and *The Three Hermits*, from an itinerant story-teller.) And if we doubted whether his new-found convictions were genuine, no better proof of their genuineness need be looked for than these tales; for they are fairly plainly works of genius, and such works cannot be produced dishonestly. (For me, just at moments, *What Men Live By* dips into cloying religiosity; but only at moments, and that first smile of the angel has always haunted me.) No question, then, of Tolstoy's being a hypocrite. His weakness lay elsewhere, in the region of wilfulness. This vehement philosophical opponent of the Will and the Napoleonic will-to-power was himself an excessively wilful man, capable of wilfully deceiving himself on a vast scale – for a time at least, for there was another underlying Tolstoy which did not bother with consistency and which reaffirmed opposite and balancing truths.

No serious crisis, whether spiritual or psychological, arrives out of the blue; the materials for it will have been there, in the victim's life, and this is markedly so in the case of Tolstoy. Already in 1869, several years before his crisis, he had passed a terrifying night at an inn at Arzamas during which, so it seemed to him, the mind's normal censorship of the thought of death had relaxed and he had looked at death face to face. But indeed we need only consider that early story *The Raid* (based on his own experience as an artillery cadet in the Caucasus) to observe a perennial pattern in his thought. We could express it thus: he equated life with unconsciousness and carefree ignorance, and death with knowledge. The look of 'astonishment and reproof' that the dying young ensign Alanin gives to the army doctor attending him is, as we sense, not just directed at the doctor's drunken clumsiness but at life itself, the truth about which he is only just grasping. Hitherto he has existed (and this is his charm) in almost complete unconsciousness, or in naïve self-consciousness and self-admiration which are the same thing.

He smiled in passing, nodded to the captain, and flourished his whip. I only had time to notice that he sat his horse and held his reins with peculiar grace, that he had beautiful black eyes, a fine nose, and only the first indications of a moustache. What specially pleased me about him was that he could not repress a smile when he noticed our admiration. This smile alone showed him to be very young.

This was an essential insight of Tolstoy's, from his earliest writings, the insubstantialness and volatility of young men's characters – no more than a few quickly acquired notions and conventions, stretched over an abyss of unknowingness and unconsciousness. In the fragment *The Cossacks* (the greatest of his fictions before *War and Peace*, though too long to include here) the hero Olenin, a young cadet – sanguine, commonplace and full of young-mannish *savoir-faire* – sets out from Moscow to take up duty in a Cossack village, and already by the end of his journey, by dint of continuous daydreaming, his fluid personality has been altered. And when, many months later, after adventures outward and inward of every kind, he leaves his village, we see that his vaunted 'experience' and 'development' have amounted to nothing at all. Whatever really happened is something quite different, and something he will never understand. As he leaves, he turns round to look at his two old village acquaintances, and neither is looking his way; they have already forgotten him.

Tolstoy had much tenderness for this, and other, kinds of unconsciousness. His friend and biographer Aylmer Maude recorded of him that he could never bring himself to wake a sleeping person. And, by contrast, if he thought of death as knowledge, it was as the most dangerous of knowledges. *A Confession* shows him trying to come to terms with this knowledge and to turn it to profit. And it is curious to notice how what is said about mortal illness, for the purposes of simile, in *A Confession* is a few years later translated into literal terms in the harrowing story *The Death of Ivan Ilych* (1886). 'Then occurred what happens to everyone sickening with a mortal internal disease,' he writes in *A Confession*.

At first trivial signs of indisposition appear to which the sick man pays no attention; then these signs reappear more and more often and merge into one uninterrupted period of suffering. The suffering increases and, before the sick man can look round, what he took for a mere indisposition has already become more important to him than anything else in the world – it is death!

This illustrates the strength of Tolstoy's 'Realist' fictional principles. It is a realism which achieves all the benefits of allegory without the need to adopt the allegorical mode. The snow-storm in *Master and Man* (1895) is a similar case. We instinctively read into it an allegorical reference to the mental storm and bewilderment of his crisis years, without any need to think of this aspect of the story as more 'profound' than the literal one.

The wish to turn the 'knowledge' of death to profit very plainly underlies many of his later tales – for instance *The Death of Ivan Ilych* and *Master and Man*, both of them tales of death-bed redemption. And we should notice that, in both tales, this redemption, only to be achieved through dying, serves also as a solution of the social problem, the question of master and worker. This is the central point of *Master and Man*, and indirectly suggested too in the dying Ivan Ilych's new-found friendship with his servant Gerasim.

Many of the later Tolstoy's attitudes, indeed, relate to a determination to put the 'knowledge' of death to profit. It was this, for instance, that underlay his pacifism. In a sense Tolstoy was a pacifist most of his life, but in another sense it is just here that the later Tolstoy differs from the earlier. At the time of the Crimean war, having been serving with the Army of the Danube, Tolstoy (as he wrote to his brother at the time) suffered a 'bad attack' of patriotism and volunteered for transfer to Sevastopol, then under fierce siege from the Allies. His motive was also partly curiosity, and he went about note-taking in Sevastopol with great recklessness and fearlessness and not much respect for authority, altogether rather puzzling his fellow-officers. His first sketch, written at the time, was read and admired by the new emperor Alexander II, who sent instructions to 'take care of the life of that young man'. However, by the time of his second sketch (the one printed in this selection) his patriotism had been much quenched; and this impartial account of the horrors, inefficiencies and casual human vanities of war so shocked the censors that they not only mangled it (as they had done previously with *The Raid*) but practically rewrote it for him. It also effectively wrecked his army career. His theme was by now Truth, truth at all costs; and we need to ask what he meant by this. It is helpful to compare a comment he made in 1908, in a Preface to another writer's *Recollections of Sevastopol*:

Here are all the horrors of war – they are in this lad with his fresh face, his little shoulder-straps (under which the ends of his hood are so neatly tucked), his well-cleaned boots, his naïve eyes, and with so perverted a conception of life.

This is the real horror of war!

This reminds us of *The Raid*, and again of parts of *Sevastopol in May 1855* (1855), and yet it is not after all the same thought, but the thought of the later Tolstoy. In *Sevastopol in May 1855* only a child picking flowers suddenly appreciates the full horrors of war – he and the *writer*, who makes them the basis of his credo as a novelist:

There, I have said what I wished to say this time. But I am seized by an oppressive doubt. Perhaps I ought to have left it unsaid. What I have said perhaps belongs to that class of evil truths that lie unconsciously hidden in the soul of each man and should not be uttered lest they become harmful, as the dregs in a bottle must not be disturbed for fear of spoiling the wine. . . .

Where in this tale is the evil that should be avoided, and where is the good that should be imitated? Who is the villain and who the hero of the story? All are good and all are bad.

Not Kalugin, with his brilliant courage – *bravoure de gentilhomme* – and the vanity that influences all his actions, not Praskukhin, the empty harmless fellow (though he fell in battle for faith, throne, and fatherland), not Mikhaylov with his shyness, nor Pesth, a child without firm principles or convictions, can be either the villain or the hero of the tale.

The hero of my tale – whom I love with all the power of my soul, whom I have tried to portray in all his beauty, who has been, is, and will be beautiful – is Truth.

And in this (the point is) the 'oppressive doubt' he speaks of is meant to have some force. He is clear that the *writer* must dwell on evil truths as much as any other truths. But it is not clear that it is the duty of the acting and suffering man. There is a most expressive touch or device in *Sevastopol in May 1855*. We read how Prince Galtsin, though not at all a coward, halts in the first room of the field hospital at the sight of the wounded and dead and 'involuntarily turned back and ran out into the street: it was too terrible'; and then the next words (after a paragraph sign) imperturbably proceed to delineate the appalling scene. Thus, the soldier flees, and the reader is compelled to stay; it is his plain duty – and an easy enough one, after all, for a mere *novel-reader*. Any wish to have rubbed Prince Galtsin's nose into that hospital's horrors would have been quite alien to the Tolstoy of 1855. Nor is Tolstoy intending, in *The Raid*, to expose ensign Alanin's 'perverted conception of life'. Such thoughts belong to the later and didactic Tolstoy.

Yet there is a fact which reassures us that the later Tolstoy was still essentially the same man, and still ready to admit the claims of unconsciousness as well as of consciousness and knowledge. In his very last years he wrote (though significantly he did not publish) the great short novel *Hadji Murad*, which is in a sense a direct counterblast or complement to *Master and Man* and *The Death of Ivan Ilych*. For this story of the Chechen leader who surrendered to the Russians (for devious motives) and later died a violent death at their hands, is a tribute to joyous and savage energies, glorious exactly in proportion to the hero's utter indifference to the idea of death.

Tolstoy, for all his grumbles at high art and vilification of Shakespeare and Beethoven, never abandoned high art himself. And one reason why I have included the story *Albert* (1858) is because it epitomizes his notion of art and its value. The point is put explicitly in a story closely akin to *Albert*, *Lucerne*. In this, the well-fed occupants of a Swiss hotel, having listened entranced to an itinerant Tyrolean street-singer, meanly pay him not a penny. The narrator is enraged, rushes out and hauls the singer back into the hotel, fills him with champagne, and picks a violent quarrel with the waiters, who look down on this shabby intruder – and all with no result save dreadfully to embarrass the hapless singer, who has borne the hotel-guests no malice and whose one idea is to escape as fast as he decently can. The narrator soon realizes he has made a fool of himself. Nevertheless, as he reflects, the truth remains:

This is the strange fate of Art! All seek it and love it – it is the one thing everybody wants and tries to find in life, yet nobody acknowledges its power, nobody values this greatest blessing in the world, nor esteems or is grateful to those who give it to mankind.

In *Albert* Tolstoy imagines the alternative outcome. Say that, unlike the mean-minded Lucerne tourists, you feel a proper gratitude for art – as Delesov does, when Albert's playing has reduced him to tears. What then? What do you do about it? All Delesov can think of is to take Albert over, to clean him up and settle him down and 'in general rescue him from his sordid condition'. It is one of those passing impulses for good, which, so commonly in Tolstoy, are shown to bear no fruit, because they do not fit the facts of existence. (We remember Karenin's abortive 'redemption' and forgiveness of his enemies in *Anna Karenina*.) Delesov's feeling, genuine in itself, quickly turns into self-satisfaction ('Really I'm not altogether a bad fellow'), then into irritation, and by the third day it has almost got forgotten, in the press of other ordinary concerns. And anyway it was all absurd, and his gratitude was useless to Albert. Important as art is, there is nothing you can, or need, 'do' about it; it does not belong in the sphere of obligation and exchange and is its own reward, as virtue is supposed to be. Indeed as soon as we enter Albert's rapturous and drunken daydream we get a sense of the nature of this reward.

If, as *Albert* implies, it is impossible and wrong to dream of possessing or annexing others, it is perhaps on some similar principle (of non-possessiveness and non-interference) that Tolstoy never writes in a comic mode, a mode *asking* you to laugh (like, say, Dickens) – indeed never writes in any mode save that of impartial realism. For it is a cardinal principle with him to allow his characters full rights and full freedom – so that if they condemn themselves, it must be out of their own mouths. But this should not blind us to the fact that Tolstoy has an admirable comic vein. Typically, even in that anguished and heartfelt socio-political tract *What Then Must We Do?* there is one splendidly funny touch. Tolstoy is describing how he recruited aristocratic acquaintances for a hare-brained scheme of his, according to which, while acting as census-takers, they should solve the problem of urban poverty in Moscow by each adopting so many of the poor. His recruits, in their hearts, don't believe a word of it, but they are ashamed not to show enthusiasm, and for their visit to night-lodging-houses they dress themselves in 'shooting jackets and high travelling boots' (which they somehow feel appropriate) and equip themselves with 'peculiar notebooks and extraordinary pencils'.

I need hardly dwell on the fine sardonic humour of *How Much Land Does a Man Need?*, of which James Joyce once wrote to his daughter that it was 'the greatest story that the literature of the world knows'. The effect, of course, depends on Tolstoy's imperturbable neutrality of tone, sustained even to those implacable final sentences: 'His servant picked up the spade and dug a grave long enough for Pakhom to lie in, and buried him in it. Six feet from his head to his heels was all he needed.' As for *The Three Hermits*, it so happens I had never read it till I was making this selection, and it charmed me greatly. It strikes me as a wonderful and profound little joke; and in the unforced way it unfolds it seems a perfect specimen of Tolstoy's very personal, wholly uncoercive, style of humour.

P. N. FURBANK

SELECT BIBLIOGRAPHY

Bayley, John, *Tolstoy and the Novel* (London, 1966).

Berlin, Isaiah, *The Hedgehog and the Fox: An Essay on Tolstoy's View of History* (London, 1954).

Christian, R. F., *Tolstoy: A Critical Introduction* (Cambridge, 1969).

—— (ed.), *Tolstoy's Letters*, 2 vols. (New York, 1978).

—— (ed.), *Tolstoy's Diaries*, 2 vols. (New York, 1985).

Ciatati, Pietro, *Tolstoy*, trans. Raymond Rosenthal (New York, 1986).

Gifford, Henry (ed.), *Leo Tolstoy: A Critical Anthology* (Harmondsworth, 1971).

Gustafson, Richard F., *Leo Tolstoy, Resident and Stranger* (Princeton, 1986).

Hayman, Ronald, *Tolstoy* (New York, 1970).

Knowles, A. V., *Tolstoy: The Critical Heritage* (London, 1978)

Matlaw, Ralph E., *Tolstoy: A Collection of Critical Essays* (Englewood Cliffs, NJ, 1967).

Maude, Aylmer, *The Life of Tolstoy*, 2 vols. (London, 1929–30).

Merejkowski, Dmitri, *Tolstoy as Man and Artist, with an Essay on Dostoievski* (New York, 1902).

Noyes, George Rapall, *Tolstoy* (New York, 1918).

Orwin, Donna Tussing, *Tolstoy's Art and Thought, 1847–1880* (Princeton, 1993).

Rolland, Romain, *The Life of Tolstoy*, trans. B. Miall (New York, 1911).

Shklovsky, Victor, *Leo Tolstoy*, trans. from Russian (Moscow, 1978).

Simmons, Ernest J., *Leo Tolstoy* (Boston, 1946).

—— *Introduction to Tolstoy's Writings* (Chicago, 1968).

Troyat, Henri, *Tolstoy*, trans. Nancy Amphoux (Garden City, NY, 1967).

Wasiolek, Edward, *Tolstoy's Major Fiction* (Chicago, 1978).

Wilson, A. N., *Tolstoy* (London, 1988).

A CHRONOLOGY OF LEO TOLSTOY

1828   28 August (os): born at Yásnaya Polyána, province of Tula, fourth son of Count Nikoláy Tolstoy. Mother dies 1830, father 1837.

1844–7 Studies at University of Kazan (Oriental Languages, then Law). Leaves without graduating.

1851   Goes to Caucasus with elder brother. Participates in army raid on local village. Begins to write *Childhood* (pub. 1852).

1854   Commissioned. *Boyhood.** Active service on Danube; gets posting to Sevastopol.

1855   After its fall returns to Petersburg, already famous for his first two *Sevastopol Sketches*. Literary and social life in the capital.

1856   Leaves army. *A Landlord's Morning.*

1857   Visits Western Europe. August: returns to Yásnaya Polyána.

1859   His interest and success in literature wane. Founds on his estate a school for peasant children. *Three Deaths*; *Family Happiness*.

1860–1 Second visit to Western Europe, in order to study educational methods.

1861   Serves as Arbiter of the Peace, to negotiate land settlements after Emancipation of Serfs.

1862   Death of two brothers. Marries Sophia Behrs, daughter of a Moscow physician. There were to be thirteen children of the marriage, only eight growing up. Publishes educational magazine *Yásnaya Polyána*.

1863   *The Cossacks, Polikúshka*. Begins *War and Peace*.

1865–6 *1805* (first part of *War and Peace*).

1866   Unsuccessfully defends at court martial soldier who had struck officer.

1869   *War and Peace* completed; final vols. published.

1870   Studies drama and Greek.

1871–2 Working on *Primer* for children.

* Tolstoy's works are dated, unless otherwise indicated, according to the year of publication.

1872   *A Prisoner in the Caucasus.*

1873   Goes with family to visit new estate in Samara. Publicizes Samara famine. Begins *Anna Karénina* (completed 1877).

1877   His growing religious problems. Dismay over Russo-Turkish War.

1879   Begins *A Confession* (completed 1882).

1881   Letter to new tsar asking for clemency towards assassins of Alexander II.

1882   *What Men Live By.* Begins *Death of Iván Ilých* and *What Then Must We Do?* (completed 1886).

1883   Meets Chertkóv, afterwards his leading disciple.

1885   Founds with Chertkóv's help the *Intermediary*, to publish edifying popular works, including his own stories. Vegetarian, gives up hunting.

1886   *The Death of Iván Ilých.* Writes play *The Power of Darkness.*

1889   *The Kreutzer Sonata* completed. Begins *Resurrection.*

1891–2 Organizes famine relief.

1893   *The Kingdom of God is Within You* pub. abroad.

1897   Begins *What is Art?* (pub. 1898) and *Hadji Murád.*

1899   *Resurrection.*

1901   Excommunicated from Orthodox Church. Seriously ill. In Crimea meets Chékhov and Górky.

1902   *What is Religion?* completed. Working on play *The Light Shineth in Darkness.*

1903   Denounces pogroms against Jews.

1904   *Shakespeare and the Drama* completed. Also *Hadji Murád* (pub. after his death). Pamphlet on Russo-Japanese War, *Bethink Yourselves!*

1906   Death of favourite daughter Másha. Increasing tension with wife.

1908   *I Cannot Be Silent*, opposing capital punishment. 28 August: celebrations for eightieth birthday.

1909   Frequent disputes with wife. Draws up will relinquishing copyrights. His secretary Gúsev arrested and exiled.

1910   Flight from home, followed by death at Astápovo railway station, 7 November (os).

THE RAID

A VOLUNTEER'S STORY

Набег

I

[WAR always interested me: not war in the sense of manœuvres devised by great generals – my imagination refused to follow such immense movements, I did not understand them – but the reality of war, the actual killing. I was more interested to know in what way and under the influence of what feeling one soldier kills another than to know how the armies were arranged at Austerlitz and Borodino.

I had long passed the time when, pacing the room alone and waving my arms, I imagined myself a hero instantaneously slaughtering an immense number of men and receiving a generalship as well as imperishable glory for so doing. The question now occupying me was different: under the influence of what feeling does a man, with no apparent advantage to himself, decide to subject himself to danger and, what is more surprising still, to kill his fellow men? I always wished to think that this is done under the influence of anger, but we cannot suppose that all those who fight are angry all the time, and I had to postulate feelings of self-preservation and duty.

What is courage – that quality respected in all ages and among all nations? Why is this good quality – contrary to all others – sometimes met with in vicious men? Can it be that to endure danger calmly is merely a physical capacity and that people respect it in the same way that they do a man's tall stature or robust frame? Can a horse be called brave, which fearing the whip throws itself down a steep place where it will be smashed to pieces; or a child who fearing to be punished runs into a forest where it will lose itself; or a woman who for fear of shame kills her baby and has to endure penal prosecution; or a man who from vanity resolves to kill a fellow creature and exposes himself to the danger of being killed?

In every danger there is a choice. Does it not depend on whether the choice is prompted by a noble feeling or a base one whether it should be called courage or cowardice? These were the questions and the doubts that occupied my mind and to decide which I intended to avail myself of the first opportunity to go into action.

In the summer of 184- I was living in the Caucasus at the small fortified post of N——.][1]

On the twelfth of July Captain Khlopov entered the low door of my earth-hut. He was wearing epaulettes and carrying a sword, which I had never before seen him do since I had reached the Caucasus.

'I come straight from the colonel's,' he said in answer to my questioning look. 'Tomorrow our battalion is to march.'

'Where to?' I asked.

'To M. The forces are to assemble there.'

'And from there I suppose they will go into action?'

'I expect so.'

'In what direction? What do you think?'

'What is there to think about? I am telling you what I know. A Tartar galloped here last night and brought orders from the general for the battalion to march with two days' rations of rusks. But where to, why, and for how long, we do not ask, my friend. We are told to go – and that's enough.'

'But if you are to take only two days' rations of rusks it proves that the troops won't be out longer than that.'

'It proves nothing at all!'

'How is that?' I asked with surprise.

'Because it is so. We went to Dargo and took one week's rations of rusks, but we stayed there nearly a month.'

'Can I go with you?' I asked after a pause.

'You could, no doubt, but my advice is, don't. Why run risks?'

'Oh, but you must allow me not to take your advice. I have been here a whole month solely on the chance of seeing an action, and you wish me to miss it!'

'Well, you must please yourself. But really you had better stay behind. You could wait for us here and might go hunting – and we would go our way, and it would be splendid,' he said with such con-

---

[1] The parts of this story enclosed in square brackets are those originally suppressed by the censor.

viction that for a moment it really seemed to me too that it would be 'splendid'. However, I told him decidedly that nothing would induce me to stay behind.

'But what is there for you to see?' the captain went on, still trying to dissuade me. 'Do you want to know what battles are like? Read Mikhaylovski Danilevski's *Description of War*. It's a fine book, it gives a detailed account of everything. It gives the position of every corps and describes how battles are fought.'

'All that does not interest me,' I replied.

'What is it then? Do you simply wish to see how people are killed? – In 1832 we had a fellow here, also a civilian, a Spaniard I think he was. He took part with us in two campaigns, wearing some kind of blue mantle. Well, they did for the fine fellow. You won't astonish anyone here, friend!'

Humiliating though it was that the captain so misjudged my motives, I did not try to disabuse him.

'Was he brave?' I asked.

'Heaven only knows: he always used to ride in front, and where there was firing there he always was.'

'Then he must have been brave,' said I.

'No. Pushing oneself in where one is not needed does not prove one to be brave.'

'Then what do you call brave?'

'Brave? . . . Brave?' repeated the captain with the air of one to whom such a question presents itself for the first time. 'He who does what he ought to do is brave,' he said after thinking awhile.

I remembered that Plato defines courage as 'The knowledge of what should and what should not be feared', and despite the looseness and vagueness of the captain's definition I thought that the fundamental ideas of the two were not so different as they might appear, and that the captain's definition was even more correct than that of the Greek philosopher. For if the captain had been able to express himself like Plato he would no doubt have said that, 'He is brave who fears only what should be feared and not what should not be feared'.

I wished to explain my idea to the captain.

'Yes,' said I, 'it seems to me that in every danger there is a choice, and a choice made under the influence of a sense of duty is courage, but a choice made under the influence of a base motive is cowardice. Therefore a man who risks his life from vanity, curiosity, or greed, cannot be called brave; while on the other hand he who avoids a danger from honest consideration for his family, or simply from conviction, cannot be called a coward.'

The captain looked at me with a curious expression while I was speaking.

'Well, that I cannot prove to you,' he said, filling his pipe, 'but we have a cadet here who is fond of philosophizing. You should have a talk with him. He also writes verses.'

I had known of the captain before I left Russia, but I had only made his acquaintance in the Caucasus. His mother, Mary Ivanovna Khlopova, a small and poor landowner, lives within two miles of my estate. Before I left for the Caucasus I had called on her. The old lady was very glad to hear that I should see her 'Pashenka', by which pet name she called the grey-haired elderly captain, and that I, 'a living letter', could tell him all about her and take him a small parcel from her. Having treated me to excellent pie and smoked goose, Mary Ivanovna went into her bedroom and returned with a black bag to which a black silk ribbon was attached.

'Here, this is the icon of our Mother Mediatress of the Burning Bush,' said she, crossing herself and kissing the icon of the Virgin and placing it in my hands. 'Please let him have it. You see, when he went to the Caucasus I had a Mass said for him and promised, if he remained alive and safe, to order this icon of the Mother of God for him. And now for eighteen years the Mediatress and the Holy Saints have had mercy on him, he has not been wounded once, and yet in what battles has he not taken part? . . . What Michael who went with him told me was enough, believe me, to make one's hair stand on end. You see, what I know about him is only from others. He, my pet, never writes me about his campaigns for fear of frightening me.'

(After I reached the Caucasus I learnt, and then not from the captain himself, that he had been severely wounded four times and of course never wrote to his mother either about his wounds or his campaigns.)

'So let him now wear this holy image,' she continued. 'I give it him with my blessing. May the Most Holy Mediatress guard him. Especially when going into battle let him wear it. Tell him so, dear friend. Say "Your mother wishes it."'

I promised to carry out her instructions carefully.

'I know you will grow fond of my Pashenka,' continued the old lady. 'He is such a splendid fellow. Will you believe it, he never lets a year pass without sending me some money, and he also helps my daughter Annushka a good deal, and all out of his pay! I thank God for having given me such a child,' she continued with tears in her eyes.

'Does he often write to you?' I asked.

'Seldom, my dear: perhaps once a year. Only when he sends the money, not otherwise. He says, "If I don't write to you, mother, that means I am alive and well. Should anything befall me, which God forbid, they'll tell you without me."'

When I handed his mother's present to the captain (it was in my own quarters) he asked for a bit of paper, carefully wrapped it up, and then put it away. I told him many things about his mother's life. He remained silent, and when I had finished speaking he went to a corner of the room and busied himself for what seemed a long time, filling his pipe.

'Yes, she's a splendid old woman!' he said from there in a rather muffled voice. 'Will God ever let me see her again?'

These simple words expressed much love and sadness.

'Why do you serve here?' I asked.

'One has to serve,' he answered with conviction.

['You should transfer to Russia. You would then be nearer to her.'

'To Russia? To Russia?' repeated the captain, dubiously swaying his head and smiling mournfully. 'Here I am still of some use, but there I should be the least of the officers. And besides, the double pay we get here also means something to a poor man.'

'Can it be, Pavel Ivanovich, that living as you do the ordinary pay would not suffice?'

'And does the double pay suffice?' interjected the captain. 'Look at our officers! Have any of them a brass farthing? They all go on tick at the sutler's, and are all up to their ears in debt. You say "living as I do".... Do you really think that living as I do I have anything over out of my salary? Not a farthing! You don't yet know what prices are like here; everything is three times dearer....']

The captain lived economically, did not play cards, rarely went carousing, and smoked the cheapest tobacco (which for some reason he called home-grown tobacco). I had liked him before – he had one of those simple, calm, Russian faces which are easy and pleasant to look straight in the eyes – and after this talk I felt a sincere regard for him.

II

NEXT morning at four o'clock the captain came for me. He wore an old threadbare coat without epaulettes, wide Caucasian trousers, a white sheepskin cap the wool of which had grown yellow and limp, and had a shabby Asiatic sword strapped round his shoulder. The small white horse he rode ambled along with short strides, hanging its head down and swinging its thin tail. Although the worthy captain's figure was not very martial or even good-looking, it expressed such equanimity towards everything around him that it involuntarily inspired respect.

I did not keep him waiting a single moment, but mounted my horse at once, and we rode together through the gates of the fort.

The battalion was some five hundred yards ahead of us and looked like a dense, oscillating, black mass. It was only possible to guess that it was an infantry battalion by the bayonets which looked like needles standing close together, and by the sound of the soldiers' songs which occasionally reached us, the beating of a drum, and the delightful voice of the Sixth Company's second tenor, which had often charmed me at the fort. The road lay along the middle of a deep and broad ravine by the side of a stream which had overflowed its banks. Flocks of wild pigeons whirled above it, now alighting on the rocky banks, now turning in the air in rapid circles and vanishing out of sight. The sun was not yet visible, but the crest of the right side of the ravine was just beginning to be lit up. The grey and whitish rock, the yellowish-green moss, the dew-covered bushes of Christ's Thorn, dogberry, and dwarf elm, appeared extraordinarily distinct and salient in the golden morning light, but the other side and the valley, wrapped in thick mist which floated in uneven layers, were damp and gloomy and presented an indefinite mingling of colours: pale purple, almost black, dark green, and white. Right in front of us, strikingly distinct against the dark-blue horizon, rose the bright, dead-white masses of the snowy mountains, with their shadows and outlines fantastic and yet exquisite in every detail. Crickets, grasshoppers, and thousands of other insects, awoke in the tall grasses and filled the air with their clear and ceaseless sounds: it was as if innumerable tiny bells were ringing inside our very ears. The air was full of the scent of water, grass, and mist: the scent of a lovely early summer morning. The captain struck a light and lit his pipe, and the smell of his cheap tobacco and of the tinder seemed to me extraordinarily pleasant.

To overtake the infantry more quickly we left the road. The captain appeared more thoughtful than usual, did not take his Daghestan pipe from his mouth, and at every step touched with his heels his horse, which swaying from side to side left a scarcely perceptible green track in the tall wet grass. From under its very feet, with the cry and the whirr of wings which involuntarily sends a thrill through every sportsman, a pheasant rose, and flew slowly upwards. The captain did not take the least notice of it.

We had nearly overtaken the battalion when we heard the thud of a horse galloping behind us, and that same moment a good-looking youth in an officer's uniform and white sheepskin cap galloped past us. He smiled in passing, nodded to the captain, and flourished his whip. I only had time to notice that he sat his horse and held his reins with peculiar grace, that he had beautiful black eyes, a fine nose, and only the first indications of a moustache. What specially pleased me about him was that he could not repress a smile when he noticed our admiration. This smile alone showed him to be very young.

'Where is he galloping to?' muttered the captain with a dissatisfied air, without taking the pipe from his mouth.

'Who is he?' I replied.

'Ensign Alanin, a subaltern in my company. He came from the Cadet Corps only a month ago.'

'I suppose he is going into action for the first time,' I said.

'That's why he is so delighted,' answered the captain, thoughtfully shaking his head. 'Youth!'

'But how could he help being pleased? I can fancy how interesting it must be for a young officer.'

The captain remained silent for a minute or two.

'That is just why I say "youth",' he added in a deep voice. 'What is there to be pleased at without ever having seen the thing? When one has seen it many times one is not so pleased. There are now, let us say, twenty of us officers here: one or other is sure to be killed or wounded, that is quite certain. Today it may be I, tomorrow he, the next day a third. So what is there to be pleased about?'

III

As soon as the bright sun appeared above the hill and lit up the valley along which we were marching, the wavy clouds of mist

cleared and it grew hot. The soldiers, with muskets and sacks on their
shoulders, marched slowly along the dusty road. Now and then
Ukrainian words and laughter could be heard in their ranks. Several
old soldiers in white blouses (most of them non-commissioned
officers) walked together by the roadside, smoking their pipes and
conversing gravely. Heavily laden wagons drawn by three horses
moved steadily along, raising thick clouds of dust that hung motionless in the air. The officers rode in front: some of them caracoled –
whipping their horses, making them take three or four leaps and then,
pulling their heads round, stopping abruptly. Others were occupied
with the singers, who in spite of the heat and sultriness sang song
after song.

With the mounted Tartars, about two hundred yards ahead of the
infantry, rode a tall handsome lieutenant in Asiatic costume on a large
white horse. He was known in the regiment as a desperate dare-
devil who would spit the truth out at anybody. He wore a black
tunic trimmed with gold braid, leggings to match, soft closely fitting
gold-braided oriental shoes, a yellow coat and a tall sheepskin cap
pushed back from his forehead. Fastened to the silver strap that lay
across his chest and back, he carried a powder-flask, and a pistol
behind him. Another pistol and a silver-mounted dagger hung from
his girdle, and above these a sword in a red leather sheath, and a
musket in a black cover, were slung over his shoulder. By his clothing,
by the way he sat his horse, by his general bearing, in fact by his every
movement, one could see that he tried to resemble a Tartar. He even
spoke to the Tartars with whom he was riding in a language I did not
know, and from the bewildered and amused looks with which they
glanced at one another I surmised that they did not understand him
either. He was one of our young officers, dare-devil braves who shape
their lives on the model of Lermontov's and Marlinsky's heroes.
These officers see the Caucasus only through the prism of such books
as *A Hero of our Time*, and *Mullah-Nur*,[2] and are guided in their
actions not by their own inclinations but by the examples of their
models.

The lieutenant, for instance, may perhaps have liked the company
of well-bred women and men of rank: generals, colonels, and aides-
de-camp (it is even my conviction that he liked such society very
much, for he was exceedingly ambitious), but he considered it his
imperative duty to turn his roughest side to all important men, though

[2] Novels by the above-mentioned authors.

he was strictly moderate in his rudeness to them; and when any lady came to the fort he considered it his duty to walk before her window with his bosom friends, in a red shirt and with slippers on his bare feet, and shout and swear at the top of his voice. But all this he did not so much with the intention of offending her as to let her see what beautiful white feet he had, and how easy it would be to fall in love with him should he desire it. Or he would often go with two or three friendly Tartars to the hills at night to lie in ambush by the roadside to watch for passing hostile Tartars and kill them: and though his heart told him more than once that there was nothing valiant in this, he considered himself bound to cause suffering to people with whom he affected to be disillusioned and whom he chose to hate and despise. He always carried two things: a large icon hanging round his neck, and a dagger which he wore over his shirt even when in bed. He sincerely believed that he had enemies. To persuade himself that he must avenge himself on someone and wash away some insult with blood was his greatest enjoyment. He was convinced that hatred, vengeance, and contempt for the human race were the noblest and most poetic of emotions. But his mistress (a Circassian of course), whom I happened to meet subsequently, used to say that he was the kindest and mildest of men, and that every evening he wrote down his dismal thoughts in his diary, as well as his accounts on ruled paper, and prayed to God on his knees. And how much he suffered merely to appear in his own eyes what he wished to be! For his comrades and the soldiers could never see him as he wished to appear. Once on one of his nocturnal expeditions on the road with his bosom friends he happened to wound a hostile Chechen with a bullet in the leg, and took him prisoner. After that the Chechen lived for seven weeks with the lieutenant, who attended to him and nursed him as he would have nursed his dearest friend, and when the Chechen recovered he gave him presents and set him free. After that, during one of our expeditions when the lieutenant was retreating with the soldiers of the cordon and firing to keep back the foe, he heard someone among the enemy call him by name, and the man he had wounded rode forward and made signs to the lieutenant to do the same. The lieutenant rode up to his friend and pressed his hand. The hillsmen stood some way back and did not fire, but scarcely had the lieutenant turned his horse to return before several men shot at him and a bullet grazed the small of his back. Another time, at night, when a fire had broken out in the fort and two companies of soldiers were putting it out, I myself saw how the tall figure of a man mounted on a black horse and lit up by the red glow of the fire suddenly appeared among the crowd and, pushing through, rode up to the very flames. When quite close the lieutenant jumped from his horse and rushed into the house, one side of which was burning. Five minutes later he came out with singed hair and scorched elbow, carrying in his bosom two pigeons he had rescued from the flames.

His name was Rosenkranz, yet he often spoke of his descent, deducing it somehow from the Varangians (the first rulers of Russia), and clearly demonstrated that he and his ancestors were pure Russians.

IV

THE sun had done half its journey, and cast its hot rays through the glowing air onto the dry earth. The dark blue sky was perfectly clear, and only the base of the snowy mountains began to clothe itself in lilac-tinged white clouds. The motionless air seemed full of transparent dust, the heat was becoming unbearable.

Half-way on their march the troops reached a small stream and halted. The soldiers stacked their muskets and rushed to the stream; the commander of the battalion sat down in the shade on a drum, his full face assuming the correct expression denoting the greatness of his rank. He, together with some other officers, prepared to have a snack. The captain lay down on the grass under his company's wagon. The brave Lieutenant Rosenkranz and some other young officers disposed themselves on their outspread cloaks and got ready for a drinking-bout, as could be gathered from the bottles and flasks arranged round them, as well as from the peculiar animation of the singers who, standing before them in a semicircle, sang a Caucasian dance-song with a whistling obbligato interjected:

> Shamyl, he began to riot
> In the days gone by,
> Try-ry-rataty,
> In the days gone by!

Among these officers was the young ensign who had overtaken us in the morning. He was very amusing: his eyes shone, he spoke rather thickly, and he wished to kiss and declare his love to everyone. Poor boy! He did not know that he might appear funny in such a situation, that the frankness and tenderness with which he assailed everyone predisposed them not to the affection he so longed for, but to ridicule; nor did he know that when, quite heated, he at last threw himself down on the cloak and rested on his elbow with his thick black hair thrown back, he looked uncommonly charming.

[In a word, everyone was cheerful, except perhaps one officer who, sitting under his company's cart, had lost the horse he was riding to another officer at cards and had agreed to hand it over when they reached headquarters. He was vainly trying to induce the other to play again, offering to stake a casket which everyone could confirm he had bought for thirty rubles from a Jew, but which – merely because he was in difficulties – he was now willing to stake for fifteen. His opponent looked casually into the distance and persistently remained silent, till at last he remarked that he was terribly anxious to have a doze.

I confess that from the time I started from the fort and decided to take part in this action, gloomy reflections involuntarily rose in my mind, and so – since one has a tendency to judge of others by oneself] I listened with curiosity to the conversation of the soldiers and officers and attentively watched the expression of their faces, but could find absolutely no trace of the anxiety I myself experienced: jokes, laughter and anecdotes, gambling and drunkenness, expressed the general carelessness and indifference to the impending danger [as if all these people had long ago finished their affairs in this world. What was this – firmness, habituation to danger, or carelessness and indifference to life? Or was it all these things together as well as others I did not know, forming a complex but powerful moral motive of human nature termed *esprit de corps* – a subtle code embracing within itself a general expression of all the virtues and vices of men banded together in any permanent condition, a code each new member involuntarily submits to unmurmuringly and which does not change with the individuals, since whoever they may be the sum total of human tendencies everywhere and always remains the same?]

V

TOWARDS seven that evening, dusty and tired, we entered the wide fortified gate of Fort M. The sun was already setting and threw its rosy slanting rays on the picturesque little batteries, on the gardens with their tall poplars which surrounded the fortress, on the yellow gleaming cultivated fields, and on the white clouds that crowding round the snowy peaks had, as if trying to imitate them, formed a range not less fantastic and beautiful. On the horizon the new moon appeared delicate as a little cloud. In the Tartar village, from the roof of a hut, a Tartar was calling the faithful to prayer, and our singers raised their voices with renewed energy and vigour.

After a rest and after tidying myself up a bit, I went to an adjutant of my acquaintance to ask him to let the general know of my intention. On my way from the suburb where I had put up I noticed in Fort M. something I did not at all expect: a pretty little brougham overtook me, in which I caught sight of a fashionable bonnet and from which I overheard some French words. The sounds of some 'Lizzie' or 'Katenka' polka, played on a bad ramshackle piano, reached me through the windows of the commander's house. In a little grocery and wine shop which I passed, some clerks with cigarettes in their fingers sat drinking wine, and I heard one of them say to another, 'No, excuse me, as to politics, Mary Gregorevna is first of our ladies.' A Jew in a worn-out coat, with a bent back and sickly countenance, was dragging along a wheezy barrel-organ and the whole suburb resounded to the tones of the finale of 'Lucia'. Two women in rustling dresses with silk kerchiefs on their heads and carrying bright-coloured parasols passed by along the planks that did duty for a pavement. Two girls, one in a pink, the other in a blue dress, stood bareheaded beside the earth-embankments of a low-roofed house, and shrieked with high-pitched, forced laughter, evidently to attract the attention of passing officers. Officers, dressed in new uniforms with glittering epaulettes and white gloves, flaunted along the street and on the boulevard.

I found my acquaintance on the ground floor of the general's house. I had scarcely had time to explain my wish to him and to get his reply that it could easily be fulfilled, when the pretty little brougham I had noticed outside rattled past the window we were sitting at. A tall, well-built man in an infantry major's uniform and epaulettes got out and entered the house.

'Oh, please excuse me,' said the adjutant, rising, 'I must go and announce them to the general.'

'Who is it?' I asked.

'The countess,' he replied, and buttoning his uniform he rushed upstairs.

A few minutes later a very handsome man in a frock coat without epaulettes and with a white cross in his buttonhole went out into the porch. He was not tall but remarkably good-looking. He was followed by the major, an adjutant, and a couple of other officers. The general's gait, voice, and all his movements, showed him to be a man well aware of his own value.

'*Bonsoir, madame la comtesse,*'[3] he said, offering his hand through the carriage window.

A small hand in a kid glove pressed his, and a pretty smiling face in a yellow bonnet appeared at the carriage window.

Of the conversation which lasted several minutes I only overheard the general say laughingly as I passed by:

'*Vous savez que j'ai fait vœu de combattre les infidèles; prenez donc garde de la devenir.*'[4]

A laugh replied from inside the carriage.

'*Adieu donc, cher général!*'[5]

'*Non, au revoir,*' said the general, ascending the steps of the porch. '*N'oubliez pas, que je m'invite pour la soirée de demain.*'[6]

The carriage rattled off [and the general went into the sitting-room with the major. Passing by the open window of the adjutant's room, he noticed my un-uniformed figure and turned his kind attention to me. Having heard my request he announced his complete agreement with it and passed on into his room.]

'There again', I thought as I walked home, 'is a man who possesses all that Russians strive after: rank, riches, distinction; and this man, the day before an engagement the outcome of which is known only to God, jokes with a pretty woman and promises to have tea with her next day, just as if they had met at a ball!'

[I remembered a reflection I had heard a Tartar utter, to the effect that only a pauper can be brave. '*Become rich, become a coward,*' said he, not at all to offend his comrade but as a common and unquestionable rule. But the general could lose, together with his life, much more than anyone else I had had an opportunity of observing and, contrary to the Tartar's rule, no one had shown such a pleasant,

[3] 'Good evening, Countess.'

[4] 'You know I have sworn to fight the infidels (the unfaithful), so beware of becoming one.'

[5] 'Goodbye then, dear general.'

[6] 'No, *au revoir*. Don't forget that I am inviting myself for tomorrow's soirée.'

graceful indifference and confidence as he. My conceptions of courage became completely confused.]

At that same adjutant's I met a young man who surprised me even more. He was a young lieutenant of the K. regiment who was noted for his almost feminine meekness and timidity and who had come to the adjutant to pour out his vexation and resentment against those who, he said, had intrigued against him to keep him from taking part in the impending action. He said it was mean to behave in that way, that it was unfriendly, that he would not forget it, and so forth. Intently as I watched the expression of his face and listened to the sound of his voice, I could not help feeling convinced that he was not pretending but was genuinely filled with indignation and grief at not being allowed to go and shoot Circassians and expose himself to their fire. He was grieving like a little child who has been unjustly birched . . . I could make nothing at all of it.

VI

THE troops were to start at ten in the evening. At half-past eight I mounted and rode to the general's, but thinking that he and his adjutant were busy I tied my horse to the fence and sat down on an earth-bank intending to catch the general when he came out.

The heat and glare of the sun were now replaced by the coolness of night and the soft light of the young moon, which had formed a pale glimmering semicircle around itself on the deep blue of the starry sky and was already setting. Lights appeared in the windows of the houses and shone through cracks in the shutters of the earth huts. The stately poplars, beyond the white moonlit earth huts with their rush-thatched roofs, looked darker and taller than ever against the horizon.

The long shadows of the houses, the trees, and the fences, stretched out daintily on the dusty road. . . . From the river came the ringing voices of frogs;[7] along the street came the sound of hurried steps and voices talking, or the gallop of a horse, and from the suburb the tones of a barrel-organ playing now 'The winds are blowing', now some 'Aurora Waltz'.

I will not say in what meditations I was absorbed: first, because I

[7] Frogs in the Caucasus make a noise quite different from the croaking of frogs elsewhere. L. T.

should be ashamed to confess the gloomy waves of thought that insistently flooded my soul while around me I noticed nothing but gaiety and joy, and secondly, because it would not suit my story. I was so absorbed in thought that I did not even notice the bell strike eleven and the general with his suite ride past me.

[Hastily mounting my horse I set out to overtake the detachment.] The rearguard was still within the gates of the fort. I had great difficulty in making my way across the bridge among the guns, ammunition wagons, carts of different companies, and officers noisily giving orders. Once outside the gates I trotted past the troops who, stretching out over nearly three-quarters of a mile, were silently moving on amid the darkness, and I overtook the general. As I rode past the guns drawn out in single file, and the officers who rode between them, I was hurt as by a discord in the quiet and solemn harmony by the German accents of a voice shouting, 'A linstock, you devil!' and the voice of a soldier hurriedly exclaiming, 'Shevchenko, the lieutenant wants a light!'

The greater part of the sky was now overcast by long strips of dark grey clouds; it was only here and there that a few stars twinkled dimly among them. The moon had already sunk behind the near horizon of the black hills visible to the right and threw a faint trembling light on their peaks, in sharp contrast to the impenetrable darkness enveloping their base. The air was so warm and still that it seemed as if not a single blade of grass, not a single cloudlet, was moving. It was so dark that even objects close at hand could not be distinguished. By the sides of the road I seemed to see now rocks, now animals, now some strange kind of men, and I discovered that they were merely bushes only when I heard them rustle, or felt the dew with which they were sprinkled.

Before me I saw a dense heaving wall followed by some dark moving spots; this was the cavalry vanguard and the general with his suite. Another similar dark mass, only lower, moved beside us; this was the infantry.

The silence that reigned over the whole division was so great that all the mingling sounds of night with their mysterious charm were distinctly audible: the far-off mournful howling of jackals, now like agonized weeping, now like chuckling; the monotonous resounding song of crickets, frogs, and quails; a sort of rumbling I could not at all account for but which seemed to draw nearer; and all those scarcely audible motions of Nature which can neither be understood

nor defined, mingled into one beautiful harmony which we call the
stillness of night. This stillness was interrupted by, or rather combined with, the dull thud of hoofs and the rustling of the tall grass
caused by the slowly advancing detachment.

Only very occasionally could the clang of a heavy gun, the sound
of bayonets touching one another, hushed voices, or the snorting of
a horse, be heard. [By the scent of the wet juicy grass which sank
under our horses' feet, by the light steam rising from the ground and
by the horizons seen on two sides of us, it was evident that we were
moving across a wide, luxuriant meadow.] Nature seemed to breathe
with pacifying beauty and power.

Can it be that there is not room for all men on this beautiful earth
under those immeasurable starry heavens? Can it be possible that in
the midst of this entrancing Nature feelings of hatred, vengeance, or
the desire to exterminate their fellows, can endure in the souls of
men? All that is unkind in the hearts of men should, one would think,
vanish at contact with Nature – that most direct expression of beauty
and goodness.

[War! What an incomprehensible phenomenon! When one's
reason asks: 'Is it just, is it necessary?' an inner voice always replies
'No'. Only the persistence of this unnatural occurrence makes it
seem natural, and a feeling of self-preservation makes it seem just.

Who will doubt that in the war of the Russians against the
mountain-tribes, justice – resulting from a feeling of self-preservation
– is on our side? Were it not for this war, what would secure the
neighbouring rich and cultured Russian territories from robbery,
murder, and raids by wild and warlike tribes? But consider two
private persons. On whose side is the feeling of self-preservation and
consequently of justice? Is it on the side of this ragamuffin – some
Djemi or other – who hearing of the approach of the Russians
snatches down his old gun from the wall, puts three or four charges
(which he will only reluctantly discharge) in his pouch and runs to
meet the giaours, and on seeing that the Russians still advance,
approaching the fields he has sown which they will tread down and
his hut which they will burn, and the ravine where his mother, his
wife, and his children have hidden themselves, shaking with fear –
seeing that he will be deprived of all that constitutes his happiness – in
impotent anger and with a cry of despair tears off his tattered jacket,
flings down his gun, and drawing his sheepskin cap over his eyes
sings his death-song and flings himself headlong onto the Russian

bayonets with only a dagger in his hand? Is justice on his side or on
that of this officer on the general's staff who is singing French chan-
sonettes so well just as he rides past us? He has a family in Russia,
relations, friends, serfs, and obligations towards them, but has no
reason or desire to be at enmity with the hillsmen, and has come to the
Caucasus just by chance and to show his courage. Or is it on the side
of my acquaintance the adjutant, who only wishes to obtain a cap-
taincy and a comfortable position as soon as possible and for that
reason has become the hillsmen's enemy? Or is it on the side of this
young German who, with a strong German accent, is demanding a
linstock from the artillerymen? What devil has brought him from his
fatherland and set him down in this distant region? Why should this
Saxon, Kaspar Lavrentich, mix himself up in our bloodthirsty con-
flict with these turbulent neighbours?]

VII

WE had been riding for more than two hours. I was beginning to
shiver and feel drowsy. Through the gloom I still seemed to see the
same indefinite forms; a little way in front the same black wall and
the moving spots. Close in front of me I could see the crupper of a
white horse which swung its tail and threw its hind legs wide apart,
the back of a white Circassian coat on which could be discerned a
musket in a black case, and the glimmering butt of a pistol in an
embroidered holster; the glow of a cigarette lit up a fair moustache,
a beaver collar and a hand in a chamois glove. Every now and then
I leant over my horse's neck, shutting my eyes and forgetting myself
for a few minutes, then startled by the familiar tramping and rustling
I glanced round, and felt as if I were standing still and the black wall
in front was moving towards me, or that it had stopped and I should
in a moment ride into it. At one such moment the rumbling which
increased and seemed to approach, and the cause of which I could not
guess, struck me forcibly: it was the sound of water. We were
entering a deep gorge and approaching a mountain-stream that was
overflowing its banks.[8] The rumbling increased, the damp grass
became thicker and taller and the bushes closer, while the horizon
gradually narrowed. Now and then bright lights appeared here and
there against the dark background of the hills, and vanished instantly.

[8] In the Caucasus rivers are apt to overflow in July. L. T.

'Tell me, please, what are those lights?' I asked in a whisper of a Tartar riding beside me.

'Don't you know?' he replied.

'No.'

'The hillsmen have tied straw to poles and are waving it about alight.'

'Why are they doing that?'

'So that everyone should know that the Russians have come. Oh, oh! What a bustle is going on now in the *aouls*! Everybody's dragging his belongings into the ravine,' he said laughing.

'Why, do they already know in the mountains that a detachment is on its way?' I asked him.

'How can they help knowing? They always know. Our people are like that.'

'Then Shamyl[9] too is preparing for action?' I asked.

'No,' he answered, shaking his head, 'Shamyl won't go into action; Shamyl will send his *naibs*,[10] and he himself will look on through a telescope from above.'

'Does he live far away?'

'Not far. Some eight miles to the left.'

'How do you know?' I asked. 'Have you been there?'

'I have. Our people have all been.'

'Have you seen Shamyl?'

'Such as we don't see Shamyl! There are a hundred, three hundred, a thousand *murids*[11] all round him, and Shamyl is in the centre,' he said, with an expression of servile admiration.

Looking up, it was possible to discern that the sky, now cleared, was beginning to grow lighter in the east and the pleiades to sink towards the horizon, but the ravine through which we were marching was still damp and gloomy.

Suddenly a little way in front of us several lights flashed through the darkness; at the same moment some bullets flew whizzing past amid the surrounding silence [and sharp abrupt firing could be heard and loud cries, as piercing as cries of despair but expressing instead of

[9] Shamyl was the leader (in 1834–59) of the Caucasian hill-tribes in their resistance to Russia.

[10] A *naib* was a man to whom Shamyl had entrusted some administrative office. L. T.

[11] The word *murid* has several meanings, but here it denotes something between an adjutant and a bodyguard.

fear such a passion of brutal audacity and rage that one could not but shudder at hearing it]. It was the enemy's advanced picket. The Tartars who composed it whooped, fired at random, and then ran in different directions.

All became silent again. The general called up an interpreter. A Tartar in a white Circassian coat rode up to him and, gesticulating and whispering, talked with him for some time.

'Colonel Khasanov! Order the cordon to take open order,' commanded the general with a quiet but distinct drawl.

The detachment advanced to the river, the black hills and gorges were left behind, the dawn appeared. The vault of the heavens, in which a few pale stars were still dimly visible, seemed higher; the sunrise glow beyond shone brightly in the east, a fresh penetrating breeze blew from the west and the white mists rose like steam above the rushing stream.

VIII

Our guide pointed out a ford and the cavalry vanguard, followed by the general, began crossing the stream. The water which reached to the horses' chests rushed with tremendous force between the white boulders which here and there appeared on a level with its surface, and formed foaming and gurgling ripples round the horses' legs. The horses, surprised by the noise of the water, lifted their heads and pricked their ears, but stepped evenly and carefully against the current on the uneven bottom of the stream. Their riders lifted their feet and their weapons. The infantry, literally in nothing but their shirts, linked arm in arm by twenties and holding above the water their muskets to which their bundles of clothing were fastened, made great efforts (as the strained expression of their faces showed) to resist the force of the current. The mounted artillerymen with loud shouts drove their horses into the water at a trot. The guns and green ammunition wagons, over which the water occasionally splashed, rang against the stony bottom, but the sturdy little horses, churning the water, pulled at the traces in unison and with dripping manes and tails clambered out on the opposite bank.

As soon as the crossing was accomplished the general's face suddenly assumed a meditative and serious look and he turned his horse and, followed by the cavalry, rode at a trot down a broad glade which opened out before us in the midst of the forest. A cordon of mounted Cossacks was scattered along the skirts of the forest.

In the woods we noticed a man on foot dressed in a Circassian coat and wearing a tall cap – then a second and a third. One of the officers said: 'Those are Tartars.' Then a puff of smoke appeared from behind a tree, a shot, and another. . . . Our rapid fire drowns the enemy's. Only now and then a bullet, with a slow sound like the buzzing of a bee's wings, passes by and proves that the firing is not all ours. Now the infantry at a run and the guns at a trot pass into the cordon. You can hear the boom of the guns, the metallic sounds of flying grape-shot, the hissing of rockets, and the crackle of musketry. Over the wide glade on all sides you can see cavalry, infantry, and artillery. Puffs of smoke mingle with the dew-covered verdure and the mist. Colonel Khasanov, approaching the general at full gallop, suddenly reins in his horse.

'Your Excellency, shall we order the cavalry to charge?' he says, raising his hand to his cap. 'The enemy's colours[12] are in sight,' and he points with his whip to some mounted Tartars in front of whom ride two men on white horses with bits of blue and red stuff fastened to poles in their hands.

'Go, and God be with you, Ivan Mikhaylovich!' says the general.

The colonel turns his horse sharply round, draws his sword, and shouts 'Hurrah!'

'Hurrah! Hurrah! Hurrah!' comes from the ranks, and the cavalry gallop after him. . . .

Everyone looks on with interest: there is a colour, another, a third and a fourth. . . .

The enemy, not waiting for the attack, hides in the wood and thence opens a small-arms fire. Bullets come flying more and more frequently.

'Quel charmant coup d'œil!'[13] says the general, rising slightly, English fashion, in his saddle on his slim-legged black horse.

'Charmant!' answers the major, rolling his r's, and striking his horse he rides up to the general: 'C'est un vrai plaisir que la guerre dans un aussi beau pays,'[14] he says.

[12] The colours among the hillsmen correspond to those of our troops, except that every dzhigit or 'brave' among them may make his own colours and carry them. L. T.

[13] 'What a charming view.'

[14] 'Charming . . . War in such beautiful country is a real pleasure.'

'*Et surtout en bonne compagnie*,'[15] replies the general with a pleasant smile.

The major bows.

At that moment a hostile cannon-ball flies past with a disagreeable whiz, and strikes something. We hear behind us the moan of a wounded man.

This moaning strikes me so strangely that the warlike scene instantly loses all its charm for me. But no one except myself seems to notice it: the major laughs with apparently greater gusto, another officer repeats with perfect calm the first words of a sentence he had just been saying, the general looks the other way and with the quietest smile says something in French.

'Shall we reply to their fire?' asks the commander of the artillery, galloping up.

'Yes, frighten them a bit!' carelessly replies the general, lighting a cigar.

The battery takes up its position and the firing begins. The earth groans under the shots, the discharges flash out incessantly, and smoke, through which it is scarcely possible to distinguish the artillerymen moving round their guns, veils your sight.

The *aoul* has been bombarded. Colonel Khasanov rides up again, and at the general's command gallops towards the *aoul*. The war-cry is again heard and the cavalry disappears in the cloud of dust it has raised.

The spectacle was truly magnificent. The one thing that spoilt the general impression for me – who took no part in the affair and was unaccustomed to it – was that this movement and the animation and the shouting appeared unnecessary. The comparison involuntarily suggested itself to me of a man swinging his arms vigorously to cut the air with an axe.

IX

OUR troops had taken possession of the village and not a single soul of the enemy remained in it when the general and his suite, to which I had attached myself, rode up to it.

The long clean huts, with their flat earthen roofs and shapely chimneys, stood on irregular stony mounds between which flowed a

15 'Especially in good company.'

small stream. On one side were green gardens with enormous pear and small plum trees brightly lit up by the sun, on the other strange upright shadows, the perpendicular stones of the cemetery, and long poles with balls and many-coloured flags fastened to their ends. (These marked the graves of *dzhigits*.)

The troops were drawn up outside the gates.

['Well, how about it, Colonel?' said the general. 'Let them loot. I see they are terribly anxious to,' he added with a smile, pointing at the Cossacks.

You cannot imagine how striking was the contrast between the carelessness with which the general uttered these words, and their import and the military surroundings.]

A moment later, dragoons, Cossacks, and infantry spread with evident delight through the crooked lanes and in an instant the empty village was animated again. Here a roof crashes, an axe rings against the hard wood of a door that is being forced open, here a stack of hay, a fence, a hut, is set on fire and a pillar of thick smoke rises up in the clear air. Here is a Cossack dragging along a sack of flour and a carpet, there a soldier, with a delighted look on his face, brings a tin basin and some rag out of a hut, another is trying with outstretched arms to catch two hens that struggle and cackle beside a fence, a third has somewhere discovered an enormous pot of milk and after drinking some of it throws the rest on the ground with a loud laugh.

The battalion with which I had come from Fort N. was also in the *aoul*. The captain sat on the roof of a hut and sent thin whiffs of cheap tobacco smoke through his short pipe with such an expression of indifference on his face that on seeing him I forgot that I was in a hostile *aoul* and felt quite at home.

'Ah, you are here too?' he said when he noticed me.

The tall figure of Lieutenant Rosenkranz flitted here and there in the village. He gave orders unceasingly and appeared exceedingly engrossed in his task. I saw him with a triumphant air emerge from a hut followed by two soldiers leading an old Tartar. The old man, whose only clothing consisted of a mottled tunic all in rags and patchwork trousers, was so frail that his arms, tightly bound behind his bent back, seemed scarcely to hold onto his shoulders, and he could scarcely drag his bare crooked legs along. His face and even part of his shaven head were deeply furrowed. His wry toothless mouth kept moving beneath his close-cut moustache and beard, as if he were chewing something; but a gleam still sparkled in his red lashless eyes which clearly expressed an old man's indifference to life.

Rosenkranz asked him, through an interpreter, why he had not gone away with the others.

'Where should I go?' he answered, looking quietly away.

'Where the others have gone,' someone remarked.

'The *dzhigits* have gone to fight the Russians, but I am an old man.'

'Are you not afraid of the Russians?'

'What will the Russians do to me? I am old,' he repeated, again glancing carelessly round the circle that had formed about him.

Later, as I was returning, I saw that old man bareheaded, with his arms tied, being jolted along behind the saddle of a Cossack, and he was looking round with the same expression of indifference on his face. He was needed for the exchange of prisoners.

I climbed onto the roof and sat down beside the captain.

[A bugler who had vodka and provisions was sent for. The captain's calmness and equanimity involuntarily produced an effect on me. We ate roasted pheasant and chatted, without at all reflecting that the owners of that hut had not merely no desire to see us there but could hardly have imagined our existence.]

'There don't seem to have been many of the enemy,' I said, wishing to know his opinion of the action that had taken place.

'The enemy?' he repeated with surprise. 'The enemy was not there at all! Do you call those the enemy? . . . Wait till the evening when we go back, and you will see how they will speed us on our way: what a lot of them will pour out from there,' he said, pointing to a thicket we had passed in the morning.

'What is that?' I asked anxiously, interrupting the captain and pointing to a group of Don Cossacks who had collected round something not far from us.

A sound of something like a child's cry came from there, and the words:

'Stop . . . don't hack it . . . you'll be seen . . . Have you a knife, Evstigneich . . . Lend me a knife. . . .'

'They are up to something, the scoundrels . . .' replied the captain calmly.

But at that moment the young ensign, his comely face flushed and frightened, came suddenly running from behind a corner and rushed towards the Cossacks waving his arms.

'Don't touch it! Don't kill it!' he cried in a childish voice.

Seeing the officer, the Cossacks stepped apart and released a little white kid. The young ensign was quite abashed, muttered something, and stopped before us with a confused face. Seeing the captain and me on the roof he blushed still more and ran leaping towards us.

'I thought they were killing a child,' he said with a bashful smile.

X

THE general went ahead with the cavalry. The battalion with which I had come from Fort N. remained in the rearguard. Captain Khlopov's and Lieutenant Rosenkranz's battalions retired together.

The captain's prediction was fully justified. No sooner had we entered the narrow thicket he had mentioned, than on both sides of us we caught glimpses of hillsmen mounted and on foot, and so near were they that I could distinctly see how some of them ran stooping, rifle in hand, from one tree to another.

The captain took off his cap and piously crossed himself, some of the older soldiers did the same. From the wood were heard war-cries and the words 'Iay giaour', 'Urus! iay!' Sharp short rifle-shots, following one another fast, whizzed on both sides of us. Our men answered silently with a running fire, and only now and then remarks like the following were made in the ranks: 'See where *he*[16] fires from! It's all right for him inside the wood. We ought to use cannon,' and so forth.

Our ordnance was brought out, and after some grape-shot had been fired the enemy seemed to grow weaker, but a moment later and at every step taken by our troops, the enemy's fire again grew hotter and the shouting louder.

We had hardly gone seven hundred yards from the village before enemy cannon-balls began whistling over our heads. I saw a soldier killed by one. . . . But why should I describe the details of that terrible picture which I would myself give much to be able to forget!

Lieutenant Rosenkranz kept firing, and incessantly shouted in a hoarse voice at the soldiers and galloped from one end of the cordon to the other. He was rather pale and this suited his martial countenance very well.

The good-looking young ensign was in raptures: his beautiful dark eyes shone with daring, his lips were slightly smiling, and he kept riding up to the captain and begging permission to charge.

[16] *He* is a collective noun by which the soldiers indicate the enemy. L. T.

'We will repel them,' he said persuasively, 'we certainly will.'

'It's not necessary,' replied the captain abruptly. 'We must retreat.'

The captain's company held the skirts of the wood, the men lying down and replying to the enemy's fire. The captain in his shabby coat and shabby cap sat silent on his white horse, with loose reins, bent knees, his feet in the stirrups, and did not stir from his place. (The soldiers knew and did their work so well that there was no need to give them any orders.) Only at rare intervals he raised his voice to shout at those who exposed their heads. There was nothing at all martial about the captain's appearance, but there was something so sincere and simple in it that I was unusually struck by it. 'It is he who is really brave,' I involuntarily said to myself.

He was just the same as I had always seen him: the same calm movements, the same guileless expression on his plain but frank face, only his eyes, which were brighter than usual, showed the concentration of one quietly engaged on his duties. 'As I had always seen him' is easily said, but how many different shades have I noticed in the behaviour of others; one wishing to appear quieter, another sterner, a third merrier, than usual, but the captain's face showed that he did not even see why he should appear anything but what he was.

The Frenchman at Waterloo who said, 'La garde meurt, mais ne se rend pas,'[17] and other, particularly French, heroes who uttered memorable sayings were brave, and really uttered remarkable words, but between their courage and the captain's there was this difference, that even if a great saying had in any circumstance stirred in the soul of my hero, I am convinced that he would not have uttered it: first because by uttering a great saying he would have feared to spoil a great deed, and secondly because when a man feels within himself the capacity to perform a great deed no talk of any kind is needed. That, I think, is a peculiar and a lofty characteristic of Russian courage, and that being so, how can a Russian heart help aching when our young Russian warriors utter trivial French phrases intended to imitate antiquated French chivalry?

Suddenly from the side where our young ensign stood with his platoon we heard a not very hearty or loud 'Hurrah!' Looking round to where the shout came from, I saw some thirty soldiers with sacks on their shoulders and muskets in their hands managing with very great difficulty to run across a ploughed field. They kept stumbling,

[17] 'The Guard is dying, but does not surrender.'

but nevertheless ran on and shouted. In front of them, sword in hand, galloped the young ensign.

They all disappeared into the wood. . . .

After a few minutes of whooping and clatter a frightened horse ran out of the wood, and soldiers appeared bringing back the dead and wounded. Among the latter was the young ensign. Two soldiers supported him under his arms. He was as pale as a sheet, and his pretty head, on which only a shadow remained of the warlike enthusiasm that had animated him a few minutes before, was dreadfully sunk between his shoulders and drooped on his chest. There was a small spot of blood on the white shirt beneath his unbuttoned coat.

'Ah, what a pity!' I said, involuntarily turning away from this sad spectacle.

'Of course it's a pity,' said an old soldier, who stood leaning on his musket beside me with a gloomy expression on his face. 'He's not afraid of anything. How can one do such things?' he added, looking intently at the wounded lad. 'He was still foolish and now he has paid for it!'

'And you?' I asked. 'Are you afraid?'

'What do you expect?'

XI

FOUR soldiers were carrying the ensign on a stretcher and behind them an ambulance soldier was leading a thin, broken-winded horse with two green boxes on its back containing surgical appliances. They waited for the doctor. Some officers rode up to the stretcher and tried to cheer and comfort the wounded lad.

'Well, friend Alanin, it will be some time before you will dance again with castanets,' said Lieutenant Rosenkranz, riding up to the stretcher with a smile.

He probably supposed that these words would raise the young ensign's spirits, but as far as one could judge by the latter's coldly sad look the words had not the desired effect.

The captain rode up too. He looked intently at the wounded man and his usually calm and cold face expressed sincere sympathy. 'Well, my dear Anatol Ivanich,' he said, in a voice of tender sympathy such as I never expected from him, 'evidently it was God's will.'

The wounded lad looked round and his pale face lit up with a sad smile. 'Yes, I disobeyed you.'

'Say rather, it was God's will,' repeated the captain.

The doctor when he arrived, [as far as could be judged by the shakiness of his legs and the redness of his eyes, was in no fit condition to bandage the patient: however, he] took from his assistant bandages, a probe, and another instrument, rolled up his sleeves and stepped up to the ensign with an encouraging smile.

'So it seems they have made a hole in a sound spot for you too,' he said in a carelessly playful tone. 'Let me see.'

The ensign obeyed, but the look he gave the merry doctor expressed astonishment and reproof which the inebriated practitioner did not notice. He touched the wound so awkwardly, quite unnecessarily pressing on it with his unsteady fingers, that the wounded ensign, driven beyond the limits of endurance, pushed away his hand with a deep groan.

'Let me alone!' he said in a scarcely audible voice. 'I shall die anyway.'

[Then, addressing the captain, he said with difficulty: 'Please, Captain . . . yesterday I lost . . . twenty rubles to Dronov. . . . When my things are sold . . . let him be paid.']

With those words he fell back, and five minutes later when I passed the group that had formed around him, and asked a soldier, 'How is the ensign?' the answer was, 'Passing away.'

XII

IT was late in the day when the detachment, formed into a broad column and singing, approached the Fort.

[The general rode in front and by his merry countenance one could see that the raid had been successful. In fact, with little loss, we had that day been in Mukay *aoul* – where from immemorial times no Russian foot had trod.

The Saxon, Kaspar Lavrentich, narrated to another officer that he had himself seen how three Chechens had aimed straight at his breast. In the mind of Ensign Rosenkranz a complete story of the day's action had formulated itself. Captain Khlopov walked with thoughtful face in front of his company, leading his little white horse by its bridle.]

The sun had hidden behind the snowy mountain range and threw its last rosy beams on a long thin cloud stretching motionless across the clear horizon. The snow peaks began to disappear in purple mist and only their top outline was visible, wonderfully distinct in the crimson sunset glow. The delicate moon, which had risen long since, began to grow pale against the deep azure. The green of the grass and trees was turning black and becoming covered with dew. The dark masses of troops moved with measured sounds over the luxuriant meadows. Tambourines, drums, and merry songs were heard from various sides. The voice of the second tenor of the Sixth Company rang out with full force and the sounds of his clear chest-notes, full of feeling and power, floated through the clear evening air.

1852

SEVASTOPOL IN MAY 1855

Севастополь в мае 1855 года

I

Six months have passed since the first cannon-ball went whistling from the bastions of Sevastopol and threw up the earth of the enemy's entrenchments. Since then bullets, balls, and bombs by the thousand have flown continually from the bastions to the entrenchments and from the entrenchments to the bastions, and above them the angel of death has hovered unceasingly.

Thousands of human ambitions have had time to be mortified, thousands to be gratified and extend, thousands to be lulled to rest in the arms of death. What numbers of pink coffins and linen palls! And still the same sounds from the bastions fill the air; the French still look from their camp with involuntary trepidation and fear at the yellowy earth of the bastions of Sevastopol and count the embrasures from which the iron cannon frown fiercely; as before, through the fixed telescope on the elevation of the signal-station the pilot still watches the bright-coloured figures of the French, their batteries, their tents, their columns on the green hill, and the puffs of smoke that rise from the entrenchments; and as before, crowds of different men, with a still greater variety of desires, stream with the same ardour from many parts of the world to this fatal spot. But the question the diplomatists did not settle still remains unsettled by powder and blood.

II

A regimental band was playing on the boulevard near the pavilion in the besieged town of Sevastopol, and crowds of women and military men strolled along the paths making holiday. The bright spring sun had risen in the morning above the English entrenchments, had reached the bastions, then the town and the Nicholas Barracks, shining with equal joy on all, and was now sinking down to the distant blue sea which, rocking with an even motion, glittered with silvery light.

A tall infantry officer with a slight stoop, drawing on a presentable though not very white glove, passed out of the gate of one of the small sailors' houses built on the left side of the Morskaya Street and gazing thoughtfully at the ground ascended the hill towards the boulevard. The expression of his plain face did not reveal much intellectual power, but rather good-nature, common sense, honesty, and an inclination to respectability. He was badly built, and seemed rather shy and awkward in his movements. His cap was nearly new, a gold watch-chain showed from under his thin cloak of a rather peculiar lilac shade, and he wore trousers with foot-straps, and clean, shiny calf-skin boots. He might have been a German (but that his features indicated his purely Russian origin), an adjutant, or a regimental quartermaster (but in that case he would have worn spurs), or an officer transferred from the cavalry or the Guards for the duration of the war. He was in fact an officer who had exchanged from the cavalry, and as he ascended the hill towards the boulevard he was thinking of a letter he had received from a former comrade now retired from the army, a landed proprietor in the government of T—, and of his great friend, the pale, blue-eyed Natasha, that comrade's wife. He recalled a part of the letter where his comrade wrote:

'When we receive the *Invalide*,[1] Pupka' (so the retired Uhlan called his wife) 'rushes headlong into the hall, seizes the paper, and runs with it to a seat in the arbour or the drawing-room – in which, you remember, we spent such jolly winter evenings when your regiment was stationed in our town – and reads of *your* heroic deeds with an ardour you cannot imagine. She often speaks of you. "There now," she says, "Mikhaylov is a *darling*. I am ready to cover him with kisses when I see him. He [is fighting on the bastions and] is certain to receive a St. George's Cross, and they'll write about him in the papers," &c., &c., so that I am beginning to be quite jealous of you.'

In another place he wrote: 'The papers reach us awfully late, and though there are plenty of rumours one cannot believe them all. For instance, those musical young ladies you know of, were saying yesterday that Napoleon has been captured by our Cossacks and sent to St. Petersburg, but you can imagine how much of this I believe.

[1] The Army and Navy Gazette.

One fresh arrival from Petersburg tells us for certain (he is a capital fellow, sent by the Minister on special business – and now there is no one in the town you can't think what a *resource* he is to us), that we have taken Eupatoria [so that the French are cut off from Bala-clava], and that we lost two hundred in the affair and the French as many as fifteen thousand. My wife was in such raptures that she *caroused* all night and said that a presentiment assured her that you distinguished yourself in that affair.'

In spite of the words and expressions I have purposely italicized, and the whole tone of the letter, Lieutenant-Captain Mikhaylov thought with an inexpressibly melancholy pleasure about his pale-faced pro-vincial friend and how he used to sit with her of an evening in the arbour, talking *sentiment*. He thought of his kind comrade the Uhlan: how the latter used to get angry and lose when they played cards in the study for kopek points and how his wife used to laugh at him. He recalled the friendship these people had for him (perhaps he thought there was something more on the side of the pale-faced friend): these people and their surroundings flitted through his memory in a wonderfully sweet, joyously rosy light and, smiling at the recollection, he put his hand to the pocket where this *dear* letter lay.

From these recollections Lieutenant-Captain Mikhaylov involun-tarily passed to dreams and hopes. 'How surprised and pleased Natasha will be,' he thought as he passed along a narrow side-street, 'when she reads in the *Invalide* of my being the first to climb on the cannon, and receiving the St. George! I ought to be made full captain on that former recommendation. Then I may easily become a major this year by seniority, because so many of our fellows have been killed and no doubt many more will be killed this campaign. Then there'll be more fighting and I, as a well-known man, shall be entrusted with a regiment . . . then a lieutenant-colonel, the order of St. Anna . . . a colonel' . . . and he was already a general, honouring with a visit Natasha, the widow of his comrade (who would be dead by that time according to his daydream) – when the sounds of the music on the boulevard reached his ears more distinctly, a crowd of people appeared before his eyes, and he realized that he was on the boulevard and a lieutenant-captain of infantry as before.

III

HE went first to the pavilion, beside which stood the band with soldiers of the same regiment acting as music-stands and holding open the music books, while around them clerks, cadets, nursemaids, and children formed a circle, looking on rather than listening. Most of the people who were standing, sitting, and sauntering round the pavilion were naval officers, adjutants, and white-gloved army officers. Along the broad avenue of the boulevard walked officers of all sorts and women of all sorts – a few of the latter in hats, but the greater part with kerchiefs on their heads, and some with neither kerchiefs nor hats – but it was remarkable that there was not a single old woman amongst them – all were young. Lower down, in the scented alleys shaded by the white acacias, isolated groups sat or strolled.

No one was particularly glad to meet Lieutenant-Captain Mikhaylov on the boulevard, except perhaps Captain Obzhogov of his regiment and Captain Suslikov who pressed his hand warmly, but the first of these wore camel-hair trousers, no gloves, and a shabby overcoat, and his face was red and perspiring, and the second shouted so loud and was so free and easy that one felt ashamed to be seen walking with him, especially by those white-gloved officers – to one of whom, an adjutant, Mikhaylov bowed, and he might have bowed to another, a Staff officer whom he had twice met at the house of a mutual acquaintance. Besides, what was the fun of walking with Obzhogov and Suslikov when as it was he met them and shook hands with them six times a day? Was this what he had come to hear *the music* for?

He would have liked to accost the adjutant whom he had bowed to and to talk with those gentlemen, not at all that he wanted Captains Obzhogov and Suslikov and Lieutenant Pashtetski and others to see him talking to them, but simply because they were pleasant people who knew all the news and might have told him something.

But why is Lieutenant-Captain Mikhaylov afraid and unable to muster courage to approach them? 'Supposing they don't return my greeting,' he thinks, 'or merely bow and go on talking among themselves as if I were not there, or simply walk away and leave me standing among the aristocrats?' The word aristocrats (in the sense of the highest and most select circle of any class) has lately gained great popularity in Russia, where one would think it ought not to exist. It has made its way to every part of the country, and into every grade of society which can be reached by vanity – and to what conditions of time and circumstance does this pitiful propensity not penetrate? You find it among merchants, officials, clerks, officers – in Saratov, Mamadishi, Vinnitza, in fact wherever men are to be found. And since there are many men, and consequently much vanity, in the besieged town of Sevastopol, aristocrats are to be found here too, though death hangs over everyone, be he aristocrat or not.

To Captain Obzhogov, Lieutenant-Captain Mikhaylov was an aristocrat, and to Lieutenant-Captain Mikhaylov, Adjutant Kalugin was an aristocrat, because he was an adjutant and intimate with another adjutant. To Adjutant Kalugin, Count Nordov was an aristocrat, because he was an aide-de-camp to the Emperor.

Vanity! vanity! vanity! everywhere, even on the brink of the grave and among men ready to die for a noble cause. Vanity! It seems to be the characteristic feature and special malady of our time. How is it that among our predecessors no mention was made of this passion, as of smallpox and cholera? How is it that in our time there are only three kinds of people: those who, considering vanity an inevitably existing fact and therefore justifiable, freely submit to it; those who regard it as a sad but unavoidable condition; and those who act unconsciously and slavishly under its influence? Why did the Homers and Shakespeares speak of love, glory, and suffering, while the literature of today is an endless story of snobbery and vanity?

Twice the lieutenant-captain passed irresolutely by the group of his aristocrats, but drawing near them for the third time he made an effort and walked up to them. The group consisted of four officers: Adjutant Kalugin, Mikhaylov's acquaintance, Adjutant Prince Galtsin who was rather an aristocrat even for Kalugin himself, Lieutenant-Colonel Neferdov, one of the so-called 'two hundred and twenty-two' society men who being on the retired list re-entered the army for this war, and Cavalry-Captain Praskukhin, also of the 'two hundred and twenty-two'. Luckily for Mikhaylov, Kalugin was in splendid spirits (the General had just spoken to him in a very confidential manner, and Prince Galtsin who had arrived from Petersburg was staying with him), so he did not think it beneath his dignity to shake hands with Mikhaylov, which was more than Praskukhin did though he had often met Mikhaylov on the bastion, had more than once drunk his wine and vodka, and even owed him twelve and a half rubles lost at cards. Not being yet well acquainted with Prince

Galtsin he did not like to appear to be acquainted with a mere lieutenant-captain of infantry. So he only bowed slightly.

'Well, Captain,' said Kalugin, 'when will you be visiting the bastion again? Do you remember our meeting at the Schwartz Redoubt? Things were hot, weren't they, eh?'

'Yes, very,' said Mikhaylov, and he recalled how when making his way along the trench to the bastion he had met Kalugin walking bravely along, his sabre clanking smartly.

'My turn's tomorrow by rights, but we have an officer ill', continued Mikhaylov, 'so——'

He wanted to say that it was not his turn but as the Commander of the 8th Company was ill and only the ensign was left in the company, he felt it his duty to go in place of Lieutenant Nepshisetski and would therefore be at the bastion that evening. But Kalugin did not hear him out.

'I feel sure that something is going to happen in a day or two,' he said to Prince Galtsin.

'How about today? Will nothing happen today?' Mikhaylov asked shyly, looking first at Kalugin and then at Galtsin.

No one replied. Prince Galtsin only puckered up his face in a curious way and looking over Mikhaylov's cap said after a short silence:

'Fine girl that, with the red kerchief. You know her, don't you, Captain?'

'She lives near my lodgings, she's a sailor's daughter,' answered the lieutenant-captain.

'Come, let's have a good look at her.'

And Prince Galtsin gave one of his arms to Kalugin and the other to the lieutenant-captain, being sure he would confer great pleasure on the latter by so doing, which was really quite true.

The lieutenant-captain was superstitious and considered it a great sin to amuse himself with women before going into action; but on this occasion he pretended to be a *roué*, which Prince Galtsin and Kalugin evidently did not believe and which greatly surprised the girl with the red kerchief, who had more than once noticed how the lieutenant-captain blushed when he passed her window. Praskukhin walked behind them, and kept touching Prince Galtsin's arm and making various remarks in French, but as four people could not walk abreast on the path he was obliged to go alone until, on the second round, he took the arm of a well-known brave naval officer,

Servyagin, who came up and spoke to him, being also anxious to join the aristocrats. And the well-known hero gladly passed his honest muscular hand under the elbow of Praskukhin, whom everybody, including Servyagin himself, knew to be no better than he should be. When, wishing to explain his acquaintance with this sailor, Praskukhin whispered to Prince Galtsin that this was the well-known hero, Prince Galtsin – who had been in the Fourth Bastion the day before and seen a shell burst at some twenty yards' distance – considering himself not less courageous than the newcomer, and believing that many reputations are obtained by luck, paid not the slightest attention to Servyagin.

Lieutenant-Captain Mikhaylov found it so pleasant to walk in this company that he forgot the nice letter from T—— and his gloomy forebodings at the thought of having to go to the bastion. He remained with them till they began talking exclusively among themselves, avoiding his eyes to show that he might go, and at last walked away from him. But all the same the lieutenant-captain was contented, and when he passed Cadet Baron Pesth – who was particularly conceited and self-satisfied since the previous night, when for the first time in his life he had been in the bomb-proof of the Fifth Bastion and had consequently become a hero in his own estimation – he was not at all hurt by the suspiciously haughty expression with which the cadet saluted him.

IV

BUT the lieutenant-captain had hardly crossed the threshold of his lodgings before very different thoughts entered his head. He saw his little room with its uneven earth floor, its crooked windows, the broken panes mended with paper, his old bedstead with two Tula pistols and a rug (showing a lady on horseback) nailed to the wall beside it, as well as the dirty bed of the cadet who lived with him, with its cotton quilt. He saw his man Nikita, with his rough greasy hair, rise from the floor scratching himself, he saw his old cloak, his common boots, a little bundle tied in a handkerchief ready for him to take to the bastion, from which peeped a bit of cheese and the neck of a porter bottle containing vodka – and he suddenly remembered that he had to go with his company to spend the whole night at the lodgements.

'I shall certainly be killed tonight,' thought he, 'I feel I shall. And there was really no need for me to go – I offered to do it of my own accord. And it always happens that the one who offers himself gets killed. And what is the matter with that confounded Nepshisetski? He may not be ill at all, and they'll go and kill me because of him – they're sure to. Still, if they don't kill me I shall certainly be recommended for promotion. I saw how pleased the regimental commander was when I said: "Allow me to go if Lieutenant Nepshisetski is ill." If I'm not made a major then I'll get the Order of Vladimir for certain. Why, I am going to the bastion for the thirteenth time. Oh dear, the thirteenth! Unlucky number! I am certain to be killed. I feel I shall . . . but somebody had to go: the company can't go with only an ensign. Supposing something were to happen. . . . Why, the honour of the regiment, the honour of the army is at stake. It is my *duty* to go. Yes, my sacred duty. . . . But I have a presentiment.'

The lieutenant-captain forgot that it was not the first time he had felt this presentiment: that in a greater or lesser degree he had it whenever he was going to the bastion, and he did not know that before going into action everyone has such forebodings more or less strongly. Having calmed himself by appealing to his sense of duty – which was highly developed and very strong – the lieutenant-captain sat down at the table and began writing a farewell letter to his father. Ten minutes later, having finished his letter, he rose from the table his eyes wet with tears, and repeating mentally all the prayers he knew he began to dress. His rather tipsy and rude servant lazily handed him his new cloak – the old one which the lieutenant-captain usually wore at the bastion not being mended.

'Why isn't my cloak mended? You do nothing but sleep,' said Mikhaylov angrily.

'Sleep indeed!' grumbled Nikita, 'I do nothing but run about like a dog the whole day, and when I get fagged I mayn't even go to sleep!'

'I see you are drunk again.'

'It's not at your expense if I am, so you needn't complain.'

'Hold your tongue, you dolt!' shouted the lieutenant-captain, ready to strike the man.

Already upset, he now quite lost patience and felt hurt by the rudeness of Nikita, who had lived with him for the last twelve years and whom he was fond of and even spoilt.

'Dolt? Dolt?' repeated the servant. 'And why do you, sir, abuse me and call me a dolt? You know in times like these it isn't right to abuse people.'

Recalling where he was about to go Mikhaylov felt ashamed.

'But you know, Nikita, you would try anyone's patience!' he said mildly. 'That letter to my father on the table you may leave where it is. Don't touch it,' he added reddening.

'Yes, sir,' said Nikita, becoming sentimental under the influence of the vodka he had drunk, as he said, at his own expense, and blinking with an evident inclination to weep.

But at the porch, when the lieutenant-captain said, 'Goodbye, Nikita,' Nikita burst into forced sobs and rushed to kiss his master's hand, saying, 'Goodbye, sir,' in a broken voice. A sailor's widow who was also standing in the porch could not, as a woman, help joining in this tender scene, and began wiping her eyes on her dirty sleeve, saying something about people who, though they were gentlefolk, took such sufferings upon themselves while she, poor woman, was left a widow. And she told the tipsy Nikita for the hundredth time about her sorrows; how her husband had been killed in the first *bondbarment*, and how her hut had been shattered (the one she lived in now was not her own) and so on. After his master was gone Nikita lit his pipe, asked the landlady's little girl to get some vodka, very soon left off crying, and even had a quarrel with the old woman about a pail he said she had smashed for him.

'But perhaps I shall only be wounded,' reasoned the lieutenant-captain as he drew near the bastion with his company when twilight had already begun to fall. 'But where, and how? Here or here?' he said to himself, mentally passing his chest, his stomach, and his thighs in review. 'Supposing it's here' (he thought of his thighs) 'and goes right round. . . . Or goes here with a piece of a bomb, then it will be all up.'

The lieutenant-captain passed along the trenches and reached the lodgements safely. In perfect darkness he and an officer of Engineers set the men to their work, after which he sat down in a pit under the breastwork. There was little firing; only now and again there was a lightning flash on our side or *his*, and the brilliant fuse of a bomb formed a fiery arc on the dark, star-speckled sky. But all the bombs fell far beyond or far to the right of the lodgement where the lieutenant-captain sat in his pit. He drank some vodka, ate some cheese, smoked a cigarette, said his prayers, and felt inclined to sleep for a while.

V

PRINCE GALTSIN, Lieutenant-Colonel Neferdov, and Praskukhin –
whom no one had invited and to whom no one spoke, but who still
stuck to them – went to Kalugin's to tea.

'But you did not finish telling me about Vaska Mendel,' said
Kalugin, when he had taken off his cloak and sat in a soft easy chair
by the window unbuttoning the collar of his clean starched shirt.
'How did he get married?'

'It was a joke, my boy! . . . *Je vous dis, il y avait un temps, on ne
parlait que de ça à Pétersbourg,*[2] said Prince Galtsin, laughing as he
jumped up from the piano-stool and sat down near Kalugin on the
window-sill, 'a capital joke. I know all about it.'

And he told, amusingly, cleverly, and with animation, a love story
which, as it has no interest for us, we will omit.

It was noticeable that not only Prince Galtsin but each of these
gentlemen who established themselves, one on the window-sill,
another with his legs in the air, and a third by the piano, seemed quite
different people now from what they had been on the boulevard.
There was none of the absurd arrogance and haughtiness they had
shown towards the infantry officers; here among themselves they
were natural, and Kalugin and Prince Galtsin in particular showed
themselves very pleasant, merry, and good-natured young fellows.
Their conversation was about their Petersburg fellow officers and
acquaintances.

'What of Maslovski?'

'Which one – the Leib-Uhlan, or the Horse Guard?'

'I know them both. The one in the Horse Guards I knew when he
was a boy just out of school. But the eldest – is he a captain yet?'

'Oh yes, long ago.'

'Is he still fussing about with his gipsy?'

'No, he has dropped her. . . .' And so on in the same strain.

Later on Prince Galtsin went to the piano and gave an excellent
rendering of a gipsy song. Praskukhin, chiming in unasked, put in a
second and did it so well that he was invited to continue, and this
delighted him.

A servant brought tea, cream, and cracknels on a silver tray.

'Serve the prince,' said Kalugin.

'Isn't it strange to think that we're in a besieged town,' said Galtsin,

[2] 'I tell you, at one time it was only the only thing talked of in Petersburg.'

taking his tea to the window, 'and here's a *pianerforty*, tea with cream, and a house such as I should really be glad to have in Petersburg?'

'Well, if we hadn't even that much,' said the old and ever-dissatisfied lieutenant-colonel, 'the constant uncertainty we are living in – seeing people killed day after day and no end to it – would be intolerable. And to have dirt and discomfort added to it——.'

'But our infantry officers live at the bastions with their men in the bomb-proofs and eat the soldiers' soup', said Kalugin, 'what of them?'

'What of them? Well, though it's true they don't change their shirts for ten days at a time, they are heroes all the same – wonderful fellows.'

Just then an infantry officer entered the room.

'I . . . I have orders . . . may I see the Gen . . . his Excellency? I have come with a message from General N.,' he said with a timid bow.

Kalugin rose and without returning the officer's greeting asked with an offensive, affected, official smile if he would not have the goodness to wait; and without asking him to sit down or taking any further notice of him he turned to Galtsin and began talking French, so that the poor officer left alone in the middle of the room did not in the least know what to do with himself.

'It is a matter of the utmost urgency, sir,' he said after a short silence.

'Ah! Well then, please come with me,' said Kalugin, putting on his cloak and accompanying the officer to the door.

*

'*Eh bien, messieurs, je crois que cela chauffera cette nuit,*'[3] said Kalugin when he returned from the General's.

'Ah! What is it – a sortie?' asked the others.

'That I don't know. You will see for yourselves,' replied Kalugin with a mysterious smile.

'And my commander is at the bastion, so I suppose I must go too,' said Praskukhin, buckling on his sabre.

No one replied, it was his business to know whether he had to go or not.

Praskukhin and Neferdov left to go to their appointed posts.

'Goodbye gentlemen. *Au revoir!* We'll meet again before the night

[3] 'Well, gentlemen, I think there will be warm work tonight.'

is over,' shouted Kalugin from the window as Praskukhin and Neferdov, stooping on their Cossack saddles, trotted past. The tramp of their Cossack horses soon died away in the dark street.

'*Non, dites-moi, est-ce qu'il y aura véritablement quelque chose cette nuit?*'[4] said Galtsin as he lounged in the window-sill beside Kalugin and watched the bombs that rose above the bastions.

'I can tell *you*, you see . . . you have been to the bastions?' (Galtsin nodded, though he had only been once to the Fourth Bastion). 'You remember just in front of our lunette there is a trench,' – and Kalugin, with the air of one who without being a specialist considers his military judgement very sound, began, in a rather confused way and misusing the technical terms, to explain the position of the enemy, and of our own works, and the plan of the intended action.

'But I say, they're banging away at the lodgements! Oho! I wonder if that's ours or *his*? . . . Now it's burst,' said they as they lounged on the window-sill looking at the fiery trails of the bombs crossing one another in the air, at flashes that for a moment lit up the dark sky, at puffs of white smoke, and listened to the more and more rapid reports of the firing.

'*Quel charmant coup d'œil! a?*'[5] said Kalugin, drawing his guest's attention to the really beautiful sight. 'Do you know, you sometimes can't distinguish a bomb from a star.'

'Yes, I thought that was a star just now and then saw it fall . . . there! it's burst. And that big star – what do you call it? – looks just like a bomb.'

'Do you know I am so used to these bombs that I am sure when I'm back in Russia I shall fancy I see bombs every starlight night – one gets so used to them.'

'But hadn't I better go with this sortie?' said Prince Galtsin after a moment's pause.

'Humbug, my dear fellow! Don't think of such a thing. Besides, I won't let you,' answered Kalugin. 'You will have plenty of opportunities later on.'

'Really? You think I need not go, eh?'

At that moment, from the direction in which these gentlemen were looking, amid the boom of the cannon came the terrible rattle of musketry, and thousands of little fires flaming up in quick succession flashed all along the line.

[4] 'No, tell me, will there really be anything tonight?'
[5] 'What a charming sight, eh?'

'There! Now it's the real thing!' said Kalugin. 'I can't keep cool when I hear the noise of muskets. It seems to seize one's very soul, you know. There's an *hurrah*!' he added, listening intently to the distant and prolonged roar of hundreds of voices – 'Ah – ah – ah' – which came from the bastions.

'Whose *hurrah* was it? Theirs or ours?'

'I don't know, but it's hand-to-hand fighting now, for the firing has ceased.'

At that moment an officer followed by a Cossack galloped under the window and alighted from his horse at the porch.

'Where are you from?'

'From the bastion. I want the General.'

'Come along. Well, what's happened?'

'The lodgements have been attacked – and occupied. The French brought up tremendous reserves – attacked us – we had only two battalions,' said the officer, panting. He was the same officer who had been there that evening, but though he was now out of breath he walked to the door with full self-possession.

'Well, have we retired?' asked Kalugin.

'No,' angrily replied the officer, 'another battalion came up in time – we drove them back, but the colonel is killed and many officers. I have orders to ask for reinforcements.'

And saying this he went with Kalugin to the General's, where we shall not follow him.

Five minutes later Kalugin was already on his Cossack horse (again in the semi-Cossack manner which I have noticed that all adjutants, for some reason, seem to consider the proper thing), and rode off at a trot towards the bastion to deliver some orders and await the final result of the affair. Prince Galtsin, under the influence of that oppressive excitement usually produced in a spectator by proximity to an action in which he is not engaged, went out, and began aimlessly pacing up and down the street.

VI

SOLDIERS passed carrying the wounded on stretchers or supporting them under their arms. It was quite dark in the streets, lights could be seen here and there, but only in the hospital windows or where some officers were sitting up. From the bastions still came the thunder of cannon and the rattle of muskets,[6] and flashes kept on lighting up the dark sky as before. From time to time the tramp of hoofs could be heard as an orderly galloped past, or the groans of a wounded man, the steps and voices of stretcher-bearers, or the words of some frightened women who had come out onto their porches to watch the cannonade.

Among the spectators were our friend Nikita, the old sailor's widow with whom he had again made friends, and her ten-year-old daughter.

'O Lord God! Holy Mary, Mother of God!' said the old woman, sighing as she looked at the bombs that kept flying across from side to side like balls of fire; 'What horrors! What horrors! Ah, ah! Oh, oh! Even at the first *bondbarment* it wasn't like that. Look now where the cursed thing has burst just over our house in the suburb.'

'No, that's further, they keep tumbling into Aunt Irene's garden,' said the girl.

'And where, where, is master now?' drawled Nikita, who was not quite sober yet. 'Oh! You don't know how I love that master of mine! I love him so that if he were killed in a sinful way, which God forbid, then would you believe it, granny, after that I myself don't know what I wouldn't do to myself! I don't! . . . My master is that sort, there's only one word for it. Would I change him for such as them there, playing cards? What are they? Ugh! There's only one word for it!' concluded Nikita, pointing to the lighted window of his master's room to which, in the absence of the lieutenant-captain, Cadet Zhvadchevski had invited Sub-Lieutenants Ugrovich and Nepshisetski – the latter suffering from face-ache – and where he was having a spree in honour of a medal he had received.

'Look at the stars! Look how they're rolling!' the little girl broke the silence that followed Nikita's words as she stood gazing at the sky. 'There's another rolled down. What is it a sign of, mother?'

'They'll smash up our hut altogether,' said the old woman with a sigh, leaving her daughter unanswered.

'As we went there today with uncle, mother,' the little girl continued in a sing-song tone, become loquacious, 'there was such a

[6] Rifles, except some clumsy *stutzers*, had not been introduced into the Russian army, but were used by the besiegers, who had a still greater advantage in artillery. It is characteristic of Tolstoy that, occupied with men rather than mechanics, he does not in these sketches dwell on this disparity of equipment.

b-i-g cannon-ball inside the room close to the cupboard. Must have smashed in through the passage and right into the room! Such a big one – you couldn't lift it.'

'Those who had husbands and money all moved away,' said the old woman, 'and there's the hut, all that was left me, and that's been smashed. Just look at *him* blazing away! The fiend! . . . O Lord! O Lord!'

'And just as we were going out, comes a bomb fly-ing, and goes and bur-sts and co-o-vers us with dust. A bit of it nearly hit me and uncle.'

VII

PRINCE GALTSIN met more and more wounded carried on stretchers or walking supported by others who were talking loudly.

'Up they sprang, friends,' said the bass voice of a tall soldier with two guns slung from his shoulder, 'up they sprang, shouting "Allah! Allah!"[7] and just climbing one over another. You kill one and another's there, you couldn't do anything; no end of 'em——'

But at this point in the story Galtsin interrupted him.

'You are from the bastion?'

'Yes, your Honour.'

'Well, what happened? Tell me.'

'What happened? Well, your Honour, such a force of 'em poured down on us over the rampart, it was all up. They quite overpowered us, your Honour!'

'Overpowered? . . . But you repulsed them?'

'How could we repulse them when *his* whole force came on, killed all our men, and no re'forcements were given us?'

The soldier was mistaken, the trench had remained ours; but it is a curious fact which anyone may notice, that a soldier wounded in action always thinks the affair lost and imagines it to have been a very bloody fight.

'How is that? I was told they had been repulsed,' said Galtsin irritably. 'Perhaps they were driven back after you left? Is it long since you came away?'

'I am straight from there, your Honour,' answered the soldier, 'it

---

[7] Our soldiers fighting the Turks have become so accustomed to this cry of the enemy that they now always say that the French also shout 'Allah!' L. T.

is hardly possible. They must have kept the trench, *he* quite over-powered us.'

'And aren't you ashamed to have lost the trench? It's terrible!' said Galtsin, provoked by such indifference.

'Why, if the strength is on their side . . .' muttered the soldier.

'Ah, your Honour,' began a soldier from a stretcher which had just come up to them, 'how could we help giving it up when *he* had killed almost all our men? If we'd had the strength we wouldn't have given it up, not on any account. But as it was, what could we do? I stuck one, and then something hits me. Oh, oh-h! Steady, lads, steady! Oh, oh!' groaned the wounded man.

'Really, there seem to be too many men returning,' said Galtsin, again stopping the tall soldier with the two guns. 'Why are you retiring? You there, stop!'

The soldier stopped and took off his cap with his left hand.

'Where are you going, and why?' shouted Galtsin severely, 'you scoun——'

But having come close up to the soldier, Galtsin noticed that no hand was visible beneath the soldier's right cuff and that the sleeve was soaked in blood to the elbow.

'I am wounded, your Honour.'

'Wounded? How?'

'Here. Must have been with a bullet,' said the man, pointing to his arm, 'but I don't know what struck my head here,' and bending his head he showed the matted hair at the back stuck together with blood.

'And whose is this other gun?'

'It's a French rifle I took, your Honour. But I wouldn't have come away if it weren't to lead this fellow – he may fall,' he added, pointing to a soldier who was walking a little in front leaning on his gun and painfully dragging his left leg.

Prince Galtsin suddenly felt horribly ashamed of his unjust suspicions. He felt himself blushing, turned away, and went to the hospital without either questioning or watching the wounded men any more.

Having with difficulty pushed his way through the porch among the wounded who had come on foot and the bearers who were carrying in the wounded and bringing out the dead, Galtsin entered the first room, gave a look round, and involuntarily turned back and ran out into the street: it was too terrible.

VIII

THE large, lofty, dark hall, lit up only by the four or five candles with which the doctors examined the wounded, was quite full. Yet the bearers kept bringing in more wounded – laying them side by side on the floor which was already so packed that the unfortunate patients were jostled together, staining one another with their blood – and going to fetch more wounded. The pools of blood visible in the unoccupied spaces, the feverish breathing of several hundred men, and the perspiration of the bearers with the stretchers, filled the air with a peculiar, heavy, thick, fetid mist, in which the candles burnt dimly in different parts of the hall. All sorts of groans, sighs, death-rattles, now and then interrupted by shrill screams, filled the whole room. Sisters with quiet faces, expressing no empty feminine tearful pity, but active practical sympathy, stepped here and there across the wounded with medicines, water, bandages, and lint, flitting among the blood-stained coats and shirts. The doctors, kneeling with rolled-up sleeves beside the wounded, by the light of the candles their assistants held, examined, felt, and probed their wounds, heedless of the terrible groans and entreaties of the sufferers. One doctor sat at a table near the door and at the moment Galtsin came in was already entering No. 532.

'Ivan Bogaev, Private, Company Three, S— Regiment, *fractura femuris complicata!*' shouted another doctor from the end of the room, examining a shattered leg. 'Turn him over.'

'Oh, oh, fathers! Oh, you're our fathers!' screamed the soldier, beseeching them not to touch him.

'*Perforatio capitis!*'

'Simon Neferdov, Lieutenant-Colonel of the N— Infantry Regiment. Have a little patience, Colonel, or it is quite impossible: I shall give it up!' said a third doctor, poking about with some kind of hook in the unfortunate colonel's skull.

'Oh, don't! Oh, for God's sake be quick! Be quick! Ah——!'

Perforatio pectoris . . . Sebastian Sereda, Private . . . what regiment? But you need not write that: *moritur*. Carry him away,' said the doctor, leaving the soldier, whose eyes turned up and in whose throat the death-rattle already sounded.

About forty soldier stretcher-bearers stood at the door waiting to carry the bandaged to the wards and the dead to the chapel. They looked on at the scene before them in silence, only broken now and then by a heavy sigh.

IX

ON his way to the bastion Kalugin met many wounded, but knowing by experience that in action such sights have a bad effect on one's spirits, he did not stop to question them but tried on the contrary not to notice them. At the foot of the hill he met an orderly-officer galloping fast from the bastion.

'Zobkin! Zobkin! Wait a bit!'

'Well, what is it?'

'Where are you from?'

'The lodgements.'

'How are things there – hot?'

'Oh, awful!'

And the orderly galloped on.

In fact, though there was now but little small-arm firing, the cannonade had recommenced with fresh heat and persistence.

'Ah, that's bad!' thought Kalugin with an unpleasant sensation, and he too had a presentiment – a very usual thought, the thought of death. But Kalugin was ambitious and blessed with nerves of oak – in a word, he was what is called brave. He did not yield to the first feeling but began to nerve himself. He recalled how an adjutant, Napoleon's he thought, having delivered an order, galloped with bleeding head full speed to Napoleon. '*Vous êtes blessé?*'[8] said Napoleon. '*Je vous demande pardon, sire, je suis mort,*'[9] and the adjutant fell from his horse, dead.

That seemed to him very fine, and he pictured himself for a moment in the role of that adjutant. Then he whipped his horse, assuming a still more dashing Cossack seat, looked back at the Cossack who, standing up in his stirrups, was trotting behind, and rode quite gallantly up to the spot where he had to dismount. Here he found four soldiers sitting on some stones smoking their pipes.

'What are you doing there?' he shouted at them.

'Been carrying off a wounded man and sat down to rest a bit, your Honour,' said one of them, hiding his pipe behind his back and taking off his cap.

'Resting, indeed! . . . To your places, march!'

And he went up the hill with them through the trench, meeting wounded men at every step.

---

[8] 'You are wounded?'

[9] 'Excuse me sire, I am dead.'

After ascending the hill he turned to the left, and a few steps farther on found himself quite alone. A splinter of a bomb whizzed near him and fell into the trench. Another bomb rose in front of him and seemed flying straight at him. He suddenly felt frightened, ran a few steps at full speed, and lay down flat. When the bomb burst a considerable distance off he felt exceedingly vexed with himself and rose, looking round to see if anyone had noticed him drop down, but no one was near.

But when fear has once entered the soul it does not easily yield to any other feeling. He, who always boasted that he never even stooped, now hurried along the trench almost on all fours. He stumbled, and thought, 'Oh, it's awful! They'll kill me for certain!' His breath came with difficulty, and perspiration broke out over his whole body. He was surprised at himself but no longer strove to master his feelings.

Suddenly he heard footsteps in front. Quickly straightening himself he raised his head, and boldly clanking his sabre went on more deliberately. He felt himself quite a different man. When he met an officer of the Engineers and a sailor, and the officer shouted to him to lie down, pointing to a bright spot which growing brighter and brighter approached more and more swiftly and came crashing down close to the trench, he only bent a little, involuntarily influenced by the frightened cry, and went on.

'That's a brave one,' said the sailor, looking quite calmly at the bomb and with experienced eye deciding at once that the splinters could not fly into the trench, 'he won't even lie down.'

It was only a few steps across open ground to the bomb-proof shelter of the Commander of the bastion, when Kalugin's mind again became clouded and the same stupid terror seized him: his heart beat more violently, the blood rushed to his head, and he had to make an effort to force himself to run to the bomb-proof.

'Why are you so out of breath?' said the General, when Kalugin had reported his instructions.

'I walked very fast, your Excellency!'

'Won't you have a glass of wine?'

Kalugin drank a glass of wine and lit a cigarette. The action was over, only a fierce cannonade still continued from both sides. In the bomb-proof sat General N——, the Commander of the bastion, and some six other officers among whom was Praskukhin. They were discussing various details of the action. Sitting in this comfortable room with blue wallpaper, a sofa, a bed, a table with papers on it, a wall-clock with a lamp burning before it, and an icon – looking at these signs of habitation, at the beams more than two feet thick that formed the ceiling, and listening to the shots that sounded faint here in the shelter, Kalugin could not understand how he had twice allowed himself to be overcome by such unpardonable weakness. He was angry with himself and wished for danger in order to test his nerve once more.

'Ah! I'm glad you are here, Captain,' said he to a naval officer with big moustaches who wore a staff-officer's coat with a St. George's Cross and had just entered the shelter and asked the General to give him some men to repair two embrasures of his battery which had become blocked. When the General had finished speaking to the captain, Kalugin said: 'The Commander-in-Chief told me to ask if your guns can fire case-shot into the trenches.'

'Only one of them can,' said the captain sullenly.

'All the same, let us go and see.'

The captain frowned and gave an angry grunt.

'I have been standing there all night and have come in to get a bit of rest – couldn't you go alone?' he added. 'My assistant, Lieutenant Kartz, is there and can show you everything.'

The captain had already been more than six months in command of this, one of the most dangerous batteries. From the time the siege began, even before the bomb-proof shelters were constructed, he had lived continuously on the bastion and had a great reputation for courage among the sailors. That is why his refusal struck and surprised Kalugin. 'So much for reputation,' thought he.

'Well then, I will go alone if I may,' he said in a slightly sarcastic tone to the captain, who however paid no attention to his words.

Kalugin did not realize that whereas he had spent some fifty hours all in all at different times on the bastions, the captain had lived there for six months. Kalugin was still actuated by vanity, the wish to shine, the hope of rewards, of gaining a reputation, and the charm of running risks. But the captain had already lived through all that: at first he had felt vain, had shown off his courage, had been foolhardy, had hoped for rewards and reputation and had even gained them, but now all these incentives had lost their power over him and he saw things differently. He fulfilled his duty exactly, but quite understanding how much the chances of life were against him after six months at the bastion, he no longer ran risks without serious need, and so the young lieutenant who had joined the battery a week ago and was now showing it to Kalugin, with whom he vied in uselessly leaning out of the embrasures and climbing out on the banquette, seemed ten times braver than the captain.

Returning to the shelter after examining the battery, Kalugin in the dark came upon the General, who accompanied by his staff officers was going to the watch-tower.

'Captain Praskukhin,' he heard the General say, 'please go to the right lodgement and tell the second battalion of the M— Regiment which is at work there to cease their work, leave the place, and noiselessly rejoin their regiment which is stationed in reserve at the foot of the hill. Do you understand? Lead them yourself to the regiment.'

'Yes, sir.'

And Praskukhin started at full speed towards the lodgements.

The firing was now becoming less frequent.

X

'Is this the second battalion of the M— Regiment?' asked Praskukhin, having run to his destination and coming across some soldiers carrying earth in sacks.

'It is, your Honour.'

'Where is the Commander?'

Mikhaylov, thinking that the commander of the company was being asked for, got out of his pit and taking Praskukhin for a commanding officer saluted and approached him.

'The General's orders are . . . that you . . . should go . . . quickly . . . and above all quietly . . . back – no not back, but to the reserves,' said Praskukhin, looking askance in the direction of the enemy's fire.

Having recognized Praskukhin and made out what was wanted, Mikhaylov dropped his hand and passed on the order. The battalion became alert, the men took up their muskets, put on their cloaks, and set out.

No one without experiencing it can imagine the delight a man feels when, after three hours' bombardment, he leaves so dangerous a spot as the lodgements. During those three hours Mikhaylov, who more than once and not without reason had thought his end at hand, had had time to accustom himself to the conviction that he would certainly be killed and that he no longer belonged to this world. But in spite of that he had great difficulty in keeping his legs from running away with him when, leading the company with Praskukhin at his side, he left the lodgement.

'*Au revoir!*' said a major with whom Mikhaylov had eaten bread and cheese sitting in the pit under the breastwork and who was remaining at the bastion in command of another battalion. 'I wish you a lucky journey.'

'And I wish you a lucky defence. It seems to be getting quieter now.'

But scarcely had he uttered these words before the enemy, probably observing the movement in the lodgement, began to fire more and more frequently. Our guns replied and a heavy firing recommenced.

The stars were high in the sky but shone feebly. The night was pitch dark, only the flashes of the guns and the bursting bombs made things around suddenly visible. The soldiers walked quickly and silently, involuntarily outpacing one another; only their measured footfall on the dry road was heard besides the incessant roll of the guns, the ringing of bayonets when they touched one another, a sigh, or the prayer of some poor soldier lad: 'Lord, O Lord! What does it mean?' Now and again the moaning of a man who was hit could be heard, and the cry, 'Stretchers!' (In the company Mikhaylov commanded artillery fire alone carried off twenty-six men that night.) A flash on the dark and distant horizon, the cry, 'Can-n-on!' from the sentinel on the bastion, and a ball flew buzzing above the company and plunged into the earth, making the stones fly.

'What the devil are they so slow for?' thought Praskukhin, continually looking back as he marched beside Mikhaylov. 'I'd really better run on. I've delivered the order. . . . But no, they might afterwards say I'm a coward. What must be will be. I'll keep beside him.'

'Now why is he walking with me?' thought Mikhaylov on his part. 'I have noticed over and over again that he always brings ill luck. Here it comes, I believe, straight for us.'

After they had gone a few hundred paces they met Kalugin, who was walking briskly towards the lodgements clanking his sabre. He had been ordered by the General to find out how the works were progressing there. But when he met Mikhaylov he thought that instead of going there himself under such a terrible fire – which he was not ordered to do – he might just as well find out all about it from an officer who had been there. And having heard from Mikhay-lov full details of the work and walked a little way with him, Kalugin turned off into a trench leading to the bomb-proof shelter.

'Well, what news?' asked an officer who was eating his supper there all alone.

'Nothing much. It seems that the affair is over.'

'Over? How so? On the contrary, the General has just gone again to the watch-tower and another regiment has arrived. Yes, there it is. Listen! The muskets again! Don't you go – why should you?' added the officer, noticing that Kalugin made a movement.

'I certainly ought to be there,' thought Kalugin, 'but I have already exposed myself a great deal today: the firing is awful!'

'Yes, I think I'd better wait here for him,' he said.

And really about twenty minutes later the General and the officers who were with him returned. Among them was Cadet Baron Pesth but not Praskukhin. The lodgements had been retaken and occupied by us.

After receiving a full account of the affair Kalugin, accompanied by Pesth, left the bomb-proof shelter.

XI

'THERE's blood on your coat! You don't mean to say you were in the hand-to-hand fight?' asked Kalugin.

'Oh, it was awful! Just fancy——'

And Pesth began to relate how he had led his company, how the company-commander had been killed, how he himself had stabbed a Frenchman, and how if it had not been for him we should have lost the day.

This tale was founded on fact: the company-commander had been killed and Pesth had bayoneted a Frenchman, but in recounting the details the cadet invented and bragged.

He bragged unintentionally, because during the whole of the affair he had been as it were in a fog and so bewildered that all he remem-bered of what had happened seemed to have happened somewhere, at some time, and to somebody. And very naturally he tried to recall the details in a light advantageous to himself. What really occurred was this:

The battalion the cadet had been ordered to join for the sortie stood under fire for two hours close to some low wall. Then the battalion-commander in front said something, the company-commanders became active, the battalion advanced from behind the breastwork, and after going about a hundred paces stopped to form into company columns. Pesth was told to take his place on the right flank of the second company.

Quite unable to realize where he was and why he was there, the cadet took his place, and involuntarily holding his breath while cold shivers ran down his back he gazed into the dark distance expecting something dreadful. He was however not so much frightened (for there was no firing) as disturbed and agitated at being in the field beyond the fortifications.

Again the battalion-commander in front said something. Again the officers spoke in whispers passing on the order, and the black wall, formed by the first company, suddenly sank out of sight. The order was to lie down. The second company also lay down and in lying down Pesth hurt his hand on a sharp prickle. Only the commander of the second company remained standing. His short figure brandishing a sword moved in front of the company and he spoke incessantly.

'Mind lads! Show them what you're made of! Don't fire, but give it them with the bayonet – the dogs! – when I cry "Hurrah!" Altogether, mind, that's the thing! We'll let them see who we are. We won't disgrace ourselves, eh lads? For our father the Tsar!'

'What's your company-commander's name?' asked Pesth of a cadet lying near him. 'How brave he is!'

'Yes he always is, in action,' answered the cadet. 'His name is Lisinkovski.'

Just then a flame suddenly flashed up right in front of the company, who were deafened by a resounding crash. High up in the air stones and splinters clattered. (Some fifty seconds later a stone fell from above and severed a soldier's leg.) It was a bomb fired from an elevated stand, and the fact that it reached the company showed that the French had noticed the column.

'You're sending bombs, are you? Wait a bit till we get at you, then you'll taste a three-edged Russian bayonet, damn you!' said the company-commander so loud that the battalion-commander had to order him to hold his tongue and not make so much noise.

After that the first company got up, then the second. They were ordered to fix bayonets and the battalion advanced. Pesth was in such a fright that he could not in the least make out how long it lasted,

where he went, or who was who. He went on as if he were drunk.
But suddenly a million fires flashed from all sides, and something
whistled and clattered. He shouted and ran somewhere, because everyone shouted and ran. Then he stumbled and fell over something. It
was the company-commander, who had been wounded at the head
of his company, and who taking the cadet for a Frenchman had seized
him by the leg. Then when Pesth had freed his leg and got up, someone else ran against him from behind in the dark and nearly knocked
him down again. 'Run him through!' someone else shouted. 'Why
are you stopping?' Then someone seized a bayonet and stuck it into
something soft. '*Ah Dieu!*' came a dreadful, piercing voice and Pesth
only then understood that he had bayoneted a Frenchman. A cold
sweat covered his whole body, he trembled as in a fever and threw
down his musket. But this lasted only a moment; the thought
immediately entered his head that he was a hero. He again seized his
musket, and shouting 'Hurrah!' ran with the crowd away from the
dead Frenchman. Having run twenty paces he came to a trench. Some
of our men were there with the battalion-commander.

'And I have killed one!' said Pesth to the commander.

'You're a fine fellow, Baron!'

XII

'Do you know Praskukhin is killed?' said Pesth, while accompanying
Kalugin on his way home.

'Impossible!'

'It is true. I saw him myself.'

'Well, goodbye . . . I must be off.'

'This is capital!' thought Kalugin, as he came to his lodgings. 'It's
the first time I have had such luck when on duty. It's first-rate. I am
alive and well, and shall certainly get an excellent recommendation
and am sure of a gold sabre. And I really have deserved it.'

After reporting what was necessary to the General he went to his
room, where Prince Galtsin, long since returned, sat awaiting him,
reading a book he had found on Kalugin's table.

It was with extraordinary pleasure that Kalugin found himself safe
at home again, and having put on his night-shirt and got into bed he
gave Galtsin all the details of the affair, telling them very naturally
from a point of view where those details showed what a capable and

brave officer he, Kalugin, was (which it seems to me it was hardly necessary to allude to, since everybody knew it and had no right or reason to question it, except perhaps the deceased Captain Praskukhin who, though he had considered it an honour to walk arm in arm with Kalugin, had privately told a friend only yesterday that though Kalugin was a first-rate fellow, yet, 'between you and me, he was awfully disinclined to go to the bastions').

Praskukhin, who had been walking beside Mikhaylov after Kalugin had slipped away from him, had scarcely begun to revive a little on approaching a safer place, when he suddenly saw a bright light flash up behind him and heard the sentinel shout 'Mortar!' and a soldier walking behind him say: 'That's coming straight for the bastion!'

Mikhaylov looked round. The bright spot seemed to have stopped at its zenith, in the position which makes it absolutely impossible to define its direction. But that only lasted a moment: the bomb, coming faster and faster, nearer and nearer, so that the sparks of its fuse were already visible and its fatal whistle audible, descended towards the centre of the battalion.

'Lie down!' shouted someone.

Mikhaylov and Praskukhin lay flat on the ground. Praskukhin, closing his eyes, only heard the bomb crash down on the hard earth close by. A second passed which seemed an hour: the bomb had not exploded. Praskukhin was afraid. Perhaps he had played the coward for nothing. Perhaps the bomb had fallen far away and it only seemed to him that its fuse was fizzing close by. He opened his eyes and was pleased to see Mikhaylov lying immovable at his feet. But at that moment he caught sight of the glowing fuse of the bomb which was spinning on the ground not a yard off. Terror, cold terror excluding every other thought and feeling, seized his whole being. He covered his face with his hands.

Another second passed – a second during which a whole world of feelings, thoughts, hopes, and memories flashed before his imagination.

'Whom will it hit – Mikhaylov or me? Or both of us? And if it's me, where? In the head? Then I'm done for. But if it's the leg, they'll cut it off (I'll certainly ask for chloroform) and I may survive. But perhaps only Mikhaylov will be hit. Then I will tell how we were going side by side and how he was killed and I was splashed with his blood. No, it's nearer to me . . . it will be I.'

Then he remembered the twelve rubles he owed Mikhaylov, remembered also a debt in Petersburg that should have been paid long ago, and the gipsy song he had sung that evening. The woman he loved rose in his imagination wearing a cap with lilac ribbons. He remembered a man who had insulted him five years ago and whom he had not yet paid out. And yet, inseparable from all these and thousands of other recollections, the present thought, the expectation of death, did not leave him for an instant. 'Perhaps it won't explode,' and with desperate decision he resolved to open his eyes. But at that instant a red flame pierced through the still closed lids and something struck him in the middle of his chest with a terrible crash. He jumped up and began to run, but stumbling over the sabre that got between his legs he fell on his side.

'Thank God, I'm only bruised!' was his first thought, and he was about to touch his chest with his hand, but his arms seemed tied to his sides and he felt as if a vice were squeezing his head. Soldiers flitted past him and he counted them unconsciously: 'One, two, three soldiers! And there's an officer with his cloak tucked up,' he thought. Then lightning flashed before his eyes and he wondered whether the shot was fired from a mortar or a cannon. 'A cannon, probably. And there's another shot and here are more soldiers – five, six, seven soldiers. . . . They all pass by!' He was suddenly seized with fear that they would crush him. He wished to shout that he was hurt, but his mouth was so dry that his tongue clove to the roof of his mouth and a terrible thirst tormented him. He felt a wetness about his chest and this sensation of being wet made him think of water, and he longed to drink even this that made him feel wet. 'I suppose I hit myself in falling and made myself bleed,' thought he, and giving way more and more to fear lest the soldiers who kept flitting past might trample on him, he gathered all his strength and tried to shout, 'Take me with you!' but instead of that he uttered such a terrible groan that the sound frightened him. Then some other red fires began dancing before his eyes and it seemed to him that the soldiers put stones on him. The fires danced less and less but the stones they put on him pressed more and more heavily. He made an effort to push off the stones, stretched himself, and saw and heard and felt nothing more. He had been killed on the spot by a bomb-splinter in the middle of his chest.

XIII

WHEN Mikhaylov dropped to the ground on seeing the bomb he too, like Praskukhin, lived through an infinitude of thoughts and feelings in the two seconds that elapsed before the bomb burst. He prayed mentally and repeated, 'Thy will be done.' And at the same time he thought, 'Why did I enter the army? And why did I join the infantry to take part in this campaign? Wouldn't it have been better to have remained with the Uhlan regiment at T— and spent my time with my friend Natasha? And now here I am . . .' and he began to count, 'One, two, three, four,' deciding that if the bomb burst at an even number he would live but if at an odd number he would be killed. 'It is all over, I'm killed!' he thought when the bomb burst (he did not remember whether at an odd or even number) and he felt a blow and a cruel pain in his head. 'Lord, forgive me my trespasses!' he muttered, folding his hands. He rose, but fell on his back senseless.

When he came to, his first sensations were that of blood trickling down his nose, and the pain in his head which had become much less violent. 'That's the soul passing,' he thought. 'How will it be *there*? Lord, receive my soul in peace! . . . Only it's strange,' thought he, 'that while dying I should hear the steps of the soldiers and the sounds of the firing so distinctly.'

'Bring stretchers! Eh, the Captain has been hit!' shouted a voice above his head, which he recognized as the voice of the drummer Ignatyev.

Someone took him by the shoulders. With an effort he opened his eyes and saw above him the sky, some groups of stars, and two bombs racing one another as they flew over him. He saw Ignatyev, soldiers with stretchers and guns, the embankment, the trenches, and suddenly realized that he was not yet in the other world.

He had been slightly wounded in the head by a stone. His first feeling was one almost of regret: he had prepared himself so well and so calmly to go *there* that the return to reality, with its bombs, stretchers, and blood, seemed unpleasant. The second feeling was unconscious joy at being alive, and the third a wish to get away from the bastion as quickly as possible. The drummer tied a handkerchief round his commander's head and taking his arm led him towards the ambulance station.

'But why and where am I going?' thought the lieutenant-captain when he had collected his senses. 'My duty is to remain with the company and not leave it behind – especially,' whispered a voice, 'as it will soon be out of range of the guns.'

'Don't trouble about me, my lad,' said he, drawing his hand away from the attentive drummer. 'I won't go to the ambulance station: I'll stay with the company.'

And he turned back.

'It would be better to have it properly bandaged, your honour,' said Ignatyev. 'It's only in the heat of the moment that it seems nothing. Mind it doesn't get worse. . . . And just see what warm work it is here. . . . Really, your honour——'

Mikhaylov stood for a moment undecided, and would probably have followed Ignatyev's advice had he not reflected how many severely wounded there must be at the ambulance station. 'Perhaps the doctors will smile at my scratch,' thought the lieutenant-captain, and in spite of the drummer's arguments he returned to his company.

'And where is the orderly officer Praskukhin, who was with me?' he asked when he met the ensign who was leading the company.

'I don't know. Killed, I think,' replied the ensign unwillingly.

'Killed? Or only wounded? How is it you don't know? Wasn't he going with us? And why didn't you bring him away?'

'How could we, under such a fire?'

'But how could you do such a thing, Michael Ivanych?' said Mikhaylov angrily. 'How could you leave him supposing he is alive? Even if he's dead his body ought to have been brought away.'

'Alive indeed, when I tell you I went up and saw him myself!' said the ensign. 'Excuse me. . . . It's hard enough to collect our own. There, those villains are at it again!' he added. 'They're sending up cannon-balls now.'

Mikhaylov sat down and lifted his hands to his head, which ached terribly when he moved.

'No, it is absolutely necessary to go back and fetch him,' he said. 'He may still be alive. It is our *duty*, Michael Ivanych.'

Michael Ivanych did not answer.

'O Lord! Just because he didn't bring him in at the time, soldiers will have to be sent back alone now . . . and yet can I possibly send them under this terrible fire? They may be killed for nothing,' thought Mikhaylov.

'Lads! Someone will have to go back to fetch the officer who was wounded out there in the ditch,' said he, not very loudly or per-emptorily, for he felt how unpleasant it would be for the soldiers to execute this order. And he was right. Since he had not named any one in particular no one came forward to obey the order.

'And after all he may be dead already. It isn't worth exposing men uselessly to such danger. It's all my fault, I ought to have seen to it. I'll go back myself and find out whether he is alive. It is my *duty*,' said Mikhaylov to himself.

'Michael Ivanych, you lead the company, I'll catch you up,' said he, and holding up his cloak with one hand while with the other he kept touching a small icon of St. Metrophanes that hung round his neck and in which he had great faith, he ran quickly along the trench.

Having convinced himself that Praskukhin was dead he dragged himself back panting, holding the bandage that had slipped on his head, which was beginning to ache very badly. When he overtook the battalion it was already at the foot of the hill and almost beyond the range of the shots. I say 'almost', for a stray bomb reached even here now and then.

'Tomorrow I had better go and be entered at the ambulance station,' thought the lieutenant-captain, while a medical assistant who had turned up was bandaging his head.

XIV

HUNDREDS of bodies, which a couple of hours before had been men full of various lofty or trivial hopes and wishes, were lying with fresh bloodstains on their stiffened limbs in the dewy, flowery valley which separated the bastions from the trenches and on the smooth floor of the mortuary chapel in Sevastopol. Hundreds of men with curses or prayers on their parched lips, crawled, writhed, and groaned, some among the dead in the flowery valley, some on stretchers, or beds, or on the blood-stained floor of the ambulance station. Yet the dawn broke behind the Sapun hill, the twinkling stars grew pale and the white mists spread from the dark roaring sea just as on other days, and the rosy morning glow lit up the east, long streaks of red clouds spread along the pale-blue horizon, and just as in the old days the sun rose in power and glory, promising joy, love, and happiness to all the awakening world.

XV

NEXT evening the Chasseurs' band was again playing on the boulevard, and officers, cadets, soldiers, and young women again promenaded round the pavilion and along the side-walks under the acacias with their sweet-scented white blossoms.

Kalugin was walking arm in arm with Prince Galtsin and a colonel near the pavilion and talking of last night's affair. The main theme of their conversation, as usual in such cases, was not the affair itself, but the part each of the speakers had taken in it. Their faces and the tone of their voices were serious, almost sorrowful, as if the losses of the night had touched and saddened them all. But to tell the truth, as none of them had lost any one very dear to him, this sorrowful expression was only an official one they considered it their duty to exhibit.

Kalugin and the colonel in fact, though they were first-rate fellows, were ready to see such an affair every day if they could gain a gold sword and be made major-general each time. It is all very well to call some conqueror a monster because he destroys millions to gratify his ambition, but go and ask any Ensign Petrushev or Sub-Lieutenant Antonov on their conscience, and you will find that everyone of us is a little Napoleon, a petty monster ready to start a battle and kill a hundred men merely to get an extra medal or one-third additional pay.

'No, I beg your pardon,' said the colonel. 'It began first on the left side. I was there myself.'

'Well, perhaps,' said Kalugin. 'I spent more time on the right. I went there twice: first to look for the General, and then just to see the lodgements. It was hot there, I can tell you!'

'Kalugin ought to know,' said Galtsin. 'By the way, V— told *me* today that you are a trump——'

'But the losses, the losses are terrible!' said the colonel. 'In my regiment we had four hundred casualties. It is astonishing that I'm still alive.'

Just then the figure of Mikhaylov, with his head bandaged, appeared at the end of the boulevard walking towards these gentlemen.

'What, are you wounded, Captain?' said Kalugin.

'Yes, slightly, with a stone,' answered Mikhaylov.

'*Est-ce que le pavillon est baissé déjà?*'[10] asked Prince Galtsin, glancing

10 'Is the flag (of truce) lowered already?'

at the lieutenant-captain's cap and not addressing anyone in particular.

'*Non, pas encore*,'[11] answered Mikhaylov, wishing to show that he understood and spoke French.

'Do you mean to say the truce still continues?' said Galtsin, politely addressing him in Russian and thereby (so it seemed to the lieutenant-captain) suggesting: 'It must no doubt be difficult for you to have to speak French, so hadn't we better simply . . .' and with that the adjutants went away. The lieutenant-captain again felt exceedingly lonely, just as he had done the day before. After bowing to various people – some of whom he did not wish and some of whom he did not venture to join – he sat down near the Kazarski monument and smoked a cigarette.

Baron Pesth also turned up on the boulevard. He mentioned that he had been at the parley and had spoken to the French officers. According to his account one of them had said to him: '*S'il n'avait pas fait clair encore pendant une demi-heure, les ambuscades auraient été reprises*,'[12] and he replied, '*Monsieur, je ne dis pas non, pour ne pas vous donner un démenti*,'[13] and he told how pat it had come out, and so on.

But though he had been at the parley he had not really managed to say anything in particular, though he much wished to speak with the French ('for it's awfully jolly to speak to those fellows'). He had paced up and down the line for a long time asking the Frenchmen near him: '*De quel régiment êtes-vous?*'[14] and had got his answer and nothing more. When he went too far beyond the line, the French sentry, not suspecting that 'that soldier' knew French, abused him in the third person singular: '*Il vient regarder nos travaux, ce sacré* ——'[15] in consequence of which Cadet Baron Pesth, finding nothing more to interest him at the parley, rode home, and on his way back composed the French phrases he now repeated.

On the boulevard was Captain Zobov talking very loud, and Captain Obzhogov, the artillery captain who never curried favour with anyone, was there too, in a dishevelled condition, and also the cadet who was always fortunate in his love affairs, and all the same

----

[11] 'No, not yet.'

[12] 'Had it remained dark for another half-hour, the ambuscades would have been recaptured.'

[13] 'Sir, I will not say no, lest I give you the lie.'

[14] 'What regiment do you belong to?'

[15] 'He's come to look at our works, the confounded ——'

people as yesterday, with the same motives as always. Only Praskukhin, Neferdov, and a few more were missing, and hardly anyone now remembered or thought of them, though there had not yet been time for their bodies to be washed, laid out, and put into the ground.

XVI

WHITE flags are hung out on our bastions and on the French trenches, and in the flowery valley between them lie heaps of mangled corpses without boots, some clad in blue and others in grey, which workmen are removing and piling onto carts. The air is filled with the smell of decaying flesh. Crowds of people have poured out from Sevastopol and from the French camp to see the sight, and with eager and friendly curiosity draw near to one another.

Listen to what these people are saying.

Here, in a circle of Russians and Frenchmen who have collected round him, a young officer, who speaks French badly but sufficiently to be understood, is examining a guardsman's pouch.

'*Eh sussy, poor quah se waso lié?*'

'*Parce que c'est une giberne d'un régiment de la garde, monsieur, qui porte l'aigle impérial.*'

'*Eh voo de la guard?*'[16]

'*Pardon, monsieur, du 6ème de ligne.*'

'*Eh sussy oo ashtay?*'[17] pointing to a cigarette-holder of yellow wood, in which the Frenchman is smoking a cigarette.

'*A Balaclava, monsieur. C'est tout simple en bois de palme.*'

'*Joli,*'[18] says the officer, guided in his remarks not so much by what he wants to say as by the French words he happens to know.

'*Si vous voulez bien garder cela comme souvenir de cette rencontre, vous m'obligerez.*'[19]

And the polite Frenchman puts out his cigarette and presents the

---

[16] 'And what is this tied bird for?'
'Because this is a cartridge pouch of a guard regiment, monsieur, and bears the Imperial eagle.'
'And do you belong to the Guards?'

[17] 'No, monsieur, to the 6th regiment of the line.'
'And where did you buy this?'

[18] 'At Balaclava, monsieur. It's only made of palm wood.' 'Pretty.'

[19] 'If you will be so good as to keep it as a souvenir of this meeting you will do me a favour.'

holder to the officer with a slight bow. The officer gives him his, and all present, both French and Russian, smile and seem pleased.

Here is a bold infantryman in a pink shirt with his cloak thrown over his shoulders, accompanied by other soldiers standing near him with their hands folded behind their backs and with merry inquisitive faces. He has approached a Frenchman and asked for a light for his pipe. The Frenchman draws at and stirs up the tobacco in his own short pipe and shakes a light into that of the Russian.

'*Tabac boon?*' says the soldier in the pink shirt, and the spectators smile. '*Oui, bon tabac, tabac turc,*' says the Frenchman. '*Chez vous autres tabac – Russe? Bon?*'[20]

'*Roos boon,*' says the soldier in the pink shirt while the onlookers shake with laughter. '*Fransay* not *boon. Bongjour, mossier!*', and having let off his whole stock of French at once, he slaps the Frenchman on the stomach and laughs. The French also laugh.

'*Ils ne sont pas jolis ces b—— de Russes,*' says a Zouave among the French.

'*De quoi est-ce qu'ils rient donc?*'[21] says another with an Italian accent, a dark man, coming up to our men.

'*Coat boon,*' says the cheeky soldier, examining the embroidery of the Zouave's coat, and everybody laughs again.

'*Ne sors pas de ta ligne, à vos places, sacré nom'!*[22] cries a French corporal, and the soldiers separate with evident reluctance.

And here, in the midst of a group of French officers, one of our cavalry officers is gushing. They are talking about some Count Sazonov, '*que j'ai beaucoup connu, monsieur,*' says a French officer with only one epaulette – '*c'est un de ces vrais comtes russes, comme nous les aimons.*'

'*Il y a un Sazonoff, que j'ai connu,*' says the cavalry officer, '*mais il n'est pas comte, à moins que je sache, un petit brun de votre âge à peu près.*'[23]

'*C'est ça, monsieur, c'est lui. Oh! que je voudrais le voir, ce cher comte.*

[20] 'Yes, good tobacco, Turkish tobacco . . . You others have Russian tobacco. Is it good?'

[21] 'They are not handsome, these d—— Russians.' . . . 'What are they laughing about?'

[22] 'Don't leave your ranks. To your places, damn it!'

[23] 'Whom I knew very intimately, monsieur. He is one of those real Russian counts of whom we are so fond.' 'I am acquainted with a Sazonov, but he is not a count, as far as I know – a small dark man, of about your age.'

Si vous le voyez, je vous prie bien de lui faire mes compliments – Capitaine Latour,' he said, bowing.

'*N'est-ce pas terrible la triste besogne que nous faisons? Ça chauffait cette nuit, n'est-ce pas?'*[24] said the cavalry officer, wishing to maintain the conversation and pointing to the corpses.

'*Oh, monsieur, c'est affreux! Mais quels gaillards vos soldats, quels gaillards! C'est un plaisir que de se battre avec des gaillards comme eux.'*

'*Il faut avouer que les vôtres ne se mouchent pas du pied non plus,'*[25] said the cavalry officer, bowing and imagining himself very agreeable.

But enough.

Let us rather look at this ten-year-old boy in an old cap (probably his father's), with shoes on his stockingless feet and nankeen trousers held up by one brace. At the very beginning of the truce he came over the entrenchments, and has been walking about the valley ever since, looking with dull curiosity at the French and at the corpses that lie on the ground and gathering the blue flowers with which the valley is strewn. Returning home with a large bunch of flowers he holds his nose to escape the smell that is borne towards him by the wind, and stopping near a heap of corpses gazes for a long time at a terrible headless body that lies nearest to him. After standing there some time he draws nearer and touches with his foot the stiff outstretched arm of the corpse. The arm trembles a little. He touches it again more boldly; it moves and falls back to its old position. The boy gives a sudden scream, hides his face in his flowers, and runs towards the fortifications as fast as his legs can carry him.

Yes, there are white flags on the bastions and the trenches but the flowery valley is covered with dead bodies. The glorious sun is sinking towards the blue sea, and the undulating blue sea glitters in the golden light. Thousands of people crowd together, look at, speak to, and smile at one another. And these people – Christians professing the one great law of love and self-sacrifice – on seeing what they have done do not at once fall repentant on their knees before Him who has given them life and laid in the soul of each a fear of death and a

[24] 'Just so, monsieur, that is he. Oh, how I should like to meet the dear count. If you should see him, please be so kind as to give him my compliments – Captain Latour.' 'Isn't it terrible, this sad duty we are engaged in? It was warm work last night, wasn't it?'

[25] 'Ah, monsieur, it is terrible! But what fine fellows your men are, what fine fellows! It is a pleasure to fight with such fellows!' 'It must be admitted that yours are no fools either.' (Literally, 'don't wipe their noses with their feet'.)

love of the good and the beautiful, and do not embrace like brothers with tears of joy and gladness.

The white flags are lowered, the engines of death and suffering are sounding again, innocent blood is flowing and the air is filled with moans and curses.

There, I have said what I wished to say this time. But I am seized by an oppressive doubt. Perhaps I ought to have left it unsaid. What I have said perhaps belongs to that class of evil truths that lie unconsciously hidden in the soul of each man and should not be uttered lest they become harmful, as the dregs in a bottle must not be disturbed for fear of spoiling the wine. . . .

Where in this tale is the evil that should be avoided, and where the good that should be imitated? Who is the villain and who the hero of the story? All are good and all are bad.

Not Kalugin, with his brilliant courage – *bravoure de gentilhomme* – and the vanity that influences all his actions, not Praskukhin, the empty harmless fellow (though he fell in battle for faith, throne, and fatherland), not Mikhaylov with his shyness, nor Pesth, a child without firm principles or convictions, can be either the villain or the hero of the tale.

The hero of my tale – whom I love with all the power of my soul, whom I have tried to portray in all his beauty, who has been, is, and will be beautiful – is Truth.

1855

TWO HUSSARS

Два гусара

'Jomini and Jomini –
Not half a word of vodka.' – D. DAVYDOV.[1]

EARLY in the nineteenth century, when there were as yet no railways
or macadamized roads, no gaslight, no stearine candles, no low
couches with sprung cushions, no unvarnished furniture, no disillusioned youths with eye-glasses, no liberalizing women philoso-
phers, nor any charming *dames aux camélias* of whom there are so
many in our times, in those naïve days, when leaving Moscow for
Petersburg in a coach or carriage provided with a kitchenful of home-
made provisions one travelled for eight days along a soft, dusty, or
muddy road and believed in chopped cutlets, sledge-bells, and plain
rolls; when in the long autumn evenings the tallow candles, around
which family groups of twenty or thirty people gathered, had to be
snuffed; when ball-rooms were illuminated by candelabra with wax
or spermaceti candles, when furniture was arranged symmetrically,
when our fathers were still young and proved it not only by the
absence of wrinkles and grey hair but by fighting duels for the sake
of a woman and rushing from the opposite corner of a room to pick
up a bit of a handkerchief purposely or accidentally dropped; when
our mothers wore short-waisted dresses and enormous sleeves and
decided family affairs by drawing lots, when the charming *dames aux
camélias* hid from the light of day – in those naïve days of Masonic
lodges,[2] Martinists, and Tugendbunds, the days of Miloradoviches
and Davydovs and Pushkins – a meeting of landed proprietors was
held in the Government town of K——, and the nobility elections[3]
were being concluded.

---

[1] From *The Song of an old Hussar* by D. V. Davydov (1784–1839).

[2] Freemasonry in Russia was a secret association, which began as a mystical-
religious movement in the eighteenth century, became political during the
reign of Alexander I, and was suppressed in 1822.

[3] The *nobility* included not merely those who had titles, but all who in
England would be called the gentry.

I

'WELL, never mind, the saloon will do,' said a young officer in a fur cloak and hussar's cap, who had just got out of a post-sledge and was entering the best hotel in the town of K——.

'The assembly, your Excellency, is enormous,' said the boots, who had already managed to learn from the orderly that the hussar's name was Count Turbin, and therefore addressed him as 'your Excellency'.

'The proprietress of Afremovo with her daughters has said she is leaving this evening, so No. 11 will be at your disposal as soon as they go,' continued the boots, stepping softly before the count along the passage and continually looking round.

In the general saloon at a little table under the dingy full-length portrait of the Emperor Alexander the First, several men, probably belonging to the local nobility, sat drinking champagne, while at another side of the room sat some travellers – tradesmen in blue, fur-lined cloaks.

Entering the room and calling in Blücher, a gigantic grey mastiff he had brought with him, the count threw off his cloak, the collar of which was still covered with hoar-frost, called for vodka, sat down at the table in his blue satin Cossack jacket, and entered into conversation with the gentlemen there.

The handsome open countenance of the newcomer immediately predisposed them in his favour and they offered him a glass of champagne. The count first drank a glass of vodka and then ordered another bottle of champagne to treat his new acquaintances. The sledge-driver came in to ask for a tip.

'Sashka!' shouted the count. 'Give him something!'

The driver went out with Sashka but came back again with the money in his hand.

'Look here, y'r 'xcelence, haven't I done my very best for y'r honour? Didn't you promise me half a ruble, and he's only given me a quarter!'

'Give him a ruble, Sashka.'

Sashka cast down his eyes and looked at the driver's feet.

'He's had enough!' he said, in a bass voice. 'And besides, I have no more money.'

The count drew from his pocket-book the two five-ruble notes which were all it contained, and gave one of them to the driver, who kissed his hand and went off.

'I've run it pretty close!' said the count. 'These are my last five rubles.'

'Real hussar fashion, Count,' said one of the nobles who from his moustache, voice, and a certain energetic freedom about his legs, was evidently a retired cavalryman. 'Are you staying here some time, Count?

'I must get some money. I shouldn't have stayed here at all but for that. And there are no rooms to be had, devil take them, in this accursed pub.'

'Permit me, Count,' said the cavalryman. 'Will you not join me? My room is No. 7. . . . If you do not mind, just for the night. And then you'll stay a couple of days with us? It happens that the *Maréchal de la Noblesse* is giving a ball tonight. You would make him very happy by going.'

'Yes, Count, do stay,' said another, a handsome young man. 'You have surely no reason to hurry away! You know this only comes once in three years – the elections, I mean. You should at least have a look at our young ladies, Count!'

'Sashka, get my clean linen ready. I am going to the bath,' said the count, rising, 'and from there perhaps I may look in at the Marshal's.'

Then, having called the waiter and whispered something to him to which the latter replied with a smile, 'That can all be arranged,' he went out.

'So I'll order my trunk to be taken to your room, old fellow,' shouted the count from the passage.

'Please do, I shall be most happy,' replied the cavalryman, running to the door. 'No. 7 – don't forget.'

When the count's footsteps could no longer be heard the cavalryman returned to his place and sitting close to one of the group – a Government official, and looking him straight in the face with smiling eyes, said:

'It is the very man, you know!'

'No!'

'I tell you it is! It is the very same duellist hussar – the famous Turbin. He knew me – I bet you anything he knew me. Why, he and I went on the spree for three weeks without a break when I was at Lebedyani[4] for remounts. There was one thing he and I did together. . . . He's a fine fellow, eh?'

---

[4] A town in Tambov province noted for its horse fair.

'A splendid fellow. And so pleasant in his manner! Doesn't show a grain of – what d'you call it?' answered the handsome young man. 'How quickly we became intimate. . . . He's not more than twenty-five, is he?'

'Oh no, that's what he looks but he is more than that. One has to get to know him, you know. Who abducted Migunova? He. It was he who killed Sablin. It was he who dropped Matnev out of the window by his legs. It was he who won three hundred thousand rubles from Prince Nestorov. He is a regular dare-devil, you know: a gambler, a duellist, a seducer, but a jewel of an hussar – a real jewel. The rumours that are afloat about us are nothing to the reality – if anyone knew what a true hussar is! Ah yes, those were times!'

And the cavalryman told his interlocutor of such a spree with the count in Lebedyani as not only never had, but never even could have, taken place.

It could not have done so, first because he had never seen the count till that day and had left the army two years before the count entered it; and secondly because the cavalryman had never really served in the cavalry at all, but had for four years been the humblest of cadets in the Belevski regiment, and retired as soon as ever he became ensign. But ten years ago he had inherited some money and had really been in Lebedyani where he squandered seven hundred rubles with some officers who were there buying remounts. He had even gone so far as to have an uhlan uniform made with orange facings, meaning to enter an uhlan regiment. This desire to enter the cavalry, and the three weeks spent with the remount officers at Lebedyani, remained the brightest and happiest memories of his life, so he transformed the desire first into a reality and then into a reminiscence and came to believe firmly in his past as a cavalry officer – all of which did not prevent his being, as to gentleness and honesty, a most worthy man.

'Yes, those who have never served in the cavalry will never understand us fellows.'

He sat astride a chair and thrusting out his lower jaw began to speak in a bass voice. 'You ride at the head of your squadron, not a horse but the devil incarnate prancing about under you, and you just sit in devil-may-care style. The squadron commander rides up to review: "Lieutenant," he says. "We can't get on without you – please lead the squadron to parade." "All right," you say, and there you are: you turn round, shout to your moustached fellows. . . . Ah, devil take it, those were times!'

The count returned from the bath-house very red and with wet hair, and went straight to No. 7, where the cavalryman was already sitting in his dressing-gown smoking a pipe and considering with pleasure, and not without some apprehension, the happiness that had befallen him of sharing a room with the celebrated Turbin. 'Now suppose,' he thought, 'that he suddenly takes me, strips me naked, drives me to the town gates and sets me in the snow, or . . . tars me, or simply. . . . But no,' he consoled himself, 'he wouldn't do that to a comrade.'

'Sashka, feed Blücher!' shouted the count.

Sashka, who had taken a tumbler of vodka to refresh himself after the journey and was decidedly tipsy, came in.

'What, already! You've been drinking, you rascal! . . . Feed Blücher!'

'He won't starve anyway: see how sleek he is!' answered Sashka, stroking the dog.

'Silence! Be off and feed him!'

'You want the dog to be fed, but when a man drinks a glass you reproach him.'

'Hey! I'll thrash you!' shouted the count in a voice that made the window-panes rattle and even frightened the cavalryman a bit.

'You should ask if Sashka has had a bite today! Yes, beat me if you think more of a dog than of a man,' muttered Sashka.

But here he received such a terrible blow in the face from the count's fist that he fell, knocked his head against the partition, and clutching his nose fled from the room and fell on a settee in the passage.

'He's knocked my teeth out,' grunted Sashka, wiping his bleeding nose with one hand while with the other he scratched the back of Blücher, who was licking himself. 'He's knocked my teeth out, Blüchy, but still he's my count and I'd go through fire for him – I would! Because he – is my count. Do you understand, Blüchy? Want your dinner, eh?'

After lying still for a while he rose, fed the dog, and then, almost sobered, went in to wait on his count and to offer him some tea.

'I shall really feel hurt,' the cavalryman was saying meekly, as he stood before the count who was lying on the other's bed with his legs up against the partition. 'You see I also am an old army man and, if I may say so, a comrade. Why should you borrow from anyone else when I shall be delighted to lend you a couple of hundred rubles?

I haven't got them just now – only a hundred rubles – but I'll get the rest today. You would really hurt my feelings, Count.'

'Thank you, old man,' said the count, instantly discerning what kind of relations had to be established between them, and slapping the cavalryman on the shoulder: 'Thanks! Well then, we'll go to the ball if it must be so. But what are we to do now? Tell me what you have in your town. What pretty girls? What men fit for a spree? What gaming?'

The cavalryman explained that there would be an abundance of pretty creatures at the ball, that Kolkov, who had been re-elected Captain of Police, was the best hand at a spree, only he lacked the true hussar go – otherwise he was a good sort of a chap: that the Ilyushin gipsy chorus had been singing in the town since the elections began, Steshka leading, and that everybody meant to go to hear them after leaving the Marshal's that evening.

'And there's a devilish lot of card-playing too,' he went on. 'Lukhnov plays. He has money and is staying here to break his journey, and Ilyin, an uhlan cornet who has room No. 8, has lost a lot. They have already begun in his room. They play every evening. And what a fine fellow that Ilyin is! I tell you, Count, he's not mean – he'll let his last shirt go.'

'Well then, let us go to his room. Let's see what sort of people they are,' said the count.

'Yes do – pray do. They'll be devilish glad.'

II

THE uhlan cornet, Ilyin, had not long been awake. The evening before he had sat down to cards at eight o'clock and had lost pretty steadily for fifteen hours on end – till eleven in the morning. He had lost a considerable sum, but did not know exactly how much, because he had about three thousand rubles of his own, and fifteen thousand of Crown money which had long since got mixed up with his own, and he feared to count lest his fears that some of the Crown money was already gone should be confirmed. It was nearly noon when he fell asleep and he had slept that heavy dreamless sleep which only very young men sleep after a heavy loss. Waking at six o'clock (just when Count Turbin arrived at the hotel), and seeing the floor all around strewn with cards and bits of chalk, and the chalk-marked tables in the middle of the room, he recalled with horror last night's play, and the last card – a knave on which he lost five hundred rubles; but not yet quite convinced of the reality of all this, he drew his money from under the pillow and began to count it. He recognized some notes which had passed from hand to hand several times with 'corners' and 'transports', and he recalled the whole course of the game. He had none of his own three thousand rubles left, and some two thousand five hundred of the Government money was also gone.

Ilyin had been playing for four nights running.

He had come from Moscow where the Crown money had been entrusted to him, and at K—— had been detained by the superintendent of the post-house on the pretext that there were no horses, but really because the superintendent had an agreement with the hotel-keeper to detain all travellers for a day. The uhlan, a bright young lad who had just received three thousand rubles from his parents in Moscow for his equipment on entering his regiment, was glad to spend a few days in the town of K—— during the elections, and hoped to enjoy himself thoroughly. He knew one of the landed gentry there who had a family, and he was thinking of looking them up and flirting with the daughters, when the cavalryman turned up to make his acquaintance. Without any evil intention the cavalryman introduced him that same evening, in the general saloon or common room of the hotel, to his acquaintances, Lukhnov and other gamblers. And ever since then the uhlan had been playing cards, not asking at the post-station for horses, much less going to visit his acquaintance the landed proprietor, and not even leaving his room for four days on end.

Having dressed and drunk tea he went to the window. He felt that he would like to go for a stroll to get rid of the recollections that haunted him, and he put on his cloak and went out into the street. The sun was already hidden behind the white houses with their red roofs and it was getting dusk. It was warm for winter. Large wet snowflakes were falling slowly into the muddy street. Suddenly at the thought that he had slept all through the day now ending, a feeling of intolerable sadness overcame him.

'This day, now past, can never be recovered,' he thought.

'I have ruined my youth!' he suddenly said to himself, not because he really thought he had ruined his youth – he did not even think about it – but because the phrase happened to occur to him.

'And what am I to do now?' thought he. 'Borrow from someone

and go away?' A lady passed him along the pavement. 'There's a stupid woman,' thought he for some reason. 'There's no one to borrow from . . . I have ruined my youth!' He came to the bazaar. A tradesman in a fox-fur cloak stood at the door of his shop touting for customers. 'If I had not withdrawn that eight I should have recovered my losses.' An old beggar-woman followed him whimpering. 'There's no one to borrow from.' A man drove past in a bearskin cloak; a policeman was standing at his post. 'What unusual thing could I do? Fire at them? No, what's the point . . . I have ruined my youth! . . . Ah, those are fine horse-collars and trappings hanging there! Ah, if only I could drive in a troyka: Gee-up, beauties! . . . I'll go back. Lukhnov will come soon, and we'll play.'

He returned to the hotel and again counted his money. No, he had made no mistake the first time: there were still two thousand five hundred rubles of Crown money missing. 'I'll stake twenty-five rubles, then make a 'corner' . . . seven-fold it, fifteen-fold, thirty, sixty . . . three thousand rubles. Then I'll buy the horse-collars and be off. He won't let me, the rascal! I have ruined my youth!'

That is what was going on in the uhlan's head when Lukhnov actually entered the room.

'Have you been up long, Michael Vasilich?' asked Lukhnov slowly removing the gold spectacles from his skinny nose and carefully wiping them with a red silk handkerchief.

'No, I've only just got up – I slept uncommonly well.'

'Some hussar or other has arrived. He has put up with Zavalshevski – had you heard?'

'No, I hadn't. But how is it no one else is here yet?'

'They must have gone to Pryakhin's. They'll be here directly.'

And sure enough a little later there came into the room a garrison officer who always accompanied Lukhnov; a Greek merchant with an enormous brown hooked nose and sunken black eyes, and a fat puffy landowner, the proprietor of a distillery, who played whole nights, always staking 'simples' of half a ruble each. Everybody wished to begin playing as soon as possible, but the principal gamesters, especially Lukhnov who was telling about a robbery in Moscow in an exceedingly calm manner, did not refer to the subject.

'Just fancy,' he said, 'a city like Moscow, the historic capital, a metropolis, and men dressed up as devils go about there with crooks, frighten stupid people and rob the passers-by – and that's the end of it! What are the police about? That's the question.'

The uhlan listened attentively to the story about the robbers, but when a pause came he rose and quietly ordered cards to be brought. The fat landowner was the first to speak out.

'Well, gentlemen, why lose precious time? If we mean business let's begin.'

'Yes, you walked off with a pile of half-rubles last night so you like it,' said the Greek.

'I think we might start,' said the garrison officer.

Ilyin looked at Lukhnov. Lukhnov looking him in the eye quietly continued his story about robbers dressed up like devils with claws.

'Will you keep the bank?' asked the uhlan.

'Isn't it too early?'

'Belov!' shouted the uhlan, blushing for some unknown reason, 'bring me some dinner – I haven't had anything to eat yet, gentlemen – and a bottle of champagne and some cards.'

At this moment the count and Zavalshevski entered the room. It turned out that Turbin and Ilyin belonged to the same division. They took to one another at once, clinked glasses, drank champagne together, and were on intimate terms in five minutes. The count seemed to like Ilyin very much; he looked smilingly at him and teased him about his youth.

'There's an uhlan of the right sort!' he said. 'What moustaches! Dear me, what moustaches!'

Even what little down there was on Ilyin's lip was quite white.

'I suppose you are going to play?' said the count: 'Well, I wish you luck, Ilyin! I should think you are a master at it,' he added with a smile.

'Yes, they mean to start,' said Lukhnov, tearing open a bundle of a dozen packs of cards, 'and you'll join in too, Count, won't you?'

'No, not today. I should clear you all out if I did. When I begin "cornering" in earnest the bank begins to crack! But I have nothing to play with – I was cleaned out at a station near Volochok. I met some infantry fellow there with rings on his fingers – a sharper I should think – and he plucked me clean.'

'Why, did you stay at that station long?' asked Ilyin.

'I sat there for twenty-two hours. I shan't forget that accursed station! And the superintendent won't forget me either . . .'

'How's that?'

'I drive up, you know; out rushes the superintendent looking a regular brigand. "No horses!" says he. Now I must tell you that it's my rule, if there are no horses I don't take off my fur cloak but go into the superintendent's own room – not into the public room but into his private room – and I have all the doors and windows opened on the ground that it's smoky. Well, that's just what I did there. You remember what frosts we had last month? About twenty degrees! The superintendent began to argue, I punched his head. There was an old woman there, and girls and other women; they kicked up a row, snatched up their pots and pans and were rushing off to the village. . . . I went to the door and said, "Let me have horses and I'll be off. If not, no one shall go out: I'll freeze you all!"'

'That's an infernally good plan!' said the puffy squire, rolling with laughter. 'It's the way they freeze out cockroaches . . .'

'But I didn't watch carefully enough and the superintendent got away with the women. Only one old woman remained in pawn on the top of the stove; she kept sneezing and saying her prayers. Afterwards we began negotiating: the superintendent came and from a distance began persuading me to let the old woman go, but I set Blücher at him a bit. Blücher's splendid at tackling superintendents! But still the rascal didn't let me have horses until the next morning. Meanwhile that infantry fellow came along. I joined him in another room, and we began to play. You have seen Blücher? . . . Blücher! . . .' and he gave a whistle.

Blücher rushed in, and the players condescendingly paid some attention to him though it was evident that they wished to attend to quite other matters.

'But why don't you play, gentlemen? Please don't let me prevent you. I am a chatterbox, you see,' said Turbin. 'Play is play whether one likes it or not.'

III

LUKHNOV drew two candles nearer to him, took out a large brown pocket-book full of paper money, and slowly, as if performing some rite, opened it on the table, took out two one-hundred ruble notes and placed them under the cards.

'Two hundred for the bank, the same as yesterday,' said he, adjusting his spectacles and opening a pack of cards.

'Very well,' said Ilyin, continuing his conversation with Turbin without looking at Lukhnov.

The game[5] started. Lukhnov dealt the cards with machine-like precision, stopping now and then and deliberately jotting something down, or looking sternly over his spectacles and saying in low tones, 'Pass up!' The fat landowner spoke louder than anyone else, audibly deliberating with himself and wetting his plump fingers when he turned down the corner of a card. The garrison officer silently and neatly noted the amount of his stake on his card and bent down small corners under the table. The Greek sat beside the banker watching the game attentively with his sunken black eyes, and seemed to be waiting for something. Zavalshevski standing by the table would suddenly begin to fidget all over, take a red or blue bank-note out of his trouser pocket, lay a card on it, slap it with his palm and say: 'Little seven, pull me through!' Then he would bite his moustache, shift from foot to foot, and keep fidgeting till his card was dealt. Ilyin sat eating veal and pickled cucumbers, which were placed beside him on the horsehair sofa, and hastily wiping his hands on his coat laid down one card after another. Turbin, who at first was sitting on the sofa, quickly saw how matters stood. Lukhnov did not look at or speak to Ilyin, only now and then his spectacles would turn for a moment towards the latter's hand, but most of Ilyin's cards lost.

'There now, I'd like to beat that card,' said Lukhnov of a card the fat landowner, who was staking half-rubles, had put down.

'You beat Ilyin's, never mind me!' remarked the squire.

And indeed Ilyin's cards lost more often than any of the others. He would tear up the losing card nervously under the table and choose another with trembling fingers. Turbin rose from the sofa and asked the Greek to let him sit by the banker. The Greek moved to another place, the count took his chair and began watching Lukhnov's hands attentively, not taking his eyes off them.

'Ilyin!' he suddenly said in his usual voice, which quite unintentionally drowned all the others. 'Why do you keep to a routine? You don't know how to play.'

[5] The game referred to was *shtos*. The players selected cards for themselves from packs on the table, and placed their stakes on or under their cards. The banker had a pack from which he dealt to right and left alternately. Cards dealt to the right won for him, those dealt to the left won for the players. 'Pass up' was a reminder to the players to hand up stakes due to the bank. 'Simples' were single stakes. By turning down 'corners' of his card a player increased his stake two- or three-fold. A 'transport' increased it six-fold.

'It's all the same how one plays.'

'But you're sure to lose that way. Let me play for you.'

'No, please excuse me. I always do it myself. Play for yourself if you like.'

'I said I should not play for myself, but I should like to play for you. I am vexed that you are losing.'

'I suppose it's my fate.'

The count was silent, but leaning on his elbows he again gazed intently at the banker's hands.

'Abominable!' he suddenly said in a loud, long-drawn tone.

Lukhnov glanced at him.

'Abominable, quite abominable!' he repeated still louder, looking straight into Lukhnov's eyes.

The game continued.

'It is not right!' Turbin remarked again, just as Lukhnov beat a heavily-backed card of Ilyin's.

'What is it you don't like, Count?' inquired the banker with polite indifference.

'This! – that you let Ilyin win his simples and beat his corners. That's what's bad.'

Lukhnov made a slight movement with his brows and shoulders, expressing the advisability of submitting to fate in everything, and continued to play.

'Blücher!' shouted the count, rising and whistling the dog. 'At him!' he added quickly.

Blücher, bumping his back against the sofa as he leapt from under it and nearly upsetting the garrison officer, ran to his master and growled, looking round at everyone and moving his tail as if asking, 'Who is misbehaving here, eh?'

Lukhnov put down his cards and moved his chair to one side.

'One can't play like that,' he said. 'I hate dogs. What kind of a game is it when you bring a whole pack of hounds in here?'

'Especially a dog like that. I believe they are called "leeches",' chimed in the garrison officer.

'Well, are we going to play or not, Michael Vasilich?' said Lukhnov to their host.

'Please don't interfere with us, Count,' said Ilyin, turning to Turbin.

'Come here a minute,' said Turbin, taking Ilyin's arm and going behind the partition with him.

The count's words, spoken in his usual tone, were distinctly audible from there. His voice always carried across three rooms.

'Are you daft, eh? Don't you see that that gentleman in spectacles is a sharper of the first water?'

'Come now, enough! What are you saying?'

'No enough about it! Stop playing, I tell you. It's nothing to me. Another time I'd pluck you myself, but somehow I'm sorry to see you fleeced. And maybe you have Crown money too?'

'No . . . why do you imagine such things?'

'Ah, my lad, I've been that way myself so I know all those sharpers' tricks. I tell you the one in spectacles is a sharper. Stop playing! I ask you as a comrade.'

'Well then, I'll only finish this one deal.'

'I know what "one deal" means. Well, we'll see.'

They went back. In that one deal Ilyin put down so many cards and so many of them were beaten that he lost a large amount.

Turbin put his hands in the middle of the table. 'Now stop it! Come along.'

'No, I can't. Leave me alone, do!' said Ilyin, irritably shuffling some bent cards without looking at Turbin.

'Well, go to the devil! Go on losing for certain, if that pleases you. It's time for me to be off. Let's go to the Marshal's, Zavalshevski.'

They went out. All remained silent and Lukhnov dealt no more cards until the sound of their steps and of Blücher's claws on the passage floor had died away.

'What a devil of a fellow!' said the landowner laughing.

'Well, he won't interfere now,' remarked the garrison officer hastily, and still in a whisper.

And the play continued.

IV

THE band, composed of some of the Marshal's serfs standing in the pantry – which had been cleared out for the occasion – with their coat-sleeves turned up ready, had at a given signal struck up the old polonaise, 'Alexander, 'Lizabeth', and under the bright soft light of the wax-candles a Governor-General of Catherine's days, with a star on his breast, arm-in-arm with the Marshal's skinny wife, and the rest of the local grandees with their partners, had begun slowly gliding over the parquet floor of the large dancing-room in various combinations and variations, when Zavalshevski entered, wearing stockings and pumps and a blue swallow-tail coat with an immense and padded collar, and exhaling a strong smell of the frangipane with which the facings of his coat, his handkerchief, and his moustaches, were abundantly sprinkled. The handsome hussar who came with him wore tight-fitting light-blue riding-breeches and a gold-embroidered scarlet coat on which a Vladimir cross and an 1812 medal[6] were fastened. The count was not tall but remarkably well built. His clear blue and exceedingly brilliant eyes, and thick, closely curling, dark-brown hair, gave a remarkable character to his beauty. His arrival at the ball was expected, for the handsome young man who had seen him at the hotel had already prepared the Marshal for it. Various impressions had been produced by the news, for the most part not altogether pleasant.

'It's not unlikely that this youngster will hold us up to ridicule,' was the opinion of the men and of the older women. 'What if he should run away with me?' was more or less in the minds of the younger ladies, married or unmarried.

As soon as the polonaise was over and the couples after bowing to one another had separated – the women into one group and the men into another – Zavalshevski, proud and happy, introduced the count to their hostess.

The Marshal's wife, feeling an inner trepidation lest this hussar should treat her in some scandalous manner before everybody, turned away haughtily and contemptuously as she said: 'Very pleased, I hope you will dance,' and then gave him a distrustful look that said, 'Now, if you offend a woman it will show me that you are a perfect villain.' The count however soon conquered her prejudices by his amiability, attentive manner, and handsome gay appearance, so that five minutes later the expression on the face of the Marshal's wife told the company: 'I know how to manage such gentlemen. He immediately understood with whom he had to deal, and now he'll be charming to me for the rest of the evening.' Moreover at that moment the governor of the town, who had known the count's father, came up to him and very affably took him aside for a talk, which still further calmed the provincial public and raised the count in its estimation. After that Zavalshevski introduced the count to his sister, a plump young widow whose large black eyes had not left the

[6] A medal gained in the defence of his country against Napoleon.

count from the moment he entered. The count asked her to dance the waltz the band had just commenced, and the general prejudice was finally dispersed by the masterly way in which he danced.

'What a splendid dancer!' said a fat landed proprietress, watching his legs in their blue riding-breeches as they flitted across the room, and mentally counting 'one, two, three – one, two, three – splendid!'

'There he goes – jig, jig, jig,' said another, a visitor in the town whom local society did not consider genteel. 'How does he manage not to entangle his spurs? Wonderfully clever!'

The count's artistic dancing eclipsed the three best dancers of the province: the tall fair-haired adjutant of the governor, noted for the rapidity with which he danced and for holding his partner very close to him; the cavalryman, famous for the graceful swaying motion with which he waltzed and for the frequent but light tapping of his heels; and a civilian, of whom everybody said that though he was not very intellectual he was a first-rate dancer and the soul of every ball. In fact, from its very commencement this civilian would ask all the ladies in turn to dance, in the order in which they were sitting, and never stopped for a moment except occasionally to wipe the perspiration from his weary but cheerful face with a very wet cambric handkerchief. The count eclipsed them all and danced with the three principal ladies: the tall one, rich, handsome, stupid; the one of middle height, thin and not very pretty but splendidly dressed; and the little one, who was plain but very clever. He danced with others too – with all the pretty ones, and there were many of these – but it was Zavalshevski's sister, the little widow, who pleased him best. With her he danced a quadrille, an *écossaise*, and a mazurka. When they were sitting down during the quadrille he began paying her many compliments; comparing her to Venus and Diana, to a rose, and to some other flower. But all these compliments only made the widow bend her white neck, lower her eyes and look at her white muslin dress, or pass her fan from hand to hand. But when she said: 'Don't, you're only joking, Count,' and other words to that effect, there was a note of such naïve simplicity and amusing silliness in her slightly guttural voice, that looking at her it really seemed that this was not a woman but a flower, and not a rose, but some gorgeous scentless rosy-white wild flower that had grown all alone out of a snowdrift in some very remote land.

This combination of naïveté and unconventionality with her fresh beauty created such a peculiar impression on the count that several

times during the intervals of conversation, when gazing silently into
her eyes or at the beautiful outline of her neck and arms, the desire to
seize her in his arms and cover her with kisses assailed him with such
force that he had to make a serious effort to resist it. The widow
noticed with pleasure the effect she was producing, yet something in
the count's behaviour began to frighten and excite her, though the
young hussar, despite his insinuating amiability, was respectful to a
degree that in our days would be considered cloying. He ran to fetch
almond-milk for her, picked up her handkerchief, snatched a chair
from the hands of a scrofulous young squire who danced attendance
on her, to hand it her more quickly, and so forth.

When he noticed that the society attentions of the day had little
effect on the lady he tried to amuse her by telling her funny stories
and assured her that he was ready to stand on his head, to crow like a
cock, to jump out of the window or plunge into the water through a
hole in the ice, if she ordered him to do so. This proved quite a success.
The widow brightened up and burst into peals of laughter, showing
lovely white teeth, and was quite satisfied with her cavalier. The
count liked her more and more every minute, so that by the end of
the quadrille he was seriously in love with her.

When, after the quadrille, her eighteen-year-old adorer of long
standing came up to the widow (he was the same scrofulous young
man from whom Turbin had snatched the chair – a son of the richest
local landed proprietor and not yet in government service) she
received him with extreme coolness and did not show one-tenth of
the confusion she had experienced with the count.

'Well, you are a fine fellow!' she said, looking all the time at
Turbin's back and unconsciously considering how many yards of
gold cord it had taken to embroider his whole jacket. 'You are a good
one! You promised to call and fetch me for a drive and bring me
some comfits.'

'I did come, Anna Fedorovna, but you had already gone, and I
left some of the very best comfits for you,' said the young man, who
– despite his tallness – spoke in a very high-pitched voice.

'You always find excuses! . . . I don't want your bonbons. Please
don't imagine –'

'I see, Anna Fedorovna, that you have changed towards me and I
know why. But it's not right,' he added, evidently unable to finish
his speech because a strong inward agitation caused his lips to quiver
in a very strange and rapid manner.

Anna Fedorovna did not listen to him, but continued to follow Turbin with her eyes.

The master of the house, the stout, toothless, stately old Marshal, came up to the count, took him by the arm, and invited him into the study for a smoke and a drink. As soon as Turbin left the room Anna Fedorovna felt that there was absolutely nothing to do there and went out into the dressing-room arm-in-arm with a friend of hers, a bony, elderly, maiden lady.

'Well, is he nice?' asked the maiden lady.

'Only he bothers me so!' Anna Fedorovna replied walking up to the mirror and looking at herself.

Her face brightened, her eyes laughed, she even blushed, and suddenly, imitating the ballet-dancers she had seen during the elections, she twirled round on one foot, then laughed her guttural but pleasant laugh and even bent her knees and gave a jump.

'Just fancy, what a man! He actually asked me for a keepsake,' she said to her friend, 'but he will get no-o-o-thing.' She sang the last word and held up one finger in her kid glove which reached to her elbow.

In the study, where the Marshal had taken Turbin, stood bottles of different sorts of vodka, liqueurs, champagne, and *zakuski*.[7] The nobility, walking about or sitting in a cloud of tobacco smoke, were talking about the elections.

'When the whole worshipful society of our nobility has honoured him by their choice,' said the newly elected Captain of Police who had already imbibed freely, 'he should on no account transgress in the face of the whole society – he ought never . . .'

The count's entrance interrupted the conversation. Everybody wished to be introduced to him and the Captain of Police especially kept pressing the count's hand between his own for a long time, and repeatedly asked him not to refuse to accompany him to the new restaurant where he was going to treat the gentlemen after the ball, and where the gipsies were going to sing. The count promised to come without fail, and drank some glasses of champagne with him.

'But why are you not dancing, gentlemen?' said the count, as he was about to leave the room.

'We are not dancers,' replied the Captain of Police, laughing.

---

[7] *Zakuski* are snacks: caviare, salt-fish, cheese, radishes, etc., with small glasses of vodka or other spirits, sometimes served alone, but usually forming an appetizer, rather like the *hors-d'œuvre* of an English dinner.

'Wine is more in our line, Count. . . . And besides, I have seen all those young ladies grow up, Count! But I can walk through an *écossaise* now and then, Count . . . I can do it, Count.'

'Then come and walk through one now,' said Turbin. 'It will brighten us up before going to hear the gipsies.'

'Very well, gentlemen! Let's come and gratify our host.'

And three or four of the noblemen who had been drinking in the study since the commencement of the ball, put on gloves of black kid or knitted silk, and with red faces were just about to follow the count into the ball-room when they were stopped by the scrofulous young man who, pale and hardly able to restrain his tears, accosted Turbin.

'You think that because you are a count you can jostle people about as if you were in the market-place,' he said, breathing with difficulty, 'but that is impolite . . .'

And again, do what he would, his quivering lips checked the flow of his words.

'What?' cried Turbin, suddenly frowning. 'What? . . . You brat!' he cried, seizing him by the arms and squeezing them so that the blood rushed to the young man's head not so much from vexation as from fear. 'What? Do you want to fight? I am at your service!'

Hardly had Turbin released the arms he had been squeezing so hard, than two nobles caught hold of them and dragged the young man towards the back door.

'What! Are you out of your mind? You must be tipsy! Suppose we were to tell your papa! What's the matter with you?' they said to him.

'No, I'm not tipsy, but he jostles one and does not apologize. He's a swine, that's what he is!' squealed the young man, now quite in tears.

But they did not listen to him and someone took him home.

On the other side the Captain of Police and Zavalshevski were exhorting Turbin: 'Never mind him, Count, he's only a child. He still gets whipped, he's only sixteen. . . . What can have happened to him? What bee has stung him? And his father such a respectable man – and our candidate.'

'Well, let him go to the devil if he does not wish . . .'

And the count returned to the ball-room and danced the *écossaise* with the pretty widow as gaily as before, laughed with all his heart as he watched the steps performed by the gentlemen who had come with him out of the study, and burst into peals of laughter that rang across the room when the Captain of Police slipped and measured his full length in the midst of the dancers.

V

WHILE the count was in the study Anna Fedorovna had approached her brother, and supposing that she ought to pretend to be very little interested in the count began by asking:

'Who is that hussar who was dancing with me? Can you tell me, brother?'

The cavalryman explained to his sister as well as he could what a great man the hussar was, and told her at the same time that the count was only stopping in the town because his money had been stolen on the way, and that he himself had lent him a hundred rubles, but that that was not enough, so that perhaps 'sister' would lend another couple of hundred. Only Zavalshevski asked her on no account to mention the matter to anyone – especially not to the count. Anna Fedorovna promised to send her brother the money that very day and to keep the affair secret, but somehow during the *écossaise* she felt a great longing herself to offer the count as much money as he wanted. She took a long time making up her mind, and blushed, but at last with a great effort broached the subject as follows:

'My brother tells me that a misfortune befell you on the road, Count, and that you have no money by you. If you need any, won't you take it from me? I should be so glad.'

But having said this, Anna Fedorovna suddenly felt frightened of something and blushed. All gaiety instantly left the count's face.

'Your brother is a fool!' he said abruptly. 'You know when a man insults another man they fight; but when a woman insults a man, what does he do then – do you know?'

Poor Anna Fedorovna's neck and ears grew red with confusion. She lowered her eyes and said nothing.

'He kisses the woman in public,' said the count in a low voice, leaning towards her ear. 'Allow me at least to kiss your little hand,' he added in a whisper after a prolonged silence, taking pity on his partner's confusion.

'But not now!' said Anna Fedorovna, with a deep sigh.

'When then? I am leaving early tomorrow and you owe it me.'

'Well then it's impossible,' said Anna Fedorovna with a smile.

'Only allow me a chance to meet you tonight to kiss your hand. I
shall not fail to find an opportunity.'

'How can you find it?'

'That is not your business. In order to see you everything is
possible. . . . It's agreed?'

'Agreed.'

The *écossaise* ended. After that they danced a mazurka and the
count was quite wonderful: catching handkerchiefs, kneeling on one
knee, striking his spurs together in a quite special Warsaw manner,
so that all the old people left their game of boston and flocked into
the ball-room to see, and the cavalryman, their best dancer, confessed
himself eclipsed. Then they had supper after which they danced the
'Grandfather', and the ball began to break up. The count never took
his eyes off the little widow. It was not pretence when he said he was
ready to jump through a hole in the ice for her sake. Whether it was
whim, or love, or obstinacy, all his mental powers that evening were
concentrated on the one desire – to meet and love her. As soon as he
noticed that Anna Fedorovna was taking leave of her hostess he ran
out to the footmen's room, and thence – without his fur cloak – into
the courtyard to the place where the carriages stood.

'Anna Fedorovna Zaytseva's carriage!' he shouted.

A high four-seated closed carriage with lamps burning moved
from its place and approached the porch.

'Stop!' he called to the coachman, and plunging knee-deep into
the snow ran to the carriage.

'What do you want?' said the coachman.

'I want to get into the carriage,' replied the count opening the door
and trying to get in while the carriage was moving. 'Stop, I tell you,
you fool!'

'Stop, Vaska!' shouted the coachman to the postilion, and pulled
up the horses. 'What are you getting into other people's carriages
for? This carriage belongs to my mistress, to Anna Fedorovna, and
not to your honour.'

'Shut up, you blockhead! Here's a ruble for you; get down and
close the door,' said the count. But as the coachman did not stir he
lifted the steps himself and, lowering the window, managed somehow to close the door. In the carriage, as in all old carriages, especially
in those in which yellow galloon is used, there was a musty odour
something like the smell of decayed and burnt bristles. The count's
legs were wet with snow up to the knees and felt very cold in his thin

boots and riding-breeches; in fact the winter cold penetrated his whole body. The coachman grumbled on the box and seemed to be preparing to get down. But the count neither heard nor felt anything. His face was aflame and his heart beat fast. In his nervous tension he seized the yellow window strap and leant out of the side window, and all his being merged into one feeling of expectation.

This expectancy did not last long. Someone called from the porch: 'Zaytseva's carriage!' The coachman shook the reins, the body of the carriage swayed on its high springs, and the illuminated windows of the house ran one after another past the carriage windows.

'Mind, fellow,' said the count to the coachman, putting his head out of the front window, 'if you tell the footman I'm here, I'll thrash you, but hold your tongue and you shall have another ten rubles.'

Hardly had he time to close the window before the body of the carriage shook more violently and then stopped. He pressed close into the corner, held his breath, and even shut his eyes, so terrified was he lest anything should balk his passionate expectation. The door opened, the carriage steps fell noisily one after the other, he heard the rustle of a woman's dress, a smell of frangipane perfume filled the musty carriage, quick little feet ran up the carriage steps, and Anna Fedorovna, brushing the count's leg with the skirt of her cloak which had come open, sank silently onto the seat beside him breathing heavily.

Whether she saw him or not no one could tell, not even Anna Fedorovna herself, but when he took her hand and said: 'Well, now I will kiss your little hand,' she showed very little fear, gave no reply, but yielded her arm to him, which he covered much higher than the top of her glove with kisses. The carriage started.

'Say something! Are you angry, dear?' he said.

She silently pressed into her corner, but suddenly something caused her to burst into tears and of her own accord she let her head fall on his breast.

VI

THE newly elected Captain of Police and his guests the cavalryman and other nobles had long been listening to the gipsies and drinking in the new restaurant when the count, wearing a blue cloth cloak lined with bearskin which had belonged to Anna Fedorovna's late husband, joined them.

'Sure, your excellency, we have been awaiting you impatiently!'
said a dark cross-eyed gipsy, showing his white teeth, as he met the
count at the very entrance and rushed to help him off with his cloak.
'We have not seen you since the fair at Lebedyani . . . Steshka is quite
pining away for you.'

Steshka, a young, graceful little gipsy with a brick-red glow on her
brown face and deep, sparkling black eyes shaded by long lashes, also
ran out to meet him.

'Ah, little Count! Dearest! Jewel! This is a joy!' she murmured
between her teeth, smiling merrily.

Ilyushka himself ran out to greet him, pretending to be very glad
to see him. The old women, matrons, and maids, jumped from their
places and surrounded the guest, some claiming him as a fellow godfather, some as brother by baptism.[8]

Turbin kissed all the young gipsy girls on their lips; the old women
and the men kissed him on his shoulder or hand. The noblemen were
also glad of their visitor's arrival, especially as the carousal, having
reached its zenith, was beginning to flag, and everyone was beginning
to feel satiated. The wine having lost its stimulating effect on the
nerves merely weighed on the stomach. Each one had already let off
his store of swagger, and they were getting tired of one another; the
songs had all been sung and had got mixed in everyone's head,
leaving a noisy, dissolute impression behind. No matter what strange
or dashing thing anyone did, it began to occur to everyone that there
was nothing agreeable or funny in it. The Captain of Police, who lay
in a shocking state on the floor at the feet of an old woman, began
wriggling his legs and shouting: 'Champagne! . . . The Count's
come! . . . Champagne! . . . He's come . . . now then, champagne! . . .
I'll have a champagne bath and bathe in it! Noble gentlemen! . . . I
love the society of our brave old nobility . . . Steshka, sing *The
Pathway*.'

The cavalryman was also rather tipsy, but in another way. He sat
on a sofa in the corner very close to a tall handsome gipsy girl,
Lyubasha; and feeling his eyes misty with drink he kept blinking and
shaking his head and, repeating the same words over and over again
in a whisper, besought the gipsy to fly with him somewhere. Lyubasha, smiling and listening as if what he said were very amusing and
yet rather sad, glanced occasionally at her husband – the cross-eyed

[8] In Russia godparents and their godchildren, and people having the same
godfather or godmother, were considered to be related.

Sashka who was standing behind the chair opposite her – and in reply to the cavalryman's declarations of love, stooped and whispering in his ear asked him to buy her some scent and ribbons on the quiet, so that the others should not notice.

'Hurrah!' cried the cavalryman when the count entered.

The handsome young man was pacing up and down the room with laboriously steady steps and a careworn expression on his face, warbling an air from *Il Seraglio*.

An elderly paterfamilias, who had been tempted by the persistent entreaties of the nobles to come and hear the gipsies, as they said that without him the thing would be worthless and it would be better not to go at all, was lying on a sofa where he had sunk as soon as he arrived, and no one was taking any notice of him. Some official or other who was also there had taken off his swallow-tail coat and was sitting up on the table, feet and all, ruffling his hair, and thereby showing that he was very much on the spree. As soon as the count entered, this official unbuttoned the collar of his shirt and got still farther onto the table. In general on Turbin's arrival the carousal revived.

The gipsy girls, who had been wandering about the room, again gathered and sat down in a circle. The count took Steshka, the leading singer, on his knee, and ordered more champagne.

Ilyushka came and stood in front of Steshka with his guitar, and the 'dance' commenced, i.e. the gipsy songs, *When you go along the Street, O Hussars! Do you hear, do you know?*, and so on in a definite order. Steshka sang admirably. The flexible sonorous contralto that flowed from her very chest, her smiles while singing, her laughing passionate eyes, and her foot that moved involuntarily in measure with the song, her wild shriek at the commencement of the chorus – all touched some powerful but rarely-reached chord. It was evident that she lived only in the song she was singing. Ilyushka accompanied her on the guitar – his back, legs, smile, and whole being, expressing sympathy with the song – and eagerly watching her, raised and lowered his head as attentive and engrossed as though he heard the song for the first time. Then at the last melodious note he suddenly drew himself up, and as if feeling himself superior to everyone in the world, proudly and resolutely threw up his guitar with his foot, twirled it about, stamped, tossed back his hair, and looked round at the choir with a frown. His whole body from neck to heels began dancing in every muscle – and twenty energetic, powerful voices each trying to chime in more strongly and more strangely than the rest, rang through the air. The old women bobbed up and down on their chairs waving their handkerchiefs, showing their teeth, and vying with one another in their harmonious and measured shouts. The basses with strained necks and heads bent to one side boomed while standing behind the chairs.

When Steshka took a high note Ilyushka brought his guitar closer to her as if wishing to help her, and the handsome young man screamed with rapture, saying that now they were beginning the *bémols*.[9]

When a dance was struck up and Dunyasha, advancing with quivering shoulders and bosom, twirled round in front of the count and glided onwards, Turbin leapt up, threw off his jacket, and in his red shirt stepped jauntily with her in precise and measured step, accomplishing such things with his legs that the gipsies smiled with approval and glanced at one another.

The Captain of Police sat down like a Turk, beat his breast with his fist, and cried '*vivat!*' and then, having caught hold of the count's leg, began to tell him that of two thousand rubles he now had only five hundred left, but that he could do anything he liked if only the count would allow it. The elderly paterfamilias awoke and wished to go away, but was not allowed to do so. The handsome young man began persuading a gipsy to waltz with him. The cavalryman, wishing to show off his intimacy with the count, rose and embraced Turbin. 'Ah, my dear fellow,' he said, 'why did you leave us, eh?' The count was silent, evidently thinking of something else. 'Where did you go to? Ah, you rogue of a count, I know where you went to!'

For some reason this familiarity displeased Turbin. Without a smile he looked silently into the cavalryman's face and suddenly launched at him such terrible and rude abuse that the cavalryman was pained, and for a while could not make up his mind whether to take the offence as a joke or seriously. At last he decided to take it as a joke, smiled, and went back to his gipsy, assuring her that he would certainly marry her after Easter. They sang another song and another, danced again, and 'hailed the guests', and everyone continued to imagine that he was enjoying it. There was no end to the champagne.

[9] *Bémol* is French for a flat; but in Russia many people knowing nothing of musical technicalities imagined it to have something to do with excellence in music.

The count drank a great deal. His eyes seemed to grow moist, but he was not unsteady. He danced even better than before, spoke firmly, even joined in the chorus extremely well, and chimed in when Steshka sang *Friendship's Tender Emotions*. In the midst of a dance the landlord came in to ask the guests to return to their homes as it was getting on for three in the morning.

The count seized the landlord by the scruff of his neck and ordered him to dance the Russian dance. The landlord refused. The count snatched up a bottle of champagne and having stood the landlord on his head and had him held in that position, amidst general laughter, slowly emptied the bottle over him.

It was beginning to dawn. Everyone looked pale and exhausted except the count.

'Well, I must be starting for Moscow,' said he, suddenly rising. 'Come along, all of you! Come and see me off . . . and we'll have some tea together.'

All agreed except the paterfamilias (who was left behind asleep), and crowding into three large sledges that stood at the door, they all drove off to the hotel.

VII

'GET horses ready!' cried the count as he entered the saloon of his hotel followed by the guests and gipsies. 'Sashka! – not gipsy Sashka but my Sashka – tell the superintendent I'll thrash him if he gives me bad horses. And get us some tea. Zavalshevski, look after the tea: I'm going to have a look at Ilyin and see how he's getting on . . .' added Turbin, and went along the passage towards the uhlan's room.

Ilyin had just finished playing, and having lost his last kopek was lying face downwards on the sofa, pulling one hair after another from its torn horsehair cover, putting them in his mouth, biting them in two and spitting them out again.

Two tallow candles, one of which had burnt down to the paper in the socket, stood on the card-strewn table and feebly wrestled with the morning light that crept in through the window. There were no ideas in Ilyin's head: a dense mist of gambling passion shrouded all his faculties, he did not even feel penitent. He made one attempt to think of what he should do now: how being penniless he could get away, how he could repay the fifteen thousand rubles of Crown money, what his regimental commander would say, what his mother and his comrades would say, and he felt such terror and disgust with himself that wishing to forget himself he rose and began pacing up and down the room trying to step only where the floor-boards joined, and began, once more, vividly to recall every slightest detail of the course of play. He vividly imagined how he had begun to win back his money, how he withdrew a nine and placed the king of spades over two thousand rubles. A queen was dealt to the right, an ace to the left, then the king of diamonds to the right and all was lost; but if, say, a six had been dealt to the right and the king of diamonds to the left, he would have won everything back, would have played once more double or quits, would have won fifteen thousand rubles, and would then have bought himself an ambler from his regimental commander and another pair of horses besides, and a phaeton. Well, and what then? – Well it would have been a splendid, splendid thing!

And he lay down on the sofa again and began chewing the horse-hair.

'Why are they singing in No. 7?' thought he. 'There must be a spree on at Turbin's. Shall I go in and have a good drink?'

At this moment the count entered.

'Well, old fellow, cleaned out, are you? Eh?' cried he.

'I'll pretend to be asleep,' thought Ilyin, 'or else I shall have to speak to him, and I want to sleep.'

Turbin, however, came up and stroked his head.

'Well, my dear friend, cleaned out – lost everything? Tell me.'

Ilyin gave no answer.

The count pulled his arm.

'I have lost. But what is that to you?' muttered Ilyin in a sleepy, indifferent, discontented voice, without changing his position.

'Everything?'

'Well – yes. What of it? Everything. What is it to you?'

'Listen. Tell me the truth as to a comrade,' said the count, inclined to tenderness by the influence of the wine he had drunk and continuing to stroke Ilyin's hair. 'I have really taken a liking to you. Tell me the truth. If you have lost Crown money I'll get you out of your scrape: it will soon be too late. . . . Had you Crown money?'

Ilyin jumped up from the sofa.

'Well then, if you wish me to tell you, don't speak to me, because . . . please don't speak to me. . . . To shoot myself is the only thing!'

said Ilyin, with real despair, and his head fell on his hands and he burst into tears, though but a moment before he had been calmly thinking about amblers.

'What pretty girlishness! Where's the man who has not done the like? It's not such a calamity; perhaps we can mend it. Wait for me here.'

The count left the room.

'Where is Squire Lukhnov's room?' he asked the boots.

The boots offered to show him the way. In spite of the valet's remark that his master had only just returned and was undressing, the count went in. Lukhnov was sitting at a table in his dressing-gown counting several packets of paper money that lay before him. A bottle of Rhine wine, of which he was very fond, stood on the table. After winning he permitted himself that pleasure. Lukhnov looked coldly and sternly through his spectacles at the count as though not recognizing him.

'You don't recognize me, I think?' said the count, resolutely stepping up to the table.

Lukhnov made a gesture of recognition, and said: 'What is it you want?'

'I should like to play with you,' said Turbin, sitting down on the sofa.

'Now?'

'Yes.'

'Another time with pleasure, Count! But now I am tired and am going to bed. Won't you have a glass of wine? It is famous wine.'

'But I want to play a little – now.'

'I don't intend to play any more tonight. Perhaps some of the other gentlemen will, but I won't. You must please excuse me, Count.'

'Then you won't?'

Lukhnov shrugged his shoulders to express his regret at his inability to comply with the count's desire.

'Not on any account?'

The same shrug.

'But I particularly request it. . . . Well, will you play?'

Silence.

'Will you play?' the count asked again. 'Mind!'

The same silence and a rapid glance over the spectacles at the count's face which was beginning to frown.

'Will you play?' shouted the count very loud, striking the table with his hand so that the bottle toppled over and the wine was spilt. 'You know you did not win fairly. . . . Will you play? I ask you for the third time.'

'I said I would not. This is really strange, Count! And it is not at all proper to come and hold a knife to a man's throat,' remarked Lukhnov, not raising his eyes. A momentary silence followed during which the count's face grew paler and paler. Suddenly a terrible blow on the head stupefied Lukhnov. He fell on the sofa trying to seize the money and uttered such a piercingly despairing cry as no one could have expected from so calm and imposing a person. Turbin gathered up what money lay on the table, pushed aside the servant who ran in to his master's assistance, and left the room with rapid strides.

'If you want satisfaction I am at your service! I shall be in my room for another half-hour,' said the count, returning to Lukhnov's door.

'Thief! Robber! I'll have the law of you . . .' was all that was audible from the room.

Ilyin, who had paid no attention to the count's promise to help him, still lay as before on the sofa in his room choking with tears of despair. Consciousness of what had really happened, which the count's caresses and sympathy had evoked from behind the strange tangle of feelings, thoughts, and memories filling his soul, did not leave him. His youth, rich with hope, his honour, the respect of society, his dreams of love and friendship – all were utterly lost. The source of his tears began to run dry, a too passive feeling of hopelessness overcame him more and more, and thoughts of suicide, no longer arousing revulsion or horror, claimed his attention with increasing frequency. Just then the count's firm footsteps were heard.

In Turbin's face traces of anger could still be seen, his hands shook a little, but his eyes beamed with kindly merriment and self-satisfaction.

'Here you are, it's won back!' he said, throwing several bundles of paper money on the table. 'See if it's all there and then make haste and come into the saloon. I am just leaving,' he added, as though not noticing the joy and gratitude and extreme agitation on Ilyin's face, and whistling a gipsy song he left the room.

VIII

SASHKA, with a sash tied round his waist, announced that the horses were ready, but insisted that the count's cloak, which, he said, with its fur collar was worth three hundred rubles, should be recovered, and the shabby blue one returned to the rascal who had changed it for the count's at the Marshal's; but Turbin told him there was no need to look for the cloak, and went to his room to change his clothes.

The cavalryman kept hiccoughing as he sat silent beside his gipsy girl. The Captain of Police called for vodka, and invited everyone to come at once and have breakfast with him, promising that his wife would certainly dance with the gipsies. The handsome young man was profoundly explaining to Ilyushka that there is more soulfulness in pianoforte music, and that it is not possible to play *bémols* on a guitar. The official sat in a corner sadly drinking his tea, and in the daylight seemed ashamed of his debauchery. The gipsies were disputing among themselves in their own tongue as to 'hailing the guests' again, which Steshka opposed, saying that the *baroray* (in gipsy language count or prince or, more literally, 'great gentleman') would be angry. In general the last embers of the debauch were dying down in everyone.

'Well, one farewell song, and then off home!' said the count, entering the parlour in travelling dress, fresh, merry, and handsomer than ever.

The gipsies again formed their circle and were just ready to begin when Ilyin entered with a packet of paper money in his hand and took the count aside.

'I only had fifteen thousand rubles of Crown money and you have given me sixteen thousand three hundred,' he said, 'so this is yours.'

'That's a good thing. Give it here!'

Ilyin gave him the money and, looking timidly at the count, opened his lips to say something, but only blushed till tears came into his eyes and seizing the count's hand began to press it.

'You be off! . . . Ilyushka! Listen! Here's some money for you, but you must accompany me out of the town with songs!' and he threw onto the guitar the thirteen hundred rubles Ilyin had brought him. But the count quite forgot to repay the hundred rubles he had borrowed of the cavalryman the day before.

It was already ten o'clock in the morning. The sun had risen above the roofs of the houses. People were moving about in the streets. The tradesmen had long since opened their shops. Noblemen and officials were driving through the streets and ladies were shopping in the bazaar, when the whole gipsy band, with the Captain of Police, the cavalryman, the handsome young man, Ilyin, and the count in the blue bearskin cloak, came out into the hotel porch.

It was a sunny day and a thaw had set in. The large post-sledges, each drawn by three horses with their tails tied up tight, drove up to the porch splashing through the mud and the whole lively party took their places. The count, Ilyin, Steshka, and Ilyushka, with Sashka the count's orderly, got into the first sledge. Blücher was beside himself, and wagged his tail, barking at the shaft-horse. The other gentlemen got into the two other sledges with the rest of the gipsy men and women. The troykas got abreast as they left the hotel and the gipsies struck up in chorus.

The troykas with their songs and bells – forcing every vehicle they met right onto the pavements – dashed through the whole town right to the town gates.

The tradesmen and passers-by who did not know them, and especially those who did, were not a little astonished when they saw the noblemen driving through the streets in broad daylight with gipsy girls and tipsy gipsy men, singing.

When they had passed the town gates the troykas stopped and everyone began bidding the count farewell.

Ilyin, who had drunk a good deal at the leave-taking and had himself been driving the sledge all the way, suddenly became very sad, begged the count to stay another day, and when he found that this was not possible, rushed quite unexpectedly at his new friend, kissed him and promised with tears to try to exchange into the hussar regiment the count was serving in as soon as he got back. The count was particularly gay; he tumbled the calvaryman, who had become very familiar in the morning, into a snowdrift; set Blücher at the Captain of Police, took Steshka in his arms and wished to carry her off to Moscow, and finally jumped into his sledge and made Blücher, who wanted to stand up in the middle, sit down by his side. Sashka jumped on the box after having again asked the cavalryman to recover the count's cloak from *them*, and to send it on. The count cried, 'Go!', took off his cap, waved it over his head, and whistled to the horses like a post-boy. The troykas drove off in their different directions.

A monotonous snow-covered plain stretched far in front with a dirty yellowish road winding through it. The bright sunshine – playfully sparkling on the thawing snow which was coated with a transparent crust of ice – was pleasantly warm to one's face and back. Steam rose thickly from the sweating horses. The bell tinkled merrily. A peasant, with a loaded sledge that kept gliding to the side of the road, got hurriedly out of the way, jerking his rope reins and plashing with his wet bast shoes as he ran along the thawing road. A fat red-faced peasant woman, with a baby wrapped in the bosom of her sheepskin cloak, sat in another laden sledge, urging on a thin-tailed, jaded white horse with the ends of the reins. The count suddenly thought of Anna Fedorovna.

'Turn back!' he shouted.

The driver did not at once understand.

'Turn back! Back to town! Be quick!'

The troyka passed the town gates once more, and drove briskly up to the wooden porch of Anna Fedorovna's house. The count ran quickly up the steps, passed through the vestibule and the drawing-room, and having found the widow still asleep, took her in his arms, lifted her out of bed, kissed her sleepy eyes, and ran quickly back. Anna Fedorovna, only half awake, licked her lips and asked, 'What has happened?' The count jumped into his sledge, shouted to the driver, and with no further delay and without even a thought of Lukhnov, or the widow, or Steshka, but only of what awaited him in Moscow, left the town of K—— for ever.

IX

MORE than twenty years had gone by. Much water had flowed away, many people had died, many been born, many had grown up or grown old; still more ideas had been born and had died, much that was old and beautiful and much that was old and bad had perished; much that was beautiful and new had grown up and still more that was immature, monstrous, and new, had come into God's world.

Count Fedor Turbin had been killed long ago in a duel by some foreigner he had horse-whipped in the street. His son, physically as like him as one drop of water to another, was a handsome young man already twenty-three years old and serving in the Horse Guards. But morally the young Turbin did not in the least resemble his father. There was not a shade of the impetuous, passionate and, to speak frankly, depraved propensities of the past age. Together with his intelligence, culture, and the gifted nature he had inherited a love of propriety and the comforts of life; a practical way of looking at men and affairs, reasonableness and prudence were his distinguishing characteristics. The young count had got on well in the service and at twenty-three was already a lieutenant. At the commencement of the war he made up his mind that he would be more likely to secure promotion if he exchanged into the active army, and so he entered an hussar regiment as captain and was soon in command of a squadron.

In May 1848[10] the S—— hussar regiment was marching to the campaign through the province of K——, and the very squadron young Count Turbin commanded had to spend the night in the village of Morozovka, Anna Fedorovna's estate.

Anna Fedorovna was still living, but was already so far from young that she did not even consider herself young, which means a good deal for a woman. She had grown very fat, which is said to make a woman look younger, but deep soft wrinkles were apparent on her white plumpness. She never went to town now, it was an effort for her even to get into her carriage, but she was still just as kind-hearted and as silly as ever (now that her beauty no longer biases one, the truth may be told). With her lived her twenty-three year-old daughter Lisa, a Russian country belle, and her brother – our acquaintance the cavalryman – who had goodnaturedly squandered the whole of his small fortune and had found a home for his old age with Anna Fedorovna. His hair was quite grey and his upper lip had fallen in, but the moustache above it was still carefully blackened. His back was bent, and not only his forehead and cheeks but even his nose and neck were wrinkled, yet in the movements of his feeble crooked legs the manner of a cavalryman was still perceptible.

The family and household sat in the small drawing-room of the old house, with an open door leading out onto the verandah, and open windows overlooking the ancient star-shaped garden with its lime trees. Grey-haired Anna Fedorovna, wearing a lilac jacket, sat on the sofa laying out cards on a round mahogany table. Her old brother in his clean white trousers and a blue coat had settled himself by the window and was plaiting a cord out of white cotton with the aid of a wooden fork – a pastime his niece had taught him and which he liked very much, as he could no longer do anything and his eyes

---

[10] Tolstoy seems here to antedate Russia's intervention in the Hungarian insurrection. The Russian army did not enter Hungary till May 1849 and the war lasted till the end of September that year.

were too weak for newspaper reading, his favourite occupation. Pimochka, Anna Fedorovna's ward, sat by him learning a lesson – Lisa helping her and at the same time making a goat's-wool stocking for her uncle with wooden knitting needles. The last rays of the setting sun, as usual at that hour, shone through the lime-tree avenue and threw slanting gleams on the farthest window and the what-not standing near it. It was so quiet in the garden and the room that one could hear the swift flutter of a swallow's wings outside the window, and Anna Fedorovna's soft sigh or the old man's slight groan as he crossed his legs.

'How do they go? Show me, Lisa! I always forget,' said Anna Fedorovna, at a standstill in laying out her cards for patience.

Without stopping her work Lisa went to her mother and glanced at the cards:

'Ah, you've muddled them all, mamma dear!' she said, re-arranging them. 'That's the way they should go. And what you are trying your fortune about will still come true,' she added, with-drawing a card so that it was not noticed.

'Ah yes, you always deceive me and say it has come out.'

'No really, it means . . . you'll succeed. It has come out.'

'All right, all right, you sly puss! But isn't it time we had tea?'

'I have ordered the samovar to be lit. I'll see to it at once. Do you want to have it here? . . . Be quick and finish your lesson, Pimochka, and let's have a run.'

And Lisa went to the door.

'Lisa, Lizzie!' said her uncle, looking intently at his fork. 'I think I've dropped a stitch again – pick it up for me, there's a dear.'

'Directly, directly! But I must give out a loaf of sugar to be broken up.'

And really, three minutes later she ran back, went to her uncle and pinched his ear.

'That's for dropping your stitches!' she said laughing, 'and you haven't done your task!'

'Well, well, never mind, never mind. Put it right – there's a little knot or something.'

Lisa took the fork, drew a pin out of her tippet – which thereupon the breeze coming in at the door blew slightly open – and managing somehow to pick up the stitch with the pin, pulled two loops through, and returned the fork to her uncle.

'Now give me a kiss for it,' she said, holding out her rosy cheek to him and pinning up her tippet. 'You shall have rum with your tea today. It's Friday, you know.'

And she again went into the tea-room.

'Come here and look, uncle, the hussars are coming!' she called from there in her clear voice.

Anna Fedorovna came with her brother into the tea-room, the windows of which overlooked the village, to see the hussars. Very little was visible from the windows – only a crowd moving in a cloud of dust.

'It's a pity we have so little room, sister, and that the wing is not yet finished,' said the old man to Anna Fedorovna. 'We might have invited the officers. Hussar officers are such splendid, gay young fellows, you know. It would have been good to see something of them.'

'Why of course, I should have been only too glad, brother; but you know yourself we have no room. There's my bedroom, Lisa's room, the drawing-room, and this room of yours, and that's all. Really now, where could we put them? The village elder's hut has been cleaned up for them: Michael Matveev says it's quite clean now.'

'And we could have chosen a bridegroom for you from among them, Lizzie – a fine hussar!'

'I don't want an hussar; I'd rather have an uhlan. Weren't you in the uhlans, uncle? . . . I don't want to have anything to do with these hussars. They are all said to be desperate fellows.' And Lisa blushed a little but again laughed her musical laugh.

'Here comes Ustyushka running; we must ask her what she has seen,' she added.

Anna Fedorovna told her to call Ustyushka.

'It's not in you to keep to your work, you must needs run off to see the soldiers,' said Anna Fedorovna. 'Well, where have the officers put up?'

'In Eromkin's house, mistress. There are two of them, such handsome ones. One's a count, they say!'

'And what's his name?'

'Kazarov or Turbinov. . . . I'm sorry – I've forgotten.'

'What a fool; can't so much as tell us anything. You might at least have found out the name.'

'Well, I'll run back.'

'Yes, I know you're first-rate at that sort of thing. . . . No, let

Daniel go. Tell him to go and ask whether the officers want anything, brother. One ought to show them some politeness after all.
Say the mistress sent to inquire.'

The old people again sat down in the tea-room and Lisa went to
the servants' room to put into a box the sugar that had been broken
up. Ustyushka was there telling about the hussars.

'Darling miss, what a handsome man that count is!' she said. 'A
regular cherub with black eyebrows. There now, if you had a
bridegroom like that you would be a couple of the right sort.'

The other maids smiled approvingly; the old nurse sighed as she
sat knitting at a window and even whispered a prayer, drawing in her
breath.

'So you liked the hussars very much?' said Lisa. 'And you're a good
one at telling what you've seen. Go, please, and bring some of the
cranberry juice, Ustyushka, to give the hussars something sour to
drink.'

And Lisa, laughing, went out with the sugar basin in her hands.

'I should really like to have seen what that hussar is like,' she
thought, 'dark or fair? And he would have been glad to make our
acquaintance I should think. . . . And if he goes away he'll never know
that I was here and thought about him. And how many such have
already passed me by? Who sees me here except uncle and Ustyushka?
Whichever way I do my hair, whatever sleeves I put on, no one looks
at me with pleasure,' she thought with a sigh as she looked at her
plump white arm. 'I suppose he is tall, with large eyes, and certainly
small black moustaches. . . . Here am I, more than twenty-two, and
no one has fallen in love with me except pock-marked Ivan Ipatich,
and four years ago I was even prettier. . . . And so my girlhood has
passed without gladdening anyone. Oh, poor, poor country lass that
I am!'

Her mother's voice, calling her to pour out tea, roused the country
lass from this momentary meditation. She lifted her head with a start
and went into the tea-room.

The best results are often obtained accidentally, and the more one
tries the worse things turn out. In the country, people rarely try to
educate their children and therefore unwittingly usually give them
an excellent education. This was particularly so in Lisa's case. Anna
Fedorovna, with her limited intellect and careless temperament, gave
Lisa no education – did not teach her music or that very useful French
language – but having accidentally borne a healthy pretty child by

her deceased husband she gave her little daughter over to a wet-nurse and a dry-nurse, fed her, dressed her in cotton prints and goat-skin shoes, sent her out to walk and gather mushrooms and wild berries, engaged a student from the seminary to teach her reading, writing, and arithmetic, and when sixteen years had passed she casually found in Lisa a friend, an ever-kind-hearted, ever-cheerful soul, and an active housekeeper. Anna Fedorovna, being kind-hearted, always had some children to bring up – either serf children or foundlings. Lisa began looking after them when she was ten years old: teaching them, dressing them, taking them to church, and checking them when they played too many pranks. Later on the decrepit kindly uncle, who had to be tended like a child, appeared on the scene. Then the servants and peasants came to the young lady with various requests and with their ailments, which latter she treated with elderberry, peppermint, and camphorated spirits. Then there was the household management which all fell on her shoulders of itself. Then an unsatisfied longing for love awoke and found its outlet only in Nature and religion. And Lisa accidentally grew into an active, good-natured, cheerful, self-reliant, pure, and deeply religious woman. It is true that she suffered a little from vanity when she saw neighbours standing by her in church wearing fashionable bonnets brought from K——, and sometimes she was vexed to tears by her old mother's whims and grumbling. She had dreams of love, too, in most absurd and sometimes crude forms, but these were dispersed by her useful activity which had grown into a necessity, and at the age of twenty-two there was not one spot or sting of remorse in the clear calm soul of the physically and morally beautifully developed maiden. Lisa was of medium height, plump rather than thin, her eyes were hazel, not large, and had slight shadows on the lower lids, and she had a long light-brown plait of hair. She walked with big steps and with a slight sway – a 'duck's waddle' as the saying is. Her face, when she was occupied and not agitated by anything in par-ticular, seemed to say to everyone who looked into it: 'It is a joy to live in the world when one has someone to love and a clear con-science.' Even in moments of vexation, perplexity, alarm, or sorrow, in spite of herself there shone – through the tear in her eye, her frowning left eyebrow and her compressed lips – a kind straight-forward spirit unspoilt by the intellect; it shone in the dimples of her cheeks, in the corners of her mouth, and in her beaming eyes accus-tomed to smile and to rejoice in life.

X

THE air was still hot though the sun was setting when the squadron entered Morozovka. In front of them along the dusty village street trotted a brindled cow separated from its herd, looking round and now and then stopping and lowing, but never suspecting that all she had to do was to turn aside. The peasants – old men, women, and children, and the servants from the manor-house, crowded on both sides of the street and eagerly watched the hussars as the latter rode through a thick cloud of dust, curbing their horses which occasionally stamped and snorted. On the right of the squadron were two officers who sat their fine black horses carelessly. One was Count Turbin, the commander, the other a very young man recently promoted from cadet, whose name was Polozov.

An hussar in a white linen jacket came out of the best of the huts, raised his cap, and went up to the officers.

'Where are the quarters assigned us?'

'For your Excellency?' answered the quartermaster-sergeant, with a start of his whole body. 'The village elder's hut has been cleaned out. I wanted to get quarters at the manor-house, but they say there is no room there. The proprietress is such a vixen.'

'All right!' said the count, dismounting and stretching his legs as he reached the village elder's hut. 'And has my phaeton arrived?'

'It has deigned to arrive, your Excellency!' answered the quarter-master-sergeant, pointing with his cap to the leather body of a carriage visible through the gateway, and rushing forward to the entrance of the hut, which was thronged with members of the peasant family collected to look at the officer. He even pushed one old woman over as he briskly opened the door of the freshly cleaned hut and stepped aside to let the count pass.

The hut was fairly large and roomy but not very clean. The German valet, dressed like a gentleman, stood inside sorting the linen in a portmanteau after having set up an iron bedstead and made the bed.

'Faugh, what filthy lodgings!' said the count with vexation. 'Couldn't you have found anything better at some gentleman's house, Dyadenko?'

'If your Excellency desires it I will try at the manor-house,' answered the quartermaster-sergeant, 'but it isn't up to much – doesn't look much better than a hut.'

'Never mind now. Go away.'

And the count lay down on the bed and threw his arms behind his head.

'Johann!' he called to his valet. 'You've made a lump in the middle again! How is it you can't make a bed properly?'

Johann came up to put it right:

'No, never mind now. But where is my dressing-gown?' said the count in a dissatisfied tone.

The valet handed him the dressing-gown. Before putting it on the count examined the front.

'I thought so, that spot is not cleaned off. Could anyone be a worse servant than you?' he added, pulling the dressing-gown out of the valet's hands and putting it on. 'Tell me, do you do it on purpose? . . . Is the tea ready?'

'I have not had time,' said Johann.

'Fool!'

After that the count took up the French novel placed ready for him and read for some time in silence: Johann went out into the passage to prepare the samovar. The count was obviously in a bad temper, probably caused by fatigue, a dusty face, tight clothing, and an empty stomach.

'Johann!' he cried again, 'bring me the account for those ten rubles. What did you buy in the town?'

He looked over the account handed him, and made some dissatisfied remarks about the dearness of the things purchased.

'Serve rum with my tea.'

'I didn't buy any rum,' said Johann.

'That's good! . . . How many times have I told you to have rum?'

'I hadn't enough money.'

'Then why didn't Polozov buy some? You should have got some from his man.'

'Cornet Polozov? I don't know. He bought tea and sugar.'

'Idiot! . . . Get out! . . . You are the only man who knows how to make me lose my patience. . . . You know that on a march I always have rum with my tea.'

'Here are two letters for you from the staff,' said the valet.

The count opened his letters and began reading them without rising. The cornet, having quartered the squadron, came in with a merry face.

'Well, how is it, Turbin? It seems very nice here. But I must confess I'm tired. It was hot.'

'Very nice! . . . A filthy stinking hut, and thanks to your lordship no rum; your blockhead didn't buy any, nor did this one. You might at least have mentioned it.'

And he continued to read his letter. When he had finished he rolled it into a ball and threw it on the floor.

In the passage the cornet was meanwhile saying to his orderly in a whisper: 'Why didn't you buy any rum? You had money enough, you know.'

'But why should we buy everything? As it is I pay for everything, while his German does nothing but smoke his pipe.'

It was evident that the count's second letter was not unpleasant, for he smiled as he read it.

'Who is it from?' asked Polozov, returning to the room and beginning to arrange a sleeping-place for himself on some boards by the oven.

'From Mina,' answered the count gaily, handing him the letter. 'Do you want to see it? What a delightful woman she is! . . . Really she's much better than our young ladies. . . . Just see how much feeling and wit there is in that letter. Only one thing is bad – she's asking for money.'

'Yes, that's bad,' said the cornet.

'It's true I promised her some, but then this campaign came on, and besides. . . . However if I remain in command of the squadron another three months I'll send her some. It's worth it, really; such a charming creature, eh?' said he, watching the expression on Polozov's face as he read the letter.

'Dreadfully ungrammatical, but very nice, and it seems as if she really loves you,' said the cornet.

'H'm . . . I should think so! It's only women of that kind who love sincerely when once they do love.'

'And who was the other letter from?' asked the cornet, handing back the one he had read.

'Oh, that . . . there's a man, a nasty creature who won from me at cards, and he's reminding me of it for the third time. . . . I can't let him have it at present. . . . A stupid letter!' said the count, evidently vexed at the recollection.

After this both officers were silent for a while. The cornet, who was evidently under the count's influence, glanced now and then at the handsome though clouded countenance of Turbin – who was looking fixedly through the window – and drank his tea in silence, not venturing to start a conversation.

'But d'you know, it may turn out capitally,' said the count, suddenly turning to Polozov with a shake of his head. 'Supposing we get promotions by seniority this year, and take part in an action besides, I may get ahead of my own captains in the Guards.'

The conversation was still on the same topic and they were drinking their second tumblers of tea, when old Daniel entered and delivered Anna Fedorovna's message.

'And I was also to inquire if you are not Count Fedor Ivanych Turbin's son?' added Daniel on his own account, having learnt the count's name and remembering the deceased count's sojourn in the town of K——. 'Our mistress, Anna Fedorovna, was very well acquainted with him.'

'He was my father. And tell your mistress I am very much obliged to her. We want nothing, but say we told you to ask whether we could not have a cleaner room somewhere – in the manor-house, or anywhere.'

'Now, why did you do that?' asked Polozov when Daniel had gone. 'What does it matter? Just for one night – what does it matter? And they will be inconveniencing themselves.'

'What an idea! I think we've had our share of smoky huts!... It's easy to see you're not a practical man. Why not seize the opportunity when we can, and live like human beings for at least one night? And on the contrary they will be very pleased to have us. . . . The worst of it is, if this lady really knew my father . . .' continued the count with a smile which displayed his glistening white teeth. 'I always have to feel ashamed of my departed papa. There is always some scandalous story or other, or some debt he has left. That is why I hate meeting these acquaintances of my father's. However that was the way in those days,' he added, growing serious.

'Did I ever tell you,' said Polozov, 'I once met an uhlan brigade-commander, Ilyin? He was very anxious to meet you. He is awfully fond of your father.'

'That Ilyin is an awful good-for-nothing, I believe. But the worst of it is that these good people, who assure me that they knew my father in order to make my acquaintance, while pretending to be very pleasant, relate such tales about my father as make me ashamed to listen. It is true – I don't deceive myself, but look at things dispassionately – that he had too ardent a nature and sometimes did things that were not nice. However that was the way in those times. In our days he might have turned out a very successful man, for to do him justice he had extraordinary capacities.'

A quarter of an hour later the servant came back with a request from the proprietress that they would be so good as to spend the night at her house.

XI

HAVING heard that the hussar officer was the son of Count Fedor Turbin, Anna Fedorovna was all in a flutter.

'Oh, dear me! The darling boy! . . . Daniel, run quickly and say your mistress asks them to her house!' she began, jumping up and hurrying with quick steps to the servants' room. 'Lizzie! Ustyushka! . . . Your room must be got ready, Lisa, you can move into your uncle's room. And you, brother, you won't mind sleeping in the drawing-room, will you? It's only for one night.'

'I don't mind, sister. I can sleep on the floor.'

'He must be handsome if he's like his father. Only to have a look at him, the darling. . . . You must have a good look at him, Lisa! The father *was* handsome. . . . Where are you taking that table to? Leave it here,' said Anna Fedorovna, bustling about. 'Bring two beds – take one from the foreman's – and get the crystal candlestick, the one my brother gave me on my birthday – it's on the what-not – and put a stearine candle in it.'

At last everything was ready. In spite of her mother's interference Lisa arranged the room for the two officers her own way. She took out clean bed-clothes scented with mignonette, made the beds, had candles and a bottle of water placed on a small table near by, fumigated the servants' room with scented paper, and moved her own little bed into her uncle's room. Anna Fedorovna quieted down a little, settled in her own place, and even took up the cards again, but instead of laying them out she leaned her plump elbow on the table and grew thoughtful.

'Ah, time, time, how it flies!' she whispered to herself. 'Is it so long ago? It is as if I could see him now. Ah, he was a madcap! . . .' and tears came into her eyes. 'And now there's Lizzie . . . but still, she's now what I was at her age – she's a nice girl but she's not like that . . .'

'Lisa, you should put on your *mousseline-de-laine* dress for the evening.'

'Why, mother, you are not going to ask them in to see us? Better not,' said Lisa, unable to master her excitement at the thought of meeting the officers: 'Better not, mamma!'

And really her desire to see them was less strong than her fear of the agitating joy she imagined awaited her.

'Maybe they themselves will wish to make our acquaintance, Lizzie!' said Anna Fedorovna, stroking her head and thinking: 'No, her hair is not what mine was at her age. . . . Oh, Lizzie, how I should like you to. . . .' And she really did very earnestly desire something for her daughter. But she could not imagine a marriage with the count, and she could not desire for her daughter relations such as she had had with the father; but still she did desire something very much. She may have longed to relive in the soul of her daughter what she had experienced with him who was dead.

The old cavalryman was also somewhat excited by the arrival of the count. He locked himself into his room and emerged a quarter of an hour later in a Hungarian jacket and pale-blue trousers, and entered the room prepared for the visitors with the bashfully pleased expression of a girl who puts on a ball-dress for the first time in her life.

'I'll have a look at the hussars of today, sister! The late count was indeed a true hussar. I'll see, I'll see!'

The officers had already reached the room assigned to them through the back entrance.

'There, you see! Isn't this better than that hut with the cock-roaches?' said the count, lying down as he was, in his dusty boots, on the bed that had been prepared for him.

'Of course it's better; but still, to be indebted to the proprietress . . .'

'Oh, what nonsense! One must be practical in all things. They're awfully pleased, I'm sure . . . Eh, you there!' he cried. 'Ask for something to hang over this window, or it will be draughty in the night.'

At this moment the old man came in to make the officers' acquaintance. Of course, though he did it with a slight blush, he did not omit to say that he and the old count had been comrades, that he had enjoyed the count's favour, and he even added that he had more than once been under obligations to the deceased. What obligations he referred to, whether it was the count's omission to repay the hundred rubles he had borrowed, or his throwing him into a snow-heap, or swearing at him, the old man quite omitted to explain. The young count was very polite to the old cavalryman and thanked him for the night's lodging.

'You must excuse us if it is not luxurious, Count,' (he very nearly said 'your Excellency', so unaccustomed had he become to conversing with important persons), 'my sister's house is so small. But we'll hang something up there directly and it will be all right,' added the old man, and on the plea of seeing about a curtain, but mainly because he was in a hurry to give an account of the officers, he bowed and left the room.

The pretty Ustyushka came in with her mistress's shawl to cover the window, and besides, the mistress had told her to ask if the gentlemen would not like some tea.

The pleasant surroundings seemed to have a good influence on the count's spirits. He smiled merrily, joked with Ustyushka in such a way that she even called him a scamp, asked whether her young lady was pretty, and in answer to her question whether they would have any tea he said she might bring them some tea, but the chief thing was that, their own supper not being ready yet, perhaps they might have some vodka and something to eat, and some sherry if there was any.

The uncle was in raptures over the young count's politeness, and praised the new generation of officers to the skies, saying that the present men were incomparably superior to the former generation.

Anna Fedorovna did not agree – no one could be superior to Count Fedor Ivanych Turbin – and at last she grew seriously angry and drily remarked, 'The one who has last stroked you, brother, is always the best. . . . Of course people are cleverer nowadays, but Count Fedor Ivanych danced the *écossaise* in such a way and was so amiable that everybody lost their heads about him, though he paid attention to no one but me. So you see, there were good people in the old days too.'

Here came the news of the demand for vodka, light refreshments, and sherry.

'There now, brother, you never do the right thing; you should have ordered supper,' began Anna Fedorovna. 'Lisa, see to it, dear!'

Lisa ran to the larder to get some pickled mushrooms and fresh butter, and the cook was ordered to make rissoles.

'But how about sherry? Have you any left, brother?'

'No, sister, I never had any.'

'How's that? Why, what is it you take with your tea?'

'That's rum, Anna Fedorovna.'

'Isn't it all the same? Give them some of that – it's all the same. But wouldn't it after all be best to ask them in here, brother? You know all about it – I don't think they would take offence.'

The cavalryman declared he would warrant that the count was too good-natured to refuse and that he would certainly fetch them. Anna Fedorovna went and put on a silk dress and a new cap for some reason, but Lisa was so busy that she had no time to change her pink gingham dress with the wide sleeves. Besides, she was terribly excited; she felt as if something wonderful was awaiting her and as if a low black cloud hung over her soul. It seemed to her that this handsome hussar count must be a perfectly new, incomprehensible, but beautiful being. His character, his habits, his speech, must all be so unusual, so different from anything she had ever met. All he thinks or says must be wise and right, all he does must be honourable, his whole appearance must be beautiful. She never doubted that. Had he asked not merely for refreshments and sherry, but for a bath of sage-brandy and perfume, she would not have been surprised and would not have blamed him, but would have been firmly convinced that it was right and necessary.

The count at once agreed when the cavalryman informed them of his sister's wish. He brushed his hair, put on his uniform, and took his cigar-case.

'Come along,' he said to Polozov.

'Really it would be better not to go,' answered the cornet. '*Ils feront des frais pour nous recevoir.*'[11]

'Nonsense, they will be only too happy! Besides, I have made some inquiries: there is a pretty daughter. . . . Come along!' said the count, speaking in French.

'*Je vous en prie, messieurs!*'[12] said the cavalryman, merely to make the officers feel that he also knew French and had understood what they had said.

XII

LISA, afraid to look at the officers, blushed and cast down her eyes and pretended to be busy filling the teapot when they entered the room. Anna Fedorovna on the contrary jumped up hurriedly, bowed,

---

[11] They will be putting themselves to expense on our account.
[12] If you please, gentlemen.

and not taking her eyes off the count, began talking to him – now saying how unusually like his father he was, now introducing her daughter to him, now offering him tea, jam, or home-made sweet-meats. No one paid any attention to the cornet because of his modest appearance, and he was very glad of it, for he was, as far as propriety allowed, gazing at Lisa and minutely examining her beauty which evidently took him by surprise. The uncle, listening to his sister's conversation with the count, awaited, with the words ready on his lips, an opportunity to narrate his cavalry reminiscences. During tea the count lit a cigar and Lisa found it difficult to prevent herself from coughing. He was very talkative and amiable, at first slipping his stories into the intervals of Anna Fedorovna's ever-flowing speech, but at last monopolizing the conversation. One thing struck his hearers as strange; in his stories he often used words not considered improper in the society he belonged to, but which here sounded rather too bold and somewhat frightened Anna Fedorovna and made Lisa blush to her ears; but the count did not notice it and remained calmly natural and amiable.

Lisa silently filled the tumblers, which she did not give into the visitors' hands but placed on the table near them, not having quite recovered from her excitement, and she listened eagerly to the count's remarks. His stories, which were not very deep, and the hesitation in his speech gradually calmed her. She did not hear from him the very clever things she had expected, nor did she see that elegance in every-thing which she had vaguely expected to find in him. At the third glass of tea, after her bashful eyes had once met his and he had not looked down but had continued to look at her too quietly and with a slight smile, she even felt rather inimically disposed towards him, and soon found that not only was there nothing especial about him but that he was in no wise different from other people she had met, that there was no need to be afraid of him though his nails were long and clean, and that there was not even any special beauty in him. Lisa suddenly relinquished her dream, not without some inward pain, and grew calmer, and only the gaze of the taciturn cornet which she felt fixed upon her, disquieted her.

'Perhaps it's not this one, but that one!' she thought.

XIII

AFTER tea the old lady asked the visitors into the drawing-room and again sat down in her old place.

'But wouldn't you like to rest, Count?' she asked, and after receiving an answer in the negative continued: 'What can I do to entertain our dear guests? Do you play cards, Count? There now, brother, you should arrange something; arrange a set—'

'But you yourself play *préférence*,'[13] answered the cavalryman. 'Why not all play? Will you play, Count? And you too?'

The officers expressed their readiness to do whatever their kind hosts desired.

Lisa brought her old pack of cards which she used for divining when her mother's swollen face would get well, whether her uncle would return the same day when he went to town, whether a neighbour would call today, and so on. These cards, though she had used them for a couple of months, were cleaner than those Anna Fedorovna used to tell fortunes.

'But perhaps you won't play for small stakes?' inquired the uncle. 'Anna Fedorovna and I play for half-kopeks. . . . And even so she wins all our money.'

'Oh, any stakes you like – I shall be delighted,' replied the count.

'Well then, one kopek "assignats"[14] just for once, in honour of our dear visitors! Let them beat me, an old woman!' said Anna Fedorovna, settling down in her arm-chair and arranging her mantilla. 'And perhaps I'll win a ruble or so from them,' thought she, having developed a slight passion for cards in her old age.

'If you like, I'll teach you to play with "tables" and "*misère*",' said the count. 'It is capital.'

Everyone liked the new Petersburg way. The uncle was even sure

[13] In *préférence* partners play together as in whist. There is a method of scoring 'with tables' which increases the gains and losses of the players. The players compete in declaring the number of tricks the cards they hold will enable them to make. The highest bidder decides which suit is to be trumps and has to make the number of tricks he has declared, or be fined. A player declaring *misère* undertakes to make no tricks, and is fined (puts on a *remise*) for each trick he or she takes. 'Ace and king blank' means that a player holds the two highest cards and no others of a given suit.

[14] Two currencies were in use simultaneously – the depreciated 'assignats' and the 'silver rubles', usually paper, introduced in 1841. Assignats, redeemable at a rate of 3½ assignats per 'silver ruble', were still in general use in out-of-the-way provincial districts.

he knew it; it was just the same as 'boston' used to be, only he had forgotten it a bit. But Anna Fedorovna could not understand it at all, and failed to understand it for so long that at last, with a smile and a nod of approval, she felt herself obliged to assert that now she understood it and that all was quite clear to her. There was not a little laughter during the game when Anna Fedorovna, holding ace and king blank, declared *misère*, and was left with six tricks. She even became confused and began to smile shyly and hurriedly explain that she had not got quite used to the new way. But they scored against her all the same, especially as the count, being used to playing a careful game for high stakes, was cautious, skilfully played through his opponents' hands, and refused to understand the shoves the cornet gave him under the table with his foot, or the mistakes the latter made when they were partners.

Lisa brought more sweets, three kinds of jam, and some specially prepared apples that had been kept since last season, and stood behind her mother's back watching the game and occasionally looking at the officers and especially at the count's white hands with their rosy well-kept nails, which threw the cards and took up the tricks in so practised, assured, and elegant a manner.

Again Anna Fedorovna, rather irritably outbidding the others, declared seven tricks, made only four, and was fined accordingly, and having very clumsily noted down, on her brother's demand, the points she had lost, became quite confused and fluttered.

'Never mind, mamma, you'll win it back!' smilingly remarked Lisa, wishing to help her mother out of the ridiculous situation. 'Let uncle make a forfeit, and then he'll be caught.'

'If you would only help me, Lisa dear!' said Anna Fedorovna, with a frightened glance at her daughter. 'I don't know how this is . . .'

'But I don't know this way either,' Lisa answered, mentally reckoning up her mother's losses. 'You will lose a lot that way, mamma! There will be nothing left for Pimochka's new dress,' she added in jest.

'Yes, this way one may easily lose ten silver rubles,' said the cornet looking at Lisa and anxious to enter into conversation with her.

'Aren't we playing for "assignats"?' said Anna Fedorovna, looking round at them all.

'I don't know how we are playing, but I can't reckon in "assignats",' said the count. 'What is it? I mean, what are "assignats"?'

'Why, nowadays nobody counts in "assignats" any longer,'

remarked the uncle who had played very cautiously and had been
winning.

The old lady ordered some sparkling home-made wine to be
brought, drank two glasses, became very red, and seemed to resign
herself to any fate. A lock of her grey hair escaped from under her cap
and she did not even put it right. No doubt it seemed to her as if she
had lost millions and it was all up with her. The cornet touched the
count with his foot more and more often. The count scored down the
old lady's losses. At last the game ended, and in spite of Anna
Fedorovna's wicked attempts to add to her score by pretending to
make mistakes in adding it up, in spite of her horror at the amount
of her losses, it turned out at last that she had lost 920 points. 'That's
nine "assignats"?' she asked several times, and did not comprehend
the full extent of her loss until her brother told her, to her horror,
that she had lost more than thirty-two 'assignats' and that she must
certainly pay.

The count did not even add up his winnings, but rose immediately
the game was over, went over to the window at which Lisa was
arranging the *zakuski* and turning pickled mushrooms out of a jar
onto a plate for supper, and there quite quietly and simply did what
the cornet had all that evening so longed, but failed, to do – entered
into conversation with her about the weather.

Meanwhile the cornet was in a very unpleasant position. In the
absence of the count, and more especially of Lisa, who had been
keeping her in good humour, Anna Fedorovna became frankly angry.

'Really, it's too bad that we should win from you like this,' said
Polozov in order to say something. 'It is a real shame!'

'Well, of course, if you go and invent some kind of "tables" and
"*misères*" and I don't know how to play them. . . . Well then, how
much does it come to in "assignats"?' she asked.

'Thirty-two rubles, thirty-two and a quarter,' repeated the cavalryman who under the influence of his success was in a playful mood.
'Hand over the money, sister; pay up!'

'I'll pay it all, but you won't catch me again. No! . . . I shall not
win this back as long as I live.'

And Anna Fedorovna went off to her room, hurriedly swaying
from side to side, and came back bringing nine 'assignats'. It was only
on the old man's insistent demand that she eventually paid the whole
amount.

Polozov was seized with fear lest Anna Fedorovna should scold him if he spoke to her. He silently and quietly left her and joined the count and Lisa who were talking at the open window.

On the table spread for supper stood two tallow candles. Now and then the soft fresh breath of the May night caused the flames to flicker. Outside the window, which opened onto the garden, it was also light but it was a quite different light. The moon, which was almost full and already losing its golden tinge, floated above the tops of the tall lindens and more and more lit up the thin white clouds which veiled it at intervals. Frogs were croaking loudly by the pond, the surface of which, silvered in one place by the moon, was visible through the avenue. Some little birds fluttered slightly or lightly hopped from bough to bough in a sweet-scented lilac-bush whose dewy branches occasionally swayed gently close to the window.

'What wonderful weather!' the count said as he approached Lisa and sat down on the low window-sill. 'I suppose you walk a good deal?'

'Yes,' said Lisa, not feeling the least shyness in speaking with the count. 'In the morning about seven o'clock I look after what has to be attended to on the estate and take my mother's ward, Pimochka, with me for a walk.'

'It is pleasant to live in the country!' said the count, putting his eyeglass to his eye and looking now at the garden now at Lisa. 'And don't you ever go out at night, by moonlight?'

'No. But two years ago uncle and I used to walk every moonlight night. He was troubled with a strange complaint – insomnia. When there was a full moon he could not fall asleep. His little room – that one – looks straight out into the garden, the window is low but the moon shines straight into it.'

'That's strange: I thought that was your room,' said the count.

'No, I only sleep there tonight. You have my room.'

'Is it possible? Dear me, I shall never forgive myself for having disturbed you in such a way!' said the count letting the monocle fall from his eye in proof of the sincerity of his feelings. 'If I had known that I was troubling you . . .'

'It's no trouble! On the contrary I am very glad: uncle's is such a charming room, so bright, and the window is so low. I shall sit there till I fall asleep, or else I shall climb out into the garden and walk about a bit before going to bed.'

'What a splendid girl!' thought the count, replacing his eyeglass and looking at her and trying to touch her foot with his own while pretending to seat himself more comfortably on the window-sill. 'And how cleverly she has let me know that I may see her in the garden at the window if I like!' Lisa even lost much of her charm in his eyes – the conquest seemed so easy.

'And how delightful it must be', he said, looking thoughtfully at the dark avenue of trees, 'to spend a night like this in the garden with a beloved one.'

Lisa was embarrassed by these words and by the repeated, seemingly accidental, touch of his foot. Anxious to hide her confusion she said without thinking: 'Yes, it is nice to walk in the moonlight.' She was beginning to feel rather uncomfortable. She had tied up the jar out of which she had taken the mushrooms, and was going away from the window, when the cornet joined them and she felt a wish to see what kind of man he was.

'What a lovely night!' he said.

'Why, they talk of nothing but the weather,' thought Lisa.

'What a wonderful view!' continued the cornet. 'But I suppose you are tired of it,' he added, having a curious propensity to say rather unpleasant things to people he liked very much.

'Why do you think so? The same kind of food or the same dress one may get tired of, but not of a beautiful garden if one is fond of walking – especially when the moon is still higher. From uncle's window the whole pond can be seen. I shall look at it tonight.'

'But I don't think you have any nightingales?' said the count, much dissatisfied that the cornet had come and prevented his ascertaining more definitely the terms of the rendezvous.

'No, but there always were until last year when some sportsman caught one, and this year one began to sing beautifully only last week but the police-officer came here and his carriage-bells frightened it away. Two years ago uncle and I used to sit in the covered alley and listen to them for two hours or more at a time.'

'What is this chatterbox telling you?' said her uncle coming up to them. 'Won't you come and have something to eat?'

After supper, during which the count by praising the food and by his appetite had somewhat dispelled the hostess's ill humour, the officers said goodnight and went into their room. The count shook hands with the uncle and to Anna Fedorovna's surprise shook her hand also without kissing it, and even shook Lisa's looking straight into her eyes the while and slightly smiling his pleasant smile. This look again abashed the girl.

'He is very good-looking,' she thought, 'but he thinks too much of himself.'

XIV

'I SAY, aren't you ashamed of yourself?' said Polozov when they were in their room. 'I purposely tried to lose, and kept touching you under the table. Aren't you ashamed? The old lady was quite upset, you know.'

The count laughed very heartily.

'She was awfully funny, that old lady. . . . How offended she was! . . .'

And he again began laughing so merrily that even Johann, who stood in front of him, cast down his eyes and turned away with a slight smile.

'And with the son of a friend of the family! Ha-ha-ha! . . .' the count continued to laugh.

'No, really it was too bad. I was quite sorry for her,' said the cornet.

'What nonsense! How young you still are! Why, did you wish me to lose? Why should one lose? I used to lose before I knew how to play! Ten rubles may come in useful, my dear fellow. You must look at life practically or you'll always be left in the lurch.'

Polozov was silenced; besides, he wished to be quiet and to think about Lisa who seemed to him an unusually pure and beautiful creature. He undressed and lay down in the soft clean bed prepared for him.

'What nonsense all this military honour and glory is!' he thought, looking at the window curtained by the shawl through which the white moonbeams stole in. 'It would be happiness to live in a quiet nook with a dear, wise, simple-hearted wife – yes, that is true and lasting happiness!'

But for some reason he did not communicate these reflections to his friend and did not even refer to the country lass, though he was convinced that the count too was thinking of her.

'Why don't you undress?' he asked the count who was walking up and down the room.

'I don't feel sleepy yet, somehow. You can put out the candle if you like. I shall lie down as I am.'

And he continued to pace up and down.

'Don't feel sleepy yet somehow,' repeated Polozov, who after this last evening felt more dissatisfied than ever with the count's influence over him and was inclined to rebel against it. 'I can imagine,' he thought, addressing himself mentally to Turbin, 'what is now passing through that well-brushed head of yours! I saw how you admired her. But you are not capable of understanding such a simple honest creature: you want a Mina and a colonel's epaulettes. . . . I really must ask him how he liked her.'

And Polozov turned towards him – but changed his mind. He felt he would not be able to hold his own with the count, if the latter's opinion of Lisa were what he supposed it to be, and that he would even be unable to avoid agreeing with him so accustomed was he to bow to the count's influence, which he felt more and more every day to be oppressive and unjust.

'Where are you going?' he asked, when the count put on his cap and went to the door.

'I'm going to see if things are all right in the stables.'

'Strange!' thought the cornet, but put out the candle and turned over on his other side, trying to drive away the absurdly jealous and hostile thoughts that crowded into his head concerning his former friend.

Anna Fedorovna meanwhile, having as usual kissed her brother, daughter, and ward, and made the sign of the cross over each of them, had also retired to her room. It was long since the old lady had experienced so many strong impressions in one day and she could not even pray quietly: she could not rid herself of the sad and vivid memories of the deceased count and of the young dandy who had plundered her so unmercifully. However she undressed as usual, drank half a tumbler of *kvas*[15] that stood ready for her on a little table by her bed, and lay down. Her favourite cat crept softly into the room. Anna Fedorovna called her up and began to stroke her and listened to her purring, but could not fall asleep.

'It's the cat that keeps me awake,' she thought and drove her away. The cat fell softly on the floor and gently moving her bushy tail leapt onto the stove. And now the maid, who always slept in Anna Fedorovna's room, came and spread the piece of felt that served her for a mattress, put out the candle, and lit the lamp before the icon. At last the maid began to snore, but still sleep would not come to soothe Anna Fedorovna's excited imagination. When she closed her eyes the hussar's face appeared to her, and she seemed to see it in the

[15] Kvas: a non-alcoholic drink usually made from rye-malt and rye-flour.

room in various guises when she opened her eyes and by the dim
light of the lamp looked at the chest of drawers, the table, or a white
dress that was hanging up. Now she felt very hot on the feather bed,
now her watch ticked unbearably on the little table, and the maid
snored unendurably through her nose. She woke her up and told her
not to snore. Again thoughts of her daughter, of the old count and
the young one, and of the *préférence*, became curiously mixed in her
head. Now she saw herself waltzing with the old count, saw her own
round white shoulders, felt someone's kisses on them, and then saw
her daughter in the arms of the young count. Ustyushka again began
to snore.

'No, people are not the same nowadays. The other one was ready
to leap into the fire for me – and not without cause. But this one is
sleeping like a fool, no fear, glad to have won – no love-making
about him. . . . How the other one said on his knees, "What do you
wish me to do? I'll kill myself on the spot, or do anything you like!"
And he would have killed himself had I told him to.'

Suddenly she heard a patter of bare feet in the passage and Lisa,
with a shawl thrown over her, ran in pale and trembling and almost
fell onto her mother's bed.

After saying goodnight to her mother that evening Lisa had gone
alone to the room her uncle generally slept in. She put on a white
dressing-jacket and covering her long thick plait with a kerchief,
extinguished the candle, opened the window, and sat down on a
chair, drawing her feet up and fixing her pensive eyes on the pond
now all glittering in the silvery light.

All her accustomed occupations and interests suddenly appeared to
her in a new light: her capricious old mother, uncritical love for
whom had become part of her soul; her decrepit but amiable old
uncle; the domestic and village serfs who worshipped their young
mistress; the milch cows and the calves, and all this Nature which had
died and been renewed so many times and amid which she had grown
up loving and beloved – all this that had given such light and pleasant
tranquillity to her soul suddenly seemed unsatisfactory; it seemed dull
and unnecessary. It was as if someone had said to her: 'Little fool,
little fool, for twenty years you have been trifling, serving someone
without knowing why, and without knowing what life and happiness are!' As she gazed into the depths of the moonlit, motionless
garden she thought this more intensely, far more intensely, than ever

before. And what caused these thoughts? Not any sudden love for the count as one might have supposed. On the contrary she did not like him. She could have been interested in the cornet more easily, but he was plain, poor fellow, and silent. She kept involuntarily forgetting him and recalling the image of the count with anger and annoyance. 'No, that's not it,' she said to herself. Her ideal had been so beautiful. It was an ideal that could have been loved on such a night amid this Nature without impairing its beauty – an ideal never abridged to fit it to some coarse reality.

Formerly, solitude and the absence of anyone who might have attracted her attention had caused the power of love, which Providence has given impartially to each of us, to rest intact and tranquil in her bosom, and now she had lived too long in the melancholy happiness of feeling within her the presence of this something, and of now and again opening the secret chalice of her heart to contemplate its riches, to be able to lavish its contents thoughtlessly on anyone. God grant she may enjoy to her grave this chary bliss! Who knows whether it be not the best and strongest, and whether it is not the only true and possible happiness?

'O Lord my God,' she thought, 'can it be that I have lost my youth and happiness in vain and that it will never be . . . never be? Can that be true?' And she looked into the depths of the sky lit up by the moon and covered by light fleecy clouds that, veiling the stars, crept nearer to the moon. 'If that highest little white cloud touches the moon it will be a sign that it is true,' thought she. The mist-like smoky strip ran across the bottom half of the bright disk and little by little the light on the grass, on the tops of the limes, and on the pond, grew dimmer and the black shadows of the trees grew less distinct. As if to harmonize with the gloomy shadows that spread over the world outside, a light wind ran through the leaves and brought to the window the odour of dewy leaves, of moist earth, and of blooming lilacs.

'But it is not true,' she consoled herself. 'There now, if the nightingale sings tonight it will be a sign that what I'm thinking is all nonsense, and that I need not despair,' thought she. And she sat a long while in silence waiting for something, while again all became bright and full of life and again and again the cloudlets ran across the moon making everything dim. She was beginning to fall asleep as she sat by the window, when the quivering trills of a nightingale came ringing from below across the pond and awoke her. The country maiden opened her eyes. And once more her soul was renewed with fresh joy by its mysterious union with Nature which spread out so calmly and brightly before her. She leant on both arms. A sweet, languid sensation of sadness oppressed her heart, and tears of pure wide-spreading love, thirsting to be satisfied – good comforting tears – filled her eyes. She folded her arms on the window-sill and laid her head on them. Her favourite prayer rose to her mind and she fell asleep with her eyes still moist.

The touch of someone's hand aroused her. She awoke. But the touch was light and pleasant. The hand pressed hers more closely. Suddenly she became alive to reality, screamed, jumped up, and trying to persuade herself that she had not recognized the count who was standing under the window bathed in the moonlight, she ran out of the room. . . .

XV

AND it really was the count. When he heard the girl's cry and a husky sound from the watchman behind the fence, who had been roused by that cry, he rushed headlong across the wet dewy grass into the depths of the garden feeling like a detected thief. 'Fool that I am!' he repeated unconsciously, 'I frightened her. I ought to have roused her gently by speaking to her. Awkward brute that I am!' He stopped and listened: the watchman came into the garden through the gate-way, dragging his stick along the sandy path. It was necessary to hide and the count went down by the pond. The frogs made him start as they plumped from beneath his feet into the water. Though his boots were wet through, he squatted down and began to recall all he had done: how he had climbed the fence, looked for her window, and at last espied a white shadow; how, listening to the faintest rustle, he had several times approached the window and gone back again: how at one moment he felt sure she was waiting, vexed at his tardiness, and the next, that it was impossible she should so readily have agreed to a rendezvous: how at last, persuading himself that it was only the bashfulness of a country-bred girl that made her pretend to be asleep, he went up resolutely and distinctly saw how she sat, but then for some reason ran away again and only after severely taunting himself for cowardice boldly drew near to her and touched her hand.

The watchman again made a husky sound and the gate creaked as he left the garden. The girl's window was slammed to and a shutter fastened from inside. This was very provoking. The count would have given a good deal for a chance to begin all over again; he would not have acted so stupidly now. . . . 'And she is a wonderful girl – so fresh – quite charming! And I have let her slip through my fingers. . . . Awkward fool that I am!' He did not want to sleep now and went at random, with the firm tread of one who has been crossed, along the covered lime-tree avenue.

And here the night brought to him also its peaceful gifts of soothing sadness and the need of love. The straight pale beams of the moon threw spots of light through the thick foliage of the limes onto the clay path, where a few blades of grass grew, or a dead branch lay here and there. The light falling on one side of a bent bough made it seem as if covered with white moss. The silvered leaves whispered now and then. There were no lights in the house and all was silent; the voice of the nightingale alone seemed to fill the bright, still, limitless space. 'O God, what a night! What a wonderful night!' thought the count, inhaling the fragrant freshness of the garden. 'Yet I feel a kind of regret – as if I were discontented with myself and with others, discontented with life generally. A splendid, sweet girl! Perhaps she was really hurt. . . .' Here his dreams became mixed: he imagined himself in this garden with the country-bred girl in various extraordinary situations. Then the role of the girl was taken by his beloved Mina. 'Eh, what a fool I was! I ought simply to have caught her round the waist and kissed her.' And regretting that he had not done so, the count returned to his room.

The cornet was still awake. He at once turned in his bed and faced the count.

'Not asleep yet?' asked the count.

'No.'

'Shall I tell you what has happened?'

'Well?'

'No, I'd better not, or . . . all right, I'll tell you – move your legs.'

And the count having mentally abandoned the intrigue that had miscarried, sat down on his comrade's bed with an animated smile.

'Would you believe it, that young lady gave me a rendezvous!'

'What are you saying?' cried Polozov, jumping out of bed.

'No, but listen.'

'But how? When? It's impossible!'

'Why, while you were adding up after we had played *préférence*, she told me she would sit at the window in the night and that one could get in at the window. There, you see what it is to be practical!

While you were calculating with the old woman, I arranged that little matter. Why, you heard her say in your presence that she would sit by the window tonight and look at the pond.'

'Yes, but she didn't mean anything of the kind.'

'Well, that's just what I can't make out: did she say it intentionally or not? Maybe she didn't really wish to agree so suddenly, but it looked very like it. It turned out horribly. I quite played the fool,' he added, smiling contemptuously at himself.

'What do you mean? Where have you been?'

The count, omitting his manifold irresolute approaches, related everything as it had happened.

'I spoilt it myself: I ought to have been bolder. She screamed and ran from the window.'

'So she screamed and ran away,' said the cornet, smiling uneasily in answer to the count's smile, which for such a long time had had so strong an influence over him.

'Yes, but it's time to go to sleep.'

The cornet again turned his back to the door and lay silent for about ten minutes. Heaven knows what went on in his soul, but when he turned again, his face bore an expression of suffering and resolve.

'Count Turbin!' he said abruptly.

'Are you delirious?' quietly replied the count. '. . . What is it, Cornet Polozov?'

'Count Turbin, you are a scoundrel!' cried Polozov, and again jumped out of bed.

XVI

THE squadron left next day. The two officers did not see their hosts again and did not bid them farewell. Neither did they speak to one another. They intended to fight a duel at the first halting-place. But Captain Schulz, a good comrade and splendid horseman, beloved by everyone in the regiment and chosen by the count to act as his second, managed to settle the affair so well that not only did they not fight but no one in the regiment knew anything about the matter, and Turbin and Polozov, though no longer on the old friendly footing, still continued to speak in familiar terms to one another and to meet at dinners and card-parties.

1856

ALBERT

Альберт

I

FIVE wealthy young men had come, after two in the morning, to amuse themselves at a small Petersburg party.

Much champagne had been drunk, most of the men were very young, the girls were pretty, the piano and violin indefatigably played one polka after another, and dancing and noise went on unceasingly: yet for some reason it was dull and awkward, and, as often happens, everybody felt that it was all unnecessary and was not the thing.

Several times they tried to get things going, but forced merriment was worse even than boredom.

One of the five young men, more dissatisfied than the others with himself, with the others, and with the whole evening, rose with a feeling of disgust, found his hat, and went out quietly, intending to go home.

There was no one in the ante-room, but in the adjoining room he heard two voices disputing. The young man stopped to listen.

'You can't, there are guests there,' said a woman's voice.

'Let me in, please. I'm all right!' a man's weak voice entreated.

'No, I won't let you in without Madame's permission,' said the woman. 'Where are you going? Ah! What a man you are!'

The door burst open and a strange figure of a man appeared on the threshold. The servant on seeing a visitor no longer protested, and the strange figure, bowing timidly, entered the room, swaying on his bent legs. He was of medium height, with a narrow, stooping back, and long tangled hair. He wore a short overcoat, and narrow torn trousers over a pair of rough uncleaned boots. A necktie, twisted into a cord, was fastened round his long white neck. A dirty shirt showed from under his coat and hung over his thin hands. Yet despite the extreme emaciation of his body, his face was white and delicate, and freshness and colour played on his cheeks above his scanty black beard and whiskers. His unkempt hair, thrown back, revealed a rather low and extremely clear forehead. His dark languid eyes looked softly, imploringly, and yet with dignity, before him. Their expression corresponded alluringly with that of the fresh lips, curved at the corners, which showed from under his thin moustache.

Having advanced a few steps he stopped, turned to the young man, and smiled. He seemed to smile with difficulty, but when the smile lit up his face the young man – without knowing why – smiled too.

'Who is that?' he whispered to the servant, when the strange figure had passed into the room from which came the sounds of a dance.

'A crazy musician from the theatre,' replied the maid. 'He comes sometimes to see the mistress.'

'Where have you been, Delesov?' someone just then called out, and the young man, who was named Delesov, returned to the ball-room.

The musician was standing at the door and, looking at the dancers, showed by his smile, his look, and the tapping of his foot, the satis-faction the spectacle afforded him.

'Come in and dance yourself,' said one of the visitors to him.

The musician bowed and looked inquiringly at the hostess.

'Go, go . . . Why not, when the gentlemen ask you to?' she said.

The thin, weak limbs of the musician suddenly came into active motion, and winking, smiling, and twitching, he began to prance awkwardly and heavily about the room. In the middle of the quad-rille a merry officer, who danced very vivaciously and well, acciden-tally bumped into the musician with his back. The latter's weak and weary legs did not maintain their balance and after a few stumbling steps aside, he fell full length on the floor. Notwithstanding the dull thud produced by his fall, at first nearly everyone burst out laughing.

But the musician did not get up. The visitors grew silent and even the piano ceased. Delesov and the hostess were the first to run up to the fallen man. He was lying on his elbow, staring with dull eyes at the floor. When they lifted him and seated him on a chair, he brushed the hair back from his forehead with a quick movement of his bony hand and began to smile without answering their questions.

'Mr. Albert! Mr. Albert!' said the hostess. 'Have you hurt your-self? Where? There now, I said you ought not to dance. He is so weak,' she continued, addressing her guests, '– he can hardly walk. How could he dance?'

'Who is he?' they asked her.

'A poor man – an artist. A very good fellow, but pitiable, as you see.'

She said this unembarrassed by the presence of the musician. He suddenly came to himself and, as if afraid of something, shrank into a heap and pushed those around him away.

'It's all nothing!' he suddenly said, rising from his chair with an obvious effort.

And to show that he was not at all hurt he went into the middle of the room and tried to jump about, but staggered and would have fallen down again had someone not supported him.

Everyone felt awkward, and looking at him they all became silent.

The musician's eyes again grew dim, and evidently oblivious of everyone he began rubbing his knee with his hand. Suddenly he raised his head, advanced a trembling leg, threw back his hair with the same heedless movement as before, and going up to the violinist took his violin from him.

'It's nothing!' he said once more, flourishing the violin. 'Gentlemen, let's have some music!'

'What a strange person!' the visitors remarked to one another.

'Perhaps a fine talent is perishing in this unfortunate creature,' said one of the guests.

'Yes, he's pitiable, pitiable!' said a third.

'What a beautiful face! . . . There is something extraordinary about him,' said Delesov. 'Let us see . . .'

II

ALBERT meanwhile, paying no attention to anyone, pressed the violin to his shoulder and paced slowly up and down by the piano tuning it. His lips took on an impassive expression, his eyes could not be seen, but his narrow bony back, his long white neck, his crooked legs and shaggy black head, presented a queer – but for some reason not at all ridiculous – spectacle. Having tuned the violin he briskly struck a chord, and throwing back his head turned to the pianist who was preparing to accompany him.

'*Mélancolie G-dur!*' he said, addressing the pianist with a gesture of command.

Then, as if begging forgiveness for that gesture, he smiled meekly, and glanced round at the audience with that same smile. Having pushed back his hair with the hand in which he held the bow, he stopped at the corner of the piano, and with a smooth and easy movement drew the bow across the strings. A clear melodious sound was borne through the room and complete silence ensued.

After that first note the theme flowed freely and elegantly, suddenly illumining the inner world of every listener with an unexpectedly clear and tranquillizing light. Not one false or exaggerated sound impaired the acquiescence of the listeners: the notes were all clear, elegant, and significant. Everyone silently followed their development with tremulous expectation. From the state of dullness, noisy distraction and mental torpor in which they had been, these people were suddenly and imperceptibly carried into another quite different world that they had forgotten. Now a calm contemplation of the past arose in their souls, now an impassioned memory of some past happiness, now a boundless desire for power and splendour, now a feeling of resignation, of unsatisfied love and sadness. Sounds now tenderly sad, now vehemently despairing, mingled freely, flowing and flowing one after the other so elegantly, so strongly, and so unconsciously, that the sounds themselves were not noticed, but there flowed of itself into the soul a beautiful torrent of poetry, long familiar but only now expressed. At each note Albert grew taller and taller. He was far from appearing misshapen or strange. Pressing the violin with his chin and listening to his notes with an expression of passionate attention, he convulsively moved his feet. Now he straightened himself to his full height, now he strenuously bent his back. His left arm seemed to have become set in the bent position to which he had strained it and only the bony fingers moved convulsively: the right arm moved smoothly, elegantly, and almost imperceptibly. His face shone with uninterrupted, ecstatic joy; his eyes burnt with a bright, dry brilliance, his nostrils expanded, his red lips opened with delight.

Sometimes his head bent closer to the violin, his eyes closed, and his face, half covered by his hair, lit up with a smile of mild rapture. Sometimes he drew himself up rapidly, advancing one foot, and his clear brow and the beaming look he cast round the room gleamed with pride, dignity, and a consciousness of power. Once the pianist blundered and struck a wrong chord. Physical suffering was apparent in the whole face and figure of the musician. He paused for an instant and stamping his foot with an expression of childish anger, cried: '*Moll, ce moll!*' The pianist recovered himself. Albert closed his eyes, smiled, and again forgetting himself, the others, and the whole world, gave himself up rapturously to his task.

All who were in the room preserved a submissive silence while Albert was playing, and seemed to live and breathe only in his music.

The merry officer sat motionless on a chair by a window, directing a lifeless gaze upon the floor and breathing slowly and heavily. The girls sat in complete silence along the walls, and only occasionally threw approving and bewildered glances at one another. The hostess's fat smiling face expanded with pleasure. The pianist riveted his eyes on Albert's face and, with a fear of blundering which expressed itself in his whole taut figure, tried to keep up with him. One of the visitors who had drunk more than the others lay prone on the sofa, trying not to move for fear of betraying his agitation. Delesov experienced an unaccustomed sensation. It was as if a cold circle, now expanding, now contracting, held his head in a vice. The roots of his hair became sensitive, cold shivers ran up his spine, something rising higher and higher in his throat pricked his nose and palate as if with fine needles, and tears involuntarily wetted his cheeks. He shook himself, tried to restrain them and wipe them unperceived, but others rose and ran down his cheeks. By some strange concatenation of impressions the first sounds of Albert's violin carried Delesov back to his early youth. Now no longer very young, tired of life and exhausted, he suddenly felt himself a self-satisfied, good-looking, blissfully foolish and unconsciously happy lad of seventeen. He remembered his first love – for his cousin in a little pink dress; remembered his first declaration of love made in a linden avenue; remembered the warmth and incomprehensible delight of a spontaneous kiss, and the magic and undivined mystery of the Nature that then surrounded him. In the memories that returned to him *she* shone out amid a mist of vague hopes, uncomprehended desires, and questioning faith in the possibility of impossible happiness. All the unappreciated moments of that time arose before him one after another, not as insignificant moments of a fleeting present, but as arrested, growing, reproachful images of the past. He contemplated them with joy, and wept – wept not because the time was past that he might have spent better (if he had it again he would not have undertaken to employ it better), but merely because it was past and would never return. Memories rose up of themselves, and Albert's violin repeated again and again: 'For you that time of vigour, love, and happiness has passed for ever, and will not return. Weep for it, shed all your tears, die weeping for that time – that is the best happiness left for you.'

Towards the end of the last variation Albert's face grew red, his eyes burnt and glowed, and large drops of perspiration ran down his cheeks. The veins of his forehead swelled up, his whole body came more and more into motion, his pale lips no longer closed, and his whole figure expressed ecstatic eagerness for enjoyment.

Passionately swaying his whole body and tossing back his hair he lowered the violin, and with a smile of proud dignity and happiness surveyed the audience. Then his back sagged, his head hung down, his lips closed, his eyes grew dim, and he timidly glanced round as if ashamed of himself, and made his way stumblingly into the other room.

III

SOMETHING strange occurred with everyone present and something strange was felt in the dead silence that followed Albert's playing. It was as if each would have liked to express what all this meant, but was unable to do so. What did it mean – this bright hot room, brilliant women, the dawn in the windows, excitement in the blood, and the pure impression left by sounds that had flowed past? But no one even tried to say what it all meant: on the contrary everyone, unable to dwell in those regions which the new impression had revealed to them, rebelled against it.

'He really plays well, you know!' said the officer.

'Wonderfully!' replied Delesov, stealthily wiping his cheek with his sleeve.

'However, it's time for us to be going,' said the man who was lying on the sofa, having somewhat recovered. 'We must give him something. Let's make a collection.'

Meanwhile Albert sat alone on a sofa in the next room. Leaning his elbows on his bony knees he stroked his face and ruffled his hair with his moist and dirty hands, smiling happily to himself.

They made a good collection, which Delesov offered to hand to Albert.

Moreover it had occurred to Delesov, on whom the music had made an unusual and powerful impression, to be of use to this man. It occurred to him to take him home, dress him, get him a place somewhere, and in general rescue him from his sordid condition.

'Well, are you tired?' he asked, coming up to him.

Albert smiled.

'You have real talent. You ought to study music seriously and give public performances.'

'I'd like to have something to drink,' said Albert, as if just awake.

Delesov brought some wine, and the musician eagerly drank two glasses.

'What excellent wine!' he said.

'What a delightful thing that *Mélancolie* is!' said Delesov.

'Oh, yes, yes!' replied Albert with a smile – 'but excuse me: I don't know with whom I have the honour of speaking, maybe you are a count, or a prince: could you, perhaps, lend me a little money?' He paused a little. 'I have nothing . . . I am a poor man. I couldn't pay it back.'

Delesov flushed: he felt awkward, and hastily handed the musician the money that had been collected.

'Thank you very much!' said Albert, seizing the money. 'Now let's have some music. I'll play for you as much as you like – only let me have a drink of something, a drink . . .' he added, rising.

Delesov brought him some more wine and asked him to sit beside him.

'Excuse me if I am frank with you,' he said, 'your talent interests me so much. It seems to me you are not in good circumstances.'

Albert looked now at Delesov and now at his hostess who had entered the room.

'Allow me to offer you my services,' continued Delesov. 'If you are in need of anything I should be glad if you would stay with me for a time. I am living alone and could perhaps be of use to you.'

Albert smiled and made no reply.

'Why don't you thank him?' said the hostess. 'Of course it is a godsend for you. Only I should not advise you to,' she continued, turning to Delesov and shaking her head disapprovingly.

'I am very grateful to you!' said Albert, pressing Delesov's hand with his own moist ones – 'Only let us have some music now, please.'

But the other visitors were preparing to leave, and despite Albert's endeavours to persuade them to stay they went out into the hall.

Albert took leave of the hostess, put on his shabby broad-brimmed hat and old summer cloak, which was his only winter clothing, and went out into the porch with Delesov.

When Delesov had seated himself with his new acquaintance in his carriage, and became aware of the unpleasant odour of drunkenness and uncleanness which emanated so strongly from the musician, he began to repent of his action and blamed himself for childish soft-heartedness and imprudence. Besides, everything Albert said was so stupid and trivial, and the fresh air suddenly made him so disgustingly drunk that Delesov was repelled. 'What am I to do with him?' he thought.

When they had driven for a quarter of an hour Albert grew silent, his hat fell down at his feet, and he himself tumbled into a corner of the carriage and began to snore. The wheels continued to creak monotonously over the frozen snow; the feeble light of dawn hardly penetrated the frozen windows.

Delesov turned and looked at his companion. The long body covered by the cloak lay lifelessly beside him. The long head with its big black nose seemed to sway on that body, but looking closer Delesov saw that what he had taken for nose and face was hair, and that the real face hung lower. He stooped and was able to distinguish Albert's features. Then the beauty of the forehead and calmly closed lips struck him again.

Under the influence of tired nerves, restlessness from lack of sleep at that hour of the morning, and of the music he had heard, Delesov, looking at that face, let himself again be carried back to the blissful world into which he had glanced that night; he again recalled the happy and magnanimous days of his youth and no longer repented of what he had done. At that moment he was sincerely and warmly attached to Albert, and firmly resolved to be of use to him.

IV

NEXT morning when he was awakened to go to his office, Delesov with a feeling of unpleasant surprise saw around him his old screen, his old valet, and his watch lying on the small side-table. 'But what did I expect to see if not what is always around me?' he asked himself. Then he remembered the musician's black eyes and happy smile, the motif of *Mélancolie*, and all the strange experiences of the previous night passed through his mind.

He had no time however to consider whether he had acted well or badly by taking the musician into his house. While dressing he mapped out the day, took his papers, gave the necessary household orders, and hurriedly put on his overcoat and overshoes. Passing the dining-room door he looked in. Albert, after tossing about, had sunk his face in the pillow, and lay in his dirty ragged shirt, dead asleep on the leather sofa where he had been deposited unconscious the night before. 'There's something wrong!' thought Delesov involuntarily.

'Please go to Boryuzovski and ask him to lend me a violin for a couple of days,' he said to his manservant. 'When he wakes up, give him coffee and let him have some underclothing and old clothes of mine. In general, make him comfortable – please!'

On returning late in the evening Delesov was surprised not to find Albert.

'Where is he?' he asked his man.

'He went away immediately after dinner,' replied the servant. 'He took the violin and went away. He promised to be back in an hour, but he's not here yet.'

'Tut, tut! How provoking!' muttered Delesov. 'Why did you let him go, Zakhar?'

Zakhar was a Petersburg valet who had been in Delesov's service for eight years. Delesov, being a lonely bachelor, could not help confiding his intentions to him, and liked to know his opinion about all his undertakings.

'How could I dare not to let him?' Zakhar replied, toying with the fob of his watch. 'If you had told me to keep him in I might have amused him at home. But you only spoke to me about clothes.'

'Pshaw! How provoking! Well, and what was he doing here without me?'

Zakhar smiled.

'One can well call him an "artist",[1] sir. As soon as he woke he asked for Madeira, and then he amused himself with the cook and with the neighbour's manservant. He is so funny. However, he is good-natured. I gave him tea and brought him dinner. He would not eat anything himself, but kept inviting me to do so. But when it comes to playing the violin, even Izler has few artists like him. One may well befriend such a man. When he played *Down the Little Mother Volga* to us it was as if a man were weeping. It was too beautiful. Even the servants from all the flats came to our back-entrance to hear him.'

'Well, and did you get him dressed?' his master interrupted him.

[1] In addition to its proper meaning, the word 'artist' was used in Russian to denote a thief, or a man dexterous at anything, good or bad.

'Of course. I gave him a night-shirt of yours and put my own paletot on him. A man like that is worth helping – he really is a dear fellow!' Zakhar smiled.

'He kept asking me what your rank is, whether you have influential acquaintances, and how many serfs you own.'

'Well, all right, but now he must be found, and in future don't let him have anything to drink, or it'll be worse for him.'

'That's true,' Zakhar interjected. 'He is evidently feeble; our old master had a clerk like that . . .'

But Delesov who had long known the story of the clerk who took hopelessly to drink, did not let Zakhar finish, and telling him to get everything ready for the night, sent him out to find Albert and bring him back.

He then went to bed and put out the light, but could not fall asleep for a long time, thinking about Albert. 'Though it may seem strange to many of my acquaintances,' he thought, 'yet one so seldom does anything for others that one ought to thank God when such an opportunity presents itself, and I will not miss it. I will do anything – positively anything in my power – to help him. He may not be mad at all, but only under the influence of drink. It won't cost me very much. Where there's enough for one there's enough for two. Let him live with me awhile, then we'll find him a place or arrange a concert for him and pull him out of the shallows, and then see what happens.'

He experienced a pleasant feeling of self-satisfaction after this reflection.

'Really I'm not altogether a bad fellow,' he thought. 'Not at all bad even – when I compare myself with others.'

He was already falling asleep when the sound of opening doors and of footsteps in the hall roused him.

'Well, I'll be stricter with him,' he thought, 'that will be best; and I must do it.'

He rang.

'Have you brought him back?' he asked when Zakhar entered.

'A pitiable man, sir,' said Zakhar, shaking his head significantly and closing his eyes.

'Is he drunk?'

'He is very weak.'

'And has he the violin?'

'I've brought it back. The lady gave it me.'

'Well, please don't let him in here now. Put him to bed, and tomorrow be sure not to let him leave the house on any account.'

But before Zakhar was out of the room Albert entered it.

V

'Do you want to sleep already?' asked Albert with a smile. 'And I have been at Anna Ivanovna's and had a very pleasant evening. We had music, and laughed, and there was delightful company. Let me have a glass of something,' he added, taking hold of a water-bottle that stood on a little table, '– but not water.'

Albert was just the same as he had been the previous evening: the same beautiful smile in his eyes and on his lips, the same bright inspired forehead, and the same feeble limbs. Zakhar's paletot fitted him well, and the clean wide unstarched collar of the nightshirt encircled his thin white neck picturesquely, giving him a particularly childlike and innocent look. He sat down on Delesov's bed and looked at him silently with a happy and grateful smile. Delesov looked into his eyes, and again suddenly felt himself captivated by that smile. He no longer wanted to sleep, he forgot that it was his duty to be stern: on the contrary he wished to make merry, to hear music, and to chat amicably with Albert till morning. He told Zakhar to bring a bottle of wine, some cigarettes, and the violin.

'There, that's splendid!' said Albert. 'It's still early, and we'll have some music. I'll play for you as much as you like.'

Zakhar, with evident pleasure, brought a bottle of Lafitte, two tumblers, some mild cigarettes such as Albert smoked, and the violin. But instead of going to bed as his master told him to, he himself lit a cigar and sat down in the adjoining room.

'Let us have a talk,' said Delesov to the musician, who was about to take up the violin.

Albert submissively sat down on the bed and again smiled joyfully.

'Oh yes!' said he, suddenly striking his forehead with his hand and assuming an anxiously inquisitive expression. (A change of expression always preceded anything he was about to say.) – 'Allow me to ask –' he made a slight pause – 'that gentleman who was there with you last night – you called him N—, isn't he the son of the celebrated N—?'

'His own son,' Delesov answered, not at all understanding how that could interest Albert.

'Exactly!' said Albert with a self-satisfied smile. 'I noticed at once something particularly aristocratic in his manner. I love aristocrats: there is something particularly beautiful and elegant in an aristocrat. And that officer who dances so well?' he asked. 'I liked him very much too: he is so merry and so fine. Isn't he Adjutant N. N.?'

'Which one?' asked Delesov.

'The one who bumped against me when we were dancing. He must be an excellent fellow.'

'No, he's a shallow fellow,' Delesov replied.

'Oh, no!' Albert warmly defended him. 'There is something very, very pleasant about him. He is a capital musician,' he added. 'He played something there out of an opera. It's a long time since I took such a liking to anyone.'

'Yes, he plays well, but I don't like his playing,' said Delesov, wishing to get his companion to talk about music. 'He does not understand classical music – Donizetti and Bellini, you know, are not music. You think so too, no doubt?'

'Oh, no, no, excuse me!' began Albert with a gentle, pleading look. 'The old music is music, and the new music is music. There are extraordinary beauties in the new music too. *Sonnambula*, and the finale of *Lucia*, and Chopin, and *Robert*![2] I often think –' he paused, evidently collecting his thoughts – 'that if Beethoven were alive he would weep with joy listening to *Sonnambula*. There is beauty everywhere. I heard *Sonnambula* for the first time when Viardot and Rubini[3] were here. It was like this . . .' he said, and his eyes glistened as he made a gesture with both arms as though tearing something out of his breast. 'A little more and it would have been impossible to bear it.'

'And what do you think of the opera at the present time?' asked Delesov.

'Bosio[4] is good, very good,' he said, 'extraordinarily exquisite, but

[2] *Sonnambula*, opera by Bellini, produced in 1831. *Lucia di Lammermoor*, opera by Donizetti, produced in 1835. *Robert the Devil*, opera by Meyerbeer, produced in 1831; or possibly the allusion may be to *Roberto Devereux* by Donizetti.

[3] Pauline Viardot-Garcia, the celebrated operatic singer with whom Turgenev had a close friendship for many years. Rubini, an Italian tenor who had great success in Russia in the 'forties of the last century.

[4] Angidina Bosio, an Italian singer, who was in Petersburg in 1856-9.

she does not touch one here,' – pointing to his sunken chest. 'A singer needs passion, and she has none. She gives pleasure but does not torment.'

'How about Lablache?'[5]

'I heard him in Paris in the *Barbier de Séville*. He was unique then, but now he is old: he cannot be an artist, he is old.'

'Well, what if he is old? He is still good in *morceaux d'ensemble*,' said Delesov, who was in the habit of saying that of Lablache.

'How "what if he is old?" ' rejoined Albert severely. 'He should not be old. An artist should not be old. Much is needed for art, but above all, fire!' said he with glittering eyes and stretching both arms upwards.

And a terrible inner fire really seemed to burn in his whole body.

'O my God!' he suddenly exclaimed. 'Don't you know Petrov, the artist?'

'No, I don't,' Delesov replied, smiling.

'How I should like you to make his acquaintance! You would enjoy talks with him. How well he understands art, too! I used often to meet him at Anna Ivanovna's, but now she is angry with him for some reason. I should very much like you to know him. He has great talent, great talent!'

'Does he paint now?' Delesov asked.

'I don't know, I think not, but he was an Academy artist. What ideas he has! It's wonderful when he talks sometimes. Oh, Petrov has great talent, only he leads a very gay life . . . that's a pity,' Albert added with a smile. After that he got off the bed, took the violin, and began tuning it.

'Is it long since you were at the opera?' Delesov asked.

Albert looked round and sighed.

'Ah, I can't go there any more!' he said. 'I will tell you!' And clutching his head he again sat down beside Delesov and muttered almost in a whisper: 'I can't go there. I can't play there – I have nothing – nothing! No clothes, no home, no violin. It is a miserable life! A miserable life!' he repeated several times. And why should I go there? What for? No need!' he said, smiling. 'Ah! *Don Juan* . . .'

He struck his head with his hand.

'Then let us go there together sometime,' said Delesov.

Without answering, Albert jumped up, seized the violin, and began

[5] Luigi Lablache. He was regarded as the chief basso of modern times.

playing the finale of the first act of *Don Juan*, telling the story of the opera in his own words.

Delesov felt the hair stir on his head as Albert played the voice of the dying commandant.

'No!' said Albert, putting down the violin. 'I cannot play today. I have had too much to drink.'

But after that he went up to the table, filled a tumbler with wine, drank it at a gulp, and again sat down on Delesov's bed.

Delesov looked at Albert, not taking his eyes off him. Occasionally Albert smiled, and so did Delesov. They were both silent; but their looks and smiles created more and more affectionate relations between them. Delesov felt himself growing fonder of the man, and experienced an incomprehensible joy.

'Have you ever been in love?' he suddenly asked.

Albert thought for a few seconds, and then a sad smile lit up his face. He leaned over to Delesov and looked attentively in his eyes.

'Why have you asked me that?' he whispered. 'I will tell you everything, because I like you,' he continued, after looking at him for a while and then glancing round. 'I won't deceive you, but will tell you everything from the beginning, just as it happened.' He stopped, his eyes wild and strangely fixed. 'You know that my mind is weak,' he suddenly said. 'Yes, yes,' he went on. 'Anna Ivanovna is sure to have told you. She tells everybody that I am mad! That is not true; she says it as a joke, she is a kindly woman, and I have really not been quite well for some time.' He stopped again and gazed with fixed wide-open eyes at the dark doorway. 'You asked whether I have been in love? . . . Yes, I have been in love,' he whispered, lifting his brows. 'It happened long ago, when I still had my job in the theatre. I used to play second violin at the Opera, and she used to have the lower-tier box next the stage, on the left.'

He got up and leaned over to Delesov's ear.

'No, why should I name her?' he said. 'You no doubt know her – everybody knows her. I kept silent and only looked at her; I knew I was a poor artist, and she an aristocratic lady. I knew that very well. I only looked at her and planned nothing . . .'

Albert reflected, trying to remember.

'How it happened I don't remember; but I was once called in to accompany her on the violin. . . . But what was I, a poor artist?' he said, shaking his head and smiling. 'But no, I can't tell it . . .' he added, clutching his head. 'How happy I was!'

'Yes? And did you often go to her house?' Delesov asked.

'Once! Once only . . . but it was my own fault. I was mad! I was a poor artist, and she an aristocratic lady. I ought not to have said anything to her. But I went mad and acted like a fool. Since then all has been over for me. Petrov told the truth, that it would have been better for me to have seen her only at the theatre . . .'

'What was it you did?' asked Delesov.

'Ah, wait! Wait! I can't speak of that!'

With his face hidden in his hands he remained silent for some time.

'I came late to the orchestra. Petrov and I had been drinking that evening, and I was distracted. She was sitting in her box talking to a general. I don't know who that general was. She sat at the very edge of the box, with her arm on the ledge; she had on a white dress and pearls round her neck. She talked to him and looked at me. She looked at me twice. Her hair was done like this. I was not playing, but stood near the basses and looked at her. Then for the first time I felt strange. She smiled at the general and looked at me. I felt she was speaking about me, and I suddenly saw that I was not in the orchestra, but in the box beside her and holding her arm, just there. . . . How was that?' Albert asked after a short silence.

'That was vivid imagination,' said Delesov.

'No, no! . . . but I don't know how to tell it,' Albert replied, frowning. 'Even then I was poor and had no lodging, and when I went to the theatre I sometimes stayed the night there.'

'What, at the theatre? In that dark, empty place?'

'Oh, I am not afraid of such nonsense. Wait a bit. . . . When they had all gone away I would go to the box where she had been sitting and sleep there. That was my one delight. What nights I spent there! But once it began again. Many things appeared to me in the night, but I can't tell you much.' Albert glanced at Delesov with downcast eyes. 'What was it?' he asked.

'It is strange!' said Delesov.

'No, wait, wait!' he continued, whispering in Delesov's ear. 'I kissed her hand, wept there beside her, and talked much with her. I inhaled the scent of her perfume and heard her voice. She told me much in one night. Then I took my violin and played softly; and I played splendidly. But I felt frightened. I am not afraid of those foolish things and don't believe in them, but I was afraid for my head,' he said, touching his forehead with an amiable smile. 'I was frightened for my poor wits. It seemed to me that something had happened to my head. Perhaps it's nothing. What do you think?'

Both were silent for some minutes.

'Und wenn die Wolken sie verhüllen
Die Sonne bleibt doch ewig klar.'[6]

Albert sang with a soft smile. 'Is not that so?' he added.

'Ich auch habe gelebt und genossen . . .'[7]

'Ah, how well old Petrov would have explained it all to you!'

Delesov looked silently and in terror at the pale and agitated face of his companion.

'Do you know the "*Juristen-Waltzer*"?' Albert suddenly exclaimed, and without awaiting an answer he jumped up, seized the violin, and began to play the merry waltz tune, forgetting himself completely, and evidently imagining that a whole orchestra was playing with him. He smiled, swayed, shifted his feet, and played superbly.

'Eh! Enough of merrymaking!' he said when he had finished, and flourished the violin.

'I am going,' he said, after sitting silently for a while – 'won't you come with me?'

'Where to?' Delesov asked in surprise.

'Let's go to Anna Ivanovna's again. It's gay there – noise, people, music!'

At first Delesov almost consented, but bethinking himself he tried to persuade Albert not to go that night.

'Only for a moment.'

'No really, you'd better not!'

Albert sighed and put down the violin.

'So I must stay here?'

And looking again at the table (there was no wine left) he said goodnight and left the room.

Delesov rang.

'See that you don't let Mr. Albert go anywhere without my permission,' he said to Zakhar.

[6] 'And even if the clouds do hide it
The sun remains for ever clear.'
[7] 'I, too, have lived and enjoyed.'

VI

THE next day was a holiday. Delesov was already awake and sitting in his drawing-room drinking coffee and reading a book. Albert had not yet stirred in the next room.

Zakhar cautiously opened the door and looked into the dining-room.

'Would you believe it, sir? He is asleep on the bare sofa! He wouldn't have anything spread on it, really. Like a little child. Truly, an artist.'

Towards noon groaning and coughing were heard through the door.

Zakhar again went into the dining-room, and Delesov could hear his kindly voice and Albert's weak, entreating one.

'Well?' he asked, when Zakhar returned.

'He's fretting, sir, won't wash, and seems gloomy. He keeps asking for a drink.'

'No. Having taken this matter up I must show character,' said Delesov to himself.

He ordered that no wine should be given to Albert and resumed his book, but involuntarily listened to what was going on in the dining-room. There was no sound of movement there and an occasional deep cough and spitting was all that could be heard. Two hours passed. Having dressed, Delesov decided to look in at his visitor before going out. Albert was sitting motionless at the window, his head resting on his hand. He looked round. His face was yellow, wrinkled, and not merely sad but profoundly miserable. He tried to smile by way of greeting, but his face took on a still more sorrowful expression. He seemed ready to cry. He rose with difficulty and bowed.

'If I might just have a glass of simple vodka!' he said with a look of entreaty. 'I am so weak – please!'

'Coffee will do you more good. Have some of that instead.'

Albert's face suddenly lost its childlike expression; he looked coldly, dim-eyed, out of the window, and sank feebly onto his chair.

'Or would you like some lunch?'

'No thank you, I have no appetite.'

'If you wish to play the violin you will not disturb me,' said Delesov, laying the violin on the table.

Albert looked at the violin with a contemptuous smile.

'No,' he said. 'I am too weak, I can't play,' and he pushed the instrument away from him.

After that, whatever Delesov might say, offering to go for a walk with him, and to the theatre in the evening, he only bowed humbly and remained stubbornly silent. Delesov went out, paid several calls, dined with friends, and before going to the theatre returned home to change and to see what the musician was doing. Albert was sitting in the dark hall, leaning his head in his hands and looking at the heated stove. He was neatly dressed, washed, and his hair was brushed; but his eyes were dim and lifeless, and his whole figure expressed weakness and exhaustion even more than in the morning.

'Have you dined, Mr. Albert?' asked Delesov.

Albert made an affirmative gesture with his head and, after a frightened look at Delesov, lowered his eyes. Delesov felt uncomfortable.

'I spoke to the director of the theatre about you today,' he said, also lowering his eyes. 'He will be very glad to receive you if you will let him hear you.'

'Thank you, I cannot play!' muttered Albert under his breath, and went into his room, shutting the door behind him very softly.

A few minutes later the door-knob was turned just as gently, and he came out of the room with the violin. With a rapid and hostile glance at Delesov he placed the violin on a chair and disappeared again.

Delesov shrugged his shoulders and smiled.

'What more am I to do? In what am I to blame?' he thought.

'Well, how is the musician?' was his first question when he returned home late that evening.

'Bad!' said Zakhar, briefly and clearly. 'He has been sighing and coughing and says nothing, except that he started begging for vodka four or five times. At last I gave him one glass – or else we might finish him off, sir. Just like the clerk . . .'

'Has he not played the violin?'

'Didn't even touch it. I took it to him a couple of times, but he just took it up gently and brought it out again,' Zakhar answered with a smile. 'So your orders are not to give him any drink?'

'No, we'll wait another day and see what happens. And what's he doing now?'

'He has locked himself up in the drawing-room.'

Delesov went into his study and chose several French books and a German Bible. 'Put these books in his room tomorrow, and see that you don't let him out,' he said to Zakhar.

Next morning Zakhar informed his master that the musician had not slept all night: he had paced up and down the rooms, and had been into the pantry, trying to open the cupboard and the door, but he (Zakhar) had taken care to lock everything up. He said that while he pretended to be asleep he had heard Albert in the dark muttering something to himself and waving his arms about.

Albert grew gloomier and more taciturn every day. He seemed to be afraid of Delesov, and when their eyes met his face expressed sickly fear. He did not touch the books or the violin, and did not reply to questions put to him.

On the third day of the musician's stay Delesov returned home late, tired and upset. He had been driving about all day attending to a matter that had promised to be very simple and easy but, as often happens, in spite of strenuous efforts he had been quite unable to advance a single step with it. Besides that he had called in at his club and had lost at whist. He was in bad spirits.

'Well, let him go his way!' he said to Zakhar, who told him of Albert's sad plight. 'Tomorrow I'll get a definite answer out of him, whether he wants to stay here and follow my advice, or not. If not, he needn't! It seems to me that I have done all I could.'

'There now, try doing good to people!' he thought to himself. 'I put myself out for him, I keep that dirty creature in my house, so that I can't receive a visitor in the morning. I bustle and run about, and he looks on me as if I were a villain who for his own pleasure has locked him up in a cage. And above all, he won't take a single step to help himself. They are all like that.' (The 'they' referred to people in general, and especially to those with whom he had had business that day.) 'And what is the matter with him now? What is he thinking about and pining for? Pining for the debauchery from which I have dragged him? For the humiliation in which he was? For the destitution from which I have saved him? Evidently he has fallen so low that it hurts him to see a decent life . . .'

'No, it was a childish act,' Delesov concluded. 'How can I improve others, when God knows whether I can manage myself?' He thought of letting Albert go at once, but after a little reflection put it off till the next day.

During the night he was roused by the sound of a table falling in the hall, and the sound of voices and footsteps. He lighted a candle and listened in surprise.

'Wait a bit. I'll tell my master,' Zakhar was saying; Albert's voice muttered something incoherently and heatedly. Delesov jumped up and ran into the hall with the candle. Zakhar stood against the front door in his night attire, and Albert, with his hat and cloak on, was pushing him aside and shouting in a tearful voice:

'You can't keep me here! I have a passport,[8] and have taken nothing of yours. You may search me. I shall go to the chief of police! . . .'

'Excuse me, sir!' Zakhar said, addressing his master while continuing to guard the door with his back. 'He got up during the night, found the key in my overcoat pocket, and drank a whole decanter of liqueur vodka. Is that right? And now he wants to go away. You ordered me not to let him out, so I dare not let him go.'

On seeing Delesov Albert made for Zakhar still more excitedly.

'No one dare hold me! No one has a right to!' he shouted, raising his voice more and more.

'Step aside, Zakhar!' said Delesov. 'I can't and don't want to keep you, but I advise you to stay till the morning,' he said to Albert.

'No one can keep me! I'll go to the chief of police!' Albert cried louder and louder, addressing himself to Zakhar alone and not looking at Delesov. 'Help!' he suddenly screamed in a furious voice.

'What are you screaming like that for? Nobody is keeping you!' said Zakhar, opening the door.

Albert stopped shouting. 'You didn't succeed, did you? Wanted to do for me – did you!' he muttered to himself, putting on his goloshes. Without taking leave, and continuing to mutter incoherently, he went out. Zakhar held a light for him as far as the gate, and then came back.

'Well, God be thanked, sir!' he said to his master. 'Who knows what might happen? As it is I must count the silver plate . . .'

Delesov merely shook his head and did not reply. He vividly recalled the first two evenings he had spent with the musician, and recalled the last sad days which by his fault Albert had spent there, and above all he recalled that sweet, mixed feeling of surprise, affection and pity, which that strange man had aroused in him at first sight, and he felt sorry for him. 'And what will become of him now?'

[8] To be free to go from place to place it was necessary to have a properly stamped passport from the police.

he thought. 'Without money, without warm clothing, alone in the middle of the night . . .' He was about to send Zakhar after him, but it was too late.

'Is it cold outside?' he inquired.

'A hard frost, sir,' replied Zakhar. 'I forgot to inform you, but we shall have to buy more wood for fuel before the spring.'

'How is that? You said that we should have some left over.'

VII

IT was indeed cold outside, but Albert, heated by the liquor he had drunk and by the dispute, did not feel it. On reaching the street he looked round and rubbed his hands joyfully. The street was empty, but the long row of lamps still burned with ruddy light; the sky was clear and starry. 'There now!' he said, addressing the lighted window of Delesov's lodging, thrusting his hands into his trouser pockets under his cape, and stooping forward. He went with heavy, uncertain steps down the street to the right. He felt an unusual weight in his legs and stomach, something made a noise in his head, and some invisible force was throwing him from side to side, but he still went on in the direction of Anna Ivanovna's house. Strange, incoherent thoughts passed through his mind. Now he remembered his last altercation with Zakhar, then for some reason the sea and his first arrival in Russia by steamboat, then a happy night he had passed with a friend in a small shop he was passing, then suddenly a familiar motif began singing itself in his imagination, and he remembered the object of his passion and the dreadful night in the theatre. Despite their incoherence all these memories presented themselves so clearly to his mind that, closing his eyes, he did not know which was the more real: what he was doing, or what he was thinking. He did not realize or feel how his legs were moving, how he swayed and bumped against the wall, how he looked around him, or passed from street to street. He realized and felt only the things that, intermingling and fantastically following one another, rose in his imagination.

Passing along the Little Morskaya Street, Albert stumbled and fell. Coming to his senses for a moment he saw an immense and splendid building before him and went on. In the sky no stars, nor moon, nor dawn, were visible, nor were there any street lamps, but everything was clearly outlined. In the windows of the building that towered at the end of the street lights were shining, but those lights quivered like reflections. The building stood out nearer and nearer and clearer and clearer before him. But the lights disappeared directly he entered the wide portals. All was dark within. Solitary footsteps resounded under the vaulted ceiling, and some shadows slid rapidly away as he approached. 'Why have I come here?' thought he; but some irresistible force drew him on into the depths of the immense hall. There was some kind of platform, around which some small people stood silently. 'Who is going to speak?' asked Albert. No one replied, except that someone pointed to the platform. A tall thin man with bristly hair and wearing a parti-coloured dressing-gown was already standing there, and Albert immediately recognized his friend Petrov. 'How strange that he should be here!' thought he. 'No, brothers!' Petrov was saying, pointing to someone. 'You did not understand a man living among you; you have not understood him! He is not a mercenary artist, not a mechanical performer, not a lunatic or a lost man. He is a genius – a great musical genius who has perished among you unnoticed and unappreciated!' Albert at once understood of whom his friend was speaking, but not wishing to embarrass him he modestly lowered his head.

'The holy fire that we all serve has consumed him like a blade of straw!' the voice went on, 'but he has fulfilled all that God implanted in him and should therefore be called a great man. You could despise, torment, humiliate him,' the voice continued, growing louder and louder – 'but he was, is, and will be, immeasurably higher than you all. He is happy, he is kind. He loves or despises all alike, but serves only that which was implanted in him from above. He loves but one thing – beauty, the one indubitable blessing in the world. Yes, such is the man! Fall prostrate before him, all of you! On your knees!' he cried aloud.

But another voice came mildly from the opposite corner of the hall: 'I do not wish to bow my knees before him,' said the voice, which Albert immediately recognized as Delesov's. 'Wherein is he great? Why should we bow before him? Did he behave honourably and justly? Has he been of any use to society? Don't we know how he borrowed money and did not return it, and how he carried away his fellow-artist's violin and pawned it? . . .' ('O God, how does he know all that?' thought Albert, hanging his head still lower.) 'Do we not know how he flattered the most insignificant people, flattered them for the sake of money?' Delesov continued – 'Don't we know how he was expelled from the theatre? And how Anna Ivanovna wanted to send him to the police?' ('O God! That is all true, but defend me, Thou who alone knowest why I did it!' muttered Albert.)

'Cease, for shame!' Petrov's voice began again. 'What right have you to accuse him? Have you lived his life? Have you experienced his rapture?' ('True, true!' whispered Albert.) 'Art is the highest manifestation of power in man. It is given to a few of the elect, and raises the chosen one to such a height as turns the head and makes it difficult for him to remain sane. In Art, as in every struggle, there are heroes who have devoted themselves entirely to its service and have perished without having reached the goal.' Petrov stopped, and Albert raised his head and cried out: 'True, true!' but his voice died away without a sound.

'It does not concern you,' said the artist Petrov, turning to him severely. 'Yes, humiliate and despise him,' he continued, 'but yet he is the best and happiest of you all.'

Albert, who had listened to these words with rapture in his soul, could not restrain himself, and went up to his friend wishing to kiss him.

'Go away! I do not know you!' Petrov said. 'Go your way, or you won't get there.'

'Just see how the drink's got hold of you! You won't get there,' shouted a policeman at the crossroad.

Albert stopped, collected his strength and, trying not to stagger, turned into the side street.

Only a few more steps were left to Anna Ivanovna's door. From the hall of her house the light fell on the snow in the courtyard, and sledges and carriages stood at the gate.

Holding onto the banister with his numbed hands, he ran up the steps and rang. The sleepy face of a maid appeared in the opening of the doorway, and she looked angrily at Albert. 'You can't!' she cried. 'The orders are not to let you in,' and she slammed the door to. The sound of music and of women's voices reached the steps. Albert sat down, leaned his head against the wall, and closed his eyes. Immediately a throng of disconnected but kindred visions beset him with renewed force, engulfed him in their waves, and bore him away into the free and beautiful realm of dreams. 'Yes, he was the best and happiest!' ran involuntarily through his imagination. The sounds of a polka came through the door. These sounds also told him that he was the best and happiest. The bells in the nearest church rang out for early service, and these bells also said: 'Yes, he is the best and happiest!' . . . 'I will go back to the hall,' thought Albert. 'Petrov must tell me much more.' But there was no one in the hall now, and instead of the artist Petrov, Albert himself stood on the platform and played on the violin all that the voice had said before. But the violin was of strange construction; it was made of glass and it had to be held in both hands and slowly pressed to the breast to make it produce sounds. The sounds were the most delicate and delightful Albert had ever heard. The closer he pressed the violin to his breast the more joyful and tender he felt. The louder the sounds grew the faster the shadows dispersed and the brighter the walls of the hall were lit up by transparent light. But it was necessary to play the violin very warily so as not to break it. He played the glass instrument very carefully and well. He played such things as he felt no one would ever hear again. He was beginning to grow tired when another distant, muffled sound distracted his attention. It was the sound of a bell, but it spoke words: 'Yes,' said the bell, droning somewhere high up and far away, 'he seems to you pitiful, you despise him, yet he is the best and happiest of men! No one will ever again play that instrument.'

These familiar words suddenly seemed so wise, so new, and so true, to Albert that he stopped playing and, trying not to move, raised his arms and eyes to heaven. He felt that he was beautiful and happy. Although there was no one else in the hall he expanded his chest and stood on the platform with head proudly erect so that all might see him. Suddenly someone's hand lightly touched his shoulder; he turned and saw a woman in the faint light. She looked at him sadly and shook her head deprecatingly. He immediately realized that what he was doing was bad, and felt ashamed of himself. 'Whither?' he asked her. She again gave him a long fixed look and sadly inclined her head. It was she – none other than she whom he loved, and her garments were the same; on her full white neck a string of pearls, and her superb arms bare to above the elbow. She took his hand and led him out of the hall. 'The exit is on the other side,' said Albert, but without replying she smiled and led him out. At the threshold of the hall Albert saw the moon and some water. But the water was not below as it usually is, nor was the moon a white circle in one place up above as it usually is. Moon and water were together and everywhere – above, below, at the sides, and all around them both. Albert threw himself with her into the moon and the water, and realized that he could now embrace her, whom he loved more than anything in the world. He embraced her and felt unutterable happiness. 'Is this not a dream?' he asked himself. But no! It was more than reality: it was reality and recollection combined. Then he felt that the unutterable bliss he had at that moment enjoyed had passed and would never return. 'What am I weeping for?' he asked her. She looked at him silently and sadly. Albert understood what she meant by that. 'But how can it be, since I am alive?' he muttered. Without replying or moving she looked straight before her. 'This is terrible! How can I explain to her that I am alive?' he thought with horror. 'O Lord! I am alive, do understand me!' he whispered.

'He is the best and happiest!' a voice was saying. But something was pressing more and more heavily on Albert. Whether it was the moon and the water, her embraces, or his tears, he did not know, but he felt he would not be able to say all that was necessary, and that soon all would be over.

Two visitors, leaving Anna Ivanovna's house, stumbled over Albert, who lay stretched out on the threshold. One of them went back and called the hostess.

'Why, this is inhuman!' he said. 'You might let a man freeze like that!'

'Ah, that Albert! I'm sick to death of him!' replied the hostess. 'Annushka, lay him down somewhere in a room,' she said to the maid.

'But I am alive – why bury me?' muttered Albert, as they carried him insensible into the room.

1858

WHAT MEN LIVE BY

Чем люди живи

'We know that we have passed out of death unto life, because we love the brethren. He that loveth not abideth in death.' – 1 *Epistle St. John* iii. 14.

'Whoso hath the world's goods, and beholdeth his brother in need, and shutteth up his compassion from him, how doth the love of God abide in him? My little children, let us not love in word, neither with the tongue; but in deed and truth.' – iii. 17–18.

'Love is of God; and every one that loveth is begotten of God, and knoweth God. He that loveth not knoweth not God; for God is love.' – iv. 7–8.

'No man hath beheld God at any time; if we love one another, God abideth in us.' – iv. 12.

'God is love; and he that abideth in love abideth in God, and God abideth in him.' – iv. 16.

'If a man say, I love God, and hateth his brother, he is a liar; for he that loveth not his brother whom he hath seen, how can he love God whom he hath not seen?' – iv. 20.

I

A SHOEMAKER named Simon, who had neither house nor land of his own, lived with his wife and children in a peasant's hut and earned his living by his work. Work was cheap but bread was dear, and what he earned he spent for food. The man and his wife had but one sheepskin coat between them for winter wear, and even that was worn to tatters, and this was the second year he had been wanting to buy sheepskins for a new coat. Before winter Simon saved up a little money: a three-ruble note lay hidden in his wife's box, and five rubles and twenty kopeks were owed him by customers in the village.

So one morning he prepared to go to the village to buy the sheepskins. He put on over his shirt his wife's wadded nankeen jacket, and over that he put his own cloth coat. He took the three-ruble note in his pocket, cut himself a stick to serve as a staff, and started off after breakfast. 'I'll collect the five rubles that are due to me,' thought he, 'add the three I have got, and that will be enough to buy sheepskins for the winter coat.'

He came to the village and called at a peasant's hut, but the man was not at home. The peasant's wife promised that the money should be paid next week, but she would not pay it herself. Then Simon called on another peasant, but this one swore he had no money, and would only pay twenty kopeks which he owed for a pair of boots Simon had mended. Simon then tried to buy the sheepskins on credit, but the dealer would not trust him.

'Bring your money,' said he, 'then you may have your pick of the skins. We know what debt-collecting is like.'

So all the business the shoemaker did was to get the twenty kopeks for boots he had mended, and to take a pair of felt boots a peasant gave him to sole with leather.

Simon felt downhearted. He spent the twenty kopeks on vodka, and started homewards without having bought any skins. In the morning he had felt the frost; but now, after drinking the vodka, he felt warm even without a sheepskin coat. He trudged along, striking his stick on the frozen earth with one hand, swinging the felt boots with the other, and talking to himself.

'I'm quite warm,' said he, 'though I have no sheepskin coat. I've had a drop and it runs through all my veins. I need no sheepskins. I go along and don't worry about anything. That's the sort of man I am! What do I care? I can live without sheepskins. I don't need them. My wife will fret, to be sure. And, true enough, it *is* a shame; one works all day long and then does not get paid. Stop a bit! If you don't bring that money along, sure enough I'll skin you, blessed if I don't. How's that? He pays twenty kopeks at a time! What can I do with twenty kopeks? Drink it – that's all one can do! Hard up, he says he is! So he may be – but what about me? You have house, and cattle, and everything; I've only what I stand up in! You have corn of your own growing, I have to buy every grain. Do what I will, I must spend three rubles every week for bread alone. I come home and find the bread all used up and I have to fork out another ruble and a half. So just you pay up what you owe, and no nonsense about it!'

By this time he had nearly reached the shrine at the bend of the road. Looking up, he saw something whitish behind the shrine. The daylight was fading, and the shoemaker peered at the thing without being able to make out what it was. 'There was no white stone here before. Can it be an ox? It's not like an ox. It has a head like a man, but it's too white; and what could a man be doing there?'

He came closer, so that it was clearly visible. To his surprise it really was a man, alive or dead, sitting naked, leaning motionless against the shrine. Terror seized the shoemaker, and he thought, 'Some one has killed him, stripped him, and left him here. If I meddle I shall surely get into trouble.'

So the shoemaker went on. He passed in front of the shrine so that he could not see the man. When he had gone some way he looked back, and saw that the man was no longer leaning against the shrine, but was moving as if looking towards him. The shoemaker felt more frightened than before, and thought, 'Shall I go back to him or shall I go on? If I go near him something dreadful may happen. Who knows who the fellow is? He has not come here for any good. If I go near him he may jump up and throttle me, and there will be no getting away. Or if not, he'd still be a burden on one's hands. What could I do with a naked man? I couldn't give him my last clothes. Heaven only help me to get away!'

So the shoemaker hurried on, leaving the shrine behind him – when suddenly his conscience smote him and he stopped in the road.

'What are you doing, Simon?' said he to himself. 'The man may be dying of want, and you slip past afraid. Have you grown so rich as to be afraid of robbers? Ah, Simon, shame on you!'

So he turned back and went up to the man.

II

SIMON approached the stranger, looked at him, and saw that he was a young man, fit, with no bruises on his body, but evidently freezing and frightened, and he sat there leaning back without looking up at Simon, as if too faint to lift his eyes. Simon went close to him and then the man seemed to wake up. Turning his head, he opened his eyes and looked into Simon's face. That one look was enough to make Simon fond of the man. He threw the felt boots on the ground, undid his sash, laid it on the boots, and took off his cloth coat.

'It's not a time for talking,' said he. 'Come, put this coat on at once!' And Simon took the man by the elbows and helped him to rise. As he stood there, Simon saw that his body was clean and in good condition, his hands and feet shapely, and his face good and kind. He threw his coat over the man's shoulders, but the latter could not find the sleeves. Simon guided his arms into them, and drawing the coat well on, wrapped it closely about him, tying the sash round the man's waist.

Simon even took off his torn cap to put it on the man's head, but then his own head felt cold and he thought: 'I'm quite bald, while he has long curly hair.' So he put his cap on his own head again. 'It will be better to give him something for his feet,' thought he; and he made the man sit down and helped him to put on the felt boots, saying, 'There, friend, now move about and warm yourself. Other matters can be settled later on. Can you walk?'

The man stood up and looked kindly at Simon, but could not say a word.

'Why don't you speak?' said Simon. 'It's too cold to stay here, we must be getting home. There now, take my stick, and if you're feeling weak lean on that. Now step out!'

The man started walking and moved easily, not lagging behind.

As they went along, Simon asked him, 'And where do you belong to?'

'I'm not from these parts.'

'I thought as much. I know the folks hereabouts. But how did you come to be there by the shrine?'

'I cannot tell.'

'Has some one been ill-treating you?'

'No one has ill-treated me. God has punished me.'

'Of course God rules all. Still, you'll have to find food and shelter somewhere. Where do you want to go to?'

'It is all the same to me.'

Simon was amazed. The man did not look like a rogue, and he spoke gently, but yet he gave no account of himself. Still Simon thought, 'Who knows what may have happened?' And he said to the stranger: 'Well then, come home with me and at least warm yourself awhile.'

So Simon walked towards his home, and the stranger kept up with him, walking at his side. The wind had risen and Simon felt it cold under his shirt. He was getting over his tipsiness by now and began to feel the frost. He went along sniffling and wrapping his wife's coat round him, and he thought to himself: 'There now – talk about sheepskins! I went out for sheepskins and come home without even a coat to my back, and what is more, I'm bringing a naked man along with me. Matrena won't be pleased!' And when he thought of his wife he felt sad; but when he looked at the stranger and remembered how he had looked up at him at the shrine, his heart was glad.

III

SIMON's wife had everything ready early that day. She had cut wood, brought water, fed the children, eaten her own meal, and now she sat thinking. She wondered when she ought to make bread: now or tomorrow? There was still a large piece left.

'If Simon has had some dinner in town,' thought she, 'and does not eat much for supper, the bread will last out another day.'

She weighed the piece of bread in her hand again and again, and thought: 'I won't make any more today. We have only enough flour left to bake one batch. We can manage to make this last out till Friday.'

So Matrena put away the bread, and sat down at the table to patch her husband's shirt. While she worked she thought how her husband was buying skins for a winter coat.

'If only the dealer does not cheat him. My good man is much too simple; he cheats nobody, but any child can take him in. Eight rubles is a lot of money – he should get a good coat at that price. Not tanned skins, but still a proper winter coat. How difficult it was last winter to get on without a warm coat. I could neither get down to the river, nor go out anywhere. When he went out he put on all we had, and there was nothing left for me. He did not start very early today, but still it's time he was back. I only hope he has not gone on the spree!'

Hardly had Matrena thought this than steps were heard on the threshold and some one entered. Matrena stuck her needle into her work and went out into the passage. There she saw two men: Simon, and with him a man without a hat and wearing felt boots.

Matrena noticed at once that her husband smelt of spirits. 'There now, he has been drinking,' thought she. And when she saw that he was coatless, had only her jacket on, brought no parcel, stood there silent, and seemed ashamed, her heart was ready to break with disappointment. 'He has drunk the money,' thought she, 'and has been on the spree with some good-for-nothing fellow whom he has brought home with him.'

Matrena let them pass into the hut, followed them in, and saw that the stranger was a young, slight man, wearing her husband's coat. There was no shirt to be seen under it, and he had no hat. Having entered, he stood neither moving nor raising his eyes, and Matrena thought: 'He must be a bad man – he's afraid.'

Matrena frowned, and stood beside the stove looking to see what they would do.

Simon took off his cap and sat down on the bench as if things were all right.

'Come, Matrena; if supper is ready, let us have some.'

Matrena muttered something to herself and did not move, but stayed where she was, by the stove. She looked first at the one and then at the other of them and only shook her head. Simon saw that his wife was annoyed, but tried to pass it off. Pretending not to notice anything, he took the stranger by the arm.

'Sit down, friend,' said he, 'and let us have some supper.'

The stranger sat down on the bench.

'Haven't you cooked anything for us?' said Simon.

Matrena's anger boiled over. 'I've cooked, but not for you. It seems to me you have drunk your wits away. You went to buy a sheepskin coat, but come home without so much as the coat you had on, and bring a naked vagabond home with you. I have no supper for drunkards like you.'

'That's enough, Matrena. Don't wag your tongue without reason! You had better ask what sort of man —'

'And you tell me what you've done with the money?'

Simon found the pocket of the jacket, drew out the three-ruble note, and unfolded it.

'Here is the money. Trifonov did not pay, but promises to pay soon.'

Matrena got still more angry; he had bought no sheepskins, but had put his only coat on some naked fellow and had even brought him to their house.

She snatched up the note from the table, took it to put away in safety, and said: 'I have no supper for you. We can't feed all the naked drunkards in the world.'

'There now, Matrena, hold your tongue a bit. First hear what a man has to say —!'

'Much wisdom I shall hear from a drunken fool. I was right in not wanting to marry you – a drunkard. The linen my mother gave me you drank; and now you've been to buy a coat – and have drunk it too!'

Simon tried to explain to his wife that he had only spent twenty kopeks; tried to tell how he had found the man – but Matrena would not let him get a word in. She talked nineteen to the dozen, and dragged in things that had happened ten years before.

Matrena talked and talked, and at last she flew at Simon and seized him by the sleeve.

'Give me my jacket. It is the only one I have, and you must needs take it from me and wear it yourself. Give it here, you mangy dog, and may the devil take you.'

Simon began to pull off the jacket, and turned a sleeve of it inside out; Matrena seized the jacket and it burst its seams. She snatched it up, threw it over her head and went to the door. She meant to go out, but stopped undecided – she wanted to work off her anger, but she also wanted to learn what sort of a man the stranger was.

IV

MATRENA stopped and said: 'If he were a good man he would not be naked. Why, he hasn't even a shirt on him. If he were all right, you would say where you came across the fellow.'

'That's just what I am trying to tell you,' said Simon. 'As I came to the shrine I saw him sitting all naked and frozen. It isn't quite the weather to sit about naked! God sent me to him or he would have perished. What was I to do? How do we know what may have happened to him? So I took him, clothed him, and brought him along. Don't be so angry, Matrena. It is a sin. Remember, we must all die one day.'

Angry words rose to Matrena's lips, but she looked at the stranger and was silent. He sat on the edge of the bench, motionless, his hands folded on his knees, his head drooping on his breast, his eyes closed, and his brows knit as if in pain. Matrena was silent, and Simon said: 'Matrena, have you no love of God?'

Matrena heard these words, and as she looked at the stranger, suddenly her heart softened towards him. She came back from the door, and going to the stove she got out the supper. Setting a cup on the table, she poured out some *kvas*. Then she brought out the last piece of bread and set out a knife and spoons.

'Eat, if you want to,' said she.

Simon drew the stranger to the table.

'Take your place, young man,' said he.

Simon cut the bread, crumbled it into the broth, and they began to eat. Matrena sat at the corner of the table, resting her head on her hand and looking at the stranger.

And Matrena was touched with pity for the stranger and began to feel fond of him. And at once the stranger's face lit up; his brows were no longer bent, he raised his eyes and smiled at Matrena.

When they had finished supper, the woman cleared away the things and began questioning the stranger. 'Where are you from?' said she.

'I am not from these parts.'

'But how did you come to be on the road?'

'I may not tell.'

'Did some one rob you?'

'God punished me.'

'And you were lying there naked?'

'Yes, naked and freezing. Simon saw me and had pity on me. He took off his coat, put it on me, and brought me here. And you have fed me, given me drink, and shown pity on me. God will reward you!'

Matrena rose, took from the window Simon's old shirt she had been patching, and gave it to the stranger. She also brought out a pair of trousers for him.

'There,' said she, 'I see you have no shirt. Put this on, and lie down where you please, in the loft or on the stove.'

The stranger took off the coat, put on the shirt, and lay down in the loft. Matrena put out the candle, took the coat, and climbed to where her husband lay on the stove.

Matrena drew the skirts of the coat over her and lay down but could not sleep; she could not get the stranger out of her mind.

When she remembered that he had eaten their last piece of bread and that there was none for tomorrow, and thought of the shirt and trousers she had given away, she felt grieved; but when she remembered how he had smiled, her heart was glad.

Long did Matrena lie awake, and she noticed that Simon also was awake – he drew the coat towards him.

'Simon!'

'Well?'

'You have had the last of the bread and I have not put any to rise. I don't know what we shall do tomorrow. Perhaps I can borrow some of neighbour Martha.'

'If we're alive we shall find something to eat.'

The woman lay still awhile, and then said, 'He seems a good man, but why does he not tell us who he is?'

'I suppose he has his reasons.'

'Simon!'

'Well?'

'We give; but why does nobody give us anything?'

Simon did not know what to say; so he only said, 'Let us stop talking,' and turned over and went to sleep.

V

In the morning Simon awoke. The children were still asleep; his wife had gone to the neighbour's to borrow some bread. The stranger alone was sitting on the bench, dressed in the old shirt and trousers, and looking upwards. His face was brighter than it had been the day before.

Simon said to him, 'Well, friend; the belly wants bread and the naked body clothes. One has to work for a living. What work do you know?'

'I do not know any.'

This surprised Simon, but he said, 'Men who want to learn can learn anything.'

'Men work and I will work also.'

'What is your name?'

'Michael.'

'Well, Michael, if you don't wish to talk about yourself, that is your own affair; but you'll have to earn a living for yourself. If you will work as I tell you, I will give you food and shelter.'

'May God reward you! I will learn. Show me what to do.'

Simon took yarn, put it round his thumb and began to twist it.

'It is easy enough – see!'

Michael watched him, put some yarn round his own thumb in the same way, caught the knack, and twisted the yarn also.

Then Simon showed him how to wax the thread. This also Michael mastered. Next Simon showed him how to twist the bristle in, and how to sew, and this, too, Michael learned at once.

Whatever Simon showed him he understood at once, and after three days he worked as if he had sewn boots all his life. He worked without stopping and ate little. When work was over he sat silently, looking upwards. He hardly went into the street, spoke only when necessary, and neither joked nor laughed. They never saw him smile, except that first evening when Matrena gave them supper.

VI

DAY by day and week by week the year went round. Michael lived and worked with Simon. His fame spread till people said that no one sewed boots so neatly and strongly as Simon's workman, Michael; from all the district round people came to Simon for their boots, and he began to be well off.

One winter day, as Simon and Michael sat working, a carriage on sledge-runners, with three horses and with bells, drove up to the hut. They looked out of the window; the carriage stopped at their door, a fine servant jumped down from the box and opened the door. A gentleman in a fur coat got out and walked up to Simon's hut. Up jumped Matrena and opened the door wide. The gentleman stooped to enter the hut, and when he drew himself up again his head nearly reached the ceiling and he seemed quite to fill his end of the room.

Simon rose, bowed, and looked at the gentleman with astonishment. He had never seen any one like him. Simon himself was lean, Michael was thin, and Matrena was dry as a bone, but this man was like some one from another world: red-faced, burly, with a neck like a bull's, and looking altogether as if he were cast in iron.

The gentleman puffed, threw off his fur coat, sat down on the bench, and said, 'Which of you is the master bootmaker?'

'I am, your Excellency,' said Simon, coming forward.

Then the gentleman shouted to his lad, 'Hey, Fedka, bring the leather!'

The servant ran in, bringing a parcel. The gentleman took the parcel and put it on the table.

'Untie it,' said he. The lad untied it.

The gentleman pointed to the leather.

'Look here, shoemaker,' said he, 'do you see this leather?'

'Yes, your honour.'

'But do you know what sort of leather it is?'

Simon felt the leather and said, 'It is good leather.'

'Good, indeed! Why, you fool, you never saw such leather before in your life. It's German, and cost twenty rubles.'

Simon was frightened, and said, 'Where should I ever see leather like that?'

'Just so! Now, can you make it into boots for me?'

'Yes, your Excellency, I can.'

Then the gentleman shouted at him: 'You *can*, can you? Well, remember whom you are to make them for, and what the leather is. You must make me boots that will wear for a year, neither losing shape nor coming unsewn. If you can do it, take the leather and cut it up; but if you can't, say so. I warn you now, if your boots come unsewn or lose shape within a year I will have you put in prison. If they don't burst or lose shape for a year, I will pay you ten rubles for your work.'

Simon was frightened and did not know what to say. He glanced at Michael and nudging him with his elbow, whispered: 'Shall I take the work?'

Michael nodded his head as if to say, 'Yes, take it.'

Simon did as Michael advised and undertook to make boots that would not lose shape or split for a whole year.

Calling his servant, the gentleman told him to pull the boot off his left leg, which he stretched out.

'Take my measure!' said he.

Simon stitched a paper measure seventeen inches long, smoothed it out, knelt down, wiped his hands well on his apron so as not to soil the gentleman's sock, and began to measure. He measured the sole, and round the instep, and began to measure the calf of the leg, but the paper was too short. The calf of the leg was as thick as a beam.

'Mind you don't make it too tight in the leg.'

Simon stitched on another strip of paper. The gentleman twitched his toes about in his sock looking round at those in the hut, and as he did so he noticed Michael.

'Whom have you there?' asked he.

'That is my workman. He will sew the boots.'

'Mind,' said the gentleman to Michael, 'remember to make them so that they will last me a year.'

Simon also looked at Michael, and saw that Michael was not looking at the gentleman, but was gazing into the corner behind the gentleman, as if he saw some one there. Michael looked and looked, and suddenly he smiled, and his face became brighter.

'What are you grinning at, you fool?' thundered the gentleman. 'You had better look to it that the boots are ready in time.'

'They shall be ready in good time,' said Michael.

'Mind it is so,' said the gentleman, and he put on his boots and his fur coat, wrapped the latter round him, and went to the door. But he forgot to stoop, and struck his head against the lintel.

He swore and rubbed his head. Then he took his seat in the carriage and drove away.

When he had gone, Simon said: 'There's a figure of a man for you! You could not kill him with a mallet. He almost knocked out the lintel, but little harm it did him.'

And Matrena said: 'Living as he does, how should he not grow strong? Death itself can't touch such a rock as that.'

VII

THEN Simon said to Michael: 'Well, we have taken the work, but we must see we don't get into trouble over it. The leather is dear, and the gentleman hot-tempered. We must make no mistakes. Come, your eye is truer and your hands have become nimbler than mine, so you take this measure and cut out the boots. I will finish off the sewing of the vamps.'

Michael did as he was told. He took the leather, spread it out on the table, folded it in two, took a knife and began to cut out.

Matrena came and watched him cutting, and was surprised to see how he was doing it. Matrena was accustomed to seeing boots made, and she looked and saw that Michael was not cutting the leather for boots, but was cutting it round.

She wished to say something, but she thought to herself: 'Perhaps I do not understand how gentlemen's boots should be made. I suppose Michael knows more about it – and I won't interfere.'

When Michael had cut up the leather he took a thread and began to sew not with two ends, as boots are sewn, but with a single end, as for soft slippers.

Again Matrena wondered, but again she did not interfere. Michael sewed on steadily till noon. Then Simon rose for dinner, looked around, and saw that Michael had made slippers out of the gentleman's leather.

'Ah!' groaned Simon, and he thought, 'How is it that Michael, who has been with me a whole year and never made a mistake before, should do such a dreadful thing? The gentleman ordered high boots, welted, with whole fronts, and Michael has made soft slippers with single soles, and has wasted the leather. What am I to say to the gentleman? I can never replace leather such as this.'

And he said to Michael, 'What are you doing, friend? You have ruined me! You know the gentleman ordered high boots, but see what you have made!'

Hardly had he begun to rebuke Michael, when 'rat-tat' went the iron ring that hung at the door. Some one was knocking. They looked out of the window; a man had come on horseback and was fastening his horse. They opened the door, and the servant who had been with the gentleman came in.

'Good day,' said he.

'Good day,' replied Simon. 'What can we do for you?'

'My mistress has sent me about the boots.'

'What about the boots?'

'Why, my master no longer needs them. He is dead.'

'Is it possible?'

'He did not live to get home after leaving you, but died in the carriage. When we reached home and the servants came to help him alight, he rolled over like a sack. He was dead already, and so stiff that he could hardly be got out of the carriage. My mistress sent me here, saying: "Tell the bootmaker that the gentleman who ordered boots of him and left the leather for them no longer needs the boots, but that he must quickly make soft slippers for the corpse. Wait till they are ready and bring them back with you." That is why I have come.'

Michael gathered up the remnants of the leather; rolled them up, took the soft slippers he had made, slapped them together, wiped them down with his apron, and handed them and the roll of leather to the servant, who took them and said: 'Goodbye, masters, and good day to you!'

VIII

ANOTHER year passed, and another, and Michael was now living his sixth year with Simon. He lived as before. He went nowhere, only spoke when necessary, and had only smiled twice in all those years – once when Matrena gave him food, and a second time when the gentleman was in their hut. Simon was more than pleased with his workman. He never now asked him where he came from, and only feared lest Michael should go away.

They were all at home one day. Matrena was putting iron pots in the oven; the children were running along the benches and looking out of the window; Simon was sewing at one window and Michael was fastening on a heel at the other.

One of the boys ran along the bench to Michael, leant on his shoulder, and looked out of the window.

'Look, Uncle Michael! There is a lady with little girls! She seems to be coming here. And one of the girls is lame.'

When the boy said that, Michael dropped his work, turned to the window, and looked out into the street.

Simon was surprised. Michael never used to look out into the street, but now he pressed against the window, staring at something. Simon also looked out and saw that a well-dressed woman was really coming to his hut, leading by the hand two little girls in fur coats and woollen shawls. The girls could hardly be told one from the other, except that one of them was crippled in her left leg and walked with a limp.

The woman stepped into the porch and entered the passage. Feeling about for the entrance she found the latch, which she lifted and opened the door. She let the two girls go in first, and followed them into the hut.

'Good day, good folk!'

'Pray come in,' said Simon. 'What can we do for you?'

The woman sat down by the table. The two little girls pressed close to her knees, afraid of the people in the hut.

'I want leather shoes made for these two little girls, for spring.'

'We can do that. We never have made such small shoes, but we can make them; either welted or turnover shoes, linen-lined. My man, Michael, is a master at the work.'

Simon glanced at Michael and saw that he had left his work and was sitting with his eyes fixed on the little girls. Simon was surprised. It was true the girls were pretty, with black eyes, plump, and rosy-cheeked, and they wore nice kerchiefs and fur coats, but still Simon could not understand why Michael should look at them like that – just as if he had known them before. He was puzzled, but went on talking with the woman and arranging the price. Having fixed it, he prepared the measure. The woman lifted the lame girl on to her lap and said: 'Take two measures from this little girl. Make one shoe for the lame foot and three for the sound one. They both have the same-sized feet. They are twins.'

Simon took the measure and, speaking of the lame girl, said: 'How did it happen to her? She is such a pretty girl. Was she born so?'

'No, her mother crushed her leg.'

Then Matrena joined in. She wondered who this woman was and whose the children were, so she said: 'Are not you their mother, then?'

'No, my good woman; I am neither their mother nor any relation to them. They were quite strangers to me, but I adopted them.'

'They are not your children and yet you are so fond of them?'

'How can I help being fond of them? I fed them both at my own breasts. I had a child of my own, but God took him. I was not so fond of him as I now am of these.'

'Then whose children are they?'

IX

THE woman, having begun talking, told them the whole story.

'It is about six years since their parents died, both in one week: their father was buried on the Tuesday, and their mother died on the Friday. These orphans were born three days after their father's death, and their mother did not live another day. My husband and I were then living as peasants in the village. We were neighbours of theirs, our yard being next to theirs. Their father was a lonely man, a wood-cutter in the forest. When felling trees one day they let one fall on him. It fell across his body and crushed his bowels out. They hardly got him home before his soul went to God; and that same week his wife gave birth to twins – these little girls. She was poor and alone; she had no one, young or old, with her. Alone she gave them birth, and alone she met her death.

'The next morning I went to see her, but when I entered the hut, she, poor thing, was already stark and cold. In dying she had rolled on to this child and crushed her leg. The village folk came to the hut, washed the body, laid her out, made a coffin, and buried her. They were good folk. The babies were left alone. What was to be done with them? I was the only woman there who had a baby at the time. I was nursing my first-born – eight weeks old. So I took them for a time.

The peasants came together, and thought and thought what to do with them; and at last they said to me: "For the present, Mary, you had better keep the girls, and later on we will arrange what to do for them." So I nursed the sound one at my breast, but at first I did not feed this crippled one. I did not suppose she would live. But then I thought to myself, why should the poor innocent suffer? I pitied her and began to feed her. And so I fed my own boy and these two – the three of them – at my own breast. I was young and strong and had good food, and God gave me so much milk that at times it even overflowed. I used sometimes to feed two at a time, while the third was waiting. When one had had enough I nursed the third. And God so ordered it that these grew up, while my own was buried before he was two years old. And I had no more children, though we prospered. Now my husband is working for the corn merchant at the mill. The pay is good and we are well off. But I have no children of my own, and how lonely I should be without these little girls! How can I help loving them! They are the joy of my life!'

She pressed the lame little girl to her with one hand, while with the other she wiped the tears from her cheeks.

And Matrena sighed, and said: 'The proverb is true that says, "One may live without father or mother, but one cannot live without God."'

So they talked together, when suddenly the whole hut was lighted up as though by summer lightning from the corner where Michael sat. They all looked towards him and saw him sitting, his hands folded on his knees, gazing upwards and smiling.

X

THE woman went away with the girls. Michael rose from the bench, put down his work, and took off his apron. Then, bowing low to Simon and his wife, he said: 'Farewell, masters. God has forgiven me. I ask your forgiveness, too, for anything done amiss.'

And they saw that a light shone from Michael. And Simon rose, bowed down to Michael, and said: 'I see, Michael, that you are no common man, and I can neither keep you nor question you. Only tell me this: how is it that when I found you and brought you home, you were gloomy, and when my wife gave you food you smiled at her and became brighter? Then when the gentleman came to order the boots, you smiled again and became brighter still? And now, when this woman brought the little girls, you smiled a third time and have become as bright as day? Tell me, Michael, why does your face shine so, and why did you smile those three times?'

And Michael answered: 'Light shines from me because I have been punished, but now God has pardoned me. And I smiled three times, because God sent me to learn three truths, and I have learnt them. One I learnt when your wife pitied me, and that is why I smiled the first time. The second I learnt when the rich man ordered the boots, and then I smiled again. And now, when I saw those little girls, I learnt the third and last truth, and I smiled the third time.'

And Simon said, 'Tell me, Michael, what did God punish you for? and what were the three truths? that I, too, may know them.'

And Michael answered: 'God punished me for disobeying Him. I was an angel in heaven and disobeyed God. God sent me to fetch a woman's soul. I flew to earth, and saw a sick woman lying alone who had just given birth to twin girls. They moved feebly at their mother's side but she could not lift them to her breast. When she saw me, she understood that God had sent me for her soul, and she wept and said: "Angel of God! My husband has just been buried, killed by a falling tree. I have neither sister, nor aunt, nor mother: no one to care for my orphans. Do not take my soul! Let me nurse my babes, feed them, and set them on their feet before I die. Children cannot live without father or mother." And I hearkened to her. I placed one child at her breast and gave the other into her arms, and returned to the Lord in heaven. I flew to the Lord, and said: "I could not take the soul of the mother. Her husband was killed by a tree; the woman has twins and prays that her soul may not be taken." She says: "Let me nurse and feed my children, and set them on their feet. Children cannot live without father or mother." I have not taken her soul." And God said: "Go – take the mother's soul, and learn three truths: Learn *What dwells in man*, *What is not given to man*, and *What men live by*. When thou hast learnt these things, thou shalt return to heaven." So I flew again to earth and took the mother's soul. The babes dropped from her breasts. Her body rolled over on the bed and crushed one babe, twisting its leg. I rose above the village, wishing to take her soul to God, but a wind seized me and my wings drooped and dropped off. Her soul rose alone to God, while I fell to earth by the roadside.'

XI

AND Simon and Matrena understood who it was that had lived with them, and whom they had clothed and fed. And they wept with awe and with joy. And the angel said: 'I was alone in the field, naked. I had never known human needs, cold and hunger, till I became a man. I was famished, frozen, and did not know what to do. I saw, near the field I was in, a shrine built for God, and I went to it hoping to find shelter. But the shrine was locked and I could not enter. So I sat down behind the shrine to shelter myself at least from the wind. Evening drew on, I was hungry, frozen, and in pain. Suddenly I heard a man coming along the road. He carried a pair of boots and was talking to himself. For the first time since I became a man I saw the mortal face of a man, and his face seemed terrible to me and I turned from it. And I heard the man talking to himself of how to cover his body from the cold in winter, and how to feed wife and children. And I thought: "I am perishing of cold and hunger and here is a man thinking only of how to clothe himself and his wife, and how to get bread for themselves. He cannot help me. When the man saw me he frowned and became still more terrible, and passed me by on the other side. I despaired; but suddenly I heard him coming back. I looked up and did not recognize the same man: before, I had seen death in his face; but now he was alive and I recognized in him the presence of God. He came up to me, clothed me, took me with him, and brought me to his home. I entered the house; a woman came to meet us and began to speak. The woman was still more terrible than the man had been; the spirit of death came from her mouth; I could not breathe for the stench of death that spread around her. She wished to drive me out into the cold, and I knew that if she did so she would die. Suddenly her husband spoke to her of God, and the woman changed at once. And when she brought me food and looked at me, I glanced at her and saw that death no longer dwelt in her; she had become alive, and in her too I saw God.

'Then I remembered the first lesson God had set me: "*Learn what dwells in man.*" And I understood that in man dwells Love! I was glad that God had already begun to show me what He had promised, and I smiled for the first time. But I had not yet learnt all. I did not yet know *What is not given to man*, and *What men live by*.

'I lived with you and a year passed. A man came to order boots that should wear for a year without losing shape or cracking. I looked at him, and suddenly, behind his shoulder, I saw my comrade – the angel of death. None but me saw that angel; but I knew him, and knew that before the sun set he would take that rich man's soul. And I thought to myself, "The man is making preparations for a year and does not know that he will die before evening." And I remembered God's second saying, "*Learn what is not given to man.*"

'What dwells in man I already knew. Now I learnt what is not given him. It is not given to man to know his own needs. And I smiled for the second time. I was glad to have seen my comrade angel – glad also that God had revealed to me the second saying.

'But I still did not know all. I did not know *What men live by*. And I lived on, waiting till God should reveal to me the last lesson. In the sixth year came the girl-twins with the woman; and I recognized the girls and heard how they had been kept alive. Having heard the story, I thought, "Their mother besought me for the children's sake, and I believed her when she said that children cannot live without father or mother; but a stranger has nursed them, and has brought them up." And when the woman showed her love for the children that were not her own, and wept over them, I saw in her the living God, and understood *What men live by*. And I knew that God had revealed to me the last lesson, and had forgiven my sin. And then I smiled for the third time.'

XII

AND the angel's body was bared, and he was clothed in light so that eye could not look on him; and his voice grew louder, as though it came not from him but from heaven above. And the angel said:

'I have learnt that all men live not by care for themselves, but by love.

'It was not given to the mother to know what her children needed for their life. Nor was it given to the rich man to know what he himself needed. Nor is it given to any man to know whether, when evening comes, he will need boots for his body or slippers for his corpse.

'I remained alive when I was a man, not by care of myself but because love was present in a passer-by, and because he and his wife pitied and loved me. The orphans remained alive not because of their mother's care, but because there was love in the heart of a woman, a stranger to them, who pitied and loved them. And all men live not by the thought they spend on their own welfare, but because love exists in man.

'I knew before that God gave life to men and desires that they should live; now I understood more than that.

'I understood that God does not wish men to live apart, and therefore he does not reveal to them what each one needs for himself; but he wishes them to live united, and therefore reveals to each of them what is necessary for all.

'I have now understood that though it seems to men that they live by care for themselves, in truth it is love alone by which they live. He who has love, is in God, and God is in him, for God is love.'

And the angel sang praise to God, so that the hut trembled at his voice. The roof opened, and a column of fire rose from earth to heaven. Simon and his wife and children fell to the ground. Wings appeared upon the angel's shoulders and he rose into the heavens.

And when Simon came to himself the hut stood as before, and there was no one in it but his own family.

1881

MASTER AND MAN

Хозяин и человек

I

It happened in the seventies in winter, on the day after St. Nicholas's Day. There was a fête in the parish and the innkeeper, Vasili Andreevich Brekhunov, a Second Guild merchant, being a church elder had to go to church, and had also to entertain his relatives and friends at home.

But when the last of them had gone he at once began to prepare to drive over to see a neighbouring proprietor about a grove which he had been bargaining over for a long time. He was now in a hurry to start, lest buyers from the town might forestall him in making a profitable purchase.

The youthful landowner was asking ten thousand rubles for the grove simply because Vasili Andreevich was offering seven thousand. Seven thousand was, however, only a third of its real value. Vasili Andreevich might perhaps have got it down to his own price, for the woods were in his district and he had a long-standing agreement with the other village dealers that no one should run up the price in another's district, but he had now learnt that some timber-dealers from town meant to bid for the Goryachkin grove, and he resolved to go at once and get the matter settled. So as soon as the feast was over, he took seven hundred rubles from his strong box, added to them two thousand three hundred rubles of church money he had in his keeping, so as to make up the sum to three thousand; carefully counted the notes, and having put them into his pocket-book made haste to start.

Nikita, the only one of Vasili Andreevich's labourers who was not drunk that day, ran to harness the horse. Nikita, though an habitual drunkard, was not drunk that day because since the last day before the fast, when he had drunk his coat and leather boots, he had sworn off drink and had kept his vow for two months, and was still keeping it despite the temptation of the vodka that had been drunk every-where during the first two days of the feast.

Nikita was a peasant of about fifty from a neighbouring village, 'not a manager' as the peasants said of him, meaning that he was not the thrifty head of a household but lived most of his time away from home as a labourer. He was valued everywhere for his industry, dexterity, and strength at work, and still more for his kindly and pleasant temper. But he never settled down anywhere for long because about twice a year, or even oftener, he had a drinking bout, and then besides spending all his clothes on drink he became turbulent and quarrelsome. Vasili Andreevich himself had turned him away several times, but had afterwards taken him back again – valuing his honesty, his kindness to animals, and especially his cheapness. Vasili Andreevich did not pay Nikita the eighty rubles a year such a man was worth, but only about forty, which he gave him haphazard, in small sums, and even that mostly not in cash but in goods from his own shop and at high prices.

Nikita's wife Martha, who had once been a handsome vigorous woman, managed the homestead with the help of her son and two daughters, and did not urge Nikita to live at home: first because she had been living for some twenty years already with a cooper, a peasant from another village who lodged in their house; and secondly because though she managed her husband as she pleased when he was sober, she feared him like fire when he was drunk. Once when he had got drunk at home, Nikita, probably to make up for his submissive-ness when sober, broke open her box, took out her best clothes, snatched up an axe, and chopped all her under-garments and dresses to bits. All the wages Nikita earned went to his wife, and he raised no objection to that. So now, two days before the holiday, Martha had been twice to see Vasili Andreevich and had got from him wheat flour, tea, sugar, and a quart of vodka, the lot costing three rubles, and also five rubles in cash, for which she thanked him as for a special favour though he owed Nikita at least twenty rubles.

'What agreement did we ever draw up with you?' said Vasili Andreevich to Nikita. 'If you need anything, take it; you will work it off. I'm not like others to keep you waiting, and making up accounts and reckoning fines. We deal straightforwardly. You serve me and I don't neglect you.'

And when saying this Vasili Andreevich was honestly convinced that he was Nikita's benefactor, and he knew how to put it so plausibly that all those who depended on him for their money, beginning with Nikita, confirmed him in the conviction that he was their benefactor and did not overreach them.

'Yes, I understand, Vasili Andreevich. You know that I serve you and take as much pains as I would for my own father. I understand very well!' Nikita would reply. He was quite aware that Vasili Andreevich was cheating him, but at the same time he felt that it was useless to try to clear up his accounts with him or explain his side of the matter, and that as long as he had nowhere else to go he must accept what he could get.

Now, having heard his master's order to harness, he went as usual cheerfully and willingly to the shed, stepping briskly and easily on his rather turned-in feet; took down from a nail the heavy tasselled leather bridle, and jingling the rings of the bit went to the closed stable where the horse he was to harness was standing by himself.

'What, feeling lonely, feeling lonely, little silly?' said Nikita in answer to the low whinny with which he was greeted by the good-tempered, medium-sized bay stallion, with a rather slanting crupper, who stood alone in the shed. 'Now then, now then, there's time enough. Let me water you first,' he went on, speaking to the horse just as to someone who understood the words he was using, and having whisked the dusty grooved back of the well-fed young stallion with the skirt of his coat, he put a bridle on his handsome head, straightened his ears and forelock, and having taken off his halter led him out to water.

Picking his way out of the dung-strewn stable, Mukhorty frisked, and making play with his hind leg pretended that he meant to kick Nikita, who was running at a trot beside him to the pump.

'Now then, now then, you rascal!' Nikita called out, well knowing how carefully Mukhorty threw out his hind leg just to touch his greasy sheepskin coat but not to strike him – a trick Nikita much appreciated.

After a drink of the cold water the horse sighed, moving his strong wet lips, from the hairs of which transparent drops fell into the trough; then standing still as if in thought, he suddenly gave a loud snort.

'If you don't want any more, you needn't. But don't go asking for any later,' said Nikita quite seriously and fully explaining his conduct to Mukhorty. Then he ran back to the shed pulling the playful young horse, who wanted to gambol all over the yard, by the rein.

There was no one else in the yard except a stranger, the cook's husband, who had come for the holiday.

'Go and ask which sledge is to be harnessed – the wide one or the small one – there's a good fellow!'

The cook's husband went into the house, which stood on an iron foundation and was iron-roofed, and soon returned saying that the little one was to be harnessed. By that time Nikita had put the collar and brass-studded belly-band on Mukhorty and, carrying a light, painted shaft-bow in one hand, was leading the horse with the other up to two sledges that stood in the shed.

'All right, let it be the little one!' he said, backing the intelligent horse, which all the time kept pretending to bite him, into the shafts, and with the aid of the cook's husband he proceeded to harness. When everything was nearly ready and only the reins had to be adjusted, Nikita sent the other man to the shed for some straw and to the barn for a drugget.

'There, that's all right! Now, now, don't bristle up!' said Nikita, pressing down into the sledge the freshly threshed oat straw the cook's husband had brought. 'And now let's spread the sacking like this, and the drugget over it. There, like that it will be comfortable sitting,' he went on, suiting the action to the words and tucking the drugget all round over the straw to make a seat.

'Thank you, mate. Things always go quicker with two working at it!' he added. And gathering up the leather reins fastened together by a brass ring, Nikita took the driver's seat and started the impatient horse over the frozen manure which lay in the yard, towards the gate.

'Uncle Nikita! I say, Uncle, Uncle!' a high-pitched voice shouted, and a seven-year-old boy in a black sheepskin coat, new white felt boots, and a warm cap, ran hurriedly out of the house into the yard. 'Take me with you!' he cried, fastening up his coat as he ran.

'All right, come along, son!' said Nikita, and stopping the sledge he picked up the master's pale thin little son, radiant with joy, and drove out into the road.

It was past two o'clock and the day was windy, dull, and cold, with more than twenty degrees Fahrenheit of frost. Half the sky was hidden by a lowering dark cloud. In the yard it was quiet, but in the street the wind was felt more keenly. The snow swept down from a neighbouring shed and whirled about in the corner near the bath-house.

Hardly had Nikita driven out of the yard and turned the horse's head to the house, before Vasili Andreevich emerged from the high porch in front of the house with a cigarette in his mouth and wearing a cloth-covered sheepskin coat tightly girdled low at his waist, and stepped onto the hard-trodden snow which squeaked under the leather soles of his felt boots, and stopped. Taking a last whiff of his cigarette he threw it down, stepped on it, and letting the smoke escape through his moustache and looking askance at the horse that was coming up, began to tuck in his sheepskin collar on both sides of his ruddy face, clean-shaven except for the moustache, so that his breath should not moisten the collar.

'See now! The young scamp is there already!' he exclaimed when he saw his little son in the sledge. Vasili Andreevich was excited by the vodka he had drunk with his visitors, and so he was even more pleased than usual with everything that was his and all that he did. The sight of his son, whom he always thought of as his heir, now gave him great satisfaction. He looked at him, screwing up his eyes and showing his long teeth.

His wife – pregnant, thin and pale, with her head and shoulders wrapped in a shawl so that nothing of her face could be seen but her eyes – stood behind him in the vestibule to see him off.

'Now really, you ought to take Nikita with you,' she said timidly, stepping out from the doorway.

Vasili Andreevich did not answer. Her words evidently annoyed him and he frowned angrily and spat.

'You have money on you,' she continued in the same plaintive voice. 'What if the weather gets worse! Do take him, for goodness' sake!'

'Why? Don't I know the road that I must needs take a guide?' exclaimed Vasili Andreevich, uttering every word very distinctly and compressing his lips unnaturally, as he usually did when speaking to buyers and sellers.

'Really you ought to take him. I beg you in God's name!' his wife repeated, wrapping her shawl more closely round her head.

'There, she sticks to it like a leech! . . . Where am I to take him?'

'I'm quite ready to go with you, Vasili Andreevich,' said Nikita cheerfully. 'But they must feed the horses while I am away,' he added, turning to his master's wife.

'I'll look after them, Nikita dear. I'll tell Simon,' replied the mistress.

'Well, Vasili Andreevich, am I to come with you?' said Nikita, awaiting a decision.

'It seems I must humour my old woman. But if you're coming you'd better put on a warmer cloak,' said Vasili Andreevich, smiling again as he winked at Nikita's short sheepskin coat, which was torn under the arms and at the back, was greasy and out of shape, frayed to a fringe round the skirt, and had endured many things in its lifetime.

'Hey, mate, come and hold the horse!' shouted Nikita to the cook's husband, who was still in the yard.

'No, I will myself, I will myself!' shrieked the little boy, pulling his hands, red with cold, out of his pockets, and seizing the cold leather reins.

'Only don't be too long dressing yourself up. Look alive!' shouted Vasili Andreevich, grinning at Nikita.

'Only a moment, father, Vasili Andreevich!' replied Nikita, and running quickly with his inturned toes in his felt boots with their soles patched with felt, he hurried across the yard and into the workmen's hut.

'Arinushka! Get my coat down from the stove. I'm going with the master,' he said, as he ran into the hut and took down his girdle from the nail on which it hung.

The workmen's cook, who had had a sleep after dinner and was now getting the samovar ready for her husband, turned cheerfully to Nikita, and infected by his hurry began to move as quickly as he did, got down his miserable worn-out cloth coat from the stove where it was drying, and began hurriedly shaking it out and smoothing it down.

'There now, you'll have a chance of a holiday with your goodman,' said Nikita, who from kindhearted politeness always said something to anyone he was alone with.

Then, drawing his worn narrow girdle round him, he drew in his breath, pulling in his lean stomach still more, and girdled himself as tightly as he could over his sheepskin.

'There now,' he said, addressing himself no longer to the cook but the girdle, as he tucked the ends in at the waist, 'now you won't come undone!' And working his shoulders up and down to free his arms, he put the coat over his sheepskin, arched his back more strongly to ease his arms, poked himself under the armpits, and took down his leather-covered mittens from the shelf. 'Now we're all right!'

'You ought to wrap your feet up, Nikita. Your boots are very bad.'
Nikita stopped as if he had suddenly realized this.

'Yes, I ought to. . . . But they'll do like this. It isn't far!' and he
ran out into the yard.

'Won't you be cold, Nikita?' said the mistress as he came up to
the sledge.

'Cold? No, I'm quite warm,' answered Nikita as he pushed some
straw up to the forepart of the sledge so that it should cover his feet,
and stowed away the whip, which the good horse would not need,
at the bottom of the sledge.

Vasili Andreevich, who was wearing two fur-lined coats one over
the other, was already in the sledge, his broad back filling nearly its
whole rounded width, and taking the reins he immediately touched
the horse. Nikita jumped in just as the sledge started, and seated
himself in front on the left side, with one leg hanging over the edge.

II

THE good stallion took the sledge along at a brisk pace over the
smooth-frozen road through the village, the runners squeaking
slightly as they went.

'Look at him hanging on there! Hand me the whip, Nikita!'
shouted Vasili Andreevich, evidently enjoying the sight of his 'heir',
who standing on the runners was hanging on at the back of the sledge.
'I'll give it you! Be off to mamma, you dog!'

The boy jumped down. The horse increased his amble and, suddenly changing foot, broke into a fast trot.

Kresty, the village where Vasili Andreevich lived, consisted of six
houses. As soon as they had passed the blacksmith's hut, the last in
the village, they realized that the wind was much stronger than they
had thought. The road could hardly be seen. The tracks left by the
sledge-runners were immediately covered by snow and the road was
only distinguished by the fact that it was higher than the rest of the
ground. There was a whirl of snow over the fields and the line where
sky and earth met could not be seen. The Telyatin forest, usually
clearly visible, now only loomed up occasionally and dimly through
the driving snowy dust. The wind came from the left, insistently
blowing over to one side the mane on Mukhorty's sleek neck and
carrying aside even his fluffy tail, which was tied in a simple knot.

Nikita's wide coat-collar, as he sat on the windy side, pressed close to his cheek and nose.

'This road doesn't give him a chance – it's too snowy,' said Vasili Andreevich, who prided himself on his good horse. 'I once drove to Pashutino with him in half an hour.'

'What?' asked Nikita, who could not hear on account of his collar.

'I say I once went to Pashutino in half an hour,' shouted Vasili Andreevich.

'It goes without saying that he's a good horse,' replied Nikita.

They were silent for a while. But Vasili Andreevich wished to talk.

'Well, did you tell your wife not to give the cooper any vodka?' he began in the same loud tone, quite convinced that Nikita must feel flattered to be talking with so clever and important a person as himself, and he was so pleased with his jest that it did not enter his head that the remark might be unpleasant to Nikita.

The wind again prevented Nikita's hearing his master's words.

Vasili Andreevich repeated the jest about the cooper in his loud, clear voice.

'That's their business, Vasili Andreevich. I don't pry into those affairs. As long as she doesn't ill-treat our boy – God be with them.'

'That's so,' said Vasili Andreevich. 'Well, and will you be buying a horse in spring?' he went on, changing the subject.

'Yes, I can't avoid it,' answered Nikita, turning down his collar and leaning back towards his master.

The conversation now became interesting to him and he did not wish to lose a word.

'The lad's growing up. He must begin to plough for himself, but till now we've always had to hire someone,' he said.

'Well, why not have the lean-cruppered one. I won't charge much for it,' shouted Vasili Andreevich, feeling animated, and consequently starting on his favourite occupation – that of horse-dealing – which absorbed all his mental powers.

'Or you might let me have fifteen rubles and I'll buy one at the horse-market,' said Nikita, who knew that the horse Vasili Andreevich wanted to sell him would be dear at seven rubles, but that if he took it from him it would be charged at twenty-five, and then he would be unable to draw any money for half a year.

'It's a good horse. I think of your interest as of my own – according to conscience. Brekhunov isn't a man to wrong anyone. Let the loss be mine. I'm not like others. Honestly!' he shouted in the voice in which he hypnotized his customers and dealers. 'It's a real good horse.'

'Quite so!' said Nikita with a sigh, and convinced that there was nothing more to listen to, he again released his collar, which immediately covered his ear and face.

They drove on in silence for about half an hour. The wind blew sharply onto Nikita's side and arm where his sheepskin was torn.

He huddled up and breathed into the collar which covered his mouth, and was not wholly cold.

'What do you think – shall we go through Karamyshevo or by the straight road?' asked Vasili Andreevich.

The road through Karamyshevo was more frequented and was well marked with a double row of high stakes. The straight road was nearer but little used and had no stakes, or only poor ones covered with snow.

Nikita thought awhile.

'Though Karamyshevo is farther, it is better going,' he said.

'But by the straight road, when once we get through the hollow by the forest, it's good going – sheltered,' said Vasili Andreevich, who wished to go the nearest way.

'Just as you please,' said Nikita, and again let go of his collar.

Vasili Andreevich did as he had said, and having gone about half a verst came to a tall oak stake which had a few dry leaves still dangling on it, and there he turned to the left.

On turning they faced directly against the wind, and snow was beginning to fall. Vasili Andreevich, who was driving, inflated his cheeks, blowing the breath out through his moustache. Nikita dozed.

So they went on in silence for about ten minutes. Suddenly Vasili Andreevich began saying something.

'Eh, what?' asked Nikita, opening his eyes.

Vasili Andreevich did not answer, but bent over, looking behind them and then ahead of the horse. The sweat had curled Mukhorty's coat between his legs and on his neck. He went at a walk.

'What is it?' Nikita asked again.

'What is it? What is it?' Vasili Andreevich mimicked him angrily. 'There are no stakes to be seen! We must have got off the road!'

'Well, pull up then, and I'll look for it,' said Nikita, and jumping down lightly from the sledge and taking the whip from under the straw, he went off to the left from his own side of the sledge.

The snow was not deep that year, so that it was possible to walk anywhere, but still in places it was knee-deep and got into Nikita's boots. He went about feeling the ground with his feet and the whip, but could not find the road anywhere.

'Well, how is it?' asked Vasili Andreevich when Nikita came back to the sledge.

'There is no road this side. I must go to the other side and try there,' said Nikita.

'There's something there in front. Go and have a look.'

Nikita went to what had appeared dark, but found that it was earth which the wind had blown from the bare fields of winter oats and had strewn over the snow, colouring it. Having searched to the right also, he returned to the sledge, brushed the snow from his coat, shook it out of his boots, and seated himself once more.

'We must go to the right,' he said decidedly. 'The wind was blowing on our left before, but now it is straight in my face. Drive to the right,' he repeated with decision.

Vasili Andreevich took his advice and turned to the right, but still there was no road. They went on in that direction for some time. The wind was as fierce as ever and it was snowing lightly.

'It seems, Vasili Andreevich, that we have gone quite astray,' Nikita suddenly remarked, as if it were a pleasant thing. 'What is that?' he added, pointing to some potato bines that showed up from under the snow.

Vasili Andreevich stopped the perspiring horse, whose deep sides were heaving heavily.

'What is it?'

'Why, we are on the Zakharov lands. See where we've got to!'

'Nonsense!' retorted Vasili Andreevich.

'It's not nonsense, Vasili Andreevich. It's the truth,' replied Nikita. 'You can feel that the sledge is going over a potato-field, and there are the heaps of bines which have been carted here. It's the Zakharov factory land.'

'Dear me, how we have gone astray!' said Vasili Andreevich. 'What are we to do now?'

'We must go straight on, that's all. We shall come out somewhere – if not at Zakharova then at the proprietor's farm,' said Nikita.

Vasili Andreevich agreed, and drove as Nikita had indicated. So they went on for a considerable time. At times they came onto bare fields and the sledge-runners rattled over frozen lumps of earth. Sometimes they got onto a winter-rye field, or a fallow field on which they could see stalks of wormwood, and straws sticking up through the snow and swaying in the wind; sometimes they came onto deep and even white show, above which nothing was to be seen.

The snow was falling from above and sometimes rose from below. The horse was evidently exhausted, his hair had all curled up from sweat and was covered with hoar-frost, and he went at a walk. Suddenly he stumbled and sat down in a ditch or water-course. Vasili Andreevich wanted to stop, but Nikita cried to him:

'Why stop? We've got in and must get out. Hey, pet! Hey, darling! Gee up, old fellow!' he shouted in a cheerful tone to the horse, jumping out of the sledge and himself getting stuck in the ditch.

The horse gave a start and quickly climbed out onto the frozen bank. It was evidently a ditch that had been dug there.

'Where are we now?' asked Vasili Andreevich.

'We'll soon find out!' Nikita replied. 'Go on, we'll get somewhere.'

'Why, this must be the Goryachkin forest!' said Vasili Andreevich, pointing to something dark that appeared amid the snow in front of them.

'We'll see what forest it is when we get there,' said Nikita.

He saw that beside the black thing they had noticed, dry, oblong willow-leaves were fluttering, and so he knew it was not a forest but a settlement, but he did not wish to say so. And in fact they had not gone twenty-five yards beyond the ditch before something in front of them, evidently trees, showed up black, and they heard a new and melancholy sound. Nikita had guessed right: it was not a wood, but a row of tall willows with a few leaves still fluttering on them here and there. They had evidently been planted along the ditch round a threshing-floor. Coming up to the willows, which moaned sadly in the wind, the horse suddenly planted his forelegs above the height of the sledge, drew up his hind legs also, pulling the sledge onto higher ground, and turned to the left, no longer sinking up to his knees in snow. They were back on a road.

'Well, here we are, but heaven only knows where!' said Nikita.

The horse kept straight along the road through the drifted snow, and before they had gone another hundred yards the straight line of the dark wattle wall of a barn showed up black before them, its roof heavily covered with snow which poured down from it. After passing the barn the road turned to the wind and they drove into a snow-drift. But ahead of them was a lane with houses on either side, so evidently the snow had been blown across the road and they had to drive through the drift. And so in fact it was. Having driven through the snow they came out into a street. At the end house of the village some frozen clothes hanging on a line – shirts, one red and one white, trousers, leg-bands, and a petticoat – fluttered wildly in the wind. The white shirt in particular struggled desperately, waving its sleeves about.

'There now, either a lazy woman or a dead one has not taken her clothes down before the holiday,' remarked Nikita, looking at the fluttering shirts.

III

At the entrance to the street the wind still raged and the road was thickly covered with snow, but well within the village it was calm, warm, and cheerful. At one house a dog was barking, at another a woman, covering her head with her coat, came running from somewhere and entered the door of a hut, stopping on the threshold to have a look at the passing sledge. In the middle of the village girls could be heard singing.

Here in the village there seemed to be less wind and snow, and the frost was less keen.

'Why, this is Grishkino,' said Vasili Andreevich.

'So it is,' responded Nikita.

It really was Grishkino, which meant that they had gone too far to the left and had travelled some six miles, not quite in the direction they aimed at, but towards their destination for all that.

From Grishkino to Goryachkin was about another four miles.

In the middle of the village they almost ran into a tall man walking down the middle of the street.

'Who are you?' shouted the man, stopping the horse, and recognizing Vasili Andreevich he immediately took hold of the shaft, went along it hand over hand till he reached the sledge, and placed himself on the driver's seat.

He was Isay, a peasant of Vasili Andreevich's acquaintance, and well known as the principal horse-thief in the district.

'Ah, Vasili Andreevich! Where are you off to?' said Isay, enveloping Nikita in the odour of the vodka he had drunk.

'We were going to Goryachkin.'

'And look where you've got to! You should have gone through Molchanovka.'

'Should have, but didn't manage it,' said Vasili Andreevich, holding in the horse.

'That's a good horse,' said Isay, with a shrewd glance at Mukhorty, and with a practised hand he tightened the loosened knot high in the horse's bushy tail.

'Are you going to stay the night?'

'No, friend. I must get on.'

'Your business must be pressing. And who is this? Ah, Nikita Stepanych!'

'Who else?' replied Nikita. 'But I say, good friend, how are we to avoid going astray again?'

'Where can you go astray here? Turn back straight down the street and then when you come out keep straight on. Don't take to the left. You will come out onto the high road, and then turn to the right.'

'And where do we turn off the high road? As in summer, or the winter way?' asked Nikita.

'The winter way. As soon as you turn off you'll see some bushes, and opposite them there is a waymark – a large oak one with branches – and that's the way.'

Vasili Andreevich turned the horse back and drove through the outskirts of the village.

'Why not stay the night?' Isay shouted after them.

But Vasili Andreevich did not answer and touched up the horse. Four miles of good road, two of which lay through the forest, seemed easy to manage, especially as the wind was apparently quieter and the snow had stopped.

Having driven along the trodden village street, darkened here and there by fresh manure, past the yard where the clothes hung out and where the white shirt had broken loose and was now attached only by one frozen sleeve, they again came within sound of the weird moan of the willows, and again emerged on the open fields. The storm, far from ceasing, seemed to have grown yet stronger. The road was completely covered with drifting snow, and only the stakes showed that they had not lost their way. But even the stakes ahead of them were not easy to see, since the wind blew in their faces.

Vasili Andreevich screwed up his eyes, bent down his head, and looked out for the way-marks, but trusted mainly to the horse's sagacity, letting it take its own way. And the horse really did not lose the road but followed its windings, turning now to the right and now to the left and sensing it under his feet, so that though the snow fell thicker and the wind strengthened they still continued to see way-marks now to the left and now to the right of them.

So they travelled on for about ten minutes, when suddenly, through the slanting screen of wind-driven snow, something black showed up which moved in front of the horse.

This was another sledge with fellow-travellers. Mukhorty over-took them, and struck his hoofs against the back of the sledge in front of him.

'Pass on . . . hey there . . . get in front!' cried voices from the sledge.

Vasili Andreevich swerved aside to pass the other sledge. In it sat three men and a woman, evidently visitors returning from a feast. One peasant was whacking the snow-covered croup of their little horse with a long switch, and the other two sitting in front waved their arms and shouted something. The woman, completely wrapped up and covered with snow, sat drowsing and bumping at the back.

'Who are you?' shouted Vasili Andreevich.

'From A-a-a . . .' was all that could be heard.

'Where are you from, I say?'

'From A-a-a-a!' one of the peasants shouted with all his might, but still it was impossible to make out who they were.

'Get along! Keep up!' shouted another, ceaselessly beating his horse with the switch.

'So you're from a feast, it seems?'

'Go on, go on! Faster, Simon! Get in front! Faster!'

The wings of the sledges bumped against one another, almost got jammed but managed to separate, and the peasants' sledge began to fall behind.

Their shaggy, big-bellied horse, all covered with snow, breathed heavily under the low shaft-bow and, evidently using the last of its strength, vainly endeavoured to escape from the switch, hobbling with its short legs through the deep snow which it threw up under itself.

Its muzzle, young-looking, with the nether lip drawn up like that of a fish, nostrils distended and ears pressed back from fear, kept up for a few seconds near Nikita's shoulder and then began to fall behind.

'Just see what liquor does!' said Nikita. 'They've tired that little horse to death. What pagans!'

For a few minutes they heard the panting of the tired little horse and the drunken shouting of the peasants. Then the panting and the shouts died away, and around them nothing could be heard but the whistling of the wind in their ears and now and then the squeak of their sledge-runners over a windswept part of the road.

This encounter cheered and enlivened Vasili Andreevich, and he drove on more boldly without examining the way-marks, urging on the horse and trusting to him.

Nikita had nothing to do, and as usual in such circumstances he drowsed, making up for much sleepless time. Suddenly the horse stopped and Nikita nearly fell forward onto his nose.

'You know we're off the track again!' said Vasili Andreevich.

'How's that?'

'Why, there are no way-marks to be seen. We must have got off the road again.'

'Well, if we've lost the road we must find it,' said Nikita curtly, and getting out and stepping lightly on his pigeon-toed feet he started once more going about on the snow.

He walked about for a long time, now disappearing and now reappearing, and finally he came back.

'There is no road here. There may be farther on,' he said, getting into the sledge.

It was already growing dark. The snow-storm had not got worse but had not subsided either.

'If we could only hear those peasants!' said Vasili Andreevich.

'Well they haven't caught us up. We must have gone far astray. Or maybe they have lost their way too.'

'Where are we to go then?' asked Vasili Andreevich.

'Why, we must let the horse take its own way,' said Nikita. 'He will take us right. Let me have the reins.'

Vasili Andreevich gave him the reins, the more willingly because his hands were beginning to feel frozen in his thick gloves.

Nikita took the reins, but only held them, trying not to shake them and rejoicing at his favourite's sagacity. And indeed the clever horse, turning first one ear and then the other now to one side and then to the other, began to wheel round.

'The one thing he can't do is to talk,' Nikita kept saying. 'See what he is doing! Go on, go on! You know best. That's it, that's it!'

The wind was now blowing from behind and it felt warmer.

'Yes, he's clever,' Nikita continued, admiring the horse. 'A Kirgiz horse is strong but stupid. But this one – just see what he's doing with his ears! He doesn't need any telegraph. He can scent a mile off.'

Before another half-hour had passed they saw something dark ahead of them – a wood or a village – and stakes again appeared to the right. They had evidently come out onto the road.

'Why, that's Grishkino again!' Nikita suddenly exclaimed.

And indeed, there on the left was that same barn with the snow flying from it, and farther on the same line with the frozen washing, shirts and trousers, which still fluttered desperately in the wind.

Again they drove into the street and again it grew quiet, warm, and cheerful, and again they could see the manure-stained street and hear voices and songs and the barking of a dog. It was already so dark that there were lights in some of the windows.

Half-way through the village Vasili Andreevich turned the horse towards a large double-fronted brick house and stopped at the porch.

Nikita went to the lighted snow-covered window, in the rays of which flying snow-flakes glittered, and knocked at it with his whip.

'Who is there?' a voice replied to his knock.

'From Kresty, the Brekhunovs, dear fellow,' answered Nikita. 'Just come out for a minute.'

Someone moved from the window, and a minute or two later there was the sound of the passage door as it came unstuck, then the latch of the outside door clicked and a tall white-bearded peasant, with a sheepskin coat thrown over his white holiday shirt, pushed his way out holding the door firmly against the wind, followed by a lad in a red shirt and high leather boots.

'Is that you, Andreevich?' asked the old man.

'Yes, friend, we've gone astray,' said Vasili Andreevich. 'We wanted to get to Goryachkin but found ourselves here. We went a second time but lost our way again.'

'Just see how you have gone astray!' said the old man. 'Petrushka, go and open the gate!' he added, turning to the lad in the red shirt.

'All right,' said the lad in a cheerful voice, and ran back into the passage.

'But we're not staying the night,' said Vasili Andreevich.

'Where will you go in the night? You'd better stay!'

'I'd be glad to, but I must go on. It's business, and it can't be helped.'

'Well, warm yourself at least. The samovar is just ready.'

'Warm myself? Yes, I'll do that,' said Vasili Andreevich. 'It won't get darker. The moon will rise and it will be lighter. Let's go in and warm ourselves, Nikita.'

'Well, why not? Let us warm ourselves,' replied Nikita, who was stiff with cold and anxious to warm his frozen limbs.

Vasili Andreevich went into the room with the old man, and Nikita drove through the gate opened for him by Petrushka, by whose advice he backed the horse under the penthouse. The ground was covered with manure and the tall bow over the horse's head caught against the beam. The hens and the cock had already settled to roost there, and clucked peevishly, clinging to the beam with their claws. The disturbed sheep shied and rushed aside trampling the frozen manure with their hooves. The dog yelped desperately with fright and anger and then burst out barking like a puppy at the stranger.

Nikita talked to them all, excused himself to the fowls and assured them that he would not disturb them again, rebuked the sheep for being frightened without knowing why, and kept soothing the dog, while he tied up the horse.

'Now that will be all right,' he said, knocking the snow off his clothes. 'Just hear how he barks!' he added, turning to the dog. 'Be quiet, stupid! Be quiet. You are only troubling yourself for nothing. We're not thieves, we're friends. . . .'

'And these are, it's said, the three domestic counsellors,' remarked the lad, and with his strong arms he pushed under the pent-roof the sledge that had remained outside.

'Why counsellors?' asked Nikita.

'That's what is printed in Paulson. A thief creeps to a house – the dog barks, that means, "Be on your guard!" The cock crows, that means, "Get up!" The cat licks herself – that means, "A welcome guest is coming. Get ready to receive him!"' said the lad with a smile.

Petrushka could read and write and knew Paulson's primer, his only book, almost by heart, and he was fond of quoting sayings from it that he thought suited the occasion, especially when he had had something to drink, as today.

'That's so,' said Nikita.

'You must be chilled through and through,' said Petrushka.

'Yes, I am rather,' said Nikita, and they went across the yard and the passage into the house.

IV

THE household to which Vasili Andreevich had come was one of the richest in the village. The family had five allotments, besides renting other land. They had six horses, three cows, two calves, and some twenty sheep. There were twenty-two members belonging to the homestead: four married sons, six grandchildren (one of whom, Petrushka, was married), two great-grandchildren, three orphans, and four daughters-in-law with their babies. It was one of the few homesteads that remained still undivided, but even here the dull internal work of disintegration which would inevitably lead to separation had already begun, starting as usual among the women. Two sons were living in Moscow as water-carriers, and one was in the army. At home now were the old man and his wife, their second son who managed the homestead, the eldest who had come from Moscow for the holiday, and all the women and children. Besides these members of the family there was a visitor, a neighbour who was godfather to one of the children.

Over the table in the room hung a lamp with a shade, which brightly lit up the tea-things, a bottle of vodka, and some refreshments, besides illuminating the brick walls, which in the far corner were hung with icons on both sides of which were pictures. At the head of the table sat Vasili Andreevich in a black sheepskin coat, sucking his frozen moustache and observing the room and the people around him with his prominent hawk-like eyes. With him sat the old, bald, white-bearded master of the house in a white homespun shirt, and next to him the son home from Moscow for the holiday – a man with a sturdy back and powerful shoulders and clad in a thin print shirt – then the second son, also broad-shouldered, who acted as head of the house, and then a lean red-haired peasant – the neighbour.

Having had a drink of vodka and something to eat, they were about to take tea, and the samovar standing on the floor beside the brick oven was already humming. The children could be seen in the top bunks and on the top of the oven. A woman sat on a lower bunk with a cradle beside her. The old housewife, her face covered with wrinkles which wrinkled even her lips, was waiting on Vasili Andreevich.

As Nikita entered the house she was offering her guest a small tumbler of thick glass which she had just filled with vodka.

'Don't refuse, Vasili Andreevich, you mustn't! Wish us a merry feast. Drink it, dear!' she said.

The sight and smell of vodka, especially now when he was chilled through and tired out, much disturbed Nikita's mind. He frowned, and having shaken the snow off his cap and coat, stopped in front of the icons as if not seeing anyone, crossed himself three times, and bowed to the icons. Then, turning to the old master of the house and bowing first to him, then to all those at table, then to the women who stood by the oven, and muttering: 'A merry holiday!' he began taking off his outer things without looking at the table.

'Why, you're all covered with hoar-frost, old fellow!' said the eldest brother, looking at Nikita's snow-covered face, eyes, and beard.

Nikita took off his coat, shook it again, hung it up beside the oven, and came up to the table. He too was offered vodka. He went through a moment of painful hesitation and nearly took up the glass and emptied the clear fragrant liquid down his throat, but he glanced at Vasili Andreevich, remembered his oath and the boots that he had sold for drink, recalled the cooper, remembered his son for whom he had promised to buy a horse by spring, sighed, and declined it.

'I don't drink, thank you kindly,' he said frowning, and sat down on a bench near the second window.

'How's that?' asked the eldest brother.

'I just don't drink,' replied Nikita without lifting his eyes but squinting at his scanty beard and moustache and getting the icicles out of them.

'It's not good for him,' said Vasili Andreevich, munching a cracknel after emptying his glass.

'Well, then, have some tea,' said the kindly old hostess. 'You must be chilled through, good soul. Why are you women dawdling so with the samovar?'

'It is ready,' said one of the young women, and after flicking with her apron the top of the samovar which was now boiling over, she carried it with an effort to the table, raised it, and set it down with a thud.

Meanwhile Vasili Andreevich was telling how he had lost his way, how they had come back twice to this same village, and how they had gone astray and had met some drunken peasants. Their hosts were surprised, explained where and why they had missed their way, said who the tipsy people they had met were, and told them how they ought to go.

'A little child could find the way to Molchanovka from here. All you have to do is to take the right turning from the high road. There's a bush you can see just there. But you didn't even get that far!' said the neighbour.

'You'd better stay the night. The women will make up beds for you,' said the old woman persuasively.

'You could go on in the morning and it would be pleasanter,' said the old man, confirming what his wife had said.

'I can't, friend. Business!' said Vasili Andreevich. 'Lose an hour and you can't catch it up in a year,' he added, remembering the grove and the dealers who might snatch that deal from him. 'We shall get there, shan't we?' he said, turning to Nikita.

Nikita did not answer for some time, apparently still intent on thawing out his beard and moustache.

'If only we don't go astray again,' he replied gloomily.

He was gloomy because he passionately longed for some vodka, and the only thing that could assuage that longing was tea and he had not yet been offered any.

'But we have only to reach the turning and then we shan't go wrong. The road will be through the forest the whole way,' said Vasili Andreevich.

'It's just as you please, Vasili Andreevich. If we're to go, let us go,' said Nikita, taking the glass of tea he was offered.

'We'll drink our tea and be off.'

Nikita said nothing but only shook his head, and carefully pouring some tea into his saucer began warming his hands, the fingers of which were always swollen with hard work, over the steam. Then, biting off a tiny bit of sugar, he bowed to his hosts, said, 'Your health!' and drew in the steaming liquid.

'If somebody would see us as far as the turning,' said Vasili Andreevich.

'Well, we can do that,' said the eldest son. 'Petrushka will harness and go that far with you.'

'Well, then, put in the horse, lad, and I shall be thankful to you for it.'

'Oh, what for, dear man?' said the kindly old woman. 'We are heartily glad to do it.'

'Petrushka, go and put in the mare,' said the eldest brother.

'All right,' replied Petrushka with a smile, and promptly snatching his cap down from a nail he ran away to harness.

While the horse was being harnessed the talk returned to the point at which it had stopped when Vasili Andreevich drove up to the window. The old man had been complaining to his neighbour, the village elder, about his third son who had not sent him anything for the holiday though he had sent a French shawl to his wife.

'The young people are getting out of hand,' said the old man.

'And how they do!' said the neighbour. 'There's no managing them! They know too much. There's Demochkin now, who broke his father's arm. It's all from being too clever, it seems.'

Nikita listened, watched their faces, and evidently would have liked to share in the conversation, but he was too busy drinking his tea and only nodded his head approvingly. He emptied one tumbler after another and grew warmer and warmer and more and more comfortable. The talk continued on the same subject for a long time – the harmfulness of a household dividing up – and it was clearly not an abstract discussion but concerned the question of a separation in that house; a separation demanded by the second son who sat there morosely silent.

It was evidently a sore subject and absorbed them all, but out of propriety they did not discuss their private affairs before strangers. At last, however, the old man could not restrain himself, and with tears in his eyes declared that he would not consent to a break-up of the family during his lifetime, that his house was prospering, thank God, but that if they separated they would all have to go begging.

'Just like the Matveevs,' said the neighbour. 'They used to have a proper house, but now they've split up none of them has anything.'

'And that is what you want to happen to us,' said the old man, turning to his son.

The son made no reply and there was an awkward pause. The silence was broken by Petrushka, who having harnessed the horse had returned to the hut a few minutes before this and had been listening all the time with a smile.

'There's a fable about that in Paulson,' he said. 'A father gave his sons a broom to break. At first they could not break it, but when they took it twig by twig they broke it easily. And it's the same here,' and he gave a broad smile. 'I'm ready!' he added.

'If you're ready, let's go,' said Vasili Andreevich. 'And as to separating, don't you allow it, grandfather. You got everything together and you're the master. Go to the Justice of the Peace. He'll say how things should be done.'

'He carries on so, carries on so,' the old man continued in a whining tone. 'There's no doing anything with him. It's as if the devil possessed him.'

Nikita, having meanwhile finished his fifth tumbler of tea, laid it on its side instead of turning it upside down, hoping to be offered a sixth glass. But there was no more water in the samovar, so the hostess did not fill it up for him. Besides, Vasili Andreevich was putting his things on, so there was nothing for it but for Nikita to get up too, put back into the sugar-basin the lump of sugar he had nibbled all round, wipe his perspiring face with the skirt of his sheepskin, and go to put on his overcoat.

Having put it on he sighed deeply, thanked his hosts, said goodbye, and went out of the warm bright room into the cold dark passage, through which the wind was howling and where snow was blowing through the cracks of the shaking door, and from there into the yard.

Petrushka stood in his sheepskin in the middle of the yard by his horse, repeating some lines from Paulson's primer. He said with a smile:

> 'Storms with mist the sky conceal,
> Snowy circles wheeling wild.
> Now like savage beast 'twill howl,
> And now 'tis wailing like a child.'

Nikita nodded approvingly as he arranged the reins.

The old man, seeing Vasili Andreevich off, brought a lantern into the passage to show him a light, but it was blown out at once. And even in the yard it was evident that the snow-storm had become more violent.

'Well, this is weather!' thought Vasili Andreevich. 'Perhaps we may not get there after all. But there is nothing to be done. Business! Besides, we have got ready, our host's horse has been harnessed, and we'll get there with God's help!'

Their aged host also thought they ought not to go, but he had already tried to persuade them to stay and had not been listened to.

'It's no use asking them again. Maybe my age makes me timid. They'll get there all right, and at least we shall get to bed in good time and without any fuss,' he thought.

Petruskha did not think of danger. He knew the road and the whole district so well, and the lines about 'snowy circles wheeling wild' described what was happening outside so aptly that it cheered him up. Nikita did not wish to go at all, but he had been accustomed not to have his own way and to serve others for so long that there was no one to hinder the departing travellers.

V

VASILI ANDREEVICH went over to his sledge, found it with difficulty in the darkness, climbed in and took the reins.

'Go on in front!' he cried.

Petrushka kneeling in his low sledge started his horse. Mukhorty, who had been neighing for some time past, now scenting a mare ahead of him started after her, and they drove out into the street. They drove again through the outskirts of the village and along the same road, past the yard where the frozen linen had hung (which, however, was no longer to be seen), past the same barn, which was now snowed up almost to the roof and from which the snow was still endlessly pouring, past the same dismally moaning, whistling, and swaying willows, and again entered into the sea of blustering snow raging from above and below. The wind was so strong that when it blew from the side and the travellers steered against it, it tilted the sledges and turned the horses to one side. Petrushka drove his good mare in front at a brisk trot and kept shouting lustily. Mukhorty pressed after her.

After travelling so for about ten minutes, Petrushka turned round and shouted something. Neither Vasili Andreevich nor Nikita could hear anything because of the wind, but they guessed that they had arrived at the turning. In fact Petrushka had turned to the right, and now the wind that had blown from the side blew straight in their faces, and through the snow they saw something dark on their right. It was the bush at the turning.

'Well now, God speed you!'

'Thank you, Petrushka!'

'Storms with mist the sky conceal!' shouted Petrushka as he disappeared.

'There's a poet for you!' muttered Vasili Andreevich, pulling at the reins.

'Yes, a fine lad – a true peasant,' said Nikita.

They drove on.

Nikita, wrapping his coat closely about him and pressing his head down so close to his shoulders that his short beard covered his throat, sat silently, trying not to lose the warmth he had obtained while drinking tea in the house. Before him he saw the straight lines of the shafts which constantly deceived him into thinking they were a well-travelled road, and the horse's swaying crupper with his knotted tail blown to one side, and farther ahead the high shaft-bow and the swaying head and neck of the horse with its waving mane. Now and then he caught sight of a way-sign, so that he knew they were still on a road and that there was nothing for him to be concerned about.

Vasili Andreevich drove on, leaving it to the horse to keep to the road. But Mukhorty, though he had had a breathing-space in the village, ran reluctantly, and seemed now and then to get off the road, so that Vasili Andreevich had repeatedly to correct him.

'Here's a stake to the right, and another, and here's a third,' Vasili Andreevich counted, 'and here in front is the forest,' thought he, as he looked at something dark in front of him. But what had seemed to him a forest was only a bush. They passed the bush and drove on for another hundred yards but there was no fourth way-mark nor any forest.

'We must reach the forest soon,' thought Vasili Andreevich, and animated by the vodka and the tea he did not stop but shook the reins, and the good obedient horse responded, now ambling, now slowly trotting in the direction in which he was sent, though he knew that he was not going the right way. Ten minutes went by, but there was still no forest.

'There now, we must be astray again,' said Vasili Andreevich, pulling up.

Nikita silently got out of the sledge and holding his coat, which the wind now wrapped closely about him and now almost tore off, started to feel about in the snow, going first to one side and then to the other. Three or four times he was completely lost to sight. At last he returned and took the reins from Vasili Andreevich's hand.

'We must go to the right,' he said sternly and peremptorily, as he turned the horse.

'Well, if it's to the right, go to the right,' said Vasili Andreevich, yielding up the reins to Nikita and thrusting his freezing hands into his sleeves.

Nikita did not reply.

'Now then, friend, stir yourself!' he shouted to the horse, but in spite of the shake of the reins Mukhorty moved only at a walk.

The snow in places was up to his knees, and the sledge moved by fits and starts with his every movement.

Nikita took the whip that hung over the front of the sledge and struck him once. The good horse, unused to the whip, sprang forward and moved at a trot, but immediately fell back into an amble and then to a walk. So they went on for five minutes. It was dark and the snow whirled from above and rose from below, so that sometimes the shaft-bow could not be seen. At times the sledge seemed to stand still and the field to run backwards. Suddenly the horse stopped abruptly, evidently aware of something close in front of him. Nikita again sprang lightly out, throwing down the reins, and went ahead to see what had brought him to a standstill, but hardly had he made a step in front of the horse before his feet slipped and he went rolling down an incline.

'Whoa, whoa, whoa!' he said to himself as he fell, and he tried to stop his fall but could not, and only stopped when his feet plunged into a thick layer of snow that had drifted to the bottom of the hollow.

The fringe of a drift of snow that hung on the edge of the hollow, disturbed by Nikita's fall, showered down on him and got inside his collar.

'What a thing to do!' said Nikita reproachfully, addressing the drift and the hollow and shaking the snow from under his collar.

'Nikita! Hey, Nikita!' shouted Vasili Andreevich from above.

But Nikita did not reply. He was too occupied in shaking out the snow and searching for the whip he had dropped when rolling down the incline. Having found the whip he tried to climb straight up the bank where he had rolled down, but it was impossible to do so: he kept rolling down again, and so he had to go along at the foot of the hollow to find a way up. About seven yards farther on he managed with difficulty to crawl up the incline on all fours, then he followed the edge of the hollow back to the place where the horse should have been. He could not see either horse or sledge, but as he walked against the wind he heard Vasili Andreevich's shouts and Mukhorty's neighing, calling him.

'I'm coming! I'm coming! What are you cackling for?' he muttered.

Only when he had come up to the sledge could he make out the horse, and Vasili Andreevich standing beside it and looking gigantic.

'Where the devil did you vanish to? We must go back, if only to Grishkino,' he began reproaching Nikita.

'I'd be glad to get back, Vasili Andreevich, but which way are we to go? There is such a ravine here that if we once get in it we shan't get out again. I got stuck so fast there myself that I could hardly get out.'

'What shall we do, then? We can't stay here! We must go somewhere!' said Vasili Andreevich.

Nikita said nothing. He seated himself in the sledge with his back to the wind, took off his boots, shook out the snow that had got into them, and taking some straw from the bottom of the sledge, carefully plugged with it a hole in his left boot.

Vasili Andreevich remained silent, as though now leaving everything to Nikita. Having put his boots on again, Nikita drew his feet into the sledge, put on his mittens and took up the reins, and directed the horse along the side of the ravine. But they had not gone a hundred yards before the horse again stopped short. The ravine was in front of him again.

Nikita again climbed out and again trudged about in the snow. He did this for a considerable time and at last appeared from the opposite side to that from which he had started.

'Vasili Andreevich, are you alive?' he called out.

'Here!' replied Vasili Andreevich. 'Well, what now?'

'I can't make anything out. It's too dark. There's nothing but ravines. We must drive against the wind again.'

They set off once more. Again Nikita went stumbling through the snow, again he fell in, again climbed out and trudged about, and at last quite out of breath he sat down beside the sledge.

'Well, how now?' asked Vasili Andreevich.

'Why, I am quite worn out and the horse won't go.'

'Then, what's to be done?'

'Why, wait a minute.'

Nikita went away again but soon returned.

'Follow me!' he said, going in front of the horse.

Vasili Andreevich no longer gave orders but implicitly did what Nikita told him.

'Here, follow me!' Nikita shouted, stepping quickly to the right, and seizing the rein he led Mukhorty down towards a snow-drift.

At first the horse held back, then he jerked forward, hoping to leap the drift, but he had not the strength and sank into it up to his collar.

'Get out!' Nikita called to Vasili Andreevich who still sat in the sledge, and taking hold of one shaft he moved the sledge closer to the horse. 'It's hard, brother!' he said to Mukhorty, 'but it can't be helped. Make an effort! Now, now, just a little one!' he shouted.

The horse gave a tug, then another, but failed to clear himself and settled down again as if considering something.

'Now, brother, this won't do!' Nikita admonished him. 'Now once more!'

Again Nikita tugged at the shaft on his side, and Vasili Andreevich did the same on the other.

Mukhorty lifted his head and then gave a sudden jerk.

'That's it! That's it!' cried Nikita. 'Don't be afraid – you won't sink!'

One plunge, another, and a third, and at last Mukhorty was out of the snow-drift, and stood still, breathing heavily and shaking the snow off himself. Nikita wished to lead him farther, but Vasili Andreevich, in his two fur coats, was so out of breath that he could not walk farther and dropped into the sledge.

'Let me get my breath!' he said, unfastening the kerchief with which he had tied the collar of his fur coat at the village.

'It's all right here. You lie there,' said Nikita. 'I will lead him along.' And with Vasili Andreevich in the sledge he led the horse by the bridle about ten paces down and then up a slight rise, and stopped.

The place where Nikita had stopped was not completely in the hollow where the snow sweeping down from the hillocks might have buried them altogether, but still it was partly sheltered from the wind by the side of the ravine. There were moments when the wind seemed to abate a little, but that did not last long and as if to make up for that respite the storm swept down with tenfold vigour and tore and whirled the more fiercely. Such a gust struck them at the moment when Vasili Andreevich, having recovered his breath, got out of the sledge and went up to Nikita to consult him as to what they should do. They both bent down involuntarily and waited till the violence of the squall should have passed. Mukhorty too laid back his ears and shook his head discontentedly. As soon as the violence of the blast had abated a little, Nikita took off his mittens, stuck them into his belt, breathed on to his hands, and began to undo the straps of the shaft-bow.

'What's that you are doing there?' asked Vasili Andreevich.

'Unharnessing. What else is there to do? I have no strength left,' said Nikita as though excusing himself.

'Can't we drive somewhere?'

'No, we can't. We shall only kill the horse. Why, the poor beast is not himself now,' said Nikita, pointing to the horse, which was standing submissively waiting for what might come, with his steep wet sides heaving heavily. 'We shall have to stay the night here,' he said, as if preparing to spend the night at an inn, and he proceeded to unfasten the collar-straps. The buckles came undone.

'But shan't we be frozen?' remarked Vasili Andreevich.

'Well, if we are we can't help it,' said Nikita.

VI

ALTHOUGH Vasili Andreevich felt quite warm in his two fur coats, especially after struggling in the snow-drift, a cold shiver ran down his back on realizing that he must really spend the night where they were. To calm himself he sat down in the sledge and got out his cigarettes and matches.

Nikita meanwhile unharnessed Mukhorty. He unstrapped the belly-band and the back-band, took away the reins, loosened the collar-strap, and removed the shaft-bow, talking to him all the time to encourage him.

'Now come out! Come out!' he said, leading him clear of the shafts. 'Now we'll tie you up here and I'll put down some straw and take off your bridle. When you've had a bite you'll feel more cheerful.'

But Mukhorty was restless and evidently not comforted by Nikita's remarks. He stepped now on one foot and now on another, and pressed close against the sledge, turning his back to the wind and rubbing his head on Nikita's sleeve. Then, as if not to pain Nikita by refusing his offer of the straw he put before him, he hurriedly snatched a wisp out of the sledge, but immediately decided that it was now no time to think of straw and threw it down, and the wind instantly scattered it, carried it away, and covered it with snow.

'Now we will set up a signal,' said Nikita, and turning the front of the sledge to the wind he tied the shafts together with a strap and set them up on end in front of the sledge. 'There now, when the snow covers us up, good folk will see the shafts and dig us out,' he said, slapping his mittens together and putting them on. 'That's what the old folk taught us!'

Vasili Andreevich meanwhile had unfastened his coat, and holding its skirts up for shelter, struck one sulphur match after another on the steel box. But his hands trembled, and one match after another either did not kindle or was blown out by the wind just as he was lifting it to the cigarette. At last a match did burn up, and its flame lit up for a moment the fur of his coat, his hand with the gold ring on the bent forefinger, and the snow-sprinkled oat-straw that stuck out from under the drugget. The cigarette lighted, he eagerly took a whiff or two, inhaled the smoke, let it out through his moustache, and would have inhaled again, but the wind tore off the burning tobacco and whirled it away as it had done the straw.

But even these few puffs had cheered him.

'If we must spend the night here, we must!' he said with decision. 'Wait a bit, I'll arrange a flag as well,' he added, picking up the kerchief which he had thrown down in the sledge after taking it from round his collar, and drawing off his gloves and standing up on the front of the sledge and stretching himself to reach the strap, he tied the handkerchief to it with a tight knot.

The kerchief immediately began to flutter wildly, now clinging round the shaft, now suddenly streaming out, stretching and flapping.

'Just see what a fine flag!' said Vasili Andreevich, admiring his handiwork and letting himself down into the sledge. 'We should be warmer together, but there's not room enough for two,' he added.

'I'll find a place,' said Nikita. 'But I must cover up the horse first – he sweated so, poor thing. Let go!' he added, drawing the drugget from under Vasili Andreevich.

Having got the drugget he folded it in two, and after taking off the breechband and pad, covered Mukhorty with it.

'Anyhow it will be warmer, silly!' he said, putting back the breechband and the pad on the horse over the drugget. Then having finished that business he returned to the sledge, and addressing Vasili Andreevich, said: 'You won't need the sackcloth, will you? And let me have some straw.'

And having taken these things from under Vasili Andreevich, Nikita went behind the sledge, dug out a hole for himself in the snow, put straw into it, wrapped his coat well round him, covered himself with the sackcloth, and pulling his cap well down seated himself on the straw he had spread, and leant against the wooden back of the sledge to shelter himself from the wind and the snow.

Vasili Andreevich shook his head disapprovingly at what Nikita was doing, as in general he disapproved of the peasants' stupidity and lack of education, and he began to settle himself down for the night.

He smoothed the remaining straw over the bottom of the sledge, putting more of it under his side, then he thrust his hands into his sleeves and settled down, sheltering his head in the corner of the sledge from the wind in front.

He did not wish to sleep. He lay and thought: thought ever of the one thing that constituted the sole aim, meaning, pleasure, and pride of his life – of how much money he had made and might still make, of how much other people he knew had made and possessed, and of how those others had made and were making it, and how he, like them, might still make much more. The purchase of the Goryachkin grove was a matter of immense importance to him. By that one deal he hoped to make perhaps ten thousand rubles. He began mentally to reckon the value of the wood he had inspected in autumn, and on five acres of which he had counted all the trees.

'The oaks will go for sledge-runners. The undergrowth will take care of itself, and there'll still be some thirty sazheens of fire-wood left on each desyatin,' said he to himself. 'That means there will be at least two hundred and twenty-five rubles' worth left on each desyatin. Fifty-six desyatins means fifty-six hundreds, and fifty-six hundreds, and fifty-six tens, and another fifty-six tens, and then fifty-six fives. . . .' He saw that it came out to more than twelve thousand rubles, but could not reckon it up exactly without a counting-frame. 'But I won't give ten thousand, anyhow. I'll give about eight thousand with a deduction on account of the glades. I'll grease the surveyor's palm – give him a hundred rubles, or a hundred and fifty, and he'll reckon that there are some five desyatins of glade to be deducted. And he'll let it go for eight thousand. Three thousand cash down. That'll move him, no fear!' he thought, and he pressed his pocket-book with his forearm.

'God only knows how we missed the turning. The forest ought to be there, and a watchman's hut, and dogs barking. But the damned things don't bark when they're wanted.' He turned his collar down from his ear and listened, but as before only the whistling of the wind could be heard, the flapping and fluttering of the kerchief tied to the shafts, and the pelting of the snow against the woodwork of the sledge. He again covered up his ear.

'If I had known I would have stayed the night. Well, no matter, we'll get there tomorrow. It's only one day lost. And the others won't travel in such weather.' Then he remembered that on the 9th he had to receive payment from the butcher for his oxen. 'He meant to come himself, but he won't find me, and my wife won't know how to receive the money. She doesn't know the right way of doing things,' he thought, recalling how at their party the day before she had not known how to treat the police-officer who was their guest. Of course she's only a woman! Where could she have seen anything? In my father's time what was our house like? Just a rich peasant's house: just an oat-mill and an inn – that was the whole property. But what have I done in these fifteen years? A shop, two taverns, a flour-mill, a grain-store, two farms leased out, and a house with an iron-roofed barn,' he thought proudly. 'Not as it was in father's time! Who is talked of in the whole district now? Brekhunov! And why? Because I stick to business. I take trouble, not like others who lie abed or waste their time on foolishness while I don't sleep of nights. Blizzard or no blizzard I start out. So business gets done. They think money-making is a joke. No, take pains and rack your brains! You get overtaken out of doors at night, like this, or keep awake night after night till the thoughts whirling in your head make the pillow turn,' he meditated with pride. 'They think people get on through luck. After all, the Mironovs are now millionaires. And why? Take pains and God gives. If only He grants me health!'

The thought that he might himself be a millionaire like Mironov, who began with nothing, so excited Vasili Andreevich that he felt the need of talking to somebody. But there was no one to talk to. . . . If only he could have reached Goryachkin he would have talked to the landlord and shown him a thing or two.

'Just see how it blows! It will snow us up so deep that we shan't be able to get out in the morning!' he thought, listening to a gust of wind that blew against the front of the sledge, bending it and lashing the snow against it. He raised himself and looked round. All he could see through the whirling darkness was Mukhorty's dark head, his back covered by the fluttering drugget, and his thick knotted tail; while all round, in front and behind, was the same fluctuating whity darkness, sometimes seeming to get a little lighter and sometimes growing denser still.

'A pity I listened to Nikita,' he thought. 'We ought to have driven on. We should have come out somewhere, if only back to Grishkino and stayed the night at Taras's. As it is we must sit here all night. But what was I thinking about? Yes, that God gives to those who take trouble, but not to loafers, lie-abeds, or fools. I must have a smoke!'

He sat down again, got out his cigarette-case, and stretched himself flat on his stomach, screening the matches with the skirt of his coat. But the wind found its way in and put out match after match. At last he got one to burn and lit a cigarette. He was very glad that he had managed to do what he wanted, and though the wind smoked more of the cigarette than he did, he still got two or three puffs and felt more cheerful. He again leant back, wrapped himself up, started reflecting and remembering, and suddenly and quite unexpectedly lost consciousness and fell asleep.

Suddenly something seemed to give him a push and awoke him. Whether it was Mukhorty who had pulled some straw from under him, or whether something within him had startled him, at all events it woke him, and his heart began to beat faster and faster so that the sledge seemed to tremble under him. He opened his eyes. Everything around him was just as before. 'It looks lighter,' he thought. 'I expect it won't be long before dawn.' But he at once remembered that it was lighter because the moon had risen. He sat up and looked first at the horse. Mukhorty still stood with his back to the wind, shivering all over. One side of the drugget, which was completely covered with snow, had been blown back, the breeching had slipped down and the snow-covered head with its waving forelock and mane were now more visible. Vasili Andreevich leant over the back of the sledge and looked behind. Nikita still sat in the same position in which he had settled himself. The sacking with which he was covered, and his legs, were thickly covered with snow.

'If only that peasant doesn't freeze to death! His clothes are so wretched. I may be held responsible for him. What shiftless people they are – such a want of education,' thought Vasili Andreevich, and he felt like taking the drugget off the horse and putting it over Nikita, but it would be very cold to get out and move about and, moreover, the horse might freeze to death. 'Why did I bring him with me? It was all her stupidity!' he thought, recalling his unloved wife, and he rolled over into his old place at the front part of the sledge. 'My uncle once spent a whole night like this,' he reflected, 'and was all right.' But another case came at once to his mind. 'But when they dug

Sebastian out he was dead – stiff like a frozen carcass. If I'd only stopped the night in Grishkino all this would not have happened!'

And wrapping his coat carefully round him so that none of the warmth of the fur should be wasted but should warm him all over, neck, knees, and feet, he shut his eyes and tried to sleep again. But try as he would he could not get drowsy, on the contrary he felt wide awake and animated. Again he began counting his gains and the debts due to him, again he began bragging to himself and feeling pleased with himself and his position, but all this was continually disturbed by a stealthily approaching fear and by the unpleasant regret that he had not remained in Grishkino.

'How different it would be to be lying warm on a bench!' He turned over several times in his attempts to get into a more comfortable position more sheltered from the wind, he wrapped up his legs closer, shut his eyes, and lay still. But either his legs in their strong felt boots began to ache from being bent in one position, or the wind blew in somewhere, and after lying still for a short time he again began to recall the disturbing fact that he might now have been lying quietly in the warm hut at Grishkino. He again sat up, turned about, muffled himself up, and settled down once more.

Once he fancied that he heard a distant cock-crow. He felt glad, turned down his coat-collar and listened with strained attention, but in spite of all his efforts nothing could be heard but the wind whistling between the shafts, the flapping of the kerchief, and the snow pelting against the frame of the sledge.

Nikita sat just as he had done all the time, not moving and not even answering Vasili Andreevich who had addressed him a couple of times. 'He doesn't care a bit – he's probably asleep!' thought Vasili Andreevich with vexation, looking behind the sledge at Nikita who was covered with a thick layer of snow.

Vasili Andreevich got up and lay down again some twenty times. It seemed to him that the night would never end. 'It must be getting near morning,' he thought, getting up and looking around. 'Let's have a look at my watch. It will be cold to unbutton, but if I only know that it's getting near morning I shall at any rate feel more cheerful. We could begin harnessing.'

In the depth of his heart Vasili Andreevich knew that it could not yet be near morning, but he was growing more and more afraid, and wished both to get to know and yet to deceive himself. He carefully undid the fastening of his sheepskin, pushed in his hand, and felt

about for a long time before he got to his waistcoat. With great difficulty he managed to draw out his silver watch with its enamelled
flower design, and tried to make out the time. He could not see anything without a light. Again he went down on his knees and elbows
as he had done when he lighted a cigarette, got out his matches, and
proceeded to strike one. This time he went to work more carefully,
and feeling with his fingers for a match with the largest head and the
greatest amount of phosphorus, lit it at the first try. Bringing the face
of the watch under the light he could hardly believe his eyes. . . . It
was only ten minutes past twelve. Almost the whole night was still
before him.

'Oh, how long the night is!' he thought, feeling a cold shudder run
down his back, and having fastened his fur coats again and wrapped
himself up, he snuggled into a corner of the sledge intending to wait
patiently. Suddenly, above the monotonous roar of the wind, he
clearly distinguished another new and living sound. It steadily
strengthened, and having become quite clear diminished just as
gradually. Beyond all doubt it was a wolf, and he was so near that the
movement of his jaws as he changed his cry was brought down the
wind. Vasili Andreevich turned back the collar of his coat and listened
attentively. Mukhorty too strained to listen, moving his ears, and
when the wolf had ceased its howling he shifted from foot to foot and
gave a warning snort. After this Vasili Andreevich could not fall
asleep again or even calm himself. The more he tried to think of his
accounts, his business, his reputation, his worth and his wealth, the
more and more was he mastered by fear; and regrets that he had not
stayed the night at Grishkino dominated and mingled in all his
thoughts.

'Devil take the forest! Things were all right without it, thank God.
Ah, if we had only put up for the night!' he said to himself. 'They
say it's drunkards that freeze,' he thought, 'and I have had some
drink.' And observing his sensations he noticed that he was beginning
to shiver, without knowing whether it was from cold or from fear.
He tried to wrap himself up and lie down as before, but could no
longer do so. He could not stay in one position. He wanted to get up,
to do something to master the gathering fear that was rising in him
and against which he felt himself powerless. He again got out his
cigarettes and matches, but only three matches were left and they
were bad ones. The phosphorus rubbed off them all without lighting.

'The devil take you! Damned thing! Curse you!' he muttered, not knowing whom or what he was cursing, and he flung away the crushed cigarette. He was about to throw away the matchbox too, but checked the movement of his hand and put the box in his pocket instead. He was seized with such unrest that he could no longer remain in one spot. He climbed out of the sledge and standing with his back to the wind began to shift his belt again, fastening it lower down in the waist and tightening it.

'What's the use of lying and waiting for death? Better mount the horse and get away!' The thought suddenly occurred to him. 'The horse will move when he has someone on his back. As for him,' he thought of Nikita – 'it's all the same to him whether he lives or dies. What is his life worth? He won't grudge his life, but I have something to live for, thank God.'

He untied the horse, threw the reins over his neck and tried to mount, but his coats and boots were so heavy that he failed. Then he clambered up in the sledge and tried to mount from there, but the sledge tilted under his weight, and he failed again. At last he drew Mukhorty nearer to the sledge, cautiously balanced on one side of it, and managed to lie on his stomach across the horse's back. After lying like that for a while he shifted forward once and again, threw a leg over, and finally seated himself, supporting his feet on the loose breeching-straps. The shaking of the sledge awoke Nikita. He raised himself, and it seemed to Vasili Andreevich that he said something.

'Listen to such fools as you! Am I to die like this for nothing?' exclaimed Vasili Andreevich. And tucking the loose skirts of his fur coat in under his knees, he turned the horse and rode away from the sledge in the direction in which he thought the forest and the forester's hut must be.

VII

From the time he had covered himself with the sackcloth and seated himself behind the sledge, Nikita had not stirred. Like all those who live in touch with nature and have known want, he was patient and could wait for hours, even days, without growing restless or irritable. He heard his master call him, but did not answer because he did not want to move or talk. Though he still felt some warmth from the tea he had drunk and from his energetic struggle when clambering about in the snowdrift, he knew that this warmth would not last long and that he had no strength left to warm himself again by moving about.

for he felt as tired as a horse when it stops and refuses to go further in spite of the whip, and its master sees that it must be fed before it can work again. The foot in the boot with a hole in it had already grown numb, and he could no longer feel his big toe. Besides that, his whole body began to feel colder and colder.

The thought that he might, and very probably would, die that night occurred to him, but did not seem particularly unpleasant or dreadful. It did not seem particularly unpleasant because his whole life had been not a continual holiday, but on the contrary an unceasing round of toil of which he was beginning to feel weary. And it did not seem particularly dreadful because besides the masters he had served here, like Vasili Andreevich, he always felt himself dependent on the Chief Master, who had sent him into this life, and he knew that when dying he would still be in that Master's power and would not be ill-used by Him. 'It seems a pity to give up what one is used to and accustomed to. But there's nothing to be done; I shall get used to the new things.'

'Sins?' he thought, and remembered his drunkenness, the money that had gone on drink, how he had offended his wife, his cursing, his neglect of church and of the fasts, and all the things the priest blamed him for at confession. 'Of course they are sins. But then, did I take them on of myself? That's evidently how God made me. Well, and the sins? Where am I to escape to?'

So at first he thought of what might happen to him that night, and then did not return to such thoughts but gave himself up to whatever recollections came into his head of themselves. Now he thought of Martha's arrival, of the drunkenness among the workers and his own renunciation of drink, then of their present journey and of Taras's house and the talk about the breaking-up of the family, then of his own lad, and of Mukhorty now sheltered under the drugget, and then of his master who made the sledge creak as he tossed about in it. 'I expect you're sorry yourself that you started out, old chap,' he thought. 'It would seem hard to leave a life such as his! It's not like the likes of us.'

Then all these recollections began to grow confused and got mixed in his head, and he fell asleep.

But when Vasili Andreevich, getting on the horse, jerked the sledge against the back of which Nikita was leaning, and it shifted away and hit him in the back with one of its runners, he awoke and had to change his position whether he liked it or not. Straightening his legs with difficulty and shaking the snow off them he got up, and an agonizing cold immediately penetrated his whole body. On making out what was happening he called to Vasili Andreevich to leave him the drugget which the horse no longer needed, so that he might wrap himself in it.

But Vasili Andreevich did not stop, but disappeared amid the powdery snow.

Left alone, Nikita considered for a moment what he should do. He felt that he had not the strength to go off in search of a house. It was no longer possible to sit down in his old place – it was by now all filled with snow. He felt that he could not get warmer in the sledge either, for there was nothing to cover himself with, and his coat and sheepskin no longer warmed him at all. He felt as cold as though he had nothing on but a shirt. He became frightened. 'Lord, heavenly Father!' he muttered, and was comforted by the consciousness that he was not alone but that there was One who heard him and would not abandon him. He gave a deep sigh, and keeping the sackcloth over his head he got inside the sledge and lay down in the place where his master had been.

But he could not get warm in the sledge either. At first he shivered all over, then the shivering ceased and little by little he began to lose consciousness. He did not know whether he was dying or falling asleep, but felt equally prepared for the one as for the other.

VIII

MEANWHILE Vasili Andreevich, with his feet and the ends of the reins, urged the horse on in the direction in which for some reason he expected the forest and the forester's hut to be. The snow covered his eyes and the wind seemed intent on stopping him, but bending forward and constantly lapping his coat over and pushing it between himself and the cold harness pad which prevented him from sitting properly, he kept urging the horse on. Mukhorty ambled on obediently though with difficulty, in the direction in which he was driven.

Vasili Andreevich rode for about five minutes straight ahead, as he thought, seeing nothing but the horse's head and the white waste, and hearing only the whistle of the wind about the horse's ears and his coat collar.

Suddenly a dark patch showed up in front of him. His heart beat with joy, and he rode towards the object, already seeing in imagination the walls of village houses. But the dark patch was not stationary, it kept moving; and it was not a village but some tall stalks of wormwood sticking up through the snow on the boundary between two fields, and desperately tossing about under the pressure of the wind which beat it all to one side and whistled through it. The sight of that wormwood tormented by the pitiless wind made Vasili Andreevich shudder, he knew not why, and he hurriedly began urging the horse on, not noticing that when riding up to the wormwood he had quite changed his direction and was now heading the opposite way, though still imagining that he was riding towards where the hut should be. But the horse kept making towards the right, and Vasili Andreevich kept guiding it to the left.

Again something dark appeared in front of him. Again he rejoiced, convinced that now it was certainly a village. But once more it was the same boundary line overgrown with wormwood, once more the same wormwood desperately tossed by the wind and carrying unreasoning terror to his heart. But its being the same wormwood was not all, for beside it there was a horse's track partly snowed over. Vasili Andreevich stopped, stooped down and looked carefully. It was a horse-track only partially covered with snow, and could be none but his own horse's hoofprints. He had evidently gone round in a small circle. 'I shall perish like that!' he thought, and not to give way to his terror he urged on the horse still more, peering into the snowy darkness in which he saw only flitting and fitful points of light. Once he thought he heard the barking of dogs or the howling of wolves, but the sounds were so faint and indistinct that he did not know whether he heard them or merely imagined them, and he stopped and began to listen intently.

Suddenly some terrible, deafening cry resounded near his ears, and everything shivered and shook under him. He seized Mukhorty's neck, but that too was shaking all over and the terrible cry grew still more frightful. For some seconds Vasili Andreevich could not collect himself or understand what was happening. It was only that Mukhorty, whether to encourage himself or to call for help, had neighed loudly and resonantly. 'Ugh, you wretch! How you frightened me, damn you!' thought Vasili Andreevich. But even when he understood the cause of his terror he could not shake it off.

'I must calm myself and think things over,' he said to himself, but yet he could not stop, and continued to urge the horse on, without noticing that he was now going with the wind instead of against it. His body, especially between his legs where it touched the pad of the harness and was not covered by his overcoats, was getting painfully cold, especially when the horse walked slowly. His legs and arms trembled and his breathing came fast. He saw himself perishing amid this dreadful snowy waste, and could see no means of escape.

Suddenly the horse under him tumbled into something and, sinking into a snow-drift, began to plunge and fell on his side. Vasili Andreevich jumped off, and in so doing dragged to one side the breechband on which his foot was resting, and twisted round the pad to which he held as he dismounted. As soon as he had jumped off, the horse struggled to his feet, plunged forward, gave one leap and another, neighed again, and dragging the drugget and the breechband after him, disappeared, leaving Vasili Andreevich alone in the snow-drift.

The latter pressed on after the horse, but the snow lay so deep and his coats were so heavy that, sinking above his knees at each step, he stopped breathless after taking not more than twenty steps. 'The copse, the oxen, the leasehold, the shop, the tavern, the house with the iron-roofed barn, and my heir,' thought he. 'How can I leave all that? What does this mean? It cannot be!' These thoughts flashed through his mind. Then he thought of the wormwood tossed by the wind, which he had twice ridden past, and he was seized with such terror that he did not believe in the reality of what was happening to him. 'Can this be a dream?' he thought, and tried to wake up but could not. It was real snow that lashed his face and covered him and chilled his right hand from which he had lost the glove, and this was a real desert in which he was now left alone like that wormwood, awaiting an inevitable, speedy, and meaningless death.

'Queen of Heaven! Holy Father Nicholas, teacher of temperance!' he thought, recalling the service of the day before and the holy icon with its black face and gilt frame, and the tapers which he sold to be set before that icon and which were almost immediately brought back to him scarcely burnt at all, and which he put away in the store-chest.[1] He began to pray to that same Nicholas the Wonder-Worker

[1] As churchwarden Vasili Andreevich sold the tapers the worshippers bought to set before the icons. These were collected at the end of the service, and could afterwards be resold to the advantage of the church revenue.

to save him, promising him a thanksgiving service and some candles. But he clearly and indubitably realized that the icon, its frame, the candles, the priest, and the thanksgiving service, though very important and necessary in church, could do nothing for him here, and that there was and could be no connexion between those candles and services and his present disastrous plight. 'I must not despair,' he thought. 'I must follow the horse's track before it is snowed under. He will lead me out, or I may even catch him. Only I must not hurry, or I shall stick fast and be more lost than ever.'

But in spite of his resolution to go quietly, he rushed forward and even ran, continually falling, getting up and falling again. The horse's track was already hardly visible in places where the snow did not lie deep. 'I am lost!' thought Vasili Andreevich. 'I shall lose the track and not catch the horse.' But at that moment he saw something black. It was Mukhorty, and not only Mukhorty, but the sledge with the shafts and the kerchief. Mukhorty, with the sacking and the breech-band twisted round to one side, was standing not in his former place but nearer to the shafts, shaking his head which the reins he was stepping on drew downwards. It turned out that Vasili Andreevich had sunk in the same ravine Nikita had previously fallen into, and that Mukhorty had been bringing him back to the sledge and he had got off his back no more than fifty paces from where the sledge was.

IX

HAVING stumbled back to the sledge Vasili Andreevich caught hold of it and for a long time stood motionless, trying to calm himself and recover his breath. Nikita was not in his former place, but something, already covered with snow, was lying in the sledge and Vasili Andreevich concluded that this was Nikita. His terror had now quite left him, and if he felt any fear it was lest the dreadful terror should return that he had experienced when on the horse and especially when he was left alone in the snow-drift. At any cost he had to avoid that terror, and to keep it away he must do something – occupy himself with something. And the first thing he did was to turn his back to the wind and open his fur coat. Then, as soon as he recovered his breath a little, he shook the snow out of his boots and out of his left-hand glove (the right-hand glove was hopelessly lost and by this time probably lying somewhere under a dozen inches of snow), then as was his custom when going out of his shop to buy grain from the peasants, he pulled his girdle low down and tightened it and prepared for action. The first thing that occurred to him was to free Mukhorty's leg from the rein. Having done that, and tethered him to the iron cramp at the front of the sledge where he had been before, he was going round the horse's quarters to put the breechband and pad straight and cover him with the cloth, but at that moment he noticed that something was moving in the sledge and Nikita's head rose up out of the snow that covered it. Nikita, who was half frozen, rose with great difficulty and sat up, moving his hand before his nose in a strange manner just as if he were driving away flies. He waved his hand and said something, and seemed to Vasili Andreevich to be calling him. Vasili Andreevich left the cloth unadjusted and went up to the sledge.

'What is it?' he asked. 'What are you saying?'

'I'm dy . . . ing, that's what,' said Nikita brokenly and with difficulty. 'Give what is owing to me to my lad, or to my wife, no matter.'

'Why, are you really frozen?' asked Vasili Andreevich.

'I feel it's my death. Forgive me for Christ's sake . . .' said Nikita in a tearful voice, continuing to wave his hand before his face as if driving away flies.

Vasili Andreevich stood silent and motionless for half a minute. Then suddenly, with the same resolution with which he used to strike hands when making a good purchase, he took a step back and turning up his sleeves began raking the snow off Nikita and out of the sledge. Having done this he hurriedly undid his girdle, opened out his fur coat, and having pushed Nikita down, lay down on top of him, covering him not only with his fur coat but with the whole of his body, which glowed with warmth. After pushing the skirts of his coat between Nikita and the sides of the sledge, and holding down its hem with his knees, Vasili Andreevich lay like that face down, with his head pressed against the front of the sledge. Here he no longer heard the horse's movements or the whistling of the wind, but only Nikita's breathing. At first and for a long time Nikita lay motionless, then he sighed deeply and moved.

'There, and you say you are dying! Lie still and get warm, that's our way . . .' began Vasili Andreevich.

But to his great surprise he could say no more, for tears came to his eyes and his lower jaw began to quiver rapidly. He stopped speaking and only gulped down the risings in his throat. 'Seems I was badly frightened and have gone quite weak,' he thought. But this weakness was not only not unpleasant, but gave him a particular joy such as he had never felt before.

'That's our way!' he said to himself, experiencing a strange and solemn tenderness. He lay like that for a long time, wiping his eyes on the fur of his coat and tucking under his knee the right skirt, which the wind kept turning up.

But he longed so passionately to tell somebody of his joyful condition that he said: 'Nikita!'

'It's comfortable, warm!' came a voice from beneath.

'There, you see, friend, I was going to perish. And you would have been frozen, and I should have. . . .'

But again his jaws began to quiver and his eyes to fill with tears, and he could say no more.

'Well, never mind,' he thought. 'I know what I know.'

He remained silent and lay like that for a long time.

Nikita kept him warm from below, and his fur coats from above. Only his hands, with which he kept his coat-skirts down round Nikita's sides, and his legs which the wind kept uncovering, began to freeze, especially his right hand which had no glove. But he did not think of his legs or of his hands but only of how to warm the peasant who was lying under him. He looked out several times at Mukhorty and could see that his back was uncovered and the drugget and breeching lying on the snow, and that he ought to get up and cover him, but he could not bring himself to leave Nikita and disturb even for a moment the joyous condition he was in. He no longer felt any kind of terror.

'No fear, we shan't lose him this time!' he said to himself, referring to his getting the peasant warm with the same boastfulness with which he spoke of his buying and selling.

Vasili Andreevich lay in that way for one hour, another, and a third, but he was unconscious of the passage of time. At first impressions of the snow-storm, the sledge-shafts, and the horse with the shaft-bow shaking before his eyes, kept passing through his mind, then he remembered Nikita lying under him, then recollections of the festival, his wife, the police officer, and the box of candles, began to mingle with these; then again Nikita, this time lying under that box, then the peasants, customers and traders, and the white walls of his house with its iron roof with Nikita lying underneath, presented themselves to his imagination. Afterwards all these impressions blended into one nothingness. As the colours of the rainbow unite into one white light, so all these different impressions mingled into one, and he fell asleep.

For a long time he slept without dreaming, but just before dawn the visions recommenced. It seemed to him that he was standing by the box of tapers and that Tikhon's wife was asking for a five-kopek taper for the Church fête. He wished to take one out and give it to her, but his hands would not lift, being held tight in his pockets. He wanted to walk round the box but his feet would not move and his new clean goloshes had grown to the stone floor, and he could neither lift them nor get his feet out of the goloshes. Then the taper-box was no longer a box but a bed, and suddenly Vasili Andreevich saw himself lying in his bed at home. He was lying in his bed and could not get up. Yet it was necessary for him to get up because Ivan Matveich, the police officer, would soon call for him and he had to go with him – either to bargain for the forest or to put Mukhorty's breeching straight.

He asked his wife: 'Nikolaevna, hasn't he come yet?' 'No, he hasn't,' she replied. He heard someone drive up to the front steps. 'It must be him.' 'No, he's gone past.' 'Nikolaevna! I say, Nikolaevna, isn't he here yet?' 'No.' He was still lying on his bed and could not get up, but was always waiting. And this waiting was uncanny and yet joyful. Then suddenly his joy was completed. He whom he was expecting came; not Ivan Matveich the police officer, but someone else – yet it was he whom he had been waiting for. He came and called him; and it was he who had called him and told him to lie down on Nikita. And Vasili Andreevich was glad that that one had come for him.

'I'm coming!' he cried joyfully, and that cry awoke him, but woke him up not at all the same person he had been when he fell asleep. He tried to get up but could not, tried to move his arm and could not, to move his leg and also could not, to turn his head and could not. He was surprised but not at all disturbed by this. He understood that this was death, and was not at all disturbed by that either. He remembered that Nikita was lying under him and that he had got warm and was alive, and it seemed to him that he was Nikita and Nikita was he, and that his life was not in himself but in Nikita. He strained his ears and heard Nikita breathing and even slightly snoring. 'Nikita is alive, so I too am alive!' he said to himself triumphantly.

And he remembered his money, his shop, his house, the buying and selling, and Mironov's millions, and it was hard for him to understand why that man, called Vasili Brekhunov, had troubled himself with all those things with which he had been troubled.

'Well, it was because he did not know what the real thing was,' he thought, concerning that Vasili Brekhunov. 'He did not know, but now I know and know for sure. Now I know!' And again he heard the voice of the one who had called him before. 'I'm coming! Coming!' he responded gladly, and his whole being was filled with joyful emotion. He felt himself free and that nothing could hold him back any longer.

After that Vasili Andreevich neither saw, heard, nor felt anything more in this world.

All around the snow still eddied. The same whirlwinds of snow circled about, covering the dead Vasili Andreevich's fur coat, the shivering Mukhorty, the sledge, now scarcely to be seen, and Nikita lying at the bottom of it, kept warm beneath his dead master.

X

NIKITA awoke before daybreak. He was aroused by the cold that had begun to creep down his back. He had dreamt that he was coming from the mill with a load of his master's flour and when crossing the stream had missed the bridge and let the cart get stuck. And he saw that he had crawled under the cart and was trying to lift it by arching his back. But strange to say the cart did not move, it stuck to his back and he could neither lift it nor get out from under it. It was crushing the whole of his loins. And how cold it felt! Evidently he must crawl out. 'Have done!' he exclaimed, to whoever was pressing the cart down on him. 'Take out the sacks!' But the cart pressed down colder and colder, and then he heard a strange knocking, awoke completely, and remembered everything. The cold cart was his dead and frozen master lying upon him. And the knock was produced by Mukhorty, who had twice struck the sledge with his hoof.

'Andreich! Eh, Andreich!' Nikita called cautiously, beginning to realize the truth, and straightening his back. But Vasili Andreevich did not answer and his stomach and legs were stiff and cold and heavy like iron weights.

'He must have died! May the Kingdom of Heaven be his!' thought Nikita.

He turned his head, dug with his hand through the snow about him and opened his eyes. It was daylight; the wind was whistling as before between the shafts, and the snow was falling in the same way, except that it was no longer driving against the frame of the sledge but silently covered both sledge and horse deeper and deeper, and neither the horse's movements nor his breathing were any longer to be heard.

'He must have frozen too,' thought Nikita of Mukhorty, and indeed those hoof knocks against the sledge, which had awakened Nikita, were the last efforts the already numbed Mukhorty had made to keep on his feet before dying.

'O Lord God, it seems Thou art calling me too!' said Nikita. 'Thy Holy Will be done. But it's uncanny. . . . Still, a man can't die twice and must die once. If only it would come soon!'

And he again drew in his head, closed his eyes, and became unconscious, fully convinced that now he was certainly and finally dying.

*

It was not till noon that day that peasants dug Vasili Andreevich and Nikita out of the snow with their shovels, not more than seventy yards from the road and less than half a mile from the village.

The snow had hidden the sledge, but the shafts and the kerchief tied to them were still visible. Mukhorty, buried up to his belly in snow, with the breeching and drugget hanging down, stood all white, his dead head pressed against his frozen throat: icicles hung from his nostrils, his eyes were covered with hoar-frost as though filled with tears, and he had grown so thin in that one night that he was nothing but skin and bone.

Vasili Andreevich was stiff as a frozen carcass, and when they rolled him off Nikita his legs remained apart and his arms stretched out as they had been. His bulging hawk eyes were frozen, and his open mouth under his clipped moustache was full of snow. But Nikita though chilled through was still alive. When he had been brought to, he felt sure that he was already dead and that what was taking place with him was no longer happening in this world but in the next. When he heard the peasants shouting as they dug him out and rolled the frozen body of Vasili Andreevich from off him, he was at first surprised that in the other world peasants should be shouting in the same old way and had the same kind of body, and then when he realized that he was still in this world he was sorry rather than glad, especially when he found that the toes on both his feet were frozen.

Nikita lay in hospital for two months. They cut off three of his toes, but the others recovered so that he was still able to work and went on living for another twenty years, first as a farm-labourer, then in his old age as a watchman. He died at home as he had wished, only this year, under the icons with a lighted taper in his hands. Before he died he asked his wife's forgiveness and forgave her for the cooper. He also took leave of his son and grandchildren, and died sincerely glad that he was relieving his son and daughter-in-law of the burden of having to feed him, and that he was now really passing from this life of which he was weary into that other life which every year and every hour grew clearer and more desirable to him. Whether he is better or worse off there where he awoke after his death, whether he was disappointed or found there what he expected, we shall all soon learn.

1895

HOW MUCH LAND DOES A MAN NEED?

Много ли человеку земли нужно

I

AN elder sister came to visit her younger sister in the country. The elder was married to a tradesman in town, the younger to a peasant in the village. As the sisters sat over their tea talking, the elder began to boast of the advantages of town life: saying how comfortably they lived there, how well they dressed, what fine clothes her children wore, what good things they ate and drank, and how she went to the theatre, promenades, and entertainments.

The younger sister was piqued, and in turn disparaged the life of a tradesman, and stood up for that of a peasant.

'I would not change my way of life for yours,' said she. 'We may live roughly, but at least we are free from anxiety. You live in better style than we do, but though you often earn more than you need, you are very likely to lose all you have. You know the proverb, "Loss and gain are brothers twain." It often happens that people who are wealthy one day are begging their bread the next. Our way is safer. Though a peasant's life is not a fat one, it is a long one. We shall never grow rich, but we shall always have enough to eat.'

The elder sister said sneeringly:

'Enough? Yes, if you like to share with the pigs and the calves! What do you know of elegance or manners! However much your goodman may slave, you will die as you are living – on a dung heap – and your children the same.'

'Well, what of that?' replied the younger. 'Of course our work is rough and coarse. But, on the other hand, it is sure, and we need not bow to any one. But you, in your towns, are surrounded by temptations; today all may be right, but tomorrow the Evil One may tempt your husband with cards, wine, or women, and all will go to ruin. Don't such things happen often enough?'

Pakhom, the master of the house, was lying on the top of the stove and he listened to the women's chatter.

'It is perfectly true,' thought he. 'Busy as we are from childhood tilling mother earth, we peasants have no time to let any nonsense settle in our heads. Our only trouble is that we haven't land enough. If I had plenty of land, I shouldn't fear the Devil himself!'

The women finished their tea, chatted a while about dress, and then cleared away the tea-things and lay down to sleep.

But the Devil had been sitting behind the stove, and had heard all that was said. He was pleased that the peasant's wife had led her husband into boasting, and that he had said that if he had plenty of land he would not fear the Devil himself.

'All right,' thought the Devil. 'We will have a tussle. I'll give you land enough; and by means of that land I will get you into my power.'

II

CLOSE to the village there lived a lady, a small landowner who had an estate of about three hundred acres. She had always lived on good terms with the peasants until she engaged as her steward an old soldier, who took to burdening the people with fines. However careful Pakhom tried to be, it happened again and again that now a horse of his got among the lady's oats, now a cow strayed into her garden, now his calves found their way into her meadows – and he always had to pay a fine.

Pakhom paid up, but grumbled, and going home in a temper, was rough with his family. All through that summer, Pakhom had much trouble because of this steward, and he was even glad when winter came and the cattle had to be stabled. Though he grudged the fodder when they could no longer graze on the pasture-land, at least he was free from anxiety about them.

In the winter the news got about that the lady was going to sell her land and that the keeper of the inn on the high road was bargaining for it. When the peasants heard this they were very much alarmed.

'Well,' thought they, 'if the innkeeper gets the land, he will worry us with fines worse than the lady's steward. We all depend on that estate.'

So the peasants went on behalf of their commune, and asked the lady not to sell the land to the innkeeper, offering her a better price for it themselves. The lady agreed to let them have it. Then the peasants tried to arrange for the commune to buy the whole estate, so that it might be held by them all in common. They met twice to discuss it, but could not settle the matter; the Evil One sowed discord among them and they could not agree. So they decided to buy the land individually, each according to his means; and the lady agreed to this plan as she had to the other.

Presently Pakhom heard that a neighbour of his was buying fifty acres, and that the lady had consented to accept one half in cash and to wait a year for the other half. Pakhom felt envious.

'Look at that,' thought he, 'the land is all being sold, and I shall get none of it.' So he spoke to his wife.

'Other people are buying,' said he, 'and we must also buy twenty acres or so. Life is becoming impossible. That steward is simply crushing us with his fines.'

So they put their heads together and considered how they could manage to buy it. They had one hundred rubles laid by. They sold a colt and one half of their bees, hired out one of their sons as a labourer and took his wages in advance; borrowed the rest from a brother-in-law, and so scraped together half the purchase money.

Having done this, Pakhom chose out a farm of forty acres, some of it wooded, and went to the lady to bargain for it. They came to an agreement, and he shook hands with her upon it and paid her a deposit in advance. Then they went to town and signed the deeds; he paying half the price down, and undertaking to pay the remainder within two years.

So now Pakhom had land of his own. He borrowed seed, and sowed it on the land he had bought. The harvest was a good one, and within a year he had managed to pay off his debts both to the lady and to his brother-in-law. So he became a landowner, ploughing and sowing his own land, making hay on his own land, cutting his own trees, and feeding his cattle on his own pasture. When he went out to plough his fields, or to look at his growing corn, or at his grass-meadows, his heart would fill with joy. The grass that grew and the flowers that bloomed there seemed to him unlike any that grew elsewhere. Formerly, when he had passed by that land, it had appeared the same as any other land, but now it seemed quite different.

III

So Pakhom was well-contented, and everything would have been right if the neighbouring peasants would only not have trespassed on his corn-fields and meadows. He appealed to them most civilly, but they still went on: now the communal herdsmen would let the village cows stray into his meadows, then horses from the night pasture would get among his corn. Pakhom turned them out again and again, and forgave their owners, and for a long time he forbore to prosecute any one. But at last he lost patience and complained to the district court. He knew it was the peasants' want of land, and no evil intent on their part, that caused the trouble, but he thought:

'I cannot go on overlooking it or they will destroy all I have. They must be taught a lesson.'

So he had them up, gave them one lesson, and then another, and two or three of the peasants were fined. After a time Pakhom's neighbours began to bear him a grudge for this, and would now and then let their cattle on to his land on purpose. One peasant even got into Pakhom's wood at night and cut down five young lime trees for their bark. Pakhom passing through the wood one day noticed something white. He came nearer and saw the stripped trunks lying on the ground, and close by stood the stumps where the trees had been. Pakhom was furious.

'If he had only cut one here and there it would have been bad enough,' thought Pakhom, 'but the rascal has actually cut down a whole clump. If I could only find out who did this, I would pay him out.'

He racked his brains as to who it could be. Finally he decided: 'It must be Simon – no one else could have done it.' So he went to Simon's homestead to have a look round, but he found nothing, and only had an angry scene. However, he now felt more certain than ever that Simon had done it, and he lodged a complaint. Simon was summoned. The case was tried, and retried, and at the end of it all Simon was acquitted, there being no evidence against him. Pakhom felt still more aggrieved, and let his anger loose upon the elder and the judges.

'You let thieves grease your palms,' said he. 'If you were honest folk yourselves you would not let a thief go free.'

So Pakhom quarrelled with the judges and with his neighbours. Threats to burn his building began to be uttered. So though Pakhom had more land, his place in the commune was much worse than before.

About this time a rumour got about that many people were moving to new parts.

'There's no need for me to leave my land,' thought Pakhom. 'But some of the others might leave our village and then there would be more room for us. I would take over their land myself and make my estate a bit bigger. I could then live more at ease. As it is, I am still too cramped to be comfortable.'

One day Pakhom was sitting at home when a peasant, passing through the village, happened to call in. He was allowed to stay the night, and supper was given him. Pakhom had a talk with this peasant and asked him where he came from. The stranger answered that he came from beyond the Volga, where he had been working. One word led to another, and the man went on to say that many people were settling in those parts. He told how some people from his village had settled there. They had joined the commune, and had had twenty-five acres per man granted them. The land was so good, he said, that the rye sown on it grew as high as a horse, and so thick that five cuts of a sickle made a sheaf. One peasant, he said, had brought nothing with him but his bare hands, and now he had six horses and two cows of his own.

Pakhom's heart kindled with desire. He thought:

'Why should I suffer in this narrow hole, if one can live so well elsewhere? I will sell my land and my homestead here, and with the money I will start afresh over there and get everything new. In this crowded place one is always having trouble. But I must first go and find out all about it myself.'

Towards summer he got ready and started. He went down the Volga on a steamer to Samara, then walked another three hundred miles on foot, and at last reached the place. It was just as the stranger had said. The peasants had plenty of land: every man had twenty-five acres of communal land given him for his use, and any one who had money could buy, besides, at two shillings an acre as much good freehold land as he wanted.

Having found out all he wished to know, Pakhom returned home as autumn came on, and began selling off his belongings. He sold his land at a profit, sold his homestead and all his cattle, and withdrew from membership of the commune. He only waited till the spring, and then started with his family for the new settlement.

IV

As soon as Pakhom and his family reached their new abode, he applied for admission into the commune of a large village. He stood treat to the elders and obtained the necessary documents. Five shares of communal land were given him for his own and his sons' use: that is to say – 125 acres (not all together, but in different fields) besides the use of the communal pasture. Pakhom put up the buildings he needed, and bought cattle. Of the communal land alone he had three times as much as at his former home, and the land was good corn-land. He was ten times better off than he had been. He had plenty of arable land and pasturage, and could keep as many head of cattle as he liked.

At first, in the bustle of building and settling down, Pakhom was pleased with it all, but when he got used to it he began to think that even here he had not enough land. The first year, he sowed wheat on his share of the communal land and had a good crop. He wanted to go on sowing wheat, but had not enough communal land for the purpose, and what he had already used was not available; for in those parts wheat is only sown on virgin soil or on fallow land. It is sown for one or two years, and then the land lies fallow till it is again over-grown with prairie grass. There were many who wanted such land and there was not enough for all; so that people quarrelled about it. Those who were better off wanted it for growing wheat, and those who were poor wanted it to let to dealers, so that they might raise money to pay their taxes. Pakhom wanted to sow more wheat, so he rented land from a dealer for a year. He sowed much wheat and had a fine crop, but the land was too far from the village – the wheat had to be carted more than ten miles. After a time Pakhom noticed that some peasant-dealers were living on separate farms and were growing wealthy; and he thought:

'If I were to buy some freehold land and have a homestead on it, it would be a different thing altogether. Then it would all be nice and compact.'

The question of buying freehold land recurred to him again and again.

He went on in the same way for three years, renting land and sowing wheat. The seasons turned out well and the crops were good, so that he began to lay money by. He might have gone on living contentedly, but he grew tired of having to rent other people's land every year, and having to scramble for it. Wherever there was good land to be had, the peasants would rush for it and it was taken up at once, so that unless you were sharp about it you got none. It happened in the third year that he and a dealer together rented a piece of pasture land from some peasants; and they had already ploughed it up, when there was some dispute and the peasants went to law about it, and things fell out so that the labour was all lost.

'If it were my own land,' thought Pakhom, 'I should be independent, and there would not be all this unpleasantness.'

So Pakhom began looking out for land which he could buy; and he came across a peasant who had bought thirteen hundred acres, but having got into difficulties was willing to sell again cheap. Pakhom bargained and haggled with him, and at last they settled the price at 1,500 rubles, part in cash and part to be paid later. They had all but clinched the matter when a passing dealer happened to stop at Pakhom's one day to get a feed for his horses. He drank tea with Pakhom and they had a talk. The dealer said that he was just returning from the land of the Bashkirs, far away, where he had bought thirteen thousand acres of land, all for 1,000 rubles. Pakhom questioned him further, and the tradesman said:

'All one need do is to make friends with the chiefs. I gave away about one hundred rubles worth of silk robes and carpets, besides a case of tea, and I gave wine to those who would drink it; and I got the land for less than a penny an acre.' And he showed Pakhom the title-deeds, saying:

'The land lies near a river, and the whole prairie is virgin soil.'

Pakhom plied him with questions, and the tradesman said:

'There is more land there than you could cover if you walked a year, and it all belongs to the Bashkirs. They are as simple as sheep, and land can be got almost for nothing.'

'There now,' thought Pakhom, 'with my one thousand rubles, why should I get only thirteen hundred acres, and saddle myself with a debt besides? If I take it out there, I can get more than ten times as much for the money.'

V

PAKHOM inquired how to get to the place, and as soon as the tradesman had left him, he prepared to go there himself. He left his wife to look after the homestead, and started on his journey taking his man

gladly give you as much land as you want. You have only to point it out with your hand and it is yours.'

The Bashkirs talked again for a while and began to dispute. Pakhom asked what they were disputing about, and the interpreter told him that some of them thought they ought to ask their chief about the land and not act in his absence, while others thought there was no need to wait for his return.

VI

WHILE the Bashkirs were disputing, a man in a large fox-fur cap appeared on the scene. They all became silent and rose to their feet. The interpreter said, 'This is our chief himself.'

Pakhom immediately fetched the best dressing-gown and five pounds of tea, and offered these to the chief. The chief accepted them, and seated himself in the place of honour. The Bashkirs at once began telling him something. The chief listened for a while, then made a sign with his head for them to be silent, and addressing himself to Pakhom, said in Russian:

'Well, let it be so. Choose whatever piece of land you like; we have plenty of it.'

'How can I take as much as I like?' thought Pakhom. 'I must get a deed to make it secure, or else they may say, "It is yours," and afterwards may take it away again.'

'Thank you for your kind words,' he said aloud. 'You have much land, and I only want a little. But I should like to be sure which bit is mine. Could it not be measured and made over to me? Life and death are in God's hands. You good people give it to me, but your children might wish to take it away again.'

'You are quite right,' said the chief. 'We will make it over to you.'

'I heard that a dealer had been here,' continued Pakhom, 'and that you gave him a little land, too, and signed title-deeds to that effect. I should like to have it done in the same way.'

The chief understood.

'Yes,' replied he, 'that can be done quite easily. We have a scribe, and we will go to town with you and have the deed properly sealed.'

'And what will be the price?' asked Pakhom.

'Our price is always the same: one thousand rubles a day.'

Pakhom did not understand.

'A day? What measure is that? How many acres would that be?'

'We do not know how to reckon it out,' said the chief. 'We sell it by the day. As much as you can go round on your feet in a day is yours, and the price is one thousand rubles a day.'

Pakhom was surprised.

'But in a day you can get round a large tract of land,' he said.

The chief laughed.

'It will all be yours!' said he. 'But there is one condition: If you don't return on the same day to the spot whence you started, your money is lost.'

'But how am I to mark the way that I have gone?'

'Why, we shall go to any spot you like, and stay there. You must start from that spot and make your round, taking a spade with you. Wherever you think necessary, make a mark. At every turning, dig a hole and pile up the turf; then afterwards we will go round with a plough from hole to hole. You may make as large a circuit as you please, but before the sun sets you must return to the place you started from. All the land you cover will be yours.'

Pakhom was delighted. It was decided to start early next morning. They talked a while, and after drinking some more kumiss and eating some more mutton, they had tea again, and then the night came on. They gave Pakhom a feather-bed to sleep on, and the Bashkirs dispersed for the night, promising to assemble the next morning at day-break and ride out before sunrise to the appointed spot.

VII

PAKHOM lay on the feather-bed, but could not sleep. He kept thinking about the land.

'What a large tract I will mark off!' thought he. 'I can easily do thirty-five miles in a day. The days are long now, and within a circuit of thirty-five miles what a lot of land there will be! I will sell the poorer land, or let it to peasants, but I'll pick out the best and farm it. I will buy two ox-teams, and hire two more labourers. About a hundred and fifty acres shall be plough-land, and I will pasture cattle on the rest.'

Pakhom lay awake all night, and dozed off only just before dawn. Hardly were his eyes closed when he had a dream. He thought he was lying in that same tent and heard somebody chuckling outside. He wondered who it could be, and rose and went out, and he saw the Bashkir chief sitting in front of the tent holding his sides and rolling about with laughter. Going nearer to the chief, Pakhom asked: 'What are you laughing at?' But he saw that it was no longer the chief, but the dealer who had recently stopped at his house and had told him about the land. Just as Pakhom was going to ask, 'Have you been here long?' he saw that it was not the dealer, but the peasant who had come up from the Volga, long ago, to Pakhom's old home. Then he saw that it was not the peasant either, but the Devil himself with hoofs and horns, sitting there and chuckling, and before him lay a man barefoot, prostrate on the ground, with only trousers and a shirt on. And Pakhom dreamt that he looked more attentively to see what sort of a man it was that was lying there, and he saw that the man was dead, and that it was himself! He awoke horror-struck.

'What things one does dream,' thought he.

Looking round he saw through the open door that the dawn was breaking.

'It's time to wake them up,' thought he. 'We ought to be starting.'

He got up, roused his man (who was sleeping in his cart), bade him harness; and went to call the Bashkirs.

'It's time to go to the steppe to measure the land,' he said.

The Bashkirs rose and assembled, and the chief came too. Then they began drinking kumiss again, and offered Pakhom some tea, but he would not wait.

'If we are to go, let us go. It is high time,' said he.

VIII

THE Bashkirs got ready and they all started: some mounted on horses, and some in carts. Pakhom drove in his own small cart with his servant and took a spade with him. When they reached the steppe, the morning red was beginning to kindle. They ascended a hillock (called by the Bashkirs a *shikhan*) and dismounting from their carts and their horses, gathered in one spot. The chief came up to Pakhom and stretching out his arm towards the plain;

'See,' said he, 'all this, as far as your eye can reach, is ours. You may have any part of it you like.'

Pakhom's eyes glistened: it was all virgin soil, as flat as the palm of your hand, as black as the seed of a poppy, and in the hollows different kinds of grasses grew breast high.

The chief took off his fox-fur cap, placed it on the ground and said:

'This will be the mark. Start from here, and return here again. All the land you go round shall be yours.'

Pakhom took out his money and put it on the cap. Then he took off his outer coat, remaining in his sleeveless under-coat. He unfastened his girdle and tied it tight below his stomach, put a little bag of bread into the breast of his coat, and tying a flask of water to his girdle, he drew up the tops of his boots, took the spade from his man, and stood ready to start. He considered for some moments which way he had better go – it was tempting everywhere.

'No matter,' he concluded, 'I will go towards the rising sun.'

He turned his face to the east, stretched himself, and waited for the sun to appear above the rim.

'I must lose no time,' he thought, 'and it is easier walking while it is still cool.'

The sun's rays had hardly flashed above the horizon, before Pakhom, carrying the spade over his shoulder, went down into the steppe.

Pakhom started walking neither slowly nor quickly. After having gone a thousand yards he stopped, dug a hole, and placed pieces of turf one on another to make it more visible. Then he went on; and now that he had walked off his stiffness he quickened his pace. After a while he dug another hole.

Pakhom looked back. The hillock could be distinctly seen in the sunlight, with the people on it, and the glittering tyres of the cart-wheels. At a rough guess Pakhom concluded that he had walked three miles. It was growing warmer; he took off his under-coat, flung it across his shoulder, and went on again. It had grown quite warm now; he looked at the sun, it was time to think of breakfast.

'The first shift is done, but there are four in a day, and it is too soon yet to turn. But I will just take off my boots,' said he to himself.

He sat down, took off his boots, stuck them into his girdle, and went on. It was easy walking now.

'I will go on for another three miles,' thought he, 'and then turn to the left. This spot is so fine, that it would be a pity to lose it. The further one goes, the better the land seems.'

He went straight on for a while, and when he looked round, the hillock was scarcely visible and the people on it looked like black ants, and he could just see something glistening there in the sun.

'Ah,' thought Pakhom, 'I have gone far enough in this direction, it is time to turn. Besides I am in a regular sweat, and very thirsty.'

He stopped, dug a large hole, and heaped up pieces of turf. Next he untied his flask, had a drink, and then turned sharply to the left. He went on and on; the grass was high, and it was very hot.

Pakhom began to grow tired: he looked at the sun and saw that it was noon.

'Well,' he thought, 'I must have a rest.'

He sat down, and ate some bread and drank some water; but he did not lie down, thinking that if he did he might fall asleep. After sitting a little while, he went on again. At first he walked easily: the food had strengthened him; but it had become terribly hot and he felt sleepy, still he went on, thinking: 'An hour to suffer, a life-time to live.'

He went a long way in this direction also, and was about to turn to the left again, when he perceived a damp hollow: 'It would be a pity to leave that out,' he thought. 'Flax would do well there.' So he went on past the hollow, and dug a hole on the other side of it before he turned the corner. Pakhom looked towards the hillock. The heat made the air hazy: it seemed to be quivering, and through the haze the people on the hillock could scarcely be seen.

'Ah!' thought Pakhom, 'I have made the sides too long; I must make this one shorter.' And he went along the third side, stepping faster. He looked at the sun: it was nearly half-way to the horizon, and he had not yet done two miles of the third side of the square. He was still ten miles from the goal.

'No,' he thought, 'though it will make my land lop-sided, I must hurry back in a straight line now. I might go too far, and as it is I have a great deal of land.'

So Pakhom hurriedly dug a hole, and turned straight towards the hillock.

IX

PAKHOM went straight towards the hillock, but he now walked with difficulty. He was done up with the heat, his bare feet were cut and bruised, and his legs began to fail. He longed to rest, but it was impossible if he meant to get back before sunset. The sun waits for no man, and it was sinking lower and lower.

'Oh dear,' he thought, 'if only I have not blundered trying for too much! What if I am too late?'

He looked towards the hillock and at the sun. He was still far from his goal, and the sun was already near the rim.

Pakhom walked on and on; it was very hard walking but he went quicker and quicker. He pressed on, but was still far from the place. He began running, threw away his coat, his boots, his flask, and his cap, and kept only the spade which he used as a support.

'What shall I do?' he thought again, 'I have grasped too much and ruined the whole affair. I can't get there before the sun sets.'

And this fear made him still more breathless. Pakhom went on running, his soaking shirt and trousers stuck to him and his mouth was parched. His breast was working like a blacksmith's bellows, his heart was beating like a hammer, and his legs were giving way as if they did not belong to him. Pakhom was seized with terror lest he should die of the strain.

Though afraid of death, he could not stop. 'After having run all that way they will call me a fool if I stop now,' thought he. And he ran on and on, and drew near and heard the Baskhirs yelling and shouting to him, and their cries inflamed his heart still more. He gathered his last strength and ran on.

The sun was close to the rim, and cloaked in mist looked large, and red as blood. Now, yes now, it was about to set! The sun was quite low, but he was also quite near his aim. Pakhom could already see the people on the hillock waving their arms to hurry him up. He could see the fox-fur cap on the ground and the money on it, and the chief sitting on the ground holding his sides. And Pakhom remembered his dream.

'There is plenty of land,' thought he, 'but will God let me live on it? I have lost my life, I have lost my life! I shall never reach that spot!'

Pakhom looked at the sun, which had reached the earth: one side of it had already disappeared. With all his remaining strength he rushed on, bending his body forward so that his legs could hardly follow fast enough to keep him from falling. Just as he reached the hillock it suddenly grew dark. He looked up – the sun had already set! He gave a cry: 'All my labour has been in vain,' thought he, and was about to stop, but he heard the Bashkirs still shouting, and remembered that though to him, from below, the sun seemed to have set, they on the hillock could still see it. He took a long breath and ran up the hillock. It was still light there. He reached the top and saw the cap. Before it sat the chief laughing and holding his sides. Again Pakhom remembered his dream, and he uttered a cry: his legs gave way beneath him, he fell forward and reached the cap with his hands.

'Ah, that's a fine fellow!' exclaimed the chief. 'He has gained much land!'

Pakhom's servant came running up and tried to raise him, but he saw that blood was flowing from his mouth. Pakhom was dead!

The Bashkirs clicked their tongues to show their pity.

His servant picked up the spade and dug a grave long enough for Pakhom to lie in, and buried him in it. Six feet from his head to his heels was all he needed.

1886

THE DEATH OF IVAN ILYCH

Смерть Ивана Ильича

I

During an interval in the Melvinski trial in the large building of the Law Courts the members and public prosecutor met in Ivan Egorovich Shebek's private room, where the conversation turned on the celebrated Krasovski case. Fedor Vasilievich warmly maintained that it was not subject to their jurisdiction, Ivan Egorovich maintained the contrary, while Peter Ivanovich, not having entered into the discussion at the start, took no part in it but looked through the *Gazette* which had just been handed in.

'Gentlemen,' he said, 'Ivan Ilych has died!'

'You don't say so!'

'Here, read it yourself,' replied Peter Ivanovich, handing Fedor Vasilievich the paper still damp from the press. Surrounded by a black border were the words: 'Praskovya Fedorovna Golovina, with profound sorrow, informs relatives and friends of the demise of her beloved husband Ivan Ilych Golovin, Member of the Court of Justice, which occurred on February the 4th of this year 1882. The funeral will take place on Friday at one o'clock in the afternoon.'

Ivan Ilych had been a colleague of the gentlemen present and was liked by them all. He had been ill for some weeks with an illness said to be incurable. His post had been kept open for him, but there had been conjectures that in case of his death Alexeev might receive his appointment, and that either Vinnikov or Shtabel would succeed Alexeev. So on receiving the news of Ivan Ilych's death the first thought of each of the gentlemen in that private room was of the changes and promotions it might occasion among themselves or their acquaintances.

'I shall be sure to get Shtabel's place or Vinnikov's' thought Fedor Vasilievich. 'I was promised that long ago, and the promotion means an extra eight hundred rubles a year for me besides the allowance.'

'Now I must apply for my brother-in-law's transfer from Kaluga,' thought Peter Ivanovich. 'My wife will be very glad, and then she won't be able to say that I never do anything for her relations.'

'I thought he would never leave his bed again,' said Peter Ivanovich aloud. 'It's very sad.'

'But what really was the matter with him?'

'The doctors couldn't say – at least they could, but each of them said something different. When last I saw him I thought he was getting better.'

'And I haven't been to see him since the holidays. I always meant to go.'

'Had he any property?'

'I think his wife had a little – but something quite trifling.'

'We shall have to go to see her, but they live so terribly far away.'

'Far away from you, you mean. Everything's far away from your place.'

'You see, he never can forgive my living on the other side of the river,' said Peter Ivanovich, smiling at Shebek. Then, still talking of the distances between different parts of the city, they returned to the Court.

Besides considerations as to the possible transfers and promotions likely to result from Ivan Ilych's death, the mere fact of the death of a near acquaintance aroused, as usual, in all who heard of it the complacent feeling that, 'it is he who is dead and not I'.

Each one thought or felt, 'Well, he's dead but I'm alive!' But the more intimate of Ivan Ilych's acquaintances, his so-called friends, could not help thinking also that they would now have to fulfil the very tiresome demands of propriety by attending the funeral service and paying a visit of condolence to the widow.

Fedor Vasilievich and Peter Ivanovich had been his nearest acquaintances. Peter Ivanovich had studied law with Ivan Ilych and had considered himself to be under obligations to him.

Having told his wife at dinner-time of Ivan Ilych's death, and of his conjecture that it might be possible to get her brother transferred to their circuit, Peter Ivanovich sacrificed his usual nap, put on his evening clothes, and drove to Ivan Ilych's house.

At the entrance stood a carriage and two cabs. Leaning against the wall in the hall downstairs near the cloak-stand was a coffin-lid covered with cloth of gold, ornamented with gold cord and tassels, that had been polished up with metal powder. Two ladies in black were taking off their fur cloaks. Peter Ivanovich recognized one of them as Ivan Ilych's sister, but the other was a stranger to him. His colleague Schwartz was just coming downstairs, but on seeing Peter Ivanovich enter he stopped and winked at him, as if to say: 'Ivan Ilych has made a mess of things – not like you and me.'

Schwartz's face with his Piccadilly whiskers, and his slim figure in evening dress, had as usual an air of elegant solemnity which contrasted with the playfulness of his character and had a special piquancy here, or so it seemed to Peter Ivanovich.

Peter Ivanovich allowed the ladies to precede him and slowly followed them upstairs. Schwartz did not come down but remained where he was, and Peter Ivanovich understood that he wanted to arrange where they should play bridge that evening. The ladies went upstairs to the widow's room, and Schwartz with seriously compressed lips but a playful look in his eyes, indicated by a twist of his eyebrows the room to the right where the body lay.

Peter Ivanovich, like everyone else on such occasions, entered feeling uncertain what he would have to do. All he knew was that at such times it is always safe to cross oneself. But he was not quite sure whether one should make obeisances while doing so. He therefore adopted a middle course. On entering the room he began crossing himself and made a slight movement resembling a bow. At the same time, as far as the motion of his head and arm allowed, he surveyed the room. Two young men – apparently nephews, one of whom was a high-school pupil – were leaving the room, crossing themselves as they did so. An old woman was standing motionless, and a lady with strangely arched eyebrows was saying something to her in a whisper. A vigorous, resolute Church Reader, in a frock-coat, was reading something in a loud voice with an expression that precluded any contradiction. The butler's assistant, Gerasim, stepping lightly in front of Peter Ivanovich, was strewing something on the floor. Noticing this, Peter Ivanovich was immediately aware of a faint odour of a decomposing body.

The last time he had called on Ivan Ilych, Peter Ivanovich had seen Gerasim in the study. Ivan Ilych had been particularly fond of him and he was performing the duty of a sick nurse.

Peter Ivanovich continued to make the sign of the cross slightly inclining his head in an intermediate direction between the coffin, the Reader, and the icons on the table in a corner of the room. Afterwards, when it seemed to him that this movement of his arm in crossing himself had gone on too long, he stopped and began to look at the corpse.

The dead man lay, as dead men always lie, in a specially heavy way, his rigid limbs sunk in the soft cushions of the coffin, with the head forever bowed on the pillow. His yellow waxen brow with bald patches over his sunken temples was thrust up in the way peculiar to the dead, the protruding nose seeming to press on the upper lip. He was much changed and had grown even thinner since Peter Ivanovich had last seen him, but, as is always the case with the dead, his face was handsomer and above all more dignified than when he was alive. The expression on the face said that what was necessary had been accomplished, and accomplished rightly. Besides this there was in that expression a reproach and a warning to the living. This warning seemed to Peter Ivanovich out of place, or at least not applicable to him. He felt a certain discomfort and so he hurriedly crossed himself once more and turned and went out of the door – too hurriedly and too regardless of propriety, as he himself was aware.

Schwartz was waiting for him in the adjoining room with legs spread wide apart and both hands toying with his top-hat behind his back. The mere sight of that playful, well-groomed, and elegant figure refreshed Peter Ivanovich. He felt that Schwartz was above all these happenings and would not surrender to any depressing influences. His very look said that this incident of a church service for Ivan Ilych could not be a sufficient reason for infringing the order of the session – in other words, that it would certainly not prevent his unwrapping a new pack of cards and shuffling them that evening while a footman placed four fresh candles on the table: in fact, that there was no reason for supposing that this incident would hinder their spending the evening agreeably. Indeed he said this in a whisper as Peter Ivanovich passed him, proposing that they should meet for a game at Fedor Vasilievich's. But apparently Peter Ivanovich was not destined to play bridge that evening. Praskovya Fedorovna (a short, fat woman who despite all efforts to the contrary had continued to broaden steadily from her shoulders downwards and who had the same extraordinarily arched eyebrows as the lady who had been standing by the coffin), dressed all in black, her head covered with lace, came out of her own room with some other ladies, conducted them to the room where the dead body lay, and said: 'The service will begin immediately. Please go in.'

Schwartz, making an indefinite bow, stood still, evidently neither accepting nor declining this invitation. Praskovya Fedorovna, recognizing Peter Ivanovich, sighed, went close up to him, took his hand and said: 'I know you were a true friend to Ivan Ilych . . .' and looked at him awaiting some suitable response. And Peter Ivanovich knew that, just as it had been the right thing to cross himself in that room, so what he had to do here was to press her hand, sigh, and say, 'Believe me . . .'. So he did all this and as he did it felt that the desired result had been achieved: that both he and she were touched.

'Come with me. I want to speak to you before it begins,' said the widow. 'Give me your arm.'

Peter Ivanovich gave her his arm and they went to the inner rooms, passing Schwartz who winked at Peter Ivanovich compassionately. 'That does for our bridge! Don't object if we find another player. Perhaps you can cut in when you do escape,' said his playful look.

Peter Ivanovich sighed still more deeply and despondently, and Praskovya Fedorovna pressed his arm gratefully. When they reached the drawing-room, upholstered in pink cretonne and lighted by a dim lamp, they sat down at the table – she on a sofa and Peter Ivanovich on a low pouffe, the springs of which yielded spasmodically under his weight. Praskovya Fedorovna had been on the point of warning him to take another seat, but felt that such a warning was out of keeping with her present condition and so changed her mind. As he sat down on the pouffe Peter Ivanovich recalled how Ivan Ilych had arranged this room and had consulted him regarding this pink cretonne with green leaves. The whole room was full of furniture and knick-knacks, and on her way to the sofa the lace of the widow's black shawl caught on the carved edge of the table. Peter Ivanovich rose to detach it, and the springs of the pouffe, relieved of his weight, rose also and gave him a push. The widow began detaching her shawl herself, and Peter Ivanovich again sat down, suppressing the rebellious springs of the pouffe under him. But the widow had not quite freed herself and Peter Ivanovich got up again, and again the pouffe rebelled and even creaked. When this was all over she took out a clean cambric handkerchief and began to weep. The episode with the shawl and the struggle with the pouffe had cooled Peter Ivanovich's emotions and he sat there with a sullen look on his face. This awkward situation was interrupted by Sokolov, Ivan Ilych's butler, who came to report that the plot in the cemetery that Praskovya Fedorovna had chosen would cost two hundred rubles. She stopped weeping and, looking at Peter Ivanovich with the air of a victim, remarked in French that it was very hard for her. Peter Ivanovich made a silent gesture signifying his full conviction that it must indeed be so.

'Please smoke,' she said in a magnanimous yet crushed voice, and turned to discuss with Sokolov the price of the plot for the grave.

Peter Ivanovich while lighting his cigarette heard her inquiring very circumstantially into the prices of different plots in the cemetery and finally decide which she would take. When this was done she gave instructions about engaging the choir. Sokolov then left the room.

'I look after everything myself,' she told Peter Ivanovich, shifting the albums that lay on the table; and noticing that the table was endangered by his cigarette-ash, she immediately passed him an ash-tray, saying as she did so: 'I consider it an affectation to say that my grief prevents my attending to practical affairs. On the contrary, if anything can – I won't say console me, but – distract me, it is seeing to everything concerning him.' She again took out her handkerchief as if preparing to cry, but suddenly, as if mastering her feeling, she shook herself and began to speak calmly. 'But there is something I want to talk to you about.'

Peter Ivanovich bowed, keeping control of the springs of the pouffe, which immediately began quivering under him.

'He suffered terribly the last few days.'

'Did he?' said Peter Ivanovich.

'Oh, terribly! He screamed unceasingly, not for minutes but for hours. For the last three days he screamed incessantly. It was un-endurable. I cannot understand how I bore it; you could hear him three rooms off. Oh, what I have suffered!'

'Is it possible that he was conscious all that time?' asked Peter Ivanovich.

'Yes,' she whispered. 'To the last moment. He took leave of us a quarter of an hour before he died, and asked us to take Volodya away.'

The thought of the sufferings of this man he had known so intimately, first as a merry little boy, then as a school-mate, and later as a grown-up colleague, suddenly struck Peter Ivanovich with horror, despite an unpleasant consciousness of his own and this woman's dissimulation. He again saw that brow, and that nose press-ing down on the lip, and felt afraid for himself.

'Three days of frightful suffering and then death! Why, that might suddenly, at any time, happen to me,' he thought, and for a moment felt terrified. But – he did not himself know how – the customary reflection at once occurred to him that this had happened to Ivan Ilych and not to him, and that it should not and could not happen to him, and that to think that it could would be yielding to depression which he ought not to do, as Schwartz's expression plainly showed. After which reflection Peter Ivanovich felt reassured, and began to ask with interest about the details of Ivan Ilych's death, as though death was an accident natural to Ivan Ilych but certainly not to himself.

After many details of the really dreadful physical sufferings Ivan Ilych had endured (which details he learnt only from the effect those sufferings had produced on Praskovya Fedorovna's nerves) the widow apparently found it necessary to get to business.

'Oh, Peter Ivanovich, how hard it is! How terribly, terribly hard!' and she again began to weep.

Peter Ivanovich sighed and waited for her to finish blowing her nose. When she had done so he said, 'Believe me . . .', and she again began talking and brought out what was evidently her chief concern with him – namely, to question him as to how she could obtain a grant of money from the government on the occasion of her husband's death. She made it appear that she was asking Peter Ivanovich's advice about her pension, but he soon saw that she already knew about that to the minutest detail, more even than he did himself. She knew how much could be got out of the government in consequence of her husband's death, but wanted to find out whether she could not possibly extract something more. Peter Ivanovich tried to think of some means of doing so, but after reflecting for a while and, out of propriety, condemning the government for its niggardliness, he said he thought that nothing more could be got. Then she sighed and evidently began to devise means of getting rid of her visitor. Noticing this, he put out his cigarette, rose, pressed her hand, and went out into the ante-room.

In the dining-room where the clock stood that Ivan Ilych had liked so much and had bought at an antique shop, Peter Ivanovich met a priest and a few acquaintances who had come to attend the service, and he recognized Ivan Ilych's daughter, a handsome young woman. She was in black and her slim figure appeared slimmer than ever. She had a gloomy, determined, almost angry expression, and bowed to Peter Ivanovich as though he were in some way to blame. Behind her, with the same offended look, stood a wealthy young man, an examining magistrate, whom Peter Ivanovich also knew and who was her fiancé, as he had heard. He bowed mournfully to them and was about to pass into the death-chamber, when from under the stairs appeared the figure of Ivan Ilych's schoolboy son, who was extremely like his father. He seemed a little Ivan Ilych, such as Peter Ivanovich remembered when they studied law together. His tear-stained eyes had in them the look that is seen in the eyes of boys of thirteen or fourteen who are not pure-minded. When he saw Peter Ivanovich he scowled morosely and shamefacedly. Peter Ivanovich nodded to him and entered the death-chamber. The service began: candles, groans, incense, tears, and sobs. Peter Ivanovich stood looking gloomily down at his feet. He did not look once at the dead man, did not yield to any depressing influence, and was one of the first to leave the room. There was no one in the ante-room, but Gerasim darted out of the dead man's room, rummaged with his strong hands among the fur coats to find Peter Ivanovich's and helped him on with it.

'Well, friend Gerasim,' said Peter Ivanovich, so as to say something. 'It's a sad affair, isn't it?'

'It's God's will. We shall all come to it some day,' said Gerasim, displaying his teeth – the even, white teeth of a healthy peasant – and, like a man in the thick of urgent work, he briskly opened the front door, called the coachman, helped Peter Ivanovich into the sledge, and sprang back to the porch as if in readiness for what he had to do next.

Peter Ivanovich found the fresh air particularly pleasant after the smell of incense, the dead body, and carbolic acid.

'Where to, sir?' asked the coachman.

'It's not too late even now. . . . I'll call round on Fedor Vasilievich.'

He accordingly drove there and found them just finishing the first rubber, so that it was quite convenient for him to cut in.

II

IVAN ILYCH's life had been most simple and most ordinary and therefore most terrible.

He had been a member of the Court of Justice, and died at the age of forty-five. His father had been an official who after serving in various ministries and departments in Petersburg had made the sort of career which brings men to positions from which by reason of their long service they cannot be dismissed, though they are obviously unfit to hold any responsible position, and for whom therefore posts are specially created, which though fictitious carry salaries of from six to ten thousand rubles that are not fictitious, and in receipt of which they live on to a great age.

Such was the Privy Councillor and superfluous member of various superfluous institutions, Ilya Epimovich Golovin.

He had three sons, of whom Ivan Ilych was the second. The eldest son was following in his father's footsteps only in another department, and was already approaching that stage in the service at which a similar sinecure would be reached. The third son was a failure. He had ruined his prospects in a number of positions and was now serving in the railway department. His father and brothers, and still more their wives, not merely disliked meeting him, but avoided remembering his existence unless compelled to do so. His sister had married Baron Greff, a Petersburg official of her father's type. Ivan Ilych was *le phénix de la famille* as people said. He was neither as cold and formal as his elder brother nor as wild as the younger, but was a happy mean between them – an intelligent, polished, lively and agreeable man. He had studied with his younger brother at the School of Law, but the latter had failed to complete the course and was expelled when he was in the fifth class. Ivan Ilych finished the course well. Even when he was at the School of Law he was just what he remained for the rest of his life: a capable, cheerful, good-natured, and sociable man, though strict in the fulfilment of what he considered to be his duty: and he considered his duty to be what was so considered by those in authority. Neither as a boy nor as a man was he a toady, but from early youth was by nature attracted to people of high station as a fly is drawn to the light, assimilating their ways and views of life and establishing friendly relations with them. All the enthusiasms of child-hood and youth passed without leaving much trace on him; he succumbed to sensuality, to vanity, and latterly among the highest classes to liberalism, but always within limits which his instinct un-failingly indicated to him as correct.

At school he had done things which had formerly seemed to him very horrid and made him feel disgusted with himself when he did them; but when later on he saw that such actions were done by people of good position and that they did not regard them as wrong, he was able not exactly to regard them as right, but to forget about them entirely or not be at all troubled at remembering them.

Having graduated from the School of Law and qualified for the tenth rank of the civil service, and having received money from his father for his equipment, Ivan Ilych ordered himself clothes at Scharmer's, the fashionable tailor, hung a medallion inscribed *respice finem* on his watch-chain, took leave of his professor and the prince who was patron of the school, had a farewell dinner with his comrades at Donon's first-class restaurant, and with his new and fashionable portmanteau, linen, clothes, shaving and other toilet appliances, and a travelling rug, all purchased at the best shops, he set off for one of the provinces where, through his father's influence, he had been attached to the Governor as an official for special service.

In the province Ivan Ilych soon arranged as easy and agreeable a position for himself as he had had at the School of Law. He performed his official tasks, made his career, and at the same time amused himself pleasantly and decorously. Occasionally he paid official visits to country districts, where he behaved with dignity both to his superiors and inferiors, and performed the duties entrusted to him, which related chiefly to the sectarians, with an exactness and incorruptible honesty of which he could not but feel proud.

In official matters, despite his youth and taste for frivolous gaiety, he was exceedingly reserved, punctilious, and even severe; but in society he was often amusing and witty, and always good-natured, correct in his manner, and *bon enfant*, as the governor and his wife – with whom he was like one of the family – used to say of him.

In the province he had an affair with a lady who made advances to the elegant young lawyer, and there was also a milliner; and there were carousals with aides-de-camp who visited the district, and after-supper visits to a certain outlying street of doubtful reputation; and there was too some obsequiousness to his chief and even to his chief's wife, but all this was done with such a tone of good breeding that no hard names could be applied to it. It all came under the heading of the French saying: '*Il faut que jeunesse se passe*.'[1] It was all done with clean hands, in clean linen, with French phrases, and above all among people of the best society and consequently with the approval of people of rank.

So Ivan Ilych served for five years and then came a change in his official life. The new and reformed judicial institutions were introduced, and new men were needed. Ivan Ilych became such a new man. He was offered the post of examining magistrate, and he

---

[1] Youth must have its fling.

accepted it though the post was in another province and obliged him to give up the connexions he had formed and to make new ones. His friends met to give him a send-off; they had a group-photograph taken and presented him with a silver cigarette-case, and he set off to his new post.

As examining magistrate Ivan Ilych was just as *comme il faut* and decorous a man, inspiring general respect and capable of separating his official duties from his private life, as he had been when acting as an official on special service. His duties now as examining magistrate were far more interesting and attractive than before. In his former position it had been pleasant to wear an undress uniform made by Scharmer, and to pass through the crowd of petitioners and officials who were timorously awaiting an audience with the Governor, and who envied him as with free and easy gait he went straight into his chief's private room to have a cup of tea and a cigarette with him. But not many people had then been directly dependent on him – only police officials and the sectarians when he went on special missions – and he liked to treat them politely, almost as comrades, as if he were letting them feel that he who had the power to crush them was treating them in this simple, friendly way. There were then but few such people. But now, as an examining magistrate, Ivan Ilych felt that everyone without exception, even the most important and self-satisfied, was in his power, and that he need only write a few words on a sheet of paper with a certain heading, and this or that important, self-satisfied person would be brought before him in the role of an accused person or a witness, and if he did not choose to allow him to sit down, would have to stand before him and answer his questions. Ivan Ilych never abused his power; he tried on the contrary to soften its expression, but the consciousness of it and of the possibility of softening its effect, supplied the chief interest and attraction of his office. In his work itself, especially in his examinations, he very soon acquired a method of eliminating all considerations irrelevant to the legal aspect of the case, and reducing even the most complicated case to a form in which it would be presented on paper only in its externals, completely excluding his personal opinion of the matter, while above all observing every prescribed formality. The work was new and Ivan Ilych was one of the first men to apply the new Code of 1864.[2]

[2] The emancipation of the serfs in 1861 was followed by a thorough all-round reform of judicial proceedings.

On taking up the post of examining magistrate in a new town, he made new acquaintances and connexions, placed himself on a new footing, and assumed a somewhat different tone. He took up an attitude of rather dignified aloofness towards the provincial authorities, but picked out the best circle of legal gentlemen and wealthy gentry living in the town and assumed a tone of slight dissatisfaction with the government, of moderate liberalism, and of enlightened citizenship. At the same time, without at all altering the elegance of his toilet, he ceased shaving his chin and allowed his beard to grow as it pleased.

Ivan Ilych settled down very pleasantly in this new town. The society there, which inclined towards opposition to the Governor, was friendly, his salary was larger, and he began to play whist which he found added not a little to the pleasure of life, for he had a capacity for cards, played good-humouredly, and calculated rapidly and astutely, so that he usually won.

After living there for two years he met his future wife, Praskovya Fedorovna Mikhel, who was the most attractive, clever, and brilliant girl of the set in which he moved, and among other amusements and relaxations from his labours as examining magistrate, Ivan Ilych established light and playful relations with her.

While he had been an official on special service he had been accustomed to dance, but now as an examining magistrate it was exceptional for him to do so. If he danced now, he did it as if to show that though he served under the reformed order of things, and had reached the fifth official rank, yet when it came to dancing he could do it better than most people. So at the end of an evening he sometimes danced with Praskovya Fedorovna, and it was chiefly during these dances that he captivated her. She fell in love with him. Ivan Ilych had at first no definite intention of marrying, but when the girl fell in love with him he said to himself: 'Really, why shouldn't I marry?'

Praskovya Fedorovna came of a good family, was not bad looking, and had some little property. Ivan Ilych might have aspired to a more brilliant match, but even this was good. He had his salary, and she, he hoped, would have an equal income. She was well connected, and was a sweet, pretty, and thoroughly correct young woman. To say that Ivan Ilych married because he fell in love with Praskovya Fedorovna and found that she sympathized with his view of life would be as incorrect as to say that he married because his social circle approved of the match. He was swayed by both these considerations:

the marriage gave him personal satisfaction, and at the same time it was considered the right thing by the most highly placed of his associates.

So Ivan Ilych got married.

The preparations for marriage and the beginning of married life, with its conjugal caresses, the new furniture, new crockery, and new linen, were very pleasant until his wife became pregnant – so that Ivan Ilych had begun to think that marriage would not impair the easy, agreeable, gay and always decorous character of his life, approved of by society and regarded by himself as natural, but would even improve it. But from the first months of his wife's pregnancy, something new, unpleasant, depressing, and unseemly, and from which there was no way of escape, unexpectedly showed itself.

His wife, without any reason – *de gaieté de cœur* as Ivan Ilych expressed it to himself – began to disturb the pleasure and propriety of their life. She began to be jealous without any cause, expected him to devote his whole attention to her, found fault with everything, and made coarse and ill-mannered scenes.

At first Ivan Ilych hoped to escape from the unpleasantness of this state of affairs by the same easy and decorous relation to life that had served him heretofore: he tried to ignore his wife's disagreeable moods, continued to live in his usual easy and pleasant way, invited friends to his house for a game of cards, and also tried going out to his club or spending his evenings with friends. But one day his wife began upbraiding him so vigorously, using such coarse words, and continued to abuse him every time he did not fulfil her demands, so resolutely and with such evident determination not to give way till he submitted – that is, till he stayed at home and was bored just as she was – that he became alarmed. He now realized that matrimony – at any rate with Praskovya Fedorovna – was not always conducive to the pleasures and amenities of life but on the contrary often infringed both comfort and propriety, and that he must therefore entrench himself against such infringement. And Ivan Ilych began to seek for means of doing so. His official duties were the one thing that imposed upon Praskovya Fedorovna, and by means of his official work and the duties attached to it he began struggling with his wife to secure his own independence.

With the birth of their child, the attempts to feed it and the various failures in doing so, and with the real and imaginary illnesses of mother and child, in which Ivan Ilych's sympathy was demanded but about which he understood nothing, the need of securing for himself an existence outside his family life became still more imperative.

As his wife grew more irritable and exacting and Ivan Ilych transferred the centre of gravity of his life more and more to his official work, so did he grow to like his work better and became more ambitious than before.

Very soon, within a year of his wedding, Ivan Ilych had realized that marriage, though it may add some comforts to life, is in fact a very intricate and difficult affair towards which in order to perform one's duty, that is, to lead a decorous life approved of by society, one must adopt a definite attitude just as towards one's official duties.

And Ivan Ilych evolved such an attitude towards married life. He only required of it those conveniences – dinner at home, housewife, and bed – which it could give him, and above all that propriety of external forms required by public opinion. For the rest he looked for light-hearted pleasure and propriety, and was very thankful when he found them, but if he met with antagonism and querulousness he at once retired into his separate fenced-off world of official duties, where he found satisfaction.

Ivan Ilych was esteemed a good official, and after three years was made Assistant Public Prosecutor. His new duties, their importance, the possibility of indicting and imprisoning anyone he chose, the publicity his speeches received, and the success he had in all these things, made his work still more attractive.

More children came. His wife became more and more querulous and ill-tempered, but the attitude Ivan Ilych had adopted towards his home life rendered him almost impervious to her grumbling.

After seven years' service in that town he was transferred to another province as Public Prosecutor. They moved, but were short of money and his wife did not like the place they moved to. Though the salary was higher the cost of living was greater, besides which two of their children died and family life became still more unpleasant for him.

Praskovya Fedorovna blamed her husband for every inconvenience they encountered in their new home. Most of the conversations between husband and wife, especially as to the children's education, led to topics which recalled former disputes, and those disputes were apt to flare up again at any moment. There remained only those rare periods of amorousness which still came to them at times but did not last long. These were islets at which they anchored for a while and then again set out upon that ocean of veiled hostility which showed itself in their aloofness from one another. This aloofness might have grieved Ivan Ilych had he considered that it ought not to exist, but he now regarded the position as normal, and even made it the goal at which he aimed in family life. His aim was to free himself more and more from those unpleasantnesses and to give them a semblance of harmlessness and propriety. He attained this by spending less and less time with his family, and when obliged to be at home he tried to safeguard his position by the presence of outsiders. The chief thing however was that he had his official duties. The whole interest of his life now centred in the official world and that interest absorbed him. The consciousness of his power, being able to ruin anybody he wished to ruin, the importance, even the external dignity of his entry into court, or meetings with his subordinates, his success with superiors and inferiors, and above all his masterly handling of cases, of which he was conscious – all this gave him pleasure and filled his life, together with chats with his colleagues, dinners, and bridge. So that on the whole Ivan Ilych's life continued to flow as he considered it should do – pleasantly and properly.

So things continued for another seven years. His eldest daughter was already sixteen, another child had died, and only one son was left, a schoolboy and a subject of dissension. Ivan Ilych wanted to put him in the School of Law, but to spite him Praskovya Fedorovna entered him at the High School. The daughter had been educated at home and had turned out well: the boy did not learn badly either.

III

So Ivan Ilych lived for seventeen years after his marriage. He was already a Public Prosecutor of long standing, and had declined several proposed transfers while awaiting a more desirable post, when an unanticipated and unpleasant occurrence quite upset the peaceful course of his life. He was expecting to be offered the post of presiding judge in a university town, but Happe somehow came to the front and obtained the appointment instead. Ivan Ilych became irritable, reproached Happe, and quarrelled both with him and with his immediate superiors – who became colder to him and again passed him over when other appointments were made.

This was in 1880, the hardest year of Ivan Ilych's life. It was then that it became evident on the one hand that his salary was insufficient for them to live on, and on the other that he had been forgotten, and not only this, but that what was for him the greatest and most cruel injustice appeared to others a quite ordinary occurrence. Even his father did not consider it his duty to help him. Ivan Ilych felt himself abandoned by everyone, and that they regarded his position with a salary of 3,500 rubles as quite normal and even fortunate. He alone knew that with the consciousness of the injustices done him, with his wife's incessant nagging, and with the debts he had contracted by living beyond his means, his position was far from normal.

In order to save money that summer he obtained leave of absence and went with his wife to live in the country at her brother's place.

In the country, without his work, he experienced *ennui* for the first time in his life, and not only *ennui* but intolerable depression, and he decided that it was impossible to go on living like that, and that it was necessary to take energetic measures.

Having passed a sleepless night pacing up and down the veranda, he decided to go to Petersburg and bestir himself, in order to punish those who had failed to appreciate him and to get transferred to another ministry.

Next day, despite many protests from his wife and her brother, he started for Petersburg with the sole object of obtaining a post with a salary of five thousand rubles a year. He was no longer bent on any particular department, or tendency, or kind of activity. All he now wanted was an appointment to another post with a salary of five thousand rubles, either in the administration, in the banks, with the railways, in one of the Empress Marya's Institutions, or even in the customs – but it had to carry with it a salary of five thousand rubles and be in a ministry other than that in which they had failed to appreciate him.

And this quest of Ivan Ilych's was crowned with remarkable and unexpected success. At Kursk an acquaintance of his, F. I. Ilyin, got into the first-class carriage, sat down beside Ivan Ilych, and told him of a telegram just received by the Governor of Kursk announcing that a change was about to take place in the ministry: Peter Ivanovich was to be superseded by Ivan Semenovich.

The proposed change, apart from its significance for Russia, had a special significance for Ivan Ilych, because by bringing forward a new man, Peter Petrovich, and consequently his friend Zakhar Ivanovich, it was highly favourable for Ivan Ilych, since Zakhar Ivanovich was a friend and colleague of his.

In Moscow this news was confirmed, and on reaching Petersburg Ivan Ilych found Zakhar Ivanovich and received a definite promise of an appointment in his former department of Justice.

A week later he telegraphed to his wife: 'Zakhar in Miller's place. I shall receive appointment on presentation of report.'

Thanks to this change of personnel, Ivan Ilych had unexpectedly obtained an appointment in his former ministry which placed him two stages above his former colleagues besides giving him five thousand rubles salary and three thousand five hundred rubles for expenses connected with his removal. All his ill humour towards his former enemies and the whole department vanished, and Ivan Ilych was completely happy.

He returned to the country more cheerful and contented than he had been for a long time. Praskovya Fedorovna also cheered up and a truce was arranged between them. Ivan Ilych told of how he had been fêted by everybody in Petersburg, how all those who had been his enemies were put to shame and now fawned on him, how envious they were of his appointment, and how much everybody in Petersburg had liked him.

Praskovya Fedorovna listened to all this and appeared to believe it. She did not contradict anything, but only made plans for their life in the town to which they were going. Ivan Ilych saw with delight that these plans were his plans, that he and his wife agreed, and that, after a stumble, his life was regaining its due and natural character of pleasant lightheartedness and decorum.

Ivan Ilych had come back for a short time only, for he had to take up his new duties on the 10th of September. Moreover, he needed time to settle into the new place, to move all his belongings from the province, and to buy and order many additional things: in a word, to make such arrangements as he had resolved on, which were almost exactly what Praskovya Fedorovna too had decided on.

Now that everything had happened so fortunately, and that he and his wife were at one in their aims and moreover saw so little of one another, they got on together better than they had done since the first years of marriage. Ivan Ilych had thought of taking his family away with him at once, but the insistence of his wife's brother and her sister-in-law, who had suddenly become particularly amiable and friendly to him and his family, induced him to depart alone.

So he departed, and the cheerful state of mind induced by his success and by the harmony between his wife and himself, the one intensifying the other, did not leave him. He found a delightful house, just the thing both he and his wife had dreamt of. Spacious, lofty reception rooms in the old style, a convenient and dignified study, rooms for his wife and daughter, a study for his son – it might have been specially built for them. Ivan Ilych himself superintended the arrangements, chose the wallpapers, supplemented the furniture (preferably with antiques which he considered particularly *comme il faut*), and supervised the upholstering. Everything progressed and progressed and approached the ideal he had set himself: even when things were only half completed they exceeded his expectations. He saw what a refined and elegant character, free from vulgarity, it would all have when it was ready. On falling asleep he pictured to himself how the reception-room would look. Looking at the yet unfinished drawing-room he could see the fireplace, the screen, the what-not, the little chairs dotted here and there, the dishes and plates on the walls, and the bronzes, as they would be when everything was in place. He was pleased by the thought of how his wife and daughter, who shared his taste in this matter, would be impressed by it. They were certainly not expecting as much. He had been particularly successful in finding, and buying cheaply, antiques which gave a particularly aristocratic character to the whole place. But in his letters he intentionally understated everything in order to be able to surprise them. All this so absorbed him that his new duties – though he liked his official work – interested him less than he had expected. Sometimes he even had moments of absent-mindedness during the Court Sessions, and would consider whether he should have straight or curved cornices for his curtains. He was so interested in it all that he often did things himself, rearranging the furniture, or rehanging the curtains. Once when mounting a step-ladder to show the upholsterer, who did not understand, how he wanted the hangings draped, he made a false step and slipped, but being a strong and agile man he clung on and only knocked his side against the knob of the window frame. The bruised place was painful but the pain soon passed, and he felt particularly bright and well just then. He wrote: 'I feel fifteen years younger.' He thought he would have everything ready by September, but it dragged on till mid-October. But the result was charming not only in his eyes but to everyone who saw it.

In reality it was just what is usually seen in the houses of people of moderate means who want to appear rich, and therefore succeed only in resembling others like themselves: there were damasks, dark wood, plants, rugs, and dull and polished bronzes – all the things people of a certain class have in order to resemble other people of that class. His house was so like the others that it would never have been noticed, but to him it all seemed to be quite exceptional. He was very happy when he met his family at the station and brought them to the newly furnished house all lit up, where a footman in a white tie opened the door into the hall decorated with plants, and when they went on into the drawing-room and the study uttering exclamations of delight. He conducted them everywhere, drank in their praises eagerly, and beamed with pleasure. At tea that evening, when Praskovya Fedorovna among other things asked him about his fall, he laughed, and showed them how he had gone flying and had frightened the upholsterer.

'It's a good thing I'm a bit of an athlete. Another man might have been killed, but I merely knocked myself, just here; it hurts when it's touched, but it's passing off already – it's only a bruise.'

So they began living in their new home – in which, as always happens, when they got thoroughly settled in they found they were just one room short – and with the increased income, which as always was just a little (some five hundred rubles) too little, but it was all very nice.

Things went particularly well at first, before everything was finally arranged and while something had still to be done: this thing bought, that thing ordered, another thing moved, and something else adjusted. Though there were some disputes between husband and wife, they were both so well satisfied and had so much to do that it all passed off without any serious quarrels. When nothing was left to arrange it became rather dull and something seemed to be lacking, but they were then making acquaintances, forming habits, and life was growing fuller.

Ivan Ilych spent his mornings at the law court and came home to dinner, and at first he was generally in a good humour, though he occasionally became irritable just on account of his house. (Every spot on the tablecloth or the upholstery, and every broken window-blind string, irritated him. He had devoted so much trouble to arranging it all that every disturbance of it distressed him.) But on the whole his life ran its course as he believed life should do: easily, pleasantly, and decorously.

He got up at nine, drank his coffee, read the paper, and then put on his undress uniform and went to the law courts. There the harness in which he worked had already been stretched to fit him and he donned it without a hitch: petitioners, inquiries at the chancery, the chancery itself, and the sittings public and administrative. In all this the thing was to exclude everything fresh and vital, which always disturbs the regular course of official business, and to admit only official relations with people, and then only on official grounds. A man would come, for instance, wanting some information. Ivan Ilych, as one in whose sphere the matter did not lie, would have nothing to do with him: but if the man had some business with him in his official capacity, something that could be expressed on officially stamped paper, he would do everything, positively everything he could within the limits of such relations, and in doing so would maintain the semblance of friendly human relations, that is, would observe the courtesies of life. As soon as the official relations ended, so did everything else. Ivan Ilych possessed this capacity to separate his real life from the official side of affairs and not mix the two, in the highest degree, and by long practice and natural aptitude had brought it to such a pitch that sometimes, in the manner of a virtuoso, he would even allow himself to let the human and official relations mingle. He let himself do this just because he felt that he could at any time he chose resume the strictly official attitude again and drop the human relation. And he did it all easily, pleasantly, correctly, and even artistically. In the intervals between the sessions he smoked, drank tea, chatted a little about politics, a little about general topics, a little about cards, but most of all about official appointments. Tired, but with the feelings of a virtuoso – one of the first violins who has played his part in an orchestra with precision – he would return home to find that his wife and daughter had been out paying calls, or had a visitor, and that his son had been to school, had done his homework with his tutor, and was duly learning what is taught at high schools. Everything was as it should be. After dinner, if they had no visitors, Ivan Ilych sometimes read a book that was being much discussed at the time, and in the evening settled down to work, that is, read official papers, compared the depositions of witnesses, and noted paragraphs of the Code applying to them. This was neither dull nor amusing. It was dull when he might have been playing bridge, but if no bridge was available it was at any rate better than doing nothing or sitting with his wife. Ivan Ilych's chief pleasure was giving little dinners to which he invited men and women of good social position, and just as his drawing-room resembled all other drawing-rooms so did his enjoyable little parties resemble all other such parties.

Once they even gave a dance. Ivan Ilych enjoyed it and everything went off well, except that it led to a violent quarrel with his wife about the cakes and sweets. Praskovya Fedorovna had made her own plans, but Ivan Ilych insisted on getting everything from an expensive confectioner and ordered too many cakes, and the quarrel occurred because some of those cakes were left over and the confectioner's bill came to forty-five rubles. It was a great and disagreeable quarrel. Praskovya Fedorovna called him 'a fool and an imbecile', and he clutched at his head and made angry allusions to divorce.

But the dance itself had been enjoyable. The best people were there, and Ivan Ilych had danced with Princess Trufonova, a sister of the distinguished founder of the society 'Bear my Burden'.

The pleasures connected with his work were pleasures of ambition; his social pleasures were those of vanity; but Ivan Ilych's greatest pleasure was playing bridge. He acknowledged that whatever disagreeable incident happened in his life, the pleasure that beamed like a ray of light above everything else was to sit down to bridge with good players, not noisy partners, and of course to four-handed bridge (with five players it was annoying to have to stand out, though one pretended not to mind), to play a clever and serious game (when the cards allowed it) and then to have supper and drink a glass of wine. After a game of bridge, especially if he had won a little (to win a large sum was unpleasant), Ivan Ilych went to bed in specially good humour.

So they lived. They formed a circle of acquaintances among the best people and were visited by people of importance and by young folk. In their views as to their acquaintances, husband wife and daughter were entirely agreed, and tacitly and unanimously kept at arm's length and shook off the various shabby friends and relations who, with much show of affection, gushed into the drawing-room with its Japanese plates on the walls. Soon these shabby friends ceased to obtrude themselves and only the best people remained in the Golovins' set.

Young men made up to Lisa, and Petrishchev, an examining magistrate and Dmitri Ivanovich Petrishchev's son and sole heir, began to be so attentive to her that Ivan Ilych had already spoken to Praskovya Fedorovna about it, and considered whether they should not arrange a party for them, or get up some private theatricals.

So they lived, and all went well, without change, and life flowed pleasantly.

IV

THEY were all in good health. It could not be called ill health if Ivan Ilych sometimes said that he had a queer taste in his mouth and felt some discomfort in his left side.

But this discomfort increased and, though not exactly painful, grew into a sense of pressure in his side accompanied by ill humour. And his irritability became worse and worse and began to mar the agreeable, easy, and correct life that had established itself in the Golovin family. Quarrels between husband and wife became more and more frequent, and soon the ease and amenity disappeared and even the decorum was barely maintained. Scenes again became frequent, and very few of those islets remained on which husband and wife could meet without an explosion. Praskovya Fedorovna now had good reason to say that her husband's temper was trying. With characteristic exaggeration she said he had always had a dreadful temper, and that it had needed all her good nature to put up with it for twenty years. It was true that now the quarrels were started by him. His bursts of temper always came just before dinner, often just as he began to eat his soup. Sometimes he noticed that a plate or dish was chipped, or the food was not right, or his son put his elbow on the table, or his daughter's hair was not done as he liked it, and for all this he blamed Praskovya Fedorovna. At first she retorted and said disagreeable things to him, but once or twice he fell into such a rage at the beginning of dinner that she realized it was due to some physical derangement brought on by taking food, and so she restrained herself and did not answer, but only hurried to get the dinner over. She regarded this self-restraint as highly praiseworthy. Having come to the conclusion that her husband had a dreadful temper and made her life miserable, she began to feel sorry for herself, and the more she pitied herself the more she hated her husband. She began to wish he would die; yet she did not want him to die because then his salary would cease. And this irritated her against him still more. She considered herself dreadfully unhappy just because not even his death could save her, and though she concealed her exasperation, that hidden exasperation of hers increased his irritation also.

After one scene in which Ivan Ilych had been particularly unfair and after which he had said in explanation that he certainly was irritable but that it was due to his not being well, she said that if he was ill it should be attended to, and insisted on his going to see a celebrated doctor.

He went. Everything took place as he had expected and as it always does. There was the usual waiting and the important air assumed by the doctor, with which he was so familiar (resembling that which he himself assumed in court), and the sounding and listening, and the questions which called for answers that were foregone conclusions and were evidently unnecessary, and the look of importance which implied that 'if only you put yourself in our hands we will arrange everything – we know indubitably how it has to be done, always in the same way for everybody alike.' It was all just as it was in the law courts. The doctor put on just the same air towards him as he himself put on towards an accused person.

The doctor said that so-and-so indicated that there was so-and-so inside the patient, but if the investigation of so-and-so did not confirm this, then he must assume that and that. If he assumed that and that, then . . . and so on. To Ivan Ilych only one question was important: was his case serious or not? But the doctor ignored that inappropriate question. From his point of view it was not the one under consideration, the real question was to decide between a floating kidney, chronic catarrh, or appendicitis. It was not a question of Ivan Ilych's life or death, but one between a floating kidney and appendicitis. And that question the doctor solved brilliantly, as it seemed to Ivan Ilych, in favour of the appendix, with the reservation that should an examination of the urine give fresh indications the matter would be reconsidered. All this was just what Ivan Ilych had himself brilliantly accomplished a thousand times in dealing with men on trial. The doctor summed up just as brilliantly, looking over his spectacles triumphantly and even gaily at the accused. From the doctor's summing up Ivan Ilych concluded that things were bad, but that for the doctor, and perhaps for everybody else, it was a matter of indifference, though for him it was bad. And this conclusion struck him painfully, arousing in him a great feeling of pity for himself and of bitterness towards the doctor's indifference to a matter of such importance.

He said nothing of this, but rose, placed the doctor's fee on the table, and remarked with a sigh: 'We sick people probably often put inappropriate questions. But tell me, in general, is this complaint dangerous, or not? . . .'

The doctor looked at him sternly over his spectacles with one eye, as if to say: 'Prisoner, if you will not keep to the questions put to you, I shall be obliged to have you removed from the court.'

'I have already told you what I consider necessary and proper. The analysis may show something more.' And the doctor bowed.

Ivan Ilych went out slowly, seated himself disconsolately in his sledge, and drove home. All the way home he was going over what the doctor had said, trying to translate those complicated, obscure, scientific phrases into plain language and find in them an answer to the question: 'Is my condition bad? Is it very bad? Or is there as yet nothing much wrong?' And it seemed to him that the meaning of what the doctor had said was that it was very bad. Everything in the streets seemed depressing. The cabmen, the houses, the passers-by, and the shops, were dismal. His ache, this dull gnawing ache that never ceased for a moment, seemed to have acquired a new and more serious significance from the doctor's dubious remarks. Ivan Ilych now watched it with a new and oppressive feeling.

He reached home and began to tell his wife about it. She listened, but in the middle of his account his daughter came in with her hat on, ready to go out with her mother. She sat down reluctantly to listen to this tedious story, but could not stand it long, and her mother too did not hear him to the end.

'Well, I am very glad,' she said. 'Mind now to take your medicine regularly. Give me the prescription and I'll send Gerasim to the chemist's.' And she went to get ready to go out.

While she was in the room Ivan Ilych had hardly taken time to breathe, but he sighed deeply when she left it.

'Well,' he thought, 'perhaps it isn't so bad after all.'

He began taking his medicine and following the doctor's directions, which had been altered after the examination of the urine. But then it happened that there was a contradiction between the indications drawn from the examination of the urine and the symptoms that showed themselves. It turned out that what was happening differed from what the doctor had told him, and that he had either forgotten, or blundered, or hidden something from him. He could not, however, be blamed for that, and Ivan Ilych still obeyed his orders implicitly and at first derived some comfort from doing so.

From the time of his visit to the doctor, Ivan Ilych's chief occupation was the exact fulfilment of the doctor's instructions regarding hygiene and the taking of medicine, and the observation of his pain and his excretions. His chief interests came to be people's ailments and people's health. When sickness, deaths, or recoveries were mentioned in his presence, especially when the illness resembled his own, he listened with agitation which he tried to hide, asked questions, and applied what he heard to his own case.

The pain did not grow less, but Ivan Ilych made efforts to force himself to think that he was better. And he could do this so long as nothing agitated him. But as soon as he had any unpleasantness with his wife, any lack of success in his official work, or held bad cards at bridge, he was at once acutely sensible of his disease. He had formerly borne such mischances, hoping soon to adjust what was wrong, to master it and attain success, or make a grand slam. But now every mischance upset him and plunged him into despair. He would say to himself: 'There now, just as I was beginning to get better and the medicine had begun to take effect, comes this accursed misfortune, or unpleasantness . . .' And he was furious with the mishap, or with the people who were causing the unpleasantness and killing him, for he felt that this fury was killing him but could not restrain it. One would have thought that it should have been clear to him that this exasperation with circumstances and people aggravated his illness, and that he ought therefore to ignore unpleasant occurrences. But he drew the very opposite conclusion: he said that he needed peace, and he watched for everything that might disturb it and became irritable at the slightest infringement of it. His condition was rendered worse by the fact that he read medical books and consulted doctors. The progress of his disease was so gradual that he could deceive himself when comparing one day with another – the difference was so slight. But when he consulted the doctors it seemed to him that he was getting worse, and even very rapidly. Yet despite this he was continually consulting them.

That month he went to see another celebrity, who told him almost the same as the first had done but put his questions rather differently, and the interview with this celebrity only increased Ivan Ilych's doubts and fears. A friend of a friend of his, a very good doctor, diagnosed his illness again quite differently from the others, and though he predicted recovery, his questions and suppositions bewildered Ivan Ilych still more and increased his doubts. A homoeopathist diagnosed the disease in yet another way, and prescribed medicine which Ivan Ilych took secretly for a week. But after a week, not feeling any improvement and having lost confidence both in the former doctor's treatment and in this one's, he became still more despondent. One day a lady acquaintance mentioned a cure effected by a wonder-working icon. Ivan Ilych caught himself listening attentively and beginning to believe that it had occurred. This incident alarmed him. 'Has my mind really weakened to such an extent?' he asked himself. 'Nonsense! It's all rubbish. I mustn't give way to nervous fears but having chosen a doctor must keep strictly to his treatment. That is what I will do. Now it's all settled. I won't think about it, but will follow the treatment seriously till summer, and then we shall see. From now there must be no more of this wavering!' This was easy to say but impossible to carry out. The pain in his side oppressed him and seemed to grow worse and more incessant, while the taste in his mouth grew stranger and stranger. It seemed to him that his breath had a disgusting smell, and he was conscious of a loss of appetite and strength. There was no deceiving himself: something terrible, new, and more important than anything before in his life, was taking place within him of which he alone was aware. Those about him did not understand or would not understand it, but thought everything in the world was going on as usual. That tormented Ivan Ilych more than anything. He saw that his household, especially his wife and daughter who were in a perfect whirl of visiting, did not understand anything of it and were annoyed that he was so depressed and so exacting, as if he were to blame for it. Though they tried to disguise it he saw that he was an obstacle in their path, and that his wife had adopted a definite line in regard to his illness and kept to it regardless of anything he said or did. Her attitude was this: 'You know,' she would say to her friends, 'Ivan Ilych can't do as other people do, and keep to the treatment prescribed for him. One day he'll take his drops and keep strictly to his diet and go to bed in good time, but the next day unless I watch him he'll suddenly forget his medicine, eat sturgeon – which is forbidden – and sit up playing cards till one o'clock in the morning.'

'Oh, come, when was that?' Ivan Ilych would ask in vexation. 'Only once at Peter Ivanovich's.'

'And yesterday with Shebek.'

'Well even if I hadn't stayed up, this pain would have kept me awake.'

'Be that as it may you'll never get well like that, but will always make us wretched.'

Praskovya Fedorovna's attitude to Ivan Ilych's illness, as she expressed it both to others and to him, was that it was his own fault and was another of the annoyances he caused her. Ivan Ilych felt that this opinion escaped her involuntarily – but that did not make it easier for him.

At the law courts too, Ivan Ilych noticed, or thought he noticed, a strange attitude towards himself. It sometimes seemed to him that people were watching him inquisitively as a man whose place might soon be vacant. Then again, his friends would suddenly begin to chaff him in a friendly way about his low spirits, as if the awful, horrible, and unheard-of-thing that was going on within him, incessantly gnawing at him and irresistibly drawing him away, was a very agreeable subject for jests. Schwartz in particular irritated him by his jocularity, vivacity, and *savoir-faire*, which reminded him of what he himself had been ten years ago.

Friends came to make up a set and they sat down to cards. They dealt, bending the new cards to soften them, and he sorted the diamonds in his hand and found he had seven. His partner said 'No trumps' and supported him with two diamonds. What more could be wished for? It ought to be jolly and lively. They would make a grand slam. But suddenly Ivan Ilych was conscious of that gnawing pain, that taste in his mouth, and it seemed ridiculous that in such circumstances he should be pleased to make a grand slam.

He looked at his partner Michael Mikhaylovich, who rapped the table with his strong hand and instead of snatching up the tricks pushed the cards courteously and indulgently towards Ivan Ilych that he might have the pleasure of gathering them up without the trouble of stretching out his hand for them. 'Does he think I am too weak to stretch out my arm?' thought Ivan Ilych, and forgetting what he was doing he over-trumped his partner, missing the grand slam by three tricks. And what was most awful of all was that he saw how upset Michael Mikhaylovich was about it but did not himself care. And it was dreadful to realize why he did not care.

They all saw that he was suffering, and said: 'We can stop if you are tired. Take a rest.' Lie down? No, he was not at all tired, and he finished the rubber. All were gloomy and silent. Ivan Ilych felt that he had diffused this gloom over them and could not dispel it. They had supper and went away, and Ivan Ilych was left alone with the consciousness that his life was poisoned and was poisoning the lives of others, and that this poison did not weaken but penetrated more and more deeply into his whole being.

With this consciousness, and with physical pain besides the terror, he must go to bed, often to lie awake the greater part of the night. Next morning he had to get up again, dress, go to the law courts, speak, and write; or if he did not go out, spend at home those twenty-four hours a day each of which was a torture. And he had to live thus all alone on the brink of an abyss, with no one who understood or pitied him.

V

So one month passed and then another. Just before the New Year his brother-in-law came to town and stayed at their house. Ivan Ilych was at the law courts and Praskovya Fedorovna had gone shopping. When Ivan Ilych came home and entered his study he found his brother-in-law there - a healthy, florid man - unpacking his portmanteau himself. He raised his head on hearing Ivan Ilych's footsteps and looked up at him for a moment without a word. That stare told Ivan Ilych everything. His brother-in-law opened his mouth to utter an exclamation of surprise but checked himself, and that action confirmed it all.

'I have changed, eh?'

'Yes, there is a change.'

And after that, try as he would to get his brother-in-law to return to the subject of his looks, the latter would say nothing about it. Praskovya Fedorovna came home and her brother went out to her. Ivan Ilych locked the door and began to examine himself in the glass, first full face, then in profile. He took up a portrait of himself taken with his wife, and compared it with what he saw in the glass. The change in him was immense. Then he bared his arms to the elbow, looked at them, drew the sleeves down again, sat down on an ottoman, and grew blacker than night.

'No, no, this won't do!' he said to himself, and jumped up, went to the table, took up some law papers and began to read them, but could not continue. He unlocked the door and went into the reception-room. The door leading to the drawing-room was shut. He approached it on tiptoe and listened.

'No, you are exaggerating!' Praskovya Fedorovna was saying.

'Exaggerating! Don't you see it? Why, he's a dead man! Look at his eyes – there's no light in them. But what is it that is wrong with him?'

'No one knows. Nikolaevich [that was another doctor] said something, but I don't know what. And Leshchetitsky [this was the celebrated specialist] said quite the contrary . . .'

Ivan Ilych walked away, went to his own room, lay down, and began musing: 'The kidney, a floating kidney.' He recalled all the doctors had told him of how it detached itself and swayed about. And by an effort of imagination he tried to catch that kidney and arrest it and support it. So little was needed for this, it seemed to him. 'No, I'll go to see Peter Ivanovich again.' (That was the friend whose friend was a doctor.) He rang, ordered the carriage, and got ready to go.

'Where are you going, Jean?' asked his wife, with a specially sad and exceptionally kind look.

This exceptionally kind look irritated him. He looked morosely at her.

'I must go to see Peter Ivanovich.'

He went to see Peter Ivanovich, and together they went to see his friend, the doctor. He was in, and Ivan Ilych had a long talk with him.

Reviewing the anatomical and physiological details of what in the doctor's opinion was going on inside him, he understood it all.

There was something, a small thing, in the vermiform appendix. It might all come right. Only stimulate the energy of one organ and check the activity of another, then absorption would take place and everything would come right. He got home rather late for dinner, ate his dinner, and conversed cheerfully, but could not for a long time bring himself to go back to work in his room. At last, however, he went to his study and did what was necessary, but the consciousness that he had put something aside – an important, intimate matter which he would revert to when his work was done – never left him. When he had finished his work he remembered that this intimate matter was the thought of his vermiform appendix. But he did not give himself up to it, and went to the drawing-room for tea. There were callers there, including the examining magistrate who was a desirable match for his daughter, and they were conversing, playing the piano, and singing. Ivan Ilych, as Praskovya Fedorovna remarked, spent that evening more cheerfully than usual, but he never for a moment forgot that he had postponed the important matter of the appendix. At eleven o'clock he said goodnight and went to his bedroom. Since his illness he had slept alone in a small room next to his study. He undressed and took up a novel by Zola, but instead of reading it he fell into thought, and in his imagination that desired improvement in the vermiform appendix occurred. There was the absorption and evacuation and the re-establishment of normal activity. 'Yes, that's it!' he said to himself. 'One need only assist nature, that's all.' He remembered his medicine, rose, took it, and lay down on his back watching for the beneficent action of the medicine and for it to lessen the pain. 'I need only take it regularly and avoid all injurious influences. I am already feeling better, much better.' He began touching his side: it was not painful to the touch. 'There, I really don't feel it. It's much better already.' He put out the light and turned on his side... 'The appendix is getting better, absorption is occurring.' Suddenly he felt the old, familiar, dull, gnawing pain, stubborn and serious. There was the same familiar loathsome taste in his mouth. His heart sank and he felt dazed. 'My God! My God!' he muttered. 'Again, again! And it will never cease.' And suddenly the matter presented itself in a quite different aspect. 'Vermiform appendix! Kidney!' he said to himself. 'It's not a question of appendix or kidney, but of life and ... death. Yes, life was there and now it is going, going and I cannot stop it. Yes. Why deceive myself? Isn't it obvious to everyone but me that I'm dying, and that it's only a question of weeks, days ... it may happen this moment. There was light and now there is darkness. I was here and now I'm going there! Where?' A chill came over him, his breathing ceased, and he felt only the throbbing of his heart.

'When I am not, what will there be? There will be nothing. Then where shall I be when I am no more? Can this be dying? No, I don't want to!' He jumped up and tried to light the candle, felt for it with trembling hands, dropped candle and candlestick on the floor, and fell back on his pillow.

'What's the use? It makes no difference,' he said to himself, staring with wide-open eyes into the darkness. 'Death. Yes, death. And none of them know or wish to know it, and they have no pity for me. Now they are playing.' (He heard through the door the distant sound of a song and its accompaniment.) 'It's all the same to them, but they will die too! Fools! I first, and they later, but it will be the same for them. And now they are merry ... the beasts!'

Anger choked him and he was agonizingly, unbearably miserable. 'It is impossible that all men have been doomed to suffer this awful horror!' He raised himself.

'Something must be wrong. I must calm myself – must think it all over from the beginning.' And he again began thinking. 'Yes, the beginning of my illness: I knocked my side, but I was still quite well that day and the next. It hurt a little, then rather more. I saw the doctors, then followed despondency and anguish, more doctors, and I drew nearer to the abyss. My strength grew less and I kept coming nearer and nearer, and now I have wasted away and there is no light in my eyes. I think of the appendix – but this is death! I think of mending the appendix, and all the while here is death! Can it really be death?' Again terror seized him and he gasped for breath. He leant down and began feeling for the matches, pressing with his elbow on the stand beside the bed. It was in his way and hurt him, he grew furious with it, pressed on it still harder, and upset it. Breathless and in despair he fell on his back, expecting death to come immediately.

Meanwhile the visitors were leaving. Praskovya Fedorovna was seeing them off. She heard something fall and came in.

'What has happened?'

'Nothing. I knocked it over accidentally.'

She went out and returned with a candle. He lay there panting heavily, like a man who has run a thousand yards, and stared upwards at her with a fixed look.

'What is it, Jean?'

'No . . . o . . . thing. I upset it.' ('Why speak of it? She won't understand,' he thought.)

And in truth she did not understand. She picked up the stand, lit his candle, and hurried away to see another visitor off. When she came back he still lay on his back, looking upwards.

'What is it? Do you feel worse?'

'Yes.'

She shook her head and sat down.

'Do you know, Jean, I think we must ask Leshchetitsky to come and see you here.'

This meant calling in the famous specialist, regardless of expense. He smiled malignantly and said 'No'. She remained a little longer and then went up to him and kissed his forehead.

While she was kissing him he hated her from the bottom of his soul and with difficulty refrained from pushing her away.

'Goodnight. Please God you'll sleep.'

'Yes.'

VI

IVAN ILYCH saw that he was dying, and he was in continual despair.

In the depth of his heart he knew he was dying, but not only was he not accustomed to the thought, he simply did not and could not grasp it.

The syllogism he had learnt from Kiezewetter's Logic: 'Caius is a man, men are mortal, therefore Caius is mortal', had always seemed to him correct as applied to Caius, but certainly not as applied to himself. That Caius – man in the abstract – was mortal, was perfectly correct, but he was not Caius, not an abstract man, but a creature quite quite separate from all others. He had been little Vanya, with a mamma and a papa, with Mitya and Volodya, with toys, a coachman and a nurse, afterwards with Katenka and with all the joys, griefs, and delights of childhood, boyhood, and youth. What did Caius know of the smell of that striped leather ball Vanya had been so fond of? Had Caius kissed his mother's hand like that, and did the silk of her dress rustle so for Caius? Had he rioted like that at school when the pastry was bad? Had Caius been in love like that? Could Caius preside at a session as he did? 'Caius really was mortal, and it was right for him to die; but for me, little Vanya, Ivan Ilych, with all my thoughts and emotions, it's altogether a different matter. It cannot be that I ought to die. That would be too terrible.'

Such was his feeling.

'If I had to die like Caius I should have known it was so. An inner voice would have told me so, but there was nothing of the sort in me and I and all my friends felt that our case was quite different from that of Caius. And now here it is!' he said to himself. 'It can't be. It's impossible! But here it is. How is this? How is one to understand it?'

He could not understand it, and tried to drive this false, incorrect, morbid thought away and to replace it by other proper and healthy thoughts. But that thought, and not the thought only but the reality itself, seemed to come and confront him.

And to replace that thought he called up a succession of others, hoping to find in them some support. He tried to get back into the former current of thoughts that had once screened the thought of death from him. But strange to say, all that had formerly shut off, hidden, and destroyed, his consciousness of death, no longer had that effect. Ivan Ilych now spent most of his time in attempting to re-establish that old current. He would say to himself: 'I will take up my duties again – after all I used to live by them.' And banishing all doubts he would go to the law courts, enter into conversation with his colleagues, and sit carelessly as was his wont, scanning the crowd with a thoughtful look and leaning both his emaciated arms on the arms of his oak chair; bending over as usual to a colleague and draw-ing his papers nearer he would interchange whispers with him, and then suddenly raising his eyes and sitting erect would pronounce certain words and open the proceedings. But suddenly in the midst of those proceedings the pain in his side, regardless of the stage the proceedings had reached, would begin its own gnawing work. Ivan Ilych would turn his attention to it and try to drive the thought of it away, but without success. *It* would come and stand before him and look at him, and he would be petrified and the light would die out of his eyes, and he would again begin asking himself whether *It* alone was true. And his colleagues and subordinates would see with surprise and distress that he, the brilliant and subtle judge, was becoming confused and making mistakes. He would shake himself, try to pull himself together, manage somehow to bring the sitting to a close, and return home with the sorrowful consciousness that his judicial labours could not as formerly hide from him what he wanted them to hide, and could not deliver him from *It*. And what was worst of all was that *It* drew his attention to itself not in order to make him take some action but only that he should look at *It*, look it straight in the face: look at it and without doing anything, suffer inexpressibly.

And to save himself from this condition Ivan Ilych looked for consolations – new screens – and new screens were found and for a while seemed to save him, but then they immediately fell to pieces or rather became transparent, as if *It* penetrated them and nothing could veil *It*.

In these latter days he would go into the drawing-room he had arranged – that drawing-room where he had fallen and for the sake of which (how bitterly ridiculous it seemed) he had sacrificed his life – for he knew that his illness originated with that knock. He would enter and see that something had scratched the polished table. He would look for the cause of this and find that it was the bronze ornamentation of an album, that had got bent. He would take up the expensive album which he had lovingly arranged, and feel vexed with his daughter and her friends for their untidiness – for the album was torn here and there and some of the photographs turned upside down. He would put it carefully in order and bend the ornamentation back into position. Then it would occur to him to place all those things in another corner of the room, near the plants. He would call the footman, but his daughter or wife would come to help him. They would not agree, and his wife would contradict him, and he would dispute and grow angry. But that was all right, for then he did not think about *It. It* was invisible.

But then, when he was moving something himself, his wife would say: 'Let the servants do it. You will hurt yourself again.' And suddenly *It* would flash through the screen and he would see it. It was just a flash, and he hoped it would disappear, but he would involuntarily pay attention to his side. 'It sits there as before, gnawing just the same!' And he could no longer forget *It*, but could distinctly see it looking at him from behind the flowers. 'What is it all for?'

'It really is so! I lost my life over that curtain as I might have done when storming a fort. Is that possible? How terrible and how stupid. It can't be true! It can't, but it is.'

He would go to his study, lie down, and again be alone with *It*: face to face with *It*. And nothing could be done with *It* except to look at it and shudder.

VII

How it happened it is impossible to say because it came about step by step, unnoticed, but in the third month of Ivan Ilych's illness, his wife, his daughter, his son, his acquaintances, the doctors, the servants, and above all he himself, were aware that the whole interest he had for other people was whether he would soon vacate his place, and at last release the living from the discomfort caused by his presence and be himself released from his sufferings.

He slept less and less. He was given opium and hypodermic injections of morphine, but this did not relieve him. The dull depression he experienced in a somnolent condition at first gave him a little relief, but only as something new, afterwards it became as distressing as the pain itself or even more so.

Special foods were prepared for him by the doctors' orders, but all those foods became increasingly distasteful and disgusting to him.

For his excretions also special arrangements had to be made, and this was a torment to him every time – a torment from the uncleanliness, the unseemliness, and the smell, and from knowing that another person had to take part in it.

But just through this most unpleasant matter, Ivan Ilych obtained comfort. Gerasim, the butler's young assistant, always came in to carry the things out. Gerasim was a clean, fresh peasant lad, grown stout on town food and always cheerful and bright. At first the sight of him, in his clean Russian peasant costume, engaged on that disgusting task embarrassed Ivan Ilych.

Once when he got up from the commode too weak to draw up his trousers, he dropped into a soft arm-chair and looked with horror at his bare, enfeebled thighs with the muscles so sharply marked on them.

Gerasim with a firm light tread, his heavy boots emitting a pleasant smell of tar and fresh winter air, came in wearing a clean Hessian apron, the sleeves of his print shirt tucked up over his strong bare young arms; and refraining from looking at his sick master out of consideration for his feelings, and restraining the joy of life that beamed from his face, he went up to the commode.

'Gerasim!' said Ivan Ilych in a weak voice.

Gerasim started, evidently afraid he might have committed some blunder, and with a rapid movement turned his fresh, kind, simple young face which just showed the first downy signs of a beard.

'Yes, sir?'

'That must be very unpleasant for you. You must forgive me. I am helpless.'

'Oh, why, sir,' and Gerasim's eyes beamed and he showed his glistening white teeth, 'what's a little trouble? It's a case of illness with you, sir.'

And his deft strong hands did their accustomed task, and he went out of the room stepping lightly. Five minutes later he as lightly returned.

Ivan Ilych was still sitting in the same position in the arm-chair.

'Gerasim,' he said when the latter had replaced the freshly-washed utensil. 'Please come here and help me.' Gerasim went up to him. 'Lift me up. It is hard for me to get up, and I have sent Dmitri away.'

Gerasim went up to him, grasped his master with his strong arms deftly but gently, in the same way that he stepped – lifted him, supported him with one hand, and with the other drew up his trousers

and would have set him down again, but Ivan Ilych asked to be led
to the sofa. Gerasim, without an effort and without apparent pressure,
led him, almost lifting him, to the sofa and placed him on it.

'Thank you. How easily and well you do it all!'

Gerasim smiled again and turned to leave the room. But Ivan Ilych
felt his presence such a comfort that he did not want to let him go.

'One thing more, please move up that chair. No, the other one –
under my feet. It is easier for me when my feet are raised.'

Gerasim brought the chair, set it down gently in place, and raised
Ivan Ilych's legs on to it. It seemed to Ivan Ilych that he felt better
while Gerasim was holding up his legs.

'It's better when my legs are higher,' he said. 'Place that cushion
under them.'

Gerasim did so. He again lifted the legs and placed them, and again
Ivan Ilych felt better while Gerasim held his legs. When he set them
down Ivan Ilych fancied he felt worse.

'Gerasim,' he said. 'Are you busy now?'

'Not at all, sir,' said Gerasim, who had learnt from the townsfolk
how to speak to gentlefolk.

'What have you still to do?'

'What have I to do? I've done everything except chopping the logs
for tomorrow.'

'Then put my legs up a bit higher, can you?'

'Of course I can. Why not?' And Gerasim raised his master's legs
higher and Ivan Ilych thought that in that position he did not feel
any pain at all.

'And how about the logs?'

'Don't trouble about that, sir. There's plenty of time.'

Ivan Ilych told Gerasim to sit down and hold his legs, and began to
talk to him. And strange to say it seemed to him that he felt better
while Gerasim held his legs up.

After that Ivan Ilych would sometimes call Gerasim and get him
to hold his legs on his shoulders, and he liked talking to him. Gerasim
did it all easily, willingly, simply, and with a good nature that
touched Ivan Ilych. Health, strength, and vitality in other people were
offensive to him, but Gerasim's strength and vitality did not mortify
but soothed him.

What tormented Ivan Ilych most was the deception, the lie, which
for some reason they all accepted, that he was not dying but was
simply ill, and that he only need keep quiet and undergo a treatment

and then something very good would result. He however knew that
do what they would nothing would come of it, only still more
agonizing suffering and death. This deception tortured him – their
not wishing to admit what they all knew and what he knew, but
wanting to lie to him concerning his terrible condition, and wishing
and forcing him to participate in that lie. Those lies – lies enacted over
him on the eve of his death and destined to degrade this awful,
solemn act to the level of their visitings, their curtains, their sturgeon
for dinner – were a terrible agony for Ivan Ilych. And strangely
enough, many times when they were going through their antics over
him he had been within a hairbreadth of calling out to them: 'Stop
lying! You know and I know that I am dying. Then at least stop
lying about it!' But he had never had the spirit to do it. The awful,
terrible act of his dying was, he could see, reduced by those about him
to the level of a casual, unpleasant, and almost indecorous incident (as
if someone entered a drawing-room diffusing an unpleasant odour)
and this was done by that very decorum which he had served all his
life long. He saw that no one felt for him, because no one even wished
to grasp his position. Only Gerasim recognized it and pitied him. And
so Ivan Ilych felt at ease only with him. He felt comforted when
Gerasim supported his legs (sometimes all night long) and refused to
go to bed, saying: 'Don't you worry, Ivan Ilych. I'll get sleep enough
later on,' or when he suddenly became familiar and exclaimed: 'If
you weren't sick it would be another matter, but as it is, why should
I grudge a little trouble?' Gerasim alone did not lie; everything
showed that he alone understood the facts of the case and did not
consider it necessary to disguise them, but simply felt sorry for his
emaciated and enfeebled master. Once when Ivan Ilych was sending
him away he even said straight out: 'We shall all of us die, so why
should I grudge a little trouble?' – expressing the fact that he did not
think his work burdensome, because he was doing it for a dying man
and hoped someone would do the same for him when his time
came.

Apart from this lying, or because of it, what most tormented Ivan
Ilych was that no one pitied him as he wished to be pitied. At certain
moments after prolonged suffering he wished most of all (though he
would have been ashamed to confess it) for someone to pity him as a
sick child is pitied. He longed to be petted and comforted. He knew
he was an important functionary, that he had a beard turning grey,
and that therefore what he longed for was impossible, but still he

longed for it. And in Gerasim's attitude towards him there was something akin to what he wished for, and so that attitude comforted him. Ivan Ilych wanted to weep, wanted to be petted and cried over, and then his colleague Shebek would come, and instead of weeping and being petted, Ivan Ilych would assume a serious, severe, and profound air, and by force of habit would express his opinion on a decision of the Court of Cassation and would stubbornly insist on that view. This falsity around him and within him did more than anything else to poison his last days.

VIII

It was morning. He knew it was morning because Gerasim had gone, and Peter the footman had come and put out the candles, drawn back one of the curtains, and begun quietly to tidy up. Whether it was morning or evening, Friday or Sunday, made no difference, it was all just the same: the gnawing, unmitigated, agonizing pain, never ceasing for an instant, the consciousness of life inexorably waning but not yet extinguished, the approach of that ever dreaded and hateful death which was the only reality, and always the same falsity. What were days, weeks, hours, in such a case?

'Will you have some tea, sir?'

'He wants things to be regular, and wishes the gentlefolk to drink tea in the morning,' thought Ivan Ilych, and only said 'No'.

'Wouldn't you like to move onto the sofa, sir?'

'He wants to tidy up the room, and I'm in the way. I am uncleanliness and disorder,' he thought, and said only:

'No, leave me alone.'

The man went on bustling about. Ivan Ilych stretched out his hand. Peter came up, ready to help.

'What is it, sir?'

'My watch.'

Peter took the watch which was close at hand and gave it to his master.

'Half-past eight. Are they up?'

'No sir, except Vladimir Ivanich' (the son) 'who has gone to school. Praskovya Fedorovna ordered me to wake her if you asked for her. Shall I do so?'

'No, there's no need to.' 'Perhaps I'd better have some tea,' he thought, and added aloud: 'Yes, bring me some tea.'

Peter went to the door but Ivan Ilych dreaded being left alone. 'How can I keep him here? Oh, yes, my medicine.' 'Peter, give me my medicine.' 'Why not? Perhaps it may still do me some good.' He took a spoonful and swallowed it. 'No, it won't help. It's all tomfoolery, all deception,' he decided as soon as he became aware of the familiar, sickly, hopeless taste. 'No, I can't believe in it any longer. But the pain, why this pain? If it would only cease just for a moment!' And he moaned. Peter turned towards him. 'It's all right. Go and fetch me some tea.'

Peter went out. Left alone Ivan Ilych groaned not so much with pain, terrible though that was, as from mental anguish. Always and for ever the same, always these endless days and nights. If only it would come quicker! If only *what* would come quicker? Death, darkness? . . . No, no! Anything rather than death!

When Peter returned with the tea on a tray, Ivan Ilych stared at him for a time in perplexity, not realizing who and what he was. Peter was disconcerted by that look and his embarrassment brought Ivan Ilych to himself.

'Oh, tea! All right, put it down. Only help me to wash and put on a clean shirt.'

And Ivan Ilych began to wash. With pauses for rest, he washed his hands and then his face, cleaned his teeth, brushed his hair, and looked in the glass. He was terrified by what he saw, especially by the limp way in which his hair clung to his pallid forehead.

While his shirt was being changed he knew that he would be still more frightened at the sight of his body, so he avoided looking at it. Finally he was ready. He drew on a dressing-gown, wrapped himself in a plaid, and sat down in the armchair to take his tea. For a moment he felt refreshed, but as soon as he began to drink the tea he was again aware of the same taste, and the pain also returned. He finished it with an effort, and then lay down stretching out his legs, and dismissed Peter.

Always the same. Now a spark of hope flashes up, then a sea of despair rages, and always pain; always pain, always despair, and always the same. When alone he had a dreadful and distressing desire to call someone, but he knew beforehand that with others present it would be still worse. 'Another dose of morphine – to lose consciousness. I will tell him, the doctor, that he must think of something else. It's impossible, impossible, to go on like this.'

An hour and another pass like that. But now there is a ring at the door bell. Perhaps it's the doctor? It is. He comes in fresh, hearty, plump, and cheerful, with that look on his face that seems to say: 'There now, you're in a panic about something, but we'll arrange it all for you directly!' The doctor knows this expression is out of place here, but he has put it on once for all and can't take it off – like a man who has put on a frock-coat in the morning to pay a round of calls.

The doctor rubs his hands vigorously and reassuringly.

'Brr! How cold it is! There's such a sharp frost; just let me warm myself!' he says, as if it were only a matter of waiting till he was warm, and then he would put everything right.

'Well now, how are you?'

Ivan Ilych feels that the doctor would like to say: 'Well, how are our affairs?' but that even he feels that this would not do, and says instead: 'What sort of a night have you had?'

Ivan Ilych looks at him as much as to say: 'Are you really never ashamed of lying?' But the doctor does not wish to understand this question, and Ivan Ilych says: 'Just as terrible as ever. The pain never leaves me and never subsides. If only something . . .'

'Yes, you sick people are always like that. . . . There, now I think I am warm enough. Even Praskovya Fedorovna, who is so particular, could find no fault with my temperature. Well, now I can say good-morning,' and the doctor presses his patient's hand.

Then, dropping his former playfulness, he begins with a most serious face to examine the patient, feeling his pulse and taking his temperature, and then begins the sounding and auscultation.

Ivan Ilych knows quite well and definitely that all this is nonsense and pure deception, but when the doctor, getting down on his knee, leans over him, putting his ear first higher then lower, and performs various gymnastic movements over him with a significant expression on his face, Ivan Ilych submits to it all as he used to submit to the speeches of the lawyers, though he knew very well that they were all lying and why they were lying.

The doctor, kneeling on the sofa, is still sounding him when Praskovya Fedorovna's silk dress rustles at the door and she is heard scolding Peter for not having let her know of the doctor's arrival.

She comes in, kisses her husband, and at once proceeds to prove that she has been up a long time already, and only owing to a mis-understanding failed to be there when the doctor arrived.

Ivan Ilych looks at her, scans her all over, sets against her the whiteness and plumpness and cleanness of her hands and neck, the gloss of her hair, and the sparkle of her vivacious eyes. He hates her with his whole soul. And the thrill of hatred he feels for her makes him suffer from her touch.

Her attitude towards him and his disease is still the same. Just as the doctor had adopted a certain relation to his patient which he could not abandon, so had she formed one towards him – that he was not doing something he ought to do and was himself to blame, and that she reproached him lovingly for this – and she could not now change that attitude.

'You see he doesn't listen to me and doesn't take his medicine at the proper time. And above all he lies in a position that is no doubt bad for him – with his legs up.'

She described how he made Gerasim hold his legs up.

The doctor smiled with a contemptuous affability that said: 'What's to be done? These sick people do have foolish fancies of that kind, but we must forgive them.'

When the examination was over the doctor looked at his watch, and then Praskovya Fedorovna announced to Ivan Ilych that it was of course as he pleased, but she had sent today for a celebrated specialist who would examine him and have a consultation with Michael Danilovich (their regular doctor).

'Please don't raise any objections. I am doing this for my own sake,' she said ironically, letting it be felt that she was doing it all for his sake and only said this to leave him no right to refuse. He remained silent, knitting his brows. He felt that he was so surrounded and involved in a mesh of falsity that it was hard to unravel anything.

Everything she did for him was entirely for her own sake, and she told him she was doing for herself what she actually was doing for herself, as if that was so incredible that he must understand the opposite.

At half-past eleven the celebrated specialist arrived. Again the sounding began and the significant conversations in his presence and in another room, about the kidneys and the appendix, and the questions and answers, with such an air of importance that again, instead of the real question of life and death which now alone confronted him, the question arose of the kidney and appendix which were not behaving as they ought to and would now be attacked by Michael Danilovich and the specialist and forced to amend their ways.

The celebrated specialist took leave of him with a serious though not hopeless look, and in reply to the timid question Ivan Ilych, with

eyes glistening with fear and hope, put to him as to whether there
was a chance of recovery, said that he could not vouch for it but there
was a possibility. The look of hope with which Ivan Ilych watched
the doctor out was so pathetic that Praskovya Fedorovna, seeing it,
even wept as she left the room to hand the doctor his fee.

The gleam of hope kindled by the doctor's encouragement did not
last long. The same room, the same pictures, curtains, wallpaper,
medicine bottles, were all there, and the same aching suffering body,
and Ivan Ilych began to moan. They gave him a subcutaneous
injection and he sank into oblivion.

It was twilight when he came to. They brought him his dinner and
he swallowed some beef tea with difficulty, and then everything was
the same again and night was coming on.

After dinner, at seven o'clock, Praskovya Fedorovna came into the
room in evening dress, her full bosom pushed up by her corset, and
with traces of powder on her face. She had reminded him in the
morning that they were going to the theatre. Sarah Bernhardt was
visiting the town and they had a box, which he had insisted on their
taking. Now he had forgotten about it and her toilet offended him,
but he concealed his vexation when he remembered that he had
himself insisted on their securing a box and going because it would be
an instructive and aesthetic pleasure for the children.

Praskovya Fedorovna came in, self-satisfied but yet with a rather
guilty air. She sat down and asked how he was but, as he saw, only
for the sake of asking and not in order to learn about it, knowing that
there was nothing to learn – and then went on to what she really
wanted to say: that she would not on any account have gone but that
the box had been taken and Helen and their daughter were going, as
well as Petrishchev (the examining magistrate, their daughter's
fiancé) and that it was out of the question to let them go alone; but
that she would have much preferred to sit with him for a while; and
he must be sure to follow the doctor's orders while she was away.

'Oh, and Fedor Petrovich' (the fiancé) 'would like to come in.
May he? And Lisa?'

'All right.'

Their daughter came in in full evening dress, her fresh young flesh
exposed (making a show of that very flesh which in his own case
caused so much suffering), strong, healthy, evidently in love, and
impatient with illness, suffering, and death, because they interfered
with her happiness.

Fedor Petrovich came in too, in evening dress, his hair curled *à la Capoul*, a tight stiff collar round his long sinewy neck, an enormous white shirt-front and narrow black trousers tightly stretched over his strong thighs. He had one white glove tightly drawn on, and was holding his opera hat in his hand.

Following him the schoolboy crept in unnoticed, in a new uniform, poor little fellow, and wearing gloves. Terribly dark shadows showed under his eyes, the meaning of which Ivan Ilych knew well.

His son had always seemed pathetic to him, and now it was dreadful to see the boy's frightened look of pity. It seemed to Ivan Ilych that Vasya was the only one besides Gerasim who understood and pitied him.

They all sat down and again asked how he was. A silence followed. Lisa asked her mother about the opera-glasses, and there was an altercation between mother and daughter as to who had taken them and where they had been put. This occasioned some unpleasantness.

Fedor Petrovich inquired of Ivan Ilych whether he had ever seen Sarah Bernhardt. Ivan Ilych did not at first catch the question, but then replied: 'No, have you seen her before?'

'Yes, in *Adrienne Lecouvreur*.'

Praskovya Fedorovna mentioned some rôles in which Sarah Bernhardt was particularly good. Her daughter disagreed. Conversation sprang up as to the elegance and realism of her acting – the sort of conversation that is always repeated and is always the same.

In the midst of the conversation Fedor Petrovich glanced at Ivan Ilych and became silent. The others also looked at him and grew silent. Ivan Ilych was staring with glittering eyes straight before him, evidently indignant with them. This had to be rectified, but it was impossible to do so. The silence had to be broken, but for a time no one dared to break it and they all became afraid that the conventional deception would suddenly become obvious and the truth become plain to all. Lisa was the first to pluck up courage and break that silence, but by trying to hide what everybody was feeling, she betrayed it.

'Well, if we are going it's time to start,' she said, looking at her watch, a present from her father, and with a faint and significant smile at Fedor Petrovich relating to something known only to them. She got up with a rustle of her dress.

They all rose, said goodnight, and went away.

When they had gone it seemed to Ivan Ilych that he felt better; the falsity had gone with them. But the pain remained – that same pain and that same fear that made everything monotonously alike, nothing harder and nothing easier. Everything was worse.

Again minute followed minute and hour followed hour. Everything remained the same and there was no cessation. And the inevitable end of it all became more and more terrible.

'Yes, send Gerasim here,' he replied to a question Peter asked.

IX

HIS wife returned late at night. She came in on tiptoe, but he heard her, opened his eyes, and made haste to close them again. She wished to send Gerasim away and to sit with him herself, but he opened his eyes and said: 'No, go away.'

'Are you in great pain?'

'Always the same.'

'Take some opium.'

He agreed and took some. She went away.

Till about three in the morning he was in a state of stupefied misery. It seemed to him that he and his pain were being thrust into a narrow, deep black sack, but though they were pushed further and further in they could not be pushed to the bottom. And this, terrible enough in itself, was accompanied by suffering. He was frightened yet wanted to fall through the sack, he struggled but yet co-operated. And suddenly he broke through, fell, and regained consciousness. Gerasim was sitting at the foot of the bed dozing quietly and patiently, while he himself lay with his emaciated stockinged legs resting on Gerasim's shoulders; the same shaded candle was there and the same unceasing pain.

'Go away, Gerasim,' he whispered.

'It's all right, sir. I'll stay a while.'

'No. Go away.'

He removed his legs from Gerasim's shoulders, turned sideways onto his arm, and felt sorry for himself. He only waited till Gerasim had gone into the next room and then restrained himself no longer but wept like a child. He wept on account of his helplessness, his terrible loneliness, the cruelty of man, the cruelty of God, and the absence of God.

'Why hast Thou done all this? Why hast Thou brought me here? Why, why dost Thou torment me so terribly?'

He did not expect an answer and yet wept because there was no answer and could be none. The pain again grew more acute, but he did not stir and did not call. He said to himself: 'Go on! Strike me! But what is it for? What have I done to Thee? What is it for?'

Then he grew quiet and not only ceased weeping but even held his breath and became all attention. It was as though he were listening not to an audible voice but to the voice of his soul, to the current of thoughts arising within him.

'What is it you want?' was the first clear conception capable of expression in words, that he heard.

'What do you want? What do you want?' he repeated to himself.

'What do I want? To live and not to suffer,' he answered.

And again he listened with such concentrated attention that even his pain did not distract him.

'To live? How?' asked his inner voice.

'Why, to live as I used to – well and pleasantly.'

'As you lived before, well and pleasantly?' the voice repeated.

And in imagination he began to recall the best moments of his pleasant life. But strange to say none of those best moments of his pleasant life now seemed at all what they had then seemed – none of them except the first recollections of childhood. There, in childhood, there had been something really pleasant with which it would be possible to live if it could return. But the child who had experienced that happiness existed no longer, it was like a reminiscence of somebody else.

As soon as the period began which had produced the present Ivan Ilych, all that had then seemed joys now melted before his sight and turned into something trivial and often nasty.

And the further he departed from childhood and the nearer he came to the present the more worthless and doubtful were the joys. This began with the School of Law. A little that was really good was still found there – there was light-heartedness, friendship, and hope. But in the upper classes there had already been fewer of such good moments. Then during the first years of his official career, when he was in the service of the Governor, some pleasant moments again occurred: they were the memories of love for a woman. Then all became confused and there was still less of what was good; later on again there was still less that was good, and the further he went the less there was. His marriage, a mere accident, then the disenchantment that followed it, his wife's bad breath and the sensuality and hypocrisy: then that deadly official life and those preoccupations about money, a year of it, and two, and ten, and twenty, and always the same thing. And the longer it lasted the more deadly it became. 'It is as if I had been going downhill while I imagined I was going up. And that is really what it was. I was going up in public opinion, but to the same extent life was ebbing away from me. And now it is all done and there is only death.'

'Then what does it mean? Why? It can't be that life is so senseless and horrible. But if it really has been so horrible and senseless, why must I die and die in agony? There is something wrong!'

'Maybe I did not live as I ought to have done,' it suddenly occurred to him. 'But how could that be, when I did everything properly?' he replied, and immediately dismissed from his mind this, the sole solution of all the riddles of life and death, as something quite impossible.

'Then what do you want now? To live? Live how? Live as you lived in the law courts when the usher proclaimed "The judge is coming!" The judge is coming, the judge!' he repeated to himself. 'Here he is, the judge. But I am not guilty!' he exclaimed angrily. 'What is it for?' And he ceased crying, but turning his face to the wall continued to ponder on the same questions: Why, and for what purpose, is there all this horror? But however much he pondered he found no answer. And whenever the thought occurred to him, as it often did, that it all resulted from his not having lived as he ought to have done, he at once recalled the correctness of his whole life and dismissed so strange an idea.

X

ANOTHER fortnight passed. Ivan Ilych now no longer left his sofa. He would not lie in bed but lay on the sofa, facing the wall nearly all the time. He suffered ever the same unceasing agonies and in his loneliness pondered always on the same insoluble question: 'What is this? Can it be that it is Death?' And the inner voice answered: 'Yes, it is Death.'

'Why these sufferings?' And the voice answered, 'For no reason – they just are so.' Beyond and besides this there was nothing.

From the very beginning of his illness, ever since he had first been to see the doctor, Ivan Ilych's life had been divided between two contrary and alternating moods: now it was despair and the expectation of this uncomprehended and terrible death, and now hope and an intently interested observation of the functioning of his organs. Now before his eyes there was only a kidney or an intestine that temporarily evaded its duty, and now only that incomprehensible and dreadful death from which it was impossible to escape.

These two states of mind had alternated from the very beginning of his illness, but the further it progressed the more doubtful and fantastic became the conception of the kidney, and the more real the sense of impending death.

He had but to call to mind what he had been three months before and what he was now, to call to mind with what regularity he had been going downhill, for every possibility of hope to be shattered.

Latterly during that loneliness in which he found himself as he lay facing the back of the sofa, a loneliness in the midst of a populous town and surrounded by numerous acquaintances and relations but that yet could not have been more complete anywhere – either at the bottom of the sea or under the earth – during that terrible loneliness Ivan Ilych had lived only in memories of the past. Pictures of his past rose before him one after another. They always began with what was nearest in time and then went back to what was most remote – to his childhood – and rested there. If he thought of the stewed prunes that had been offered him that day, his mind went back to the raw shrivelled French plums of his childhood, their peculiar flavour and the flow of saliva when he sucked their stones, and along with the memory of that taste came a whole series of memories of those days: his nurse, his brother, and their toys. 'No, I mustn't think of that. . . . It is too painful,' Ivan Ilych said to himself, and brought himself back to the present – to the button on the back of the sofa and the creases in its morocco. 'Morocco is expensive, but it does not wear well: there had been a quarrel about it. It was a different kind of quarrel and a different kind of morocco that time when we tore father's portfolio and were punished, and mamma brought us some tarts. . . .' And again his thoughts dwelt on his childhood, and again it was painful and he tried to banish them and fix his mind on something else.

Then again together with that chain of memories another series passed through his mind – of how his illness had progressed and grown worse. There also the further back he looked the more life there had been. There had been more of what was good in life and more of life itself. The two merged together. 'Just as the pain went on getting worse and worse so my life grew worse and worse,' he thought. 'There is one bright spot there at the back, at the beginning of life, and afterwards all becomes blacker and blacker and proceeds more and more rapidly – in inverse ratio to the square of the distance from death,' thought Ivan Ilych. And the example of a stone falling downwards with increasing velocity entered his mind. Life, a series of increasing sufferings, flies further and further towards its end – the most terrible suffering. 'I am flying. . . .' He shuddered, shifted himself, and tried to resist, but was already aware that resistance was impossible, and again with eyes weary of gazing but unable to cease seeing what was before them, he stared at the back of the sofa and waited – awaiting that dreadful fall and shock and destruction.

'Resistance is impossible!' he said to himself. 'If I could only understand what it is all for! But that too is impossible. An explanation would be possible if it could be said that I have not lived as I ought to. But it is impossible to say that,' and he remembered all the legality, correctitude, and propriety of his life. 'That at any rate can certainly not be admitted,' he thought, and his lips smiled ironically as if someone could see that smile and be taken in by it. 'There is no explanation! Agony, death. . . . What for?'

XI

ANOTHER two weeks went by in this way and during that fortnight an event occurred that Ivan Ilych and his wife had desired. Petrishchev formally proposed. It happened in the evening. The next day Praskovya Fedorovna came into her husband's room considering how best to inform him of it, but that very night there had been a fresh change for the worse in his condition. She found him still lying on the sofa but in a different position. He lay on his back, groaning and staring fixedly straight in front of him.

She began to remind him of his medicines, but he turned his eyes towards her with such a look that she did not finish what she was saying; so great an animosity, to her in particular, did that look express.

'For Christ's sake let me die in peace!' he said.

She would have gone away, but just then their daughter came in and went up to say good morning. He looked at her as he had done at his wife, and in reply to her inquiry about his health said dryly that he would soon free them all of himself. They were both silent and after sitting with him for a while went away.

'Is it our fault?' Lisa said to her mother. 'It's as if we were to blame! I am sorry for papa, but why should we be tortured?'

The doctor came at his usual time. Ivan Ilych answered 'Yes' and 'No', never taking his angry eyes from him, and at last said: 'You know you can do nothing for me, so leave me alone.'

'We can ease your sufferings.'

'You can't even do that. Let me be.'

The doctor went into the drawing-room and told Praskovya Fedorovna that the case was very serious and that the only resource left was opium to allay her husband's sufferings, which must be terrible.

It was true, as the doctor said, that Ivan Ilych's physical sufferings were terrible, but worse than the physical sufferings were his mental sufferings which were his chief torture.

His mental sufferings were due to the fact that that night, as he looked at Gerasim's sleepy, goodnatured face with its prominent cheek-bones, the question suddenly occurred to him: 'What if my whole life has really been wrong?'

It occurred to him that what had appeared perfectly impossible before, namely that he had not spent his life as he should have done, might after all be true. It occurred to him that his scarcely perceptible attempts to struggle against what was considered good by the most highly placed people, those scarcely noticeable impulses which he had immediately suppressed, might have been the real thing, and all the rest false. And his professional duties and the whole arrangement of his life and of his family, and all his social and official interests, might all have been false. He tried to defend all those things to himself and suddenly felt the weakness of what he was defending. There was nothing to defend.

'But if that is so,' he said to himself, 'and I am leaving this life with the consciousness that I have lost all that was given me and it is impossible to rectify it – what then?'

He lay on his back and began to pass his life in review in quite a new way. In the morning when he saw first his footman, then his wife, then his daughter, and then the doctor, their every word and movement confirmed to him the awful truth that had been revealed to him during the night. In them he saw himself – all that for which he had lived – and saw clearly that it was not real at all, but a terrible and huge deception which had hidden both life and death. This consciousness intensified his physical suffering tenfold. He groaned and tossed about, and pulled at his clothing which choked and stifled him. And he hated them on that account.

He was given a large dose of opium and became unconscious, but at noon his sufferings began again. He drove everybody away and tossed from side to side.

His wife came to him and said:

'Jean, my dear, do this for me. It can't do any harm and often helps. Healthy people often do it.'

He opened his eyes wide.

'What? Take communion? Why? It's unnecessary! However. . . .'

She began to cry.

'Yes, do, my dear. I'll send for our priest. He is such a nice man.'

'All right. Very well,' he muttered.

When the priest came and heard his confession, Ivan Ilych was softened and seemed to feel a relief from his doubts and consequently from his sufferings, and for a moment there came a ray of hope. He again began to think of the vermiform appendix and the possibility of correcting it. He received the sacrament with tears in his eyes.

When they laid him down again afterwards he felt a moment's ease, and the hope that he might live awoke in him again. He began to think of the operation that had been suggested to him. 'To live! I want to live!' he said to himself.

His wife came in to congratulate him after his communion, and when uttering the usual conventional words she added:

'You feel better, don't you?'

Without looking at her he said 'Yes'.

Her dress, her figure, the expression of her face, the tone of her voice, all revealed the same thing. 'This is wrong, it is not as it should be. All you have lived for and still live for is falsehood and deception, hiding life and death from you.' And as soon as he admitted that thought, his hatred and his agonizing physical suffering again sprang up, and with that suffering a consciousness of the unavoidable, approaching end. And to this was added a new sensation of grinding shooting pain and a feeling of suffocation.

The expression of his face when he uttered that 'yes' was dreadful. Having uttered it, he looked her straight in the eyes, turned on his face with a rapidity extraordinary in his weak state and shouted:

'Go away! Go away and leave me alone!'

XII

FROM that moment the screaming began that continued for three days, and was so terrible that one could not hear it through two closed doors without horror. At the moment he answered his wife he realized that he was lost, that there was no return, that the end had come, the very end, and his doubts were still unsolved and remained doubts.

'Oh! Oh! Oh!' he cried in various intonations. He had begun by screaming 'I won't!' and continued screaming on the letter 'o'.

For three whole days, during which time did not exist for him, he struggled in that black sack into which he was being thrust by an invisible, resistless force. He struggled as a man condemned to death struggles in the hands of the executioner, knowing that he cannot save himself. And every moment he felt that despite all his efforts he was drawing nearer and nearer to what terrified him. He felt that his agony was due to his being thrust into that black hole and still more to his not being able to get right into it. He was hindered from getting into it by his conviction that his life had been a good one. That very justification of his life held him fast and prevented his moving forward, and it caused him most torment of all.

Suddenly some force struck him in the chest and side, making it still harder to breathe, and he fell through the hole and there at the bottom was a light. What had happened to him was like the sensation one sometimes experiences in a railway carriage when one thinks one is going backwards while one is really going forwards and suddenly becomes aware of the real direction.

'Yes, it was all not the right thing,' he said to himself, 'but that's no matter. It can be done. But what *is* the right thing?' he asked himself, and suddenly grew quiet.

This occurred at the end of the third day, two hours before his death. Just then his schoolboy son had crept softly in and gone up to the bedside. The dying man was still screaming desperately and waving his arms. His hand fell on the boy's head, and the boy caught it, pressed it to his lips, and began to cry.

At that very moment Ivan Ilych fell through and caught sight of the light, and it was revealed to him that though his life had not been what it should have been, this could still be rectified. He asked himself, 'What *is* the right thing?' and grew still, listening. Then he felt that someone was kissing his hand. He opened his eyes, looked at his son, and felt sorry for him. His wife came up to him and he glanced at her. She was gazing at him open-mouthed, with undried tears on her nose and cheek and a despairing look on her face. He felt sorry for her too.

'Yes, I am making them wretched,' he thought. 'They are sorry, but it will be better for them when I die.' He wished to say this but had not the strength to utter it. 'Besides, why speak? I must act,' he thought. With a look at his wife he indicated his son and said: 'Take him away . . . sorry for him . . . sorry for you too. . . .' He tried to add, 'forgive me', but said 'forgo' and waved his hand, knowing that He whose understanding mattered would understand.

And suddenly it grew clear to him that what had been oppressing him and would not leave him was all dropping away at once from two sides, from ten sides, and from all sides. He was sorry for them, he must act so as not to hurt them: release them and free himself from these sufferings. 'How good and how simple!' he thought. 'And the pain?' he asked himself. 'What has become of it? Where are you, pain?'

He turned his attention to it.

'Yes, here it is. Well, what of it? Let the pain be.'

'And death . . . where is it?'

He sought his former accustomed fear of death and did not find it. 'Where is it? What death?' There was no fear because there was no death.

In place of death there was light.

'So that's what it is!' he suddenly exclaimed aloud. 'What joy!'

To him all this happened in a single instant, and the meaning of that instant did not change. For those present his agony continued for another two hours. Something rattled in his throat, his emaciated body twitched, then the gasping and rattle became less and less frequent.

'It is finished!' said someone near him.

He heard these words and repeated them in his soul.

'Death is finished,' he said to himself. 'It is no more!'

He drew in a breath, stopped in the midst of a sigh, stretched out, and died.

1886

THE THREE HERMITS

AN OLD LEGEND CURRENT IN THE VOLGA DISTRICT

Три старца

'And in praying use not vain repetitions, as the Gentiles do; for they think that they shall be heard for their much speaking. Be not therefore like unto them: for your Father knoweth what things ye have need of, before ye ask Him.' – *Matt.* vi, 7, 8.

A BISHOP was sailing from Archangel to the Solovetsk Monastery, and on the same vessel were a number of pilgrims on their way to visit the shrines at that place. The voyage was a smooth one. The wind favourable and the weather fair. The pilgrims lay on deck, eating, or sat in groups talking to one another. The Bishop, too, came on deck, and as he was pacing up and down he noticed a group of men standing near the prow and listening to a fisherman, who was pointing to the sea and telling them something. The Bishop stopped, and looked in the direction in which the man was pointing. He could see nothing, however, but the sea glistening in the sunshine. He drew nearer to listen, but when the man saw him, he took off his cap and was silent. The rest of the people also took off their caps and bowed.

'Do not let me disturb you, friends,' said the Bishop. 'I came to hear what this good man was saying.'

'The fisherman was telling us about the hermits,' replied one, a tradesman, rather bolder than the rest.

'What hermits?' asked the Bishop, going to the side of the vessel and seating himself on a box. 'Tell me about them. I should like to hear. What were you pointing at?'

'Why, that little island you can just see over there,' answered the man, pointing to a spot ahead and a little to the right. 'That is the island where the hermits live for the salvation of their souls.'

'Where is the island?' asked the Bishop. 'I see nothing.'

'There, in the distance, if you will please look along my hand. Do you see that little cloud? Below it, and a bit to the left, there is just a faint streak. That is the island.'

The Bishop looked carefully, but his unaccustomed eyes could make out nothing but the water shimmering in the sun.

'I cannot see it,' he said. 'But who are the hermits that live there?'

'They are holy men,' answered the fisherman. 'I had long heard tell of them, but never chanced to see them myself till the year before last.'

And the fisherman related how once, when he was out fishing, he had been stranded at night upon that island, not knowing where he was. In the morning, as he wandered about the island, he came across an earth hut, and met an old man standing near it. Presently two others came out, and after having fed him and dried his things, they helped him mend his boat.

'And what are they like?' asked the Bishop.

'One is a small man and his back is bent. He wears a priest's cassock and is very old; he must be more than a hundred, I should say. He is so old that the white of his beard is taking a greenish tinge, but he is always smiling, and his face is as bright as an angel's from heaven. The second is taller, but he also is very old. He wears a tattered, peasant coat. His beard is broad, and of a yellowish-grey colour. He is a strong man. Before I had time to help him, he turned my boat over as if it were only a pail. He too is kindly and cheerful. The third is tall, and has a beard as white as snow and reaching to his knees. He is stern, with overhanging eyebrows; and he wears nothing but a piece of matting tied round his waist.'

'And did they speak to you?' asked the Bishop.

'For the most part they did everything in silence, and spoke but little even to one another. One of them would just give a glance, and the others would understand him. I asked the tallest whether they had lived there long. He frowned, and muttered something as if he were angry; but the oldest one took his hand and smiled, and then the tall one was quiet. The oldest one only said: "Have mercy upon us," and smiled.'

While the fisherman was talking, the ship had drawn nearer to the island.

'There, now you can see it plainly, if your Lordship will please to look,' said the tradesman, pointing with his hand.

The Bishop looked, and now he really saw a dark streak – which was the island. Having looked at it a while, he left the prow of the vessel, and going to the stern, asked the helmsman:

'What island is that?'

'That one,' replied the man, 'has no name. There are many such in this sea.'

'Is it true that there are hermits who live there for the salvation of their souls?'

'So it is said, your Lordship, but I don't know if it's true. Fishermen say they have seen them; but of course they may only be spinning yarns.'

'I should like to land on the island and see these men,' said the Bishop. 'How could I manage it?'

'The ship cannot get close to the island,' replied the helmsman, 'but you might be rowed there in a boat. You had better speak to the captain.'

The captain was sent for and came.

'I should like to see these hermits,' said the Bishop. 'Could I not be rowed ashore?'

The captain tried to dissuade him.

'Of course it could be done,' said he, 'but we should lose much time. And if I might venture to say so to your Lordship, the old men are not worth your pains. I have heard say that they are foolish old fellows, who understand nothing, and never speak a word, any more than the fish in the sea.'

'I wish to see them,' said the Bishop, 'and I will pay you for your trouble and loss of time. Please let me have a boat.'

There was no help for it; so the order was given. The sailors trimmed the sails, the steersman put up the helm, and the ship's course was set for the island. A chair was placed at the prow for the Bishop, and he sat there, looking ahead. The passengers all collected at the prow, and gazed at the island. Those who had the sharpest eyes could presently make out the rocks on it, and then a mud hut was seen. At last one man saw the hermits themselves. The captain brought a telescope and, after looking through it, handed it to the Bishop.

'It's right enough. There are three men standing on the shore. There, a little to the right of that big rock.'

The Bishop took the telescope, got it into position, and he saw the three men: a tall one, a shorter one, and one very small and bent, standing on the shore and holding each other by the hand.

The captain turned to the Bishop.

'The vessel can get no nearer in than this, your Lordship. If you wish to go ashore, we must ask you to go in the boat, while we anchor here.'

The cable was quickly let out; the anchor cast, and the sails furled. There was a jerk, and the vessel shook. Then, a boat having been lowered, the oarsmen jumped in, and the Bishop descended the ladder and took his seat. The men pulled at their oars and the boat moved rapidly towards the island. When they came within a stone's throw, they saw three old men: a tall one with only a piece of matting tied round his waist: a shorter one in a tattered peasant coat, and a very old one bent with age and wearing an old cassock – all three standing hand in hand.

The oarsmen pulled in to the shore, and held on with the boathook while the Bishop got out.

The old men bowed to him, and he gave them his blessing, at which they bowed still lower. Then the Bishop began to speak to them.

'I have heard,' he said, 'that you, godly men, live here saving your own souls and praying to our Lord Christ for your fellow men. I, an unworthy servant of Christ, am called, by God's mercy, to keep and teach His flock. I wished to see you, servants of God, and to do what I can to teach you, also.'

The old men looked at each other smiling, but remained silent.

'Tell me,' said the Bishop, 'what you are doing to save your souls, and how you serve God on this island.'

The second hermit sighed, and looked at the oldest, the very ancient one. The latter smiled, and said:

'We do not know how to serve God. We only serve and support ourselves, servant of God.'

'But how do you pray to God?' asked the Bishop.

'We pray in this way,' replied the hermit. 'Three are ye, three are we, have mercy upon us.'

And when the old man said this, all three raised their eyes to heaven, and repeated:

'Three are ye, three are we, have mercy upon us!'

The Bishop smiled.

'You have evidently heard something about the Holy Trinity,' said he. 'But you do not pray aright. You have won my affection, godly men. I see you wish to please the Lord, but you do not know how to serve Him. That is not the way to pray; but listen to me, and I will teach you. I will teach you, not a way of my own, but the way in which God in the Holy Scriptures has commanded all men to pray to Him.'

And the Bishop began explaining to the hermits how God had revealed Himself to men; telling them of God the Father, and God the Son, and God the Holy Ghost.

'God the Son came down on earth,' said he, 'to save men, and this is how He taught us all to pray. Listen, and repeat after me: "Our Father."'

And the first old man repeated after him, 'Our Father', and the second said, 'Our Father', and the third said, 'Our Father.'

'Which art in heaven,' continued the Bishop.

The first hermit repeated, 'Which art in heaven', but the second blundered over the words, and the tall hermit could not say them properly. His hair had grown over his mouth so that he could not speak plainly. The very old hermit, having no teeth, also mumbled indistinctly.

The Bishop repeated the words again, and the old men repeated them after him. The Bishop sat down on a stone, and the old men stood before him, watching his mouth, and repeating the words as he uttered them. And all day long the Bishop laboured, saying a word twenty, thirty, a hundred times over, and the old men repeated it after him. They blundered, and he corrected them, and made them begin again.

The Bishop did not leave off till he had taught them the whole of the Lord's Prayer so that they could not only repeat it after him, but could say it by themselves. The middle one was the first to know it, and to repeat the whole of it alone. The Bishop made him say it again and again, and at last the others could say it too.

It was getting dark and the moon was appearing over the water, before the Bishop rose to return to the vessel. When he took leave of the old men they all bowed down to the ground before him. He raised them, and kissed each of them, telling them to pray as he had taught them. Then he got into the boat and returned to the ship.

And as he sat in the boat and was rowed to the ship he could hear the three voices of the hermits loudly repeating the Lord's Prayer. As the boat drew near the vessel their voices could no longer be heard, but they could still be seen in the moonlight, standing as he had left them on the shore, the shortest in the middle, the tallest on the right, the middle one on the left. As soon as the Bishop had reached the vessel and got on board, the anchor was weighed and the sails un-furled. The wind filled them and the ship sailed away, and the Bishop took a seat in the stern and watched the island they had left. For a time he could still see the hermits, but presently they disappeared from sight, though the island was still visible. At last it too vanished, and only the sea was to be seen, rippling in the moonlight.

The pilgrims lay down to sleep, and all was quiet on deck. The Bishop did not wish to sleep, but sat alone at the stern, gazing at the sea where the island was no longer visible, and thinking of the good old men. He thought how pleased they had been to learn the Lord's Prayer; and he thanked God for having sent him to teach and help such godly men.

So the Bishop sat, thinking, and gazing at the sea where the island had disappeared. And the moonlight flickered before his eyes, sparkling, now here, now there, upon the waves. Suddenly he saw something white and shining, on the bright path which the moon cast across the sea. Was it a seagull, or the little gleaming sail of some small boat? The Bishop fixed his eyes on it, wondering.

'It must be a boat sailing after us,' thought he, 'but it is overtaking us very rapidly. It was far, far away a minute ago, but now it is much nearer. It cannot be a boat, for I can see no sail; but whatever it may be, it is following us and catching us up.'

And he could not make out what it was. Not a boat, nor a bird, nor a fish! It was too large for a man, and besides a man could not be out there in the midst of the sea. The Bishop rose, and said to the helmsman:

'Look there, what is that, my friend? What is it?' the Bishop repeated, though he could now see plainly what it was – the three hermits running upon the water, all gleaming white, their grey beards shining, and approaching the ship as quickly as though it were not moving.

The steersman looked, and let go the helm in terror.

'Oh Lord! The hermits are running after us on the water as though it were dry land!'

The passengers, hearing him, jumped up and crowded to the stern. They saw the hermits coming along hand in hand, and the two outer ones beckoning the ship to stop. All three were gliding along upon the water without moving their feet. Before the ship could be stopped, the hermits had reached it, and raising their heads, all three as with one voice, began to say:

'We have forgotten your teaching, servant of God. As long as we kept repeating it we remembered, but when we stopped saying it for a time, a word dropped out, and now it has all gone to pieces. We can remember nothing of it. Teach us again.'

The Bishop crossed himself, and leaning over the ship's side, said:

'Your own prayer will reach the Lord, men of God. It is not for me to teach you. Pray for us sinners.'

And the Bishop bowed low before the old men; and they turned and went back across the sea. And a light shone until daybreak on the spot where they were lost to sight.

1886